Jane Wilson-Howarth is a medical doctor and a zoologist by training, and lectures and writes on international health and staying healthy while travelling. She tweets travel health tips as @longdropdoc. Jane has worked on child survival and maternal health projects in various parts of Asia for eleven years. Six of those years were in Nepal where some of her work was with communities hit by disastrous floods. She has written two travel narratives, including the autobiographical prequel to this book, *A Glimpse of Eternal Snows*, and three other books for adults. Her website is www.wilson-howarth.com.

Praise for *Snowfed Waters*

'The author's chief strength lies in her observation of Nepali culture—she is careful to avoid a patronising 'them and us' perspective. Couple her sensitive approach with a dramatically unfolding plot and breezy, easy style, and readers clamouring for more since the release of her first Nepal book, *A Glimpse of Eternal Snows*, are bound to be satisfied.'

—Saumya Balsari, author of *Summer of Blue* and *The Cambridge Curry Club*

'*Snowfed Waters* is a great read. It is an engaging love story; at times a fast-moving thriller; a thoughtful account of cultures that are baffling to one another; and a vividly detailed and observant travel book—all in one.'

—Victor Watson, author of the *Paradise Barn Quartet*

'Her great skill is to have taken a place she knows intimately and to have re-populated it with a cast of characters who leap from the pages into your memory. This book is far more than 'travel literature', it is a heartfelt examination of what it means to be an outsider—either as an individual or an entire nation. An enthralling and absorbing read.'

—Tim Hooper (Customer review on Amazon.com)

SNOWFED WATERS

JANE WILSON-HOWARTH

SPEAKING TIGER

SPEAKING TIGER PUBLISHING PVT. LTD
4381/4 Ansari Road, Daryaganj,
New Delhi–110002, India

First published by Lightning Source, UK 2014
First published in India in paperback by Speaking Tiger 2017

ISBN: 978-93-86338-21-1

10 9 8 7 6 5 4 3 2 1

For sale in the Indian subcontinent only

Typeset in Sabon Roman by SÜRYA, New Delhi
Printed at Shree Maitrey Printech Pvt. Ltd., Noida

Dedicated to all those
who lost loved ones and livelihoods
in the 2015 earthquakes

CONTENTS

PROLOGUE

Monday morning surgery in a grey, drizzly Cambridge was the usual range of problems and challenges: people struggling with low moods, snotty babies, a weepy exhausted young mum, several miserable children with tonsillitis, a chest infection, insomnia, worriers demanding unpleasant unnecessary investigations, back pain, a coil insertion, a nasty sprain, tummy ache, a toddler with a head injury and a smattering of diarrhoea and vomiting. Despite it being a fairly full-on session, the doctor had almost run to time. That was a bonus: she hated keeping people waiting. She was a bit anal like that. The out-of-hours reports had been checked, she'd finished dictating her letters and done all her phone calls.

Then in scanning through a stack of x-ray and blood test results, she clicked by mistake on the notes of a patient she'd got to know well—too well. The unfortunate Mrs Swayne had become unhealthily doctor-dependent. But had she got it together? Had she actually, finally and against all predictions, left the country?

1. BENEATH THE FOOTHILLS

Sonia

The man sitting beside me on the bus turned around with an uncertain smile. Was I talking to myself again? This Wreck-Raj Dickshit (could that really be his name?) had met me off the plane. He had saved me. I had completely lost my nerve when I saw that seething mass of people outside the terminal building. It felt as if most of them were looking at me. Everything was so strange and scary that I wanted to get straight back on the plane. Suddenly I needed bland, grey, anonymous, familiar old England.

My fine-boned, graceful, self-assured, cultured and unbelievably handsome saviour stood out from the mass of heaving bodies. He rescued and then guided me through the smelly oppressive throng. He wore a dark, perfectly pressed English-style suit, tasteful tie, a colourful little cloth hat, sunglasses and a carefully shaped moustache. He looked about twenty-five but he may have been older; I often underestimate the age of short men. Quickly, we escaped all the pushing and shoving and reached the sanctuary of a disintegrating taxi in a litter-strewn car park.

I was thankful that we hadn't needed to spend long in Kathmandu. It was busy and congested—not at all as I'd imagined. It was not a good place to unwind. We did a cursory look around a couple of temples and then caught a bus that Wreck-Raj said would take us to somewhere that sounded like 'Poke-her-err'. This was Nepal's second city and he had arranged to meet a colleague for a short time. We'd relax there overnight, he said. Then there would be an onward journey—so it would be perhaps twenty hours travelling in all.

I settled myself on the bus. The seats were quite sticky. I was quite sticky as well but this trip was going to be my stepping stone back to my old life. No, not my old life—I was heading for a better life. Once I'd recovered my self-respect at this Nepalese Teacher Training College, I'd go exploring.

I was going to find out about my dad's ancestors. My great-grandfather and also a great-great-great-grandfather had both lived in the subcontinent—during two different wars.

Unexpectedly, that foreign phrase, '*Cutty budge hay*', came into my head. It was something my great-grandfather used to say. He called it his mantra and it had been adopted into our otherwise dull, suburban family vocabulary. He'd been in north India during the Second World War and was convinced the words had kept him safe. He believed that they were connected to some kind of mysterious force. I was sure they would keep me safe too.

Surely those magical words and the ancient amulet will protect me from dysentery and cholera, rape and robbery, malaria and mugging. Maybe, somehow, I'll use them to get my life back.

I checked the duty-free package at my feet. I rummaged in my bag for my phone. I pulled out my smog mask, my rehydrating spray, migraine pills, guidebook and a slightly used tissue. Several other things fell on the floor, including, embarrassingly, my diazepam tablets and sleeping pills.

Our heads collided as we both leaned down to pick up my stuff.

'Oh, err sorry…Mr…' I felt terribly insecure about how I should address my guide. Had I misheard his name? Or was Wreck some kind of Nepalese title? Would it be all right to call him something like Raji? I certainly couldn't bring myself to call him Mr Dickshit.

Finally, my hand closed around my phone. A couple of 'good luck' texts had come up. That was nice. I replied. I wanted my texts to communicate how exotic our clapped-out bus was, but I'm sure I failed to inspire. I haven't inspired anyone for years.

Rekraj

What a strange task has been allotted to me. My big-shot cousin from Kathmandu suggested this duty. He said that mixing with foreigners would be good for me—an education—as well as politically advantageous.

He had opined thus but I have no interest in foreigners.

The young ones are shallow and uncultivated. They understand nothing about Nepal and they are ignorant about our heritage. They think our culture is ganja and gongs—and sex also. These foreigners have no knowledge of duty and loyalty and honour and how everyone must give to the poor. They think of themselves only. They do not care about the gods or their families. They do not respect the wisdom of old people. How will mixing with them enhance my reputation?

Nevertheless, I go to meet this memsahib at Tribhuvan International Airport. There is a great press of people. So many people. I check if my moustache is neat, and smooth down my hair with spit. I also rub my shoes on the backs of my trousers to polish away the dust. I step forward a little nervously, clear my throat and say, 'Missus Swine, Madam, please?'

She turns towards my voice but looks over my head. She is lost and frightened, like a child. I know I must help her but she turns back towards the building.

I repeat louder, 'Missus Swine, Madam? Yes? It is your goodself, please?'

She spins around. Finally, she sees me.

'Yes, I am Sonia Swayne.' She smiles uncertainly as I salute her.

'Welcome, welcome. You, Madam, are most welcome to Nepal!'

Now the policeman with bad teeth and a baton for beating people allows me to step forward. I want to greet her properly although it makes me feel shy and uncomfortable when she reaches out to shake me by the hand.

'I, Madam, am Rekraj Dickshit—at your service.' I bow, as is correct in such circumstances. She is more beautiful than her photograph. 'Come, let us go, Madam.' I lead her away from all the ill-mannered unwashed people. 'The car is backside please. This way come, Madam.'

I see then that she is a mature lady but nice and fat. She has a small, small scar on her forehead. She is pleasing to look at, and polite. It is obvious that she has been ill, and that the scar is new. Frequently, she pulls her hair over it. She seems ashamed. She wants to hide it. It is my idea that her husband is a violent drunkard and she is running from him. I feel sorry for her. I find it difficult to avoid her gaze because her eyes are bright and the colour of a mountain lake. I have to be careful not to look at her shapely breasts.

Guliya Tharu

I sit cross-legged on our thickest rice-straw mat. My Kancha coos and gurgles in my lap. He has seen three full moons. He is fat and he is healthy and my breasts are full. Silently, I thank the gods that they have blessed us with another son.

I love to massage rich thick mustard oil into his new skin. The sun gleams on his perfect body. It warms me and it brings the scent of the oil to my nostrils. Our cockerel crows and the neighbour's water buffalo calls to her calf. I smell the good, wet mud-and-cow dung scent from the drying floor of our house. Wood smoke mingles with the perfume of roasting cumin. I look out from the verandah. My second daughter, Moti, squats at the stone slab. She is grinding chillies for the chutney we'll have with our rice. She is singing a love song from the latest movie to come from India; sometimes she uses Hindi words—so she sounds like a film star.

A special visitor is coming from Angrez. She has been ill. Her doctors say that drinking the snowfed waters of the Himalaya will cure her. It is my idea that it would be better for her to make an offering at the eternal flame in the mountains or go on a pilgrimage to some other important holy-power place. Then again, if this foreign woman has so much money she should go to one big expensive hospital in India or America. Coming to Rajapur Island for a cure sounds like Brahmin nonsense, or one of their clever high-caste swindles but what Brahmin men do is not interesting.

This new woman might be interesting, hoina? This will be a different experience: to speak to her. If she can speak. Some of these outsiders cannot talk at all. They just chatter like monkeys.

All I know is that the money she'll give might be enough to pay off the debt that binds our family to the landlord of this place. I think it would be best to be free of the malik's bond one day, but, even if we cannot, this is our life. It is not a bad life.

Rekraj

I have come to know that people in America, they like sex very much. It must be a difficult place to live. I wonder if it is true that all western women want to make love with as many men as they can. This foreigner does not seem like that. It is my idea that she is shy but what must I do if she tries to seduce me? Would it be impolite to refuse?

Perhaps I could ask another of my cousins what I must do. He works in the Shangri-La Hotel and has a lot of dealings with foreigners. He often tells amusing stories about all the strange and unpredictable things they do.

Maybe I should hand over these lady-entertainment duties to my closest cousin, Ram Krishna. He enjoys the company of any even slightly attractive woman. He would not be uneasy about these kinds of issues. He's a womanizer like his father, and like Lord Krishna also.

The memsahib cannot sit still. She is busy with nothing. She is nervous. Always she is pulling her hair over her scar. She is checking her belongings often.

I like the film music that the driver is playing. To pass the time on this long bus journey and to make our conversation interesting, I speak a little about names. Tactfully, kindly I must correct her silly misunderstanding, also. I explain that Wreck is not a title. I spell my name to avoid further confusion.

'And Madam,' I address her most firmly, 'you are making one error. I am not Raji; this is not a good name. Nepalis are more formal.'

I teach her that names are not shortened as is the tradition in America, 'Many Nepali names are compound: Rekraj, Rajkumar, Baburam, Gaganasparsana. Like that. Me, I like the shorter names like Adik, Bhooshit or Ratish for a boy, and Bimbini—when I have a daughter that will be her name. It means the very centre of the eye. These kinds of names are most beautiful, not like your English names. But tell me one thing. Where exactly is England in America?'

She is angry when she answers. 'England is NOT in America. England, Britain actually, is very, very different!'

I do not know how I have offended her. I feel I should

apologize but I do not see what the problem is. Perhaps she has tasted some alcoholic drinks…

Next, she points through the bus window to a group who are squatting with babies tied to their backs. The women are breaking up stones with small, small hammers to make hardcore for the road base—for road improvements. They are low-caste types, dressed in rags. Maybe they are outcastes. These kinds of women cannot get skilled work. Actually, I think they are coming from India.

She says, 'Look at those poor women! Their hands are bleeding!'

Of course they are poor. Of course their hands are bleeding. This is usual in this kind of work.

'How much do they earn, Mr…?'

'No more than fifty rupees a day, Madam—the price of two and a half kilos of rice. Surely in England you also have such workers? How else can hardcore be made?'

'We have machines,' she says. I do not think she means to be rude when she speaks to me like this. I think the people of England do not understand the art of interesting conversation. Endlessly she asks stupid questions. She asks yet another. There is a sign in English, warning 'STOP!—MEN AT WORK'. She wants to know why it is in English.

She asks, 'Why does it say *Men at Work* when it is women who are working?'

So many idiotic questions. This is my first experience of spending time with a godless westerner. We Nepalis see these people as weird but they bring so much of money into our country that we forgive them.

Next she speaks of one ancestor who died in Kanpur at the time of the First War of Independence against the British. She feels for the vajra at her neck as she tells me this; often her hand goes to this object. I do not know if she is praying or simply checking that it is not lost. I am uncertain how to respond. Her moods are as unpredictable as the path of a butterfly. She uses the language of a colonial so I see that I must become a diplomat and peacemaker also.

I know those smelly uncultured Sherpa and Tibetan people have discovered how to work with westerners, and profit from them. I am not like them but I shall have to learn how to react to this foreigner.

I cannot decide what kind of person she is. Madam looks wide-eyed and bewildered. It is my idea that she is harmless. But perhaps she will cause many problems. She is like a child: innocent and helpless and scared. I shall be honourable to her, protect her. Actually, I must be many things to her.

The oddest thing is how easy it is to see what is going on in her mind. Her feelings are displayed for all to see. I think that this must be most inconvenient. I can see that she tries to be kind but she is actually most rude—probably through ignorance. She is clumsy also. Perhaps this is because of her size and her heavy bones.

Sometimes she acts like a village woman, though she must have had *some* education. I've read that all British women go to school. This is not like our women; very few are intelligent enough to go even to primary school. Sending them would be a waste of money. It is better that they help their mothers and tend the animals so they learn about household duties and cooking and that and this. Then they will have all the skills necessary to be a good attentive wife.

Sonia

Jet lag and fatigue from the long flight and the motion of the bus meant I soon dozed off. That was a surprise. I've been an insomniac for years. Perhaps it is a tonic for me to be away from all that unspoken criticism I attracted back home. Although I probably deserved it. My life was such a mess.

Once, people used to say I was fun—vivacious even. Before. But my confidence was chipped away by the man who should have done most to boost it. Lately, I have kept to familiar things and routines. Familiar is good—life is scary when it is unpredictable. It was my doctor's fault. She's the one who advised me to go on an adventure. Find my ancestors. So here I am—in Nepal, of all places!

It was madness itself to have come on this journey. Kill or cure, I suppose?

I felt for the amulet, for security.

'Mr Rekraj, I wonder if I might ask you about the work I'll be doing?'

'Certainly, Memsahib.'

'Well...?'

'Memsahib?'

'What exactly will I be doing at the Teacher Training College?'

'Teacher Training College, Madam?'

'Yes, Mr Rekraj.' This is how he had said he wanted to be addressed—it seemed awkward to me.

'What Teacher Training College, please?'

'The Teacher Training College where I'll be working?'

'There is none, Memsahib.'

I tried not to look alarmed. 'I have travelled to Nepal to help at the Teacher Training College. I have a photo. Look.' I rummaged in my bag for the printout and showed him.

'Ah—this, Memsahib, is the High School of Rajapur. A very prestigious and famous educational establishment...'

'There is no Teacher Training College?'

'There is none.'

'So...why have I come to Nepal?'

'Why have you come, Memsahib?'

'I signed up to help...'

'Exactly so, Memsahib. And help you shall!'

I started to splutter but suppressed the urge to say something provocative. I had a horrible feeling that nothing had been organized for me. Yes, it was only a two-month trip but I wanted to *do* something. Achieve something. Maybe this was the penalty for choosing the cheapest of several gap year companies. I thought I'd checked. I thought I'd researched it well enough.

'What kind of work will I help with though? I need to know what is expected of me!'

'There are many tasks, Memsahib. We need one typist also.'

'I am NOT a typist, Mr Rekraj.' I switched into teacher-mode and adopted the approach I'd honed for disorganized pupils. 'Tell me specifically how we will start.'

'We will start with one meeting. First, we will meet with our esteemed High School teachers and determine their requirements. I am thinking that you, Madam, must work with them on English grammar—teach modern English expressions. Also we must have one meeting with the committee of my charity. There will be many works for you, Memsahib!'

This didn't feel good at all. My stomach churned. My nausea returned. I tried to steady my breathing. I looked forward.

Our dilapidated bus had SUPER SONIC emblazoned across the windscreen which seemed ironic—a bad joke, even—as we negotiated treacherous, winding, mountain roads. At least the scenery was interesting.

Finally, towards the end of the day, the bus slowed and creaked and bumped over the broken tarmac on the outskirts of a fairly big town.

Mr Rekraj said, 'We have come to the edges of Pokhara city now, Madam.'

There was no way this was a city.

The bus stopped in an unpleasant dusty place. Mr Rekraj said, 'We will get down here, Memsahib.'

'Oh, have we arrived?'

'Exactly so, Madam.'

I tumbled off the bus. It stank of urine outside but it was good to take a stretch. Mr Rekraj was by my side again. He said, 'I will take you to one nice hotel—beside the lake—while I make busy with my meeting. It is my idea this will be your first chance to see our himals, Madam? This way come, please.'

Soon he installed me in a nice room overlooking a tranquil lake surrounded by tree-dotted hills. Fishermen paddled hand-crafted boats and small boys cavorted in the water.

'The view will be good in the morning only!' he said, and left me alone.

I showered and ambled out into a shanty town of interesting stalls and mouth-watering smells, where you could commission T-shirts, saying absolutely anything. I contemplated ordering one saying something really rude to send to my mother. I wandered contentedly, people-watching.

Next morning, I was woken by a tap on my bedroom door. Alarmingly, a waiter just came straight in. I opened my mouth to tell him to get out when I realized he was carrying some lovely steaming cardamom-laced tea. He was followed by Mr Rekraj.

Blushing, I pulled up the covers around me. He pulled back the curtains. Mist clung to the surface of the lake. It undulated oddly.

'I hope you are liking our mountains,' Rekraj said, pouting towards the foothills. They were nothing special. I must have frowned because he said, 'No, no, Memsahib, look up!'

I looked above the forested hills. But then I looked higher still. Emerging above the clouds was a stately pyramidal peak more beautiful and probably ten times the height of anything I'd seen on skiing holidays. Then, behind the mega-Matterhorn was a towering amphitheatre of snow-covered rock.

All I managed to say was a rather pathetic, 'Wow!'

'This pointed peak, it is Machhapuchhare because it is like the tail of a fish.' I couldn't see it, personally. 'And behind is the Annapurna himal. Beautiful, hoina?'

'They seem so close!' The scale of the mountains made me feel small but also showed me that any problem I had was totally trivial. I was mesmerized by a vision of pristine glistening snow and dazzling ice against an azure sky. The whole northern horizon was an uninterrupted line of gigantic peak after gigantic peak—the Himalayas! And it was all the more gorgeous as it contrasted so wonderfully with the blue-greys of the lake and the lush greenness of the valley and the odd lollipop-shaped trees.

'Wow,' I said again.

Mr Rekraj smiled and said, 'Machhapuchhare is a sacred mountain. No one must climb it. No one will be allowed pollute it.'

He didn't explain further and he didn't allow me much time for breakfast but the spectacular panorama had induced an unfamiliar tranquillity in me as we set off again on our journey—my anxiety had left me and I was excited by the new delights I would experience.

The bus charged on and I started clocking all the quease-inducing bends. Soon though, we broke out into the plains, which extended southward from the foothills. Then the road was straight and we tore along at a terrifying speed. Now we were heading west with the mountains on my right—to the north. A vast expanse of green flatness extended to the south. The bus only slowed to rattle and creak through some charming little village or to skirt huge potholes, or places where the road had fallen away completely. The morning sun did amusing tricks with the dust so that the countryside looked mysterious and beautiful. I felt pleased with myself that I'd at least made it this far.

I had expected that the journey would feel long and tedious but my cogitations and the anticipation made the time fly by. There was so much to see too. Huge billboards in clashing shades of pink and orange and green advertised Bollywood films. People were dressed in vibrant colours too. I figured that the trees were an odd shape because people had cut off the low branches to feed to cattle.

I thought about gentle monks and holy men. I saw a naked ascetic with flaccid ash-covered genitals. I hoped Mr Rekraj didn't see me staring at him.

The young men were nearly all so beautiful to look at, with their straight proud backs and their lovely coffee-coloured skin. Seeing them, I decided that the only British men with any elegance are gay.

My guide and guardian was graceful and polite, articulate and civilized. Perhaps he was gay, which would be a pity. Actually, his name sounded almost regal. I think 'Raja' is what they call their kings. He was such a gentleman and explained everything so beautifully for me.

I wanted to make him laugh. Often a clever witticism half-formed in my head but before I'd got it out of my mouth, it would fade from my mind, or seemed distinctly lame. I struggled for a topic of conversation and then plucked up the courage to ask about his name. He talked at length about that. Was he going to turn out to be a bore?

We passed a small pre-pubescent boy being carried shoulder-high by four men on a platform hung with spectacularly decorated red cloth. The boy was also dressed in red and wore a gold turban. There was a lot of tinsel.

'Is this a special ceremony for the boy, Mr Rekraj?'

'He's getting married, Madam.'

'What! He only looks about eight!'

'He will live in his father's house for some time. Maybe for five years more. The marriage will seal the friendship of the two families.'

'Where is the bride?'

'They will meet after some days, Madam.'

I tried to picture the child-bride. What hope did she have for a good life? She didn't even have the chance for a first love affair, poor thing. My own miseries rekindled, tears prickled my eyes.

The next time the bus stopped, an object came in through the window-hole, close to my face. It startled me. Neat white triangles of fresh coconut rocked gently on a battered enamel plate attached to a skinny girl's arm. Her nose was pierced and so were her ears; the piercings were kept open with disgusting bits of filthy, grey string. Rekraj took two pieces and gave the child a small coin. She beamed, and shuffled along to the next potential customer.

I stuck my head out of the glassless window and saw her climbing along a ledge on the bus. Most of her body-weight was supported on her two big toes. She nimbly moved along the entire length of the bus, propositioning everyone on our side. Then she jumped down lightly, without dropping any coconut, and ran around the back of the bus. Her snotty face soon appeared at the windows on the other side. She managed to canvass the whole bus before we sped off again.

The piece of coconut Rekraj gave me had a thumb print on it. I nibbled at the edge, until I had the chance to throw it out of the window. I think he saw what I'd done because he gave me a funny look. He chatted a while, then got up and moved forward to speak to the driver. He just left me on my own. Most of the other passengers were locals. There were a few tourists but they were mainly scruffy young backpackers. None of them looked worth talking to.

Wondering what the mobile signal would be like now we were away from the capital, I sent a couple more texts telling friends I'd got here. I was disappointed that the few people who had been in touch hadn't said much.

Everyone was too busy to be bothered with me now.

Then a weather-beaten Londoner with dreadlocks and a cheeky grin plonked himself in a seat across the aisle from me. He leaned towards me and started up a conversation—if you could call it that—he had to shout to make himself heard over the engine and the awful screechy local pop music.

The wind blowing in through the window exposed the scar that I always tried to keep covered. The aging hippy didn't look at it but I saw him checking that my left ring finger was naked. When I forced a smile and tried to speak back to him, he moved in to sit right beside me.

This guy's years showed as an attractive, outdoor look. I could see that he was an old hand at travelling and I wondered why he should want to talk to pale, fat, ugly me. Surely someone like me wouldn't interest someone like him? But he looked appreciatively at my breasts with a cheeky smile. It had been a very long time since anyone had looked at me like that.

He checked out my amulet too and said, 'Cool necklace! Where'd ya get it?'

'It's a family heirloom. Quite an antique, actually.'

'Yeah?'

'Yes. It belonged to my great-great-great-grandfather. A Scot. He died, in Cawnpore.' It was odd that I knew so little about it considering that, in a way, it had started me on this trip.

'Wow! What? During the Indian Mutiny?'

'Yes and no. Actually I'm not sure. A great-aunt did some research on him and found some letters. He may have died of cholera, just before the Mutiny. But that might have been a story concocted to protect his new wife. Whatever the truth, it's a sad story.' I wondered whether to continue. I doubted that my saga would appeal to this man.

'Do go on!' He smiled.

'Are you really interested?'

'Absolutely! Don't leave out the sexy scandals. Know what I mean?' He winked.

'Well I'm not—' I stopped myself from uttering some stupid prudish remark. 'This is only the bare bones of the story but my ancestor, William Campbell, had been back to Britain on home leave. There was a big family party. He met a second cousin. They fell in love. A whirlwind romance, it must have been. They married. He had to get back to his duties in Lucknow but they planned for her to join him in India after the monsoon when the weather was cooler. Their letters were full of yearning and thinly disguised passion. But while she was on the ship—on her way to join him—he died. She arrived to find him long buried. The shock started her labour pains. She delivered a son, prematurely, though he survived okay. What is really sad is that having the baby didn't stop her from going into a terrible depression. She killed herself. According to the stories of my family, she died clutching this thing.' I held the amulet tight, wondering whether it might hold a sort of memory of their love, and her sorrow, within it. 'My great-great-great-grandfather had given it to her when he proposed, saying it was the second most precious thing in his life.'

'What was the first?'

'She was, of course.'

Talking of it now gave me the shivers. Yet I was full of wonder that anyone could feel so passionately about losing a man that they'd hang themselves over it. Maybe it was post-natal depression, or culture shock. They talked of brain fever in those days too. Whatever, I couldn't imagine I'd ever find passion that deep within me.

Dreadlocks was still looking at me expectantly. 'So what happened to the child?'

'He was sent back to Britain—wearing this. I think there was an Indian wet nurse. His grandparents raised him.'

When our eyes met again, he smiled and said, 'That's some heirloom! Can I see?'

I unclasped the silver chain and handed my treasure to him, wondering why I trusted this perfect stranger.

As he examined it, I saw again what an odd object it was. It was like a tiny dumbbell but instead of solid globes at each end, there were five separate curved spokes connected to a central metal spindle. The whole thing was polished by wear but silver tarnish in the crevices highlighted the fine design.

In two or three centimetres of metal, the silversmith had achieved a superb level of detail, especially where the swirls suggested leaves.

'Your ancestor must have had some Buddhist connections. That would have been unusual in those dark days, I'd say. Especially down in Cawnpore. Maybe he had a local lover. The Plains Indians really go for the almond-eyed girls from the Hills. Maybe he had the same tastes. Maybe he found a nice Nepali "wife".'

'Mmm? Yes, you may be right. Cynics in the family said that there were rumours of other children.'

'Yeah, I reckon everyone needs a little local lovin'!' He winked again.

His flirtatiousness made me smile. 'But why do you say Buddhist—not Hindu?'

'This is a vajra, that's why!'

It had a name! 'So does it have any—err—special powers?'

'If you believe it does—if you want it to...' He leaned forward. 'I'm Paul by the way.' He handed back my precious amulet. He was so close his lips brushed my ear and I caught an attractive musky fragrance. Was this what marijuana smelled like? I'd already forgotten all about my amulet's mystic properties. Teasingly I whispered, 'You're into illegal drugs, aren't you?'

He whispered back, 'Of course I am...'cept dope isn't really illegal here.' A delightful shiver ran down my spine. Really I shouldn't be encouraging this man, my inner prude said.

He said, 'Nepali gear is the best, and so cheap. How else could I pay for these trips?' He cackled mischievously, his voice harsh from dope-smoking. 'This is Nepal. Enjoy it. Enjoy some ganja.' He dug out a spliff from his pocket and offered it to me with a grin. 'You look shocked! Chillax! And don't worry—we can atone for our sins in a little ashram I know.'

I looked over to Rekraj to make sure he wasn't watching.

Paul's laughter made me wonder if he was joking—or mocking my naivete—but I began not to care and laughed with him. I loved his easy manner. His enthusiasm for Nepal was infectious too. I wanted to ask him so many things.

'Aren't ashrams for locals?'

'No, they're lovely tranquil places,' he said, 'for anyone to get their life back together.'

'You don't look as if you ever needed to get your life back together!'

'Just goes to show…' He was laughing again. 'Nah, I was a real mess when I came to Nepal the first time. I was using—a lot. Avoiding—issues. Know what I mean?'

'Oh, I do. I really do!'

'What the people here showed me was you just have to accept stuff and get on with life. That's my mantra.'

'But aren't mantras supposed to be mystical in some way?'

'Yeah, well, Buddhist mantras are deliberately deep yet superficially meaningless—to take your mind off things. That's what they say about their *om mani padme hum*… That's good but I've taken it a step further. I reckon that blaming people fixes nothing. You're the only person that is going to sort you out. No one else really can—or really cares, enough. That's what Nepalis know—better than anyone. That's our western disease. Don't take responsibility. Take on a lawyer!'

I didn't know what else to say, except limply, 'You are quite a philosopher!' What was wonderful about Paul was I didn't *need* to say anything. I was spellbound. I was anxious to ask him if he knew anything about our family mantra but I wasn't sure that I should. And anyway, here on the subcontinent, it sounded pretentious even to call it a mantra.

Eventually I added, 'I envy you. It must be so wonderful to have lived amongst people who don't have the stresses that we suffer.'

'I guess you could say that because Nepalis are amazing. They never stop smiling—whatever happens. Must be something to do with all the praying and meditating they do. And they're fatalistic. That's liberating. Helps 'em accept things. Helps 'em live for today.'

This approach might help me too. I wanted more of his wisdom. I wanted him to keep talking. 'So you speak Nepalese well then?'

'Nah. Nepalis are like the Dutch. They don't expect

anyone to learn their language. Holland's another small country where I've spent some time—in Amsterdam—chilling. You get some good grass there, too. Nepalis expect to speak in Hindi or English with outsiders, so no, I haven't learned much. But hey, I think this is where I get off. Those are the gates of the Royal Bardiya National Park. I'm going fishing! Going to catch me an 80-kilo mahseer! See ya!' And he was gone, leaving me with a smile on my face and a warm glow inside.

The other tourists on the bus got off too. All except one.

Rekraj

I suggest we follow everyone and get down from the bus. The memsahib staggers like she is drunk. At the bottom of the steps, she stumbles, falls and rolls onto her back. She looks very funny, waving her legs and arms like an upended dung beetle. I arrange a concerned expression on my face as I help her up. Barrow-boys and traders gather around like flies to horse dung. They are excited to see the strange antics of this feeble foreigner.

I hear, 'Hey, Memsahib! You need shoe-shine!'

'No—thanks,' she replies, dusting her clothes off. She is unhurt and maybe she is amused by this small, small accident. Her worry lines are gone. She is interested also in the cheeky children, and I think this is a good thing so long as she doesn't encourage them to become too disrespectful. She says, 'But how clever of you to speak English!' He doesn't understand her accent. 'My suede sandals don't need shining!' She gives him a rupee—which he does understand.

'Are you feeling hunger, Memsahib?' he lisps, and then, indicating a busy stall behind him, adds, 'This stall is selling best samosas in all Nepal!'

'Mmm, samosas,' she says. She holds up three fingers to the stall-holder and buys for herself, for me, and for the shoe-shine boy. The boy takes great care as he eats to avoid food coming down his nose. The memsahib watches him rudely, then asks me in a whisper, 'Why doesn't he have an operation to fix his face?'

'Money, he does not have enough. It is not possible for him go to the hospital.'

'Should I give him money, Mr Rekraj?'

'It is not necessary, Memsahib. He is happy with one samosa, isn't it?'

One goat approaches the memsahib, looking full of hope.

'No, you can't have a samosa!' she says to it.

I probably frown in puzzlement, then I laugh and say, 'This goat is not understanding English, Memsahib. It want the paper...'

She laughs when I tell her this but unexpectedly—like a mad person—she shrieks in alarm as the goat snatches the paper from her. Then she is laughing again. I laugh with her. But she is most confusing to me.

Sonia

The goat snatched the greasy newspaper from my hand and devoured it with enthusiasm. Its greediness made me think of how much we have and waste at home. If someone drops food outside a chip shop, it'll lie there for days. Here, there is always some being that'll be grateful for the accident.

I'd been at once shocked and fascinated by the hole in that shoe-shine boy's face. The great gap in his top lip reached right into his nose. You could see his front teeth through it. He wasn't self-conscious. In fact, he'd pointed with his chin to tell me about the samosa stall.

I'd noticed already that Nepalis avoid pointing with their fingers or hands. Maybe they think it's rude. But even so, indicating with your face instead seemed most peculiar, especially when the face is so scarred.

Self-conscious as ever, my hand went to my scar and I pulled my hair over it. Then I felt my throat to check that my amulet was still there—safe. I also felt really, really embarrassed about my fall, though Rekraj hardly seemed to notice, and he didn't say anything to deepen my humiliation.

Back on the bus, I looked out of the window and gazed north seeing ridge after ridge of wild foothills. I reflected on all I'd seen. Luckily, it wasn't quite as overwhelming or exhausting as I'd imagined it would be. Yet life here was so unfair, especially for that shoe-shine boy. He didn't seem to mind and no one else was shocked by the look of his face.

By comparison my scar is nothing but it still marks me, and every time I look in the mirror it reminds me of that awful night.

Now *he* was back in my head again, and when he was in there the panic was never far away. His words played and replayed themselves in my brain worse than the most annoying advertising jingle.

I'd been a success—in my terms, at least. But that seemed such a long time ago now.

I had enjoyed my work but then a disturbed child's accusation ruined everything. It had been his word against mine in the end. No one believed I had been trying to help him. There was violence at home. Maybe that's why he wanted to lash out and hurt me too.

At the hearing, they simply accepted his story, made me resign—to avoid anything more official—to protect the school's reputation. My spineless Head hadn't valued me enough to consider my side of the story. Maybe I should have fought for justice—because I had pride in my work. I really did. Not now.

It was no help that my husband thought teaching wasn't a worthwhile career. No money in it, he'd say. I expect he was the cause of the 'short fuse' in me that my Head had so pointedly commented on several times.

I turned back to Rekraj, needing to think about something different. I asked him about the national park.

He replied, 'Maybe we will go—later. You may find it an interesting place. It is full of tigers and lions and elephants and rhinos and snakes and all kinds of dangerous animals.'

I didn't think he was right that there were lions inside. He'd talked of lions in Kathmandu too, or at least that's what he had called the goggle-eyed stone creatures guarding temple entrances. Actually they looked like smiling Pekinese dogs, with eyes bulging as if they'd taken drugs.

I asked him, 'Have you ever visited the park?'

'Not yet.'

With pop music blaring and the wind rushing by, it wasn't easy to have a conversation so we sat together, easy in each other's company. I smiled inwardly, recalling the encounter with Paul, which had been delightful and absolutely unexpected. Something inside me was reawakening. I was still a little sexy after all! At that moment I decided that I'd start calling myself Ms rather than Mrs.

After what happened that fateful Friday, I decided to shoot off any suggestion I was ever married. It would signal the start of getting my life back together. It was about time, too. I wondered about those ashram places that Paul had talked about. Maybe...

Unexpectedly, the bus began to slow, as if to let someone off. We were still in the forest though. There were no houses in sight. The driver was shouting something. People looked ahead, interested. We were approaching a speed bump. It was an odd place to put a speed bump. It was rather thinner than the ones we had in Britain. People inside the bus had become very animated and were pointing now. The speed bump was greenish and was moving. It was a snake; a snake that was much longer than the width of the road. Everyone in the bus watched as it slowly moved into the undergrowth, then there was head-waggling and smiles as the bus sped off again. I turned to Rekraj, 'I'm so glad we are on the bus. Such a huge snake must be so, so dangerous...'

'No, not dangerous, Madam. He guards our rivers and brings rain to our rice fields.'

After a while Rekraj leaned close to speak into my ear. He smelt intoxicatingly of incense, or something exotic like that. Now we were travelling at speed again, he had to shout to make himself heard, 'Look here now, Madam! We are coming to one most important river—the Babai.'

As we crossed over a huge, long, curved concrete weir, he put his hand to his forehead, down to his chest and up to his forehead in what I presumed was a little prayer. Several others on the bus made the same gesture. After so many hours creaking and crawling over places where the already rutted dirt road had been washed away, this short stretch of smooth new tarmac seemed almost miraculous. Maybe that is what moved the other people on the bus to pray! But I was nervous of commenting in case I put my foot in it. I'm always a bit unsure about how to respond to religious stuff. It is so easy to offend. So I just smiled. He continued, 'There have been wars with India over this very river.'

'Wars? Really? India and Nepal haven't been at war, have they?'

'Yes—ferocious political wars of words—and sanctions also. The Indians, they say they need our water and so we must not place a dam. But we prevailed and you see now this one very nice piece of modern engineering. It is sending water to irrigate our rice fields and feed our people.'

I tried to look impressed and maybe I was, just a little. It was brave of little Nepal to stand up to the might of India. And especially scary to think that India had the bomb.

'Are your people farmers, Mr Rekraj?'

'We are landowners, of course. We have our kamaiya to do the manual labour.'

'Oh. Um, what is kamaiya?'

'Our workers. We care for them, and provide one small, small house.'

'And wages, of course?'

'No, wages are not necessary. They take a share of the rice harvest. It is we landowners who take all the risk. When my great-uncle first bought land here in the Plains,' Rekraj continued, 'it was a most dangerous place.' He talked of colonizing the Plains in a way that made me think of Wild West settlers fighting the Sioux.

My interest was piqued. 'Why dangerous,' I asked, 'because of floods?'

'Exactly so. There are floods and droughts and famines, and diseases of all kinds and evil spirits and worst of all, there are dacoits. In Nepal we are having these armed bandits. There are the Thuggee also. They worship the black goddess Kali and as an offering to her, they strangle their victims using one silver rupee wrapped in a silk scarf.'

'But surely…?' I vaguely recalled something about the Thuggee caste being the origin of the word 'thug' but I didn't in a million years think they were *still* garrotting people.

'I am speaking truly, Memsahib. Many of my relatives, they died of fever also. Or disappeared, eaten by some junglee animal. These were most dangerous times!'

'And now?' I asked, unsure that I wanted an honest answer. He was making me feel really anxious.

'These days, Memsahib, this region is more civilized but the problems are still there. It is true that new bridges span all our great rivers that cut through the mountains and pour south and into India. It is easier to get help. There are even telephone lines in some villages. The army are stationed here now, and the police are here, and our politicians are here also, and everything is working nicely. Dacoits are still a problem but there are not so many cases of malaria these days. Snakebites are happening also but these are not so common—only one or two in a week in the rainy season on Rajapur Island.'

'But most people recover, of course?

'Of course they do not recover. I speak of one or two *deaths* in a week. It is a big problem for us.'

I felt queasy. I needed to focus outside the bus—on all the colour and lushness. I would feel calmer if I let my mind drift and absorb the beauty of the landscape. Now that the bus was emptier, I moved seats so that I could enjoy the view from the other side. All manner of work was going on: women pounded rice in huge mortars or carried water in pots balanced on their heads; men drove hump-backed oxen out into the rice fields. Cows and water buffaloes had such big beautiful sad eyes. It was all so exotic.

Then, I got chatting to the one other foreign passenger who remained on the bus. He was American—an anthropologist—who looked as if he had gone native, with his necklaces and bracelets and loud, jazzy pyjamas. Not my type at all. He introduced himself loudly as Herb.

'Herb?' I queried. 'As in parsley, sage, rosemary and thyme?'

'No, as in Herbert. It's a family name but I prefer Herb.'

'I can appreciate that!' I laughed but he didn't. I'd probably upset him. I wondered if he knew we Brits call ridiculous, foolish people herberts.

Why did I always offend people like this? Why couldn't I learn to be more diplomatic? Was it my bossy teacher persona?

I tried to swamp the rising feelings of distress in me by silently speaking the words that my counsellor told me to chant: 'I am worth something. I am a good person. I do care.' Then inside my head I started an argument about whether those statements were true.

Stop it! I mustn't ruminate on what I say to people, and on how people judge me. But just by thinking about ruminating, I was back in the past again—obsessing about *him* and that desperate Friday, and all my symptoms, and the way my GP had so carelessly dismissed the idea that it could all be due to cancer. How did she know? Could she know? She hadn't done enough tests.

I wanted to fill the space in my head with conversation. I needed to but the American was looking at me strangely. What had I said out loud?

I asked him, 'Who have you come to study?'

'A caste of hereditary prostitutes called the Badi. I'm really lucky. It is a brilliant catch to be able to study these women. They are unique for being the only sex workers in the world who are accepted in their society. It could only happen in a relaxed place like Nepal. It's going to be fascinating.'

I was almost sure he was talking nonsense. If Rekraj was to be believed—and I'm sure he knew more than the American—Nepal is a conservative and orthodox country. It would be strange, incongruous, unlikely even, that a tradition of prostitution passed down from mother to daughter would be accepted. I didn't say anything though.

Then it occurred to me that if this Herb was studying prostitutes, maybe he was oversexed or a pervert; maybe that's why he was being friendly to me. I pulled my blouse together to cover my curves. Then I looked at him again and saw how young he was.

Herb talked a lot—about himself. Maybe I was wrong, thinking that anthropologists needed to be good listeners. I couldn't imagine he'd listen to anyone. Eventually, I managed to butt in with, 'What do Badi men do?'

'Interesting question. Hadn't thought about them,' he said.

'I saw some men back there weaving baskets. Maybe that's what they do.'

'Maybe.'

I said, sweetly. 'I look forward to reading your book!' and smiling, added, 'Where are you staying?'

'On the island of Rajapur. It's in the middle of the largest tributary of the Ganges. I don't suppose you've heard of it...but the Badi women who live there are well-known—throughout north India and Nepal, I've been told. They're the main attraction of Rajapur town apparently.'

I think I surprised him when I responded, 'Well, I'm going there too, actually...with my friend Mr Rekraj over there. So we'll be seeing a bit more of each other!' Immediately, I regretted suggesting that there was any chance we'd ever get to know each other better. Why did I blurt out words before engaging my brain?

I returned to the safety of my seat beside Rekraj and gazed out of the window. We passed a little shack where—alarmingly—smoke was seeping through its thatched roof.

Noticing me start, Rekraj calmed me by saying, 'No, Madam, this building is not on fire. The smoke, it is coming from the cooking fire. These people are too poor and ignorant to have chimney.'

A miserable rhesus monkey was tied up outside; it was too depressed or ill to even clean its fur. I had thought Hindus were kind to animals—in case they turned out to be a reincarnated relative. But come to think of it, they didn't treat humans any better. Nearby, an equally unkempt, miserable and ill-fed small child sat in the dirt.

The bus slowed and came to a halt at a deep, fast-flowing river. It was more than 150 metres wide. It was good to stop. The backs of my legs, bum and back were stuck to the seat and I was stiff and achy from sitting for so long. I thought of taking a Nurofen and maybe even some Rescue Remedy. I still had some diazepam in reserve too.

Rekraj said, 'Come! You must stretch your legs—this is a nice English expression, no?'

I smiled and nodded, wondering what would happen next since the road didn't go any further. Rekraj helped me clamber down. He's such a gentleman. It was lucky he was holding my arm because my heels sank into the soft sand and

I nearly fell down again. But he steadied me—saved me from humiliation, this time.

I'd selected my flattest shoes for this journey but it was hard to walk even in those. I should have worn trainers but they look so silly with a skirt.

I shouldn't say 'should have' so much.

Rekraj brought me water and I gulped it down. Then with a spasm of fear, I realized that it probably wasn't safe to drink.

I suddenly felt sick. I looked around desperately, wondering how far we were from the nearest hospital. I could see a stall selling a few battered items. Some looked like medicines, including a familiar-looking red Rennies packet, except they were called Runnies.

Rekraj

The bus stops again. This time we have reached the collection of temporary winter huts and stalls at the low-water road-head. I help the memsahib down and go to bring tea from the best stall. Another Brahmin is waiting for the stall-holder to heat the tea and we talk a little.

'I feel pity for these stall-holders,' I say to him. 'They are all selling the same items: cigarettes, chewing tobacco, biscuits, fruits, sweets, tea and that and this. These places should be more entrepreneurial.'

'I am in agreement, dhai. They are copy-cats and do not see that they compete one against the other. They would make more money through diversification...but the tea is good here at this stall. Do tell me, what brings you on this journey?'

'I have a strange task. I am bringing a bideshi woman to Rajapur. I find her most odd. I must say that I was surprised and a little shocked when she started talking to two foreign men on the bus: she was being most familiar with strangers. But maybe they are coming from the same village in America or UK or Greenland. Maybe they are cousins.'

'I have also seen that foreigners do act most strangely. The women are not modest.'

'Precisely. I find it hard to know how to react to her. I am a little confused about her caste.'

'You must treat this foreigner as if she is high caste, isn't it, even although she is godless? That is my idea.'

'But really it is my feeling that they are outcastes. Sometimes, Madam Sonia doesn't act like a high-caste woman. This concerns me. She may embarrass herself. I have grown tired of her and her silly questions also. I am becoming bored.'

'You have a large burden, dai.'

'Truly!'

The tea is ready. I take my leave.

Sonia

Rekraj ambled away and there were so many people milling about that I lost sight of him. He could not have gone far but I felt even more queasy. My heart was racing. I tried to take no notice. My mind kept returning to the fact that I was so very far from home and a reliable hospital. What would happen if I got ill?

I wandered around looking for somewhere to sit. Innumerable smartly dressed people were waiting, eating, drinking tea, chatting. Children were dressed in their frilly Sunday best. Not that they'd be church-goers, of course.

Where was Rekraj?

Several groups of men were gambling over cards. Others lay about on string beds. In and beside several food stalls, women chopped vegetables and cooked. One fried tiny seeds in a huge wok. The smell reminded me of armpits. Another woman squatted down at the water's edge rinsing rice, cleaning plates and washing thick, squat, tea glasses.

I was standing near a tea stall. The man inside reached for a bamboo tube and blew into the base of a cooking fire. Good fudgey smells and steam rose from the brick-brown liquid in a handleless saucepan. My nausea was fading. The tea-shop man produced an unpleasant thing that might have been made out of an old sock and a bicycle spoke. He blew steam away as he poured the tea through it and into the glasses. It looked most unhygienic. I *had* wanted some tea but wasn't so sure now.

Two goats were kneeling to eat onion skins—desperate for even that little bit of nutrition. The smell of frying garlic and ginger, cumin and cardamom reminded me of nights out with my teaching colleagues.

I hadn't seen Rekraj for quite a long time now. What if he'd just left me here?

I wasn't even sure which was our bus—there were so many. Where was my luggage?

I was getting really, really anxious that Rekraj had abandoned me. He could have done some kind of deal, got paid and just left me alone. I couldn't stem the tide of panic rising within me. My heart pounded. My mouth was completely dry. I felt really sick. I had no idea where I was, or how to get home from here.

Trucks revved and buses horn-honked. Where were they all going?

'Hey!' I registered a voice behind me. The American grabbed me by the elbow. He startled me badly. The palpitations seemed worse. I tried to steady my breathing. Herb announced loudly, 'Great to get off that bus. Great to see the Karnali river at last!'

'Ah, Kar*na*li? I've been pronouncing it *Car*nally!' Immediately, I regretted saying that. He'd think I was obsessed with sex.

'Yeah, that's the Karnali, and that across the river is Rajapur Island. And Rajapur town is 13 kilometres further on. I guess we'll be getting those horse-drawn tanga things for the last bit of the journey.'

Rekraj miraculously reappeared and, smiling, slipped a glass of hot steaming tea into my hand. 'Actually the river here it is called Geruwa. Karnali is on the other side of the island.'

My hands trembled. I scalded myself but I didn't cry out. I hoped he didn't notice.

I changed the focus away from me by randomly commenting on a huge heap of discarded mineral water bottles piled up behind the tea stall. Rekraj pointed towards them with his chin and said laughingly, 'These, Madam, are a marker of the tourist places in Nepal! Wherever there are foreign tourists, there are these water bottles. You will see very few at our destination—on Rajapur Island.'

Rekraj

I give the memsahib tea. 'Now I think you will find this tea especially delicious, Madam.'

She is trembling. She scalds her hand. She dances around like she has a hornet in her underwears. She spills more tea.

Then she calms down a little. 'Thank you,' she says. 'But I'd like one without sugar this time—I don't take sugar.'

She runs her fingers through her hair, like a film star. Then she pulls some hair over her scar again.

'That is not possible,' I patiently explain. 'It is not possible to drink tea without sugar, yaah.'

'What? Of course it is!' she says rather rudely.

I am surprised that this woman doesn't recognize male authority. 'No, Madam—here you are mistaken. Without sugar, tea has no taste. And also the didi inside the tea-shop she cannot make tea for you only.'

She looks angry. Again she touches the vajra at her neck. She does this so many times.

She says, 'I need one without sugar. Couldn't you manage to get one without sugar?'

Why does she ask when she has already tasted the sugar? I tell her again, 'Tea without sugar is not possible.'

She does not look pleased. I have a feeling of foreboding. She is going to be very, very difficult to look after.

Next she says, 'It tastes very strange! And it is much too sweet for me.'

'Memsahib doesn't like tea?'

'Yes, I like tea but without sugar. What else is in it?'

I say, 'This is good dust tea, with buffalo milk, sugar and paper, isn't it.'

'Paper!'

'Paper—the spice, yaah?'

'Oh,' she says, *'Pepper!'* That was the odd taste I couldn't identify.' She laughs and so I think there is no problem. Probably.

Then there is a horrible rasping noise. I look up towards the sound and into the branches of a dead tree. Two big black birds are perched there. These vultures are a bad omen and I start to feel most uneasy in the pit of my stomach.

But then I see her laughing as she watches the ferrymen at work. Her whole face shines and she looks like a film star again. Admiring her lifts my spirits also. She makes me laugh inside.

Conversation with the memsahib is more entertaining than talking to this American man. For her sake, I must offer the American the usual platitudes. We talk for a while but this young man doesn't appreciate the art of conversation and the pleasures of eating the air together.

Sonia

The tea was too hot for me but Rekraj slurped his tea down noisily—at a tremendous rate. I sipped tentatively. It was dreadfully sweet. It was odd that my glass contained so little. I wondered about complaining then thought better of it. People tell me that I'm inclined to complain too much. I also wondered about how hygienic it was but I didn't say anything. I didn't want to insult anyone.

Rekraj chatted amiably to the dull American while I looked beyond them. The tree that shaded us was propped up by spectacular fin-like buttresses. Rekraj called it a 'simal'. A woodpecker galloped up the trunk. Sunlight reflected on its wing feathers made them glisten so they looked carved from gold. The sun also picked out men in wobbly looking dugout boats struggling with fishing nets. Strange-looking stream-lined ducks were fishing too. Bee-eaters, gorgeous in their greens and blues and oranges, were playing exuberant dive-bombing games over the sparkling river. I wished I had that much energy.

'Mr Rekraj?'

'Hunccha, didi?' he responded absentmindedly.

'That child—the toddler—what is she drinking? Is it alcohol in that stained glass?'

'This is hard drinks, Madam. Spirit alcohol.'

'But that is dreadful. You must take it from her! In England this wouldn't be allowed.'

'It is my idea that the mother is too busy and uses alcohol to keep the child quiet.'

'But that's not right!'

He looked away from me towards the river. He wasn't going to do anything, so I thought perhaps I shouldn't interfere either.

A crude water craft chugged towards us—some sort of ferry, it seemed—with people on it. In the middle sat what appeared to be a rusting truck engine. It belched black smoke and drove a propeller by way of a prop-shaft that turned dangerously amongst the passengers. The ferry was run aground—deliberately I think—and everyone on it jumped ashore.

The engine stalled, and the ferryman started remonstrating with the passengers and others nearby. He seemed to be angry with them. I couldn't make out what was happening. At first I thought that an argument had broken out but eventually I realized he was organizing help.

He wrapped a thick rope around the prop-shaft and directed six men to run up the beach to restart the engine. They ran up the beach five times before the black-belching engine came to life again. This really was a frontier if this ferry was our link with the outside world. This was pioneering stuff!

2. A WITCH AMONG US

Guliya Tharu

That Brahmin boy, Ram Krishna, comes to the house again. He has already brought things to make the room ready for the memsahib: a new charpoy, a quilt with a fine cover, and he has found one chair also. Now he struts, as proud as a fighting-cock. I do not know what he wants this time.

Moti is hiding from him amongst the growing maize. It is time he was married; it is necessary for his mother to arrange a suitable bride and then—maybe—his eyes will stop roaming over Moti. I hate the way he looks at my daughter. He is like a dog hanging around a bitch on heat.

He is so sure of himself yet so young. He is confident and has authority because he is the nephew of the chairman of the Village Development Committee. His whole family is used to giving orders.

Last time he came to our house, he was angry. He shouted. He had given money to buy special food to welcome the foreign visitor. He criticized the quality of the foods I had bought. These high-caste men are always very difficult to please. He said that the new memsahib must have top quality.

He asked me how much I had spent. I did not know and he was not satisfied. I had kept the change for each and every item separately even though this was difficult for me. I have no pockets. First I gave him the change for the rice purchase. Next I gave him the change for the lentils and the lentil flour. Then I gave him the change for the small, small items.

He said that I am as stupid as a buffalo. Whenever I try to explain about the money he had given me, he shouts. He makes me nervous. He confuses me. I never went to school. He knows that. He never stops telling me I am uneducated. He should show me some little bit of respect because of my age. He is the worst kind of Brahmin. He has too much prejudice.

He speaks not one word of the Tharu language—doesn't even know how to offer one simple greeting. Our language is beautiful though. It is the language my husband wooed me in. It is more poetic than Nepali or Hindi.

This time, today only, the Brahmin seems to be in a better mood. He carries a large paper bag—the usual kind, made from old newspapers glued together. The bag contains two kilos of good Basmati rice, a kilo of the expensive yellow lentils and a few onions, potatoes, garlic and root ginger. He has brought mustard oil also. He says that these ingredients must be cooked nicely for the memsahib. I wonder whether I should buy one small bottle of raksi for this newcomer. Such strong drinks are good for putting cheer into the heart. Poor thing, she is troubled. Demons speak to her in the night. She wears a small, small vajra at her neck that she fingers constantly.

When yesterday only, I had showed the new memsahib the room I'd prepared for her, she hadn't looked pleased. I cannot understand why. The floor is smooth, freshly replastered. Flowers arranged in one nice yellow oil can look beautiful. Their perfume fills the room. I'd found a fine picture of Lord Krishna playing his flute and had pinned it up on the wall. The new charpoy and quilt look very smart too.

Maybe the reason she is displeased is because she is a miserable person. Some people are like that. Perhaps it is the fault of her demons. It is not important why. I have to give Kancha my milk, and must finish cooking rice for my husband. He will come from the landlord's fields soon.

Sonia

I was wrenched awake at the tail-end of a stifled scream. I fought my way up from a deep dark dream. 'Who's that?'

Heart thumping, mouth open, I strained to catch the tiniest sound. No one was there. The scream had been mine.

Fidgeting allowed me to feel the reassuring softness of the muslin against my sweat-dampened face. I caught my breath. Remembered—finally—where I was. My hand went to the reassuring swirls of the amulet at my neck. At first I could hear nothing but my heartbeat. Then the silence was punctuated by little scratchings and ferretings.

I didn't want to move from the safety of the covers but I

had to now. No choice. My bladder was full to bursting. That was what had woken me. I must've slept for quite a while.

I cursed my timidity. I'd been too scared to use that hole-in-the-ground toilet before I'd settled for the night. Should've gone then. Stupid not to have.

Imagining the awful things my hand might meet in the dark, I reached out for the hurricane lamp and found cold metal and disgusting oiliness. I groped for matches, struck one and as it flared, the room unfolded. It was marvellous to see again. I checked the shadowy corners of the cell-like room. Nothing.

The match burned my fingers and I dropped it. Darkness again. Unidentifiable noises again. I smelt phosphorus, kerosene and burnt skin. Small feet were scampering over the floor.

I sat up. I swung my legs around so I was perched on the edge of my strange string bed. I reached once more for the matches; struck another; raised the blackened lamp-glass; turned up the wick; lit the lamp. There. I was really quite competent. I could do this. I held the light high to see my way to the silent, deserted outside.

The area where the women had been cooking was clean and tidy. All the hens were under baskets. Everyone was asleep. I wouldn't need to use the dreaded lean-to. I could just pee in the spinach patch. Carefully, I picked my way between knee-high leaves that sprouted from the ground. I found a gap, set down the lamp and squatted. Relief at last.

As my stream slowed, I registered sounds coming from the direction of the verandah. Something was moving over there. It sounded large. A predator. Maybe several nocturnal creatures were hunting, hunting me.

The reality was worse.

I'd assumed this was the middle of the night and that everyone would be asleep. They were giggling. They'd seen. They'd tell everyone that the clumsy foreigner had peed on their vegetables. I pulled up my pyjamas. Wet running down my legs made them stick. I scuttled inside, not daring to look towards the verandah. Back in bed, safe under the soft cosy covers like a small child, I hid from my shame.

Other painful and embarrassing scenes crowded into my head: my bloodied face in the mirror; the hospital; the hearing; the accusations; that bitter child. This was to have been my escape but it had been a mistake. I was disgusted with myself.

Noises started again. A nasty rasping could have been a snake. There were definitely creatures moving in the thatch. Bits of straw fell down on me. There were scuttlings that sounded like mice on the floor. Or scorpions. Or, worse, rats. I froze at the thought of things climbing into bed with me, or falling on me from the ceiling.

My hand went to the object I prized most in the world: the talisman at my neck. I felt the familiar reassuring intricacies of its design. I steadied my breathing.

I wondered again about its origins and what sort of power it held. Our family lore was that my great-great-great-grandfather had brought it back from the foothills of the Himalayas.

And here I am, staying in a traditional house only 30 kilometres from where those very mountains rise sheer out of the Gangetic Plains. Even the sound of that is exotic.

I grew up in stultifying London suburbs under the thumb of a manipulative, self-obsessed mother. She undermined my confidence with every comment she made but I had escaped into dreams of misty Indian plains rising to the hill stations of the British Raj where my great-great-great-grandfather had lived, loved and died. He was from my dad's side of the family, of course.

What might happen if I met an eligible prince? Maybe his betrothed had died unexpectedly? 'I should feel sad but I hadn't known her well. I'd only met her once. She wasn't alone, and she was veiled. The first time I set eyes on you, Sonia, was so different. I saw you from afar…a golden vision, a gentle breeze moving your flaxen hair, the setting sun making you even more radiant.'

He told me how I was so different from the brown-skinned, almond-eyed beauties he'd always known. His smile, turned on just for me, was dazzling, his dark cheeks colouring charmingly as he blushed. He was fascinated by me, enchanted by my exoticness.

His family disapproved, of course. Our feelings had to be kept secret. He furtively courted me, so shy at first. But then one day, while riding in the Himalayas together, he slipped gracefully from his stallion. My prince helped me down. Without a word he drew me to him. Urgently, passionately he kissed me and...

Next time I awoke, daylight was stabbing through tiny oval openings that served as windows. In the sleepy fog of coming back into the real world, the acrid smell of cow dung rising from the mud floor penetrated my consciousness. I'd expected that the thatch would make the inside of the house smell of fresh hay but it was musty and stale—unhygienic, as well as stark. This hadn't been what I'd imagined.

With some effort, I forced my eyes to focus on the few dusty, wilted flowers that had been stuffed in an old oil can. I suppose these were intended as decoration. They were plonked on a battered wooden crate that was my bedside table. A picture of a woman with blue skin that had been clumsily torn out of a magazine was secured to the wall with rusty nails. But they hadn't even provided a peg or nail to hang my jacket on.

I'd had a good sleep though. The string bed was surprisingly comfortable, and the cotton-stuffed quilt and soft muslin cover were cosier than I had expected them to be.

Suddenly I realized what had woken me this time. Some predator or type of vermin was clawing at the fabric of the house, as if scratching to get in through my bedroom door. But there was no door.

I tensed as I heard it again, then, 'Bad tea, Memsahib!'

'What?'

'I am bringing bad tea, Memsahib!'

A teenage girl pulled back the cloth that acted as a door and she came smiling to my bedside with a glass of steaming milky-brown liquid.

'What's wrong with it?'

'Memsahib?'

'Why is it bad tea?'

She looked puzzled. 'I am bringing tea for you to drink in your bad—bad tea.'

'Ah tea-in-bed!'

'Exactly so, Memsahib!' She left before I thought to thank her. The bad tea was syrupy thick and deliciously spicy. I'd only been in the country a few days and I was getting used to the sweetness already. I used it to wash down my Well Woman vitamins. Actually, this was a perfect start to the day. In fact, this morning, things felt better: better than they had in a very long time. I'd slept all right—eventually—and awoken feeling really quite good.

Outside in the garden was much nicer; the early morning sun was glorious. The greens and reds were deeper and richer than back home, the flowers more beautiful. I found myself tracking the most enormous and gorgeous butterflies. Peculiar twitterings said that strange birds watched me.

There was a mouthwatering smell of toasting. The woman of the house was busy stirring something in a strange round-bottomed pan propped over the fire. I walked over to see maize miraculously transforming into popcorn. I smiled and rubbed my tummy.

She smiled back and mimed eating. 'Khana,' she said waggling her head amiably. Her sideways head-rocking reminded me of one of those stupid nodding dogs that people sometimes have in the backs of cars. Her neck movements were so fluid that I thought that maybe the Nepalese were double-jointed.

Before I could eat breakfast though I knew I'd need to brave that toilet. I stretched and, with theatrical casualness, strolled over to the sorry-looking little lean-to. It was leaning, too. It had been made of sticks and woven grass and looked as if it would fall into the hole beneath it any second. There was no door but where a door should have been, a revolting bit of tattered floral cloth dangled threateningly.

Holding my amulet and mumbling '*Cutty budgie hay*' was a small comfort.

I tried squeezing around the curtain without touching it. The thought of the filth and contamination within made me gag. I needed to get done and get out. I tried to hold my breath but finally I had to take a gulp of air. It smelt of earth. It wasn't that bad. I dropped my drawers. I stepped astride the deep dark hole and enjoyed the wonderful *schhweee* sound as amber fluid cascaded downwards with surprising beauty. Someone had put a pink loo-roll on a stick in a handy spot.

Peering between my legs, I saw that the bottom of the pit was moving. I looked again, presuming that I must be imagining it. I could tell what it was now—a writhing sea of maggots.

I stretched out my hand towards the pink toilet-roll. Something moved—at shoulder level. I'd mistaken it for a bit of wood. A thick, taut, brown snake. It seemed to watch me as it slid silently along one of the horizontal timbers that made up the wall of the lean-to.

To hell with loo paper. Coming here had been a dreadful, dreadful mistake. I pulled up my knickers and fled.

Rekraj

The memsahib had asked me to buy her one bicycle, so I arose early and, with my cousin Ram Krishna, met some of my relatives in the bazaar. We went hither and thither. Everywhere. Mostly the bikes were of poor quality. Very few were suitable for ladies. Finally, we managed to buy a fine bike: well-made, heavy, Indian, top quality.

Pleased with our find, I wheel it into the garden of the Tharu woman. There the memsahib is already eating a little popped corn. Mrs Swine rises and offers a greeting. I think that British people and Nepalis have this in common. We appreciate good manners and proper behaviour. She seems very happy to see me also.

She is talking very fast and I cannot make out what she says until I realize she is babbling about a snake. She describes a harmless rat snake. I do not understand why she is upset about this. I accept tea from the Tharu woman, demonstrating how broad-minded I am.

Then the memsahib looks at the bike I have brought. I read disapproval in her face.

'You don't like, Madam?' I say, feeling impatient with her. I need to explain its advantages. 'It is made in India—extra high quality. Export quality. Full suspension. Comfortable modern ladies' saddle. Very strong—heavy also.'

'Yes thanks. It's fine. I'll try it out—after breakfast.' She speaks in a monotone, with no smile. 'And I wish you would stop calling me Madam. You don't need to be so formal.'

'It is as you like, Memsahib,' I reply, irritated by her rudeness. Clearly, she doesn't appreciate all the trouble I had gone to for her only.

I see also that Ram Krishna is leering at the Tharu's grown-up daughter again; he has the sexual appetite of a dog. He is not ashamed to pursue such low-caste, uneducated village women. I do not understand why he acts this way.

He is well named—after Lord Krishna who also likes the ladies too much. It is odd. The Brahmins tell that Krishna's blue colour shows his depth of character—like the ocean, they say—whereas it is my idea that being a ladies' man does not show depth of character…but I must not think such sacrilegious things.

I do not know where these ideas come from. These are not our holy teachings. What our teachings say is that evil acts will be punished—in this world or the next. My cousin does not fear that his karma will be to suffer, that he will be repaid.

I think how ironical it is that in our language the word for love can also mean deceit. It makes me think of the cheap wheedling greasiness of the laddoo-seller, sitting at his stall in front of his pan of hot oil, determined to make a sale by promising anything.

The Tharu woman has put so much of kohl around the eyes of her baby son to ward off the Evil Eye. She is wise. This family is in need of protection. Already they have experienced too much of sorrow. I know that their suffering is not yet over.

The memsahib has finished her snack. I say to her, 'I shall take you to the bazaar also and we can buy some personal effects to make your room comfortable. We first will buy tasty sweet laddoos for you to try. And I think you are needing one mirror?'

Today she looks untidy. No longer beautiful; no longer a film star. I am bored with looking after her.

Her hand goes to her hair and she says, 'Okay, we'll go to the bazaar first.'

'We will go. And let me tell you one thing, Memsahib. When you go to the bathroom in the night, it is better you not taking light. If you go to the bathroom beside the light, it is like you are on stage and all the people are seeing and that is a great shame for you. I think it is better you use latrine next time. It is more hygienic also.' It is better that I explain everything nicely to her. 'Okay, Madam, I will come after half an hour and we will go together, yaah?'

Then the memsahib says an astonishing thing. She says she might like to explore with one of the Tharu women.

'That is not possible,' I tell her. 'They cannot speak English.'

Mostly these Tharus do not understand the value of schooling so they don't know numbers and they cannot write. They cannot even speak our national language nicely. Unexpectedly, the Tharu woman's brazen daughter steps forward and mumbles something.

'Kire? Speak up!' I tell her.

She repeats, 'I can spick English, please, Sahib.'

I can't believe that she—a young Tharu girl—can be so arrogant. I have to leave. You give these people a little education and they act as if they are as good as us. I have more important things to do than act as mother to this stupid foreigner and eat the air with these low-caste people.

Sonia

It was my hostess' grown-up daughter, the one who'd brought my bad tea, who had spoken out. Like the woman I now called Sister Sweet, this younger woman had also tied her hair into an uncomfortably tight bun, and she wore a short blouse with a full gathered skirt that had a blue band around the bottom. The daughter was someone I was going to be able to talk to. Until the bad tea announcement she had been mute but I could see she could be quietly assertive. She'd look after me. Any remnant feelings of isolation melted away. I knew that everything was going to be all right now. The young woman stood modestly in the background, smiling warmly.

Rekraj stiffened though, and walked away without saying anything more. He looked furious.

I vacillated. Should I go after him? I looked to the young woman for advice. She stifled a smile but kept her eyes on the ground.

A nice Nepalese man I'd sat next to on the plane had told me that if you're not sure what to say in Nepal, it is best to say nothing. I said nothing. I desperately hoped that I hadn't been the cause of some rift, though. There certainly seemed to be tension between Rekraj and my hostess. Probably this was because they belonged to different castes. The Brahmin seemed to look down on her family.

What I found very odd was that she hadn't wanted to tell me her name. The day before, when I had pressed Rekraj to tell me her name, he had shouted out to a neighbour, who replied, 'Guliya Tharu!' Then he explained that Guliya means sweet: like sugar, like laddoos. He didn't bother to explain what a laddoo was.

That was when I decided to call her Sister Sweet. She has such a sweet smile and it was easier to remember than her Nepalese name. In my head, that's what I'd call her, or didi. That means older sister. Everyone seems to call each other brother or sister so I don't think I'd offend anyone by calling her didi.

The Tharu women visibly relaxed as Rekraj walked away. I turned and spoke to the daughter, 'I am so pleased that we can talk to each other—so pleased! I hope that we will become good friends.'

'It is as you wish, Memsahib.' She now sounded strangely dismissive.

'But please don't call me Memsahib.'

'No, Memsahib.'

She didn't want to talk but I could at least ask her to get rid of the snake in the loo. She followed me to the lean-to and I showed her. She smiled, 'This snake has been living in this place for last two monsoons. It is his home only. He like this place.'

'Aren't you frightened it will bite?'

'He will not bite, Memsahib. He want to sleep there only.'

I wasn't convinced or reassured but I was desperate to continue this conversation. As we wandered back to the verandah, I tried a question I'd already heard Nepalese children chant at me, 'What is your name?' Everyone seemed to know this much English. She giggled and only answered after I pressed her, 'My friends call me Moti.'

'Then I shall call you Moti!'

She giggled with her hand over her mouth and said something to Sister Sweet that made her laugh too. I wondered if I had said the wrong thing, so added, 'If that is all right?'

'It is as you wish, Memsahib.'

I wasn't sure whether I'd done wrong or not. I wished they'd tell me—explain things. Not knowing what to say next, I ventured, 'So...please tell me about your family.'

This was a good question. She introduced her mother and father. She told me about the other children. She had two older brothers and two younger—including the baby—and an elder and younger sister. I was losing count. She had two nieces, a nephew and lots and lots of cousins. She smiled so much when she talked about her family. She had so much joy in her life. I dreaded her asking about my family because just thinking about home made me feel utterly miserable. I feared another panic attack too.

He'd left me alone. Completely utterly alone, that awful night back in Cambridge. A caterwauling had made me look out into our little English garden. The heartbreaking sound came from the beautiful tomcat who often came for titbits. He sat outside our back door. He'd been in a scrap and one ear was bleeding. I felt for him. He wanted me to help him. Fate was treating me kindly, after all; this creature had come to comfort me. We'd comfort each other. I squatted down and scooped him into my arms. He looked into my eyes. He meowed a thank you. Then—claws out—he lashed at my face. Pain seared across my brow. The cat fled, slashing at my forearms as it leapt clear. I was hurt physically but I was more distressed psychologically because even that cat hated me. I had no one, nothing. When I put my hand to where it hurt, it felt wet. I started to cry. I staggered inside to the bathroom. It smelled of sick.

The face I saw in the mirror wasn't me. It was something out of a horror film. Streaks of blood ran down it and you could see where tears had made two tracks. Blood still pumped out of long claw marks across the forehead. I'd be scarred for life, I knew.

I've no idea how long I stood there, shaking.

I filled a tumbler half-full of gin and downed the lot. It didn't do much. I needed help. I phoned for a taxi to get myself to the hospital but the taxi driver refused to take me at first. He argued, saying I should call an ambulance but finally—when I offered him an extra couple of ten pound notes—he agreed. I was desperate. I would have given anything to get out of that house.

The vision of that face in the mirror returned to me, haunting me as it had ever since that dreadful night. I was scarred—and I was scared too. I was scared of the future. I was scared of being on my own. I didn't want to live alone. Why had he left me? I didn't deserve to be treated this way, not with all my health problems. I wasn't a bad person, just a bit dull—and not terribly intelligent, or attractive. I was even less attractive now, with the scar.

'Memsahib...? Memsahib?'

'Mmm? What?'

'You need go to bazaar now, Memsahib? You will take bicycle, maybe?'

'Oh.' I swallowed down the nausea. 'No, Moti. Let's walk together.' I'd resolved to start a programme of exercise to distract me and shake off the lethargy of recent years. But the hefty black sit-up-and-beg bike that Rekraj had brought me had been a big disappointment. There was a television series set in the Yorkshire Dales between the wars. The district nurse cycled around on a clumsy great bike just like that one, with a basket on the front.

I had thought Rekraj would find a bike that would help me to get me fit—something more suitable for the mountains. We were, after all, at the foot of the foothills of the Himalayas.

'We will go after some time,' Moti said as she wandered off towards the toilet-shack.

Meanwhile, I popped into my room to tidy up and find my bag.

When I re-emerged into the sunshine, Moti and her mother

had disappeared, so I sat out in the sun and thought I'd try texting my mother again. It was odd she hadn't replied. She never lost a chance to tell me what to do, normally, but all I got was a 'message failed' signal. And the battery was low.

I had assumed there would be electricity here and hadn't imagined there would be a problem recharging my phone. But then it occurred to me that it might be quite exciting to be out of touch completely—and so good not to have my mother's nagging messages. It was amazing that she still had the capacity to wind me up and make me feel awful about myself, even now with just the thought of her, even when so far away.

She's always keen to advise me—even when she doesn't know what she's talking about. And she's forever worried about keeping up appearances, about what the neighbours think. In recent years she had taken to talking about her loveless childhood. What a rich new area for her to whinge about! Maybe that's why my mother's always been cold, never cuddled me as a child, and always complained about children being a nuisance. Too easily spoiled, she always said they were. My mother's never happier than when she's complaining about something. What a way to live!

I looked around, trying to shrug off the sense of oppression and irritation I tended to feel when I thought of her. Two huge bougainvillea bushes grew in the garden along with bottlebrushes and papaya trees. Neat rows of spinach, aubergines and carrots were happily growing too—where I'd peed in the moonlight. The memory of that humiliation made me cringe—again.

A tiny navy blue bird came to drink at some red trumpet flowers. It didn't care what I'd done in the vegetable patch. It hovered like a hummingbird and when the sun caught its feathers, they glinted like they were made of oiled metal. Everything here was so wonderfully exotic.

Why should I care about my mother or the past? Why should the outside world matter to me anymore? This was a lovely place.

I was standing on an expanse of flattened, recently swept mud. I could see the brush marks. This was where the women did most of their housework but they hadn't concreted or paved the area—or even put down any cobblestones. They drew water from a cast-iron hand-pump, of the kind you see in museums and TV period dramas set in the countryside. There were cobbles around the pump and a small pool of water beneath it. Astonishingly beautiful butterflies came to drink there.

My new home—Sister Sweet's house—seemed sturdy enough. However, it looked as if it had been carved out of red mud. The design was ingeniously simple: a real mediaeval wattle-and-daub cottage with walls made of woven reeds supported by big timbers. The thatched roof projected out over small verandahs on two sides of the little house so that things left there could be kept out of both rain and sun. On either side of the doorway someone had made lovely geometrical patterns of mythical animals or some such.

Maybe these people love wildlife as much as I do. Or do they entertain each other with intricate mythological tales about these fantasy animals during their long evenings? Without television, they must do something like that...

Life would be good here, I decided. And I'd escaped the daily drudgery of ironing and cleaning and all those pointless household chores that I used get so obsessed by—in my other life. It would be good for me—to find out what was necessary just to survive and how many material things I *really* needed.

It already seemed such a very long time ago that my GP had encouraged me to come here. I'd gone to see her quite a few times but when she mentioned antidepressants I told her straight that I wouldn't take them—never, ever. I'd read about what they do to you. Pill-popping wouldn't give me my life back, I knew, and I wasn't going to be dismissed with a quick fix.

I was indignant actually. 'How do you know it isn't a brain tumour that's causing my symptoms?' I challenged her.

Something horrible had certainly taken me over. I'd done all I could to avoid stress but even then I had remained in a dark place and couldn't see a way out.

In frustration, I told her it would be far better to take off to India or Nepal with this company that arranged working trips in the developing world. I had family connections there, after all.

It turned out that she had spent time there too. Enthusiasm shone from her as she exclaimed, 'How wonderful! You *must* go! A trip like that will help you find yourself again. I'm sure of it. It'll give you a boost and with your interest in flowers, I know you'll love it.'

I told her I wasn't interested in anything. Still, she rambled on at me. I expect she was fed up listening to my whining, and wanted to get rid of me any which way she could. I would have been the same. Even I was fed up with me.

Life had been a round of infections and new allergies and also my back had been bad—too bad to do anything active and certainly not gardening. She had kept telling me to get out in the garden. But what was the point? I wasn't great before that devastating Friday. Afterwards, everything got so much worse. It wasn't so surprising because the nightmare didn't stop with the cat-scratch.

The Accident and Emergency Department that Friday night was horrible, full of drunks. No one noticed the state I was in. No one saw that I needed help. I waited forever. The doctors were too young and too busy to care. They thought I had been slashing at myself, although I told them the cat had done it to me. I suppose they just saw another dead loss, self-harming female. I had vomit down my front. I probably smelt awful. I heard them talking about me, calling me a drunk. No doubt they'd judged that the scar wouldn't matter, given my alcohol problem. No one wanted to hear my explanations.

After that, almost any little change in my routine made me ache all over—or brought up a rash. My GP seemed to have forgotten all of this. She had brushed aside all my objections, 'You really must go. This trip will help you break out of this cycle of self-loathing. It'll give you something to be proud of. Might kick-start the process of healing. At the very least, you'll avoid the dismal drizzle of an English winter and it'll give you time to soak up some sunshine in an unspoilt village. Boost your vitamin-D stores.'

When I blustered about not being well enough for the jabs and not up to such a trip, she said dismissively, 'I'll give you diazepam—for the flight.'

I couldn't see how I could possibly cope with such a journey but then, on the way home from her surgery, I had a bit of an epiphany. I read 'Reality is closer than you think' on the back of a bus. I was sure that this was a message especially for me. You see, I hadn't wanted to think about reality, especially if there was any chance of it creeping up and grabbing me.

Looking further, I saw that it was only an ad for new kitchens. How sad that civilization has come to this. Reality meant a new kitchen, or a TV show. How pathetic. Then I thought, seeing meaning in back-of-bus advertising was a sign of madness, wasn't it?

Deep down, I knew I had to do something, even if it was—literally—the death of me.

Not that anyone would care if I died. Not now. My life was over. No one spent any time with me anymore. My mother ignored me or just went on and on and on about all the things I did wrong. How I was to blame for all my problems. How—especially after what had happened—I must do something to improve my appearance. Must try to create a better impression. Bloody woman.

The baby in his swinging basket under the verandah started to cry and soon the whimpers turned to lusty, full-blooded howling. I went over to check on it. There were two babies! I hadn't realized there were twins! One was very red in the face. It was probably the infant I'd seen Sister Sweet suckling. I picked him up. Pieces of cloth were wrapped around his nether regions and seemed to be functioning as a crude nappy. They were sodden and filthy and fell to the ground with a splat as I cuddled him. He seemed immediately happier to have shed them. Even then, he didn't smell too good. The other child also looked happier, having lost its crib-mate. They had probably been kicking each other.

I walked over to the hand-pump, worked the handle and rinsed the child's bottom clean. He seemed grubby all over, so I filled a bowl and gave him a good wash. He protested again—more loudly than before. I had imagined these children would be tough and used to this but I suppose it was reacting to the cold.

Sister Sweet suddenly appeared by my side. She snatched her baby from me, saying nothing but making tut-tutting noises. I was trying to help but she acted as if I had done something wrong.

Maybe I shouldn't have interfered but that's what I do—I try to help, and I'm misjudged, misunderstood.

Sister Sweet dried her son, wrapped him up again and put him to her sagging breast. The crying roused the other child, whom she scooped up and suckled as well.

Guliya

I do not know if this memsahib is too old to have children. Maybe that is her problem. It is difficult to know the age foreigners have achieved because even some of the young ones have white hair. This memsahib's hair is light in colour so she may be old. She is also hunched like an old woman: her shoulders are curled around her chest. Perhaps her belly aches. Perhaps she feels pain also. Maybe this is why this queerie doesn't laugh.

It is my idea that this foreign woman is mad—or possessed. Or maybe she is a witch. My husband's cousin says she is. It is a shocking thing that she has done to my Kancha. Imagine doing something as dangerous as washing him all over in cold water like that. Now he will get a fever and he might also die. What to do? The Brahmins in the temple must be given yet more money. It is a blessing that she didn't immerse my niece's baby also.

As I am thinking these things, my neighbour calls out to me. She is complaining yet again that little Atti has wandered into her garden and is playing there with Siru and another Tharu child. These Brahmins do not like that we Tharus live amongst them now. They are troubled to think that we are as good as them.

I walk into the Brahmin's garden, eyes lowered, and quietly take Atti's hand. I steal a glance at the Brahmin woman. She has one of those small smile-shaped sickles sticking out of her cummerbund. I laugh inside—at the irony. Brahmins should not use these implements for they never smile—except when they are making money from others' misfortunes.

That gets me thinking about all the pain and anguish that Brahmins have caused our people over the years. It is odd that Brahmins and Muslims don't laugh when they have so much. I do not know why they are miserable. They do very little work also. I don't mind; I am used to miserable people. It is their karma to be miserable and it is my karma to be content. Maybe people become miserable if they do not drink alcohol.

As I return to my work, I think about the celebrations we have enjoyed. I think about how important our extended family is and what good people the Tharus are. I was thinking like this when a new stranger arrives. He is an outsider, a townie. He walks up to where I am squatting at my chores by the hand-pump. I stand to show my respect.

He wears a city coat-pant outfit but he does not look smart or wealthy. He spends a long time on the preliminaries. He talks about nothing for so long that in my mind I am able to list all the possible reasons for his visit.

I have heard about outsiders who ask lots of questions. My relatives have warned me about new taxes and land swindles so I say little. I try to be vague. I give him no information. This is difficult though. He is highly educated and clever and uses lots of words I do not understand. It is fancy Brahmin language. He doesn't speak ordinary Nepali like we all speak in the bazaar. Maybe everyone speaks like that in the big cities like Nepalgunj and Kathmandu—I don't know.

Then as I am getting more and more suspicious, he starts talking about himself. He is a government man with good prospects. He will have a government pension. He is ripe for promotion. I begin to understand that the reason for his visit isn't about money or work or our land.

He explains that because he's always worked away so much, the opportunities for marriage had come and gone. However, he is now in an excellent financial position and he is the right age to take a wife. Now he's said that, I am very surprised and confused, until he blurts out, 'I have come to ask about your daughter Kamala. Has a marriage been arranged for her? Or perhaps she has feelings for one certain man?'

My head is whirring. I feel weak. I know that it is best not to say too much in situations like this. Would such a marriage mean that my Moti would go away with him? And then, if his financial position is so good, why isn't he already married? Perhaps he already has one or two wives in his hometown.

It is so difficult because one can never know about outsiders. One doesn't know their parents and uncles and cannot know if they are good people. I say, 'It is not correct for you to talk to me about these things, Sahib.'

'You are right, didi. I must talk to your honourable husband. But I also hope that you will say some nice things about me to your esteemed daughter.'

'Kamala is very young, Sahib. She is still studying also.'

'I am pleased to know that she is studying.'

I ask, 'May I know your caste, Sahib?'

'I am Newar, Madam. A Shrestha, actually.'

That is the surname that low-caste Newars take when they want to leave their roots behind. I don't like this kind of dishonesty. Even if he is educated—and rich also—I am not interested in him. He may have influence, of course. He might protect us from the Brahmins I suppose, but Moti's happiness is more important than anything. I know it is best to marry within one's own caste.

Newars are so different from us. They have such a strange and difficult language.

I don't know what to say next. I make an excuse. I say, 'My husband will come from the fields soon. I have to cook rice.'

This Newar man understands that I do not want to speak further. He makes me promise that I will talk to Moti—and to my husband. He says his name is Dhan Sing.

An eagle flies overhead and that makes it certain: a union with this Newar will not be favoured by the gods.

I will need to be very careful also about what I tell my husband. He is gullible. He is naive and will not give good advice to Moti. He is too kind for his own good, and will want the best for Moti only. He won't be able to think beyond the man's status and government pension.

Sonia

The 'main road' to the bazaar was bordered by hedgerows of bright red hibiscus and cobalt-blue trumpet-shaped convolvulus that transformed into royal purple through the course of the day.

How different this was to the drab smelly privet hedges of England. African marigolds grew everywhere. Gorgeous green parakeets squawked. Magnificent mango trees and giant bamboo groves gave welcome shade. I wondered if I should share what I was thinking with Moti. She was so young, and she was very quiet—unusually quiet—and I thought it best to keep my peace. Maybe she was angry with me for bathing her baby brother.

A buffalo-cart came towards us. I love the huge, sad brown eyes of water buffaloes and the way they steadily, surely plod onwards unperturbed by their enormously heavy loads. A pair of them was pulling about thirty sacks of grain.

Moti grabbed my elbow and guided me to the side of the road. I'd been so mesmerized that the buffaloes had been about to run me down!

As they ploughed past, a cloud of dust engulfed us. I began to choke. Moti had already put her sleeve over her nose and mouth. She said we should let the dust settle before we walked on. As the dust cleared, another superb bee-eater flew over.

Moti must have been watching me because she said, 'You like birds, Memsahib?'

'I do—very much.'

'Then come—look.' Again she tugged at my sleeve; she pulled me across the road and pointed into the hibiscus hedgerow. 'Can you see, Memsahib?'

I could see nothing.

'There!' The movement of her hand activated a huddle of scraggy nestlings. Suddenly, they stretched up, squawking. Their yellow-lined mouths gaped wide as they strained towards us, hoping we'd stuff regurgitated insects into their mouths. I counted five of them.

'Wow!'

She beamed, clearly delighted that she'd delighted me. She

pouted her mouth towards another part of the hedgerow and said, 'That is Mummy.'

A scarlet-bottomed bulbul scolded us noisily for going too close. Suddenly I was choked with emotion. I vividly recalled from nowhere a perfect moment in my childhood when my father had shown me nestlings. They, too, were all straining towards us, hoping we'd stuff them full of pre-chewed worms. I could still occasionally conjure up that feeling of wonder we both shared at seeing such little miracles. It hadn't stopped him deserting his brood though.

The childhood memory that still clouds my horizons is sometimes there in my worst dreams. It was the day my father didn't come home. Mum said he'd gone to hell. I was eleven. I didn't understand why, if he'd died, Mum didn't cry. Imagine my surprise when he phoned! I asked him what hell was like and he said that he wasn't in hell; he was in heaven—living with a beautiful angel. It was only much later that I worked out that he'd just gone off with a younger, less bossy woman. They're still together too. She's quite nice actually, although I can never think of anything to say to her.

I should probably write. Maybe they'll be impressed at my finally summoning the pluck to do this trip. It would be nice if someone was impressed. That would make a nice change. But should I write, though? My counsellor always said that I've got to stop doing things to impress other people. I must do things so that I'm proud of myself, which is pointless really.

How am I ever going to do anything to impress hypercritical, anal me?

There I go again, forever putting myself down.

My counsellor told me repeatedly that I must make myself the centre of my life. I should say things like 'I feel good.' 'I am good.' 'I am a nice person.' Actually I *was* beginning to feel better about myself, a little. But then my mind would wander back to my mother and the way she blamed me entirely for the divorce.

She'd forgotten that I'd done everything for him—and his precious career. I'd given him the confidence to be ambitious. I'd put up with those fashionable other wives who were so impossible to impress. I should have been more devious: I should have tantalized and teased him more, denied him more. But I didn't want to be like that. I was happy devoting my life to him. Maybe that was an excuse though—for having no high or worthy ambitions of my own.

I see now that he was shallow and that my sense of wonder came from my father. It's been a long time since life felt wonderful, though. Maybe here I will feel it again.

'Thank you, Moti. They are wonderful!'

She smiled—as proud as if they were hers, and hers alone.

She walked on. It was hard keeping up, but that didn't matter too much as Guliya's house was less than a mile from Rajapur's central market. This was the route that all traffic took, yet it was nothing more than a sandy strip between houses and storm ditches. My open-toe shoes sank into the sand with each step. I was glad I hadn't brought the bike.

3. TOO OLD FOR LOVEMAKING

Guliya

What have I done to offend the gods? First, the memsahib bathes my baby Kancha in water so that he will get ill. Now there is this new problem of the Newar man who wants to marry Moti, isn't it? I do not know what to say to him to make him go away. It will be useless for my husband to talk to him. My husband will be impressed by his city clothes only.

It might be dangerous to talk to Moti about him also. She may be seduced by the idea of going away with an exotic husband. She is too young and cannot make a good judgement. I do not think she will be happy with him for long: not if she has to live far from her family.

He looks like a weakling to me. There is no meat on his body. What to do? Suddenly there are a lot of problems in my life. There are so many outsiders. Perhaps they have caused this change and have taken away my contentment.

I am puzzled about the new memsahib's illness also. Up close she looks fat and healthy. Her skin is as smooth and pale as a film star's but it is my idea that perhaps she is very old. This woman breathes heavily as if her blood has become thin.

This is a common problem for all women. Some of my girl-cousins are also suffering from this problem of thin blood. They cannot do their work properly.

Perhaps there is some terrible disease in the memsahib's legs or perhaps she has had some accident that has broken her back because she has difficulty walking. Actually, I have heard that there is some problem that these white-skinned foreigners have that they cannot walk—none of them. This is why they always need to travel by car.

Maybe that is why these bideshis get angry so easily. The memsahib seems angry and she doesn't greet everyone properly. I don't care—it doesn't matter. Little Kancha is crying. Moti can't quieten him; he needs his mother.

My husband is also complaining and making a fuss. He has come from digging out the landlord's canal and he is hungry. When I try to say something to pacify him, he cheekily touches my plump breasts; he likes it when I have milk. He makes me laugh also.

Now that he is old—he is forty—I wonder whether he'll become less interested in lovemaking. Sometimes I think I should arrange a younger wife for him. She could help with the chores so that Moti could study more. But really I prefer to keep my husband to myself. He is a good man. He has a fine moustache, and other pleasing attributes. We've had seven children together, as well as the three who died.

It is interesting to think on how hard it was giving birth in days gone by. Me myself, I was born in a cowshed but when it came to my time to deliver our first child, we didn't even have a cowshed. I just had to manage outside—on my own. It is necessary to go outside while giving birth so that the house is not polluted. If the child comes out dead, then his spirit will kill all future babies.

There was great pain in this first labour of mine—for three days. Then finally, our first son was born. Little Jhetta. My husband was pleased and proud but I was weak for a long, long time afterwards.

Things are better for women now. These days that old Tharu woman from Gumna village stays with us when we bear children. She brings all kinds of modern things to help. She brings a big sheet of plastic to squat on and she brings a new clean blade and string to tie the cord also. And her old bent hands are skilled. She knows how to help and how to make the birth easier and quicker. She has been to the big hospital in Nepalgunj for training. She has saved a lot of women from days and days of pain, and I think she has also saved lives. She has become every woman's friend—except, of course, the Brahmins are critical of her. The Brahmins are critical of everyone—they even criticize each other. They say that the old Tharu woman from Gumna helps out wicked unmarried girls. They say that she is sinful—and polluted also. But because of her, I lost few babies.

Thinking about the children I've lost makes me sad.

Losing the first was the worst. We were so happy with our firstborn son. I still remember his carefree sunshine smile, his delighted giggles when he chased geckoes and the way we all laughed at him as he toddled around clutching my skirts or riding on his father's shoulders.

This boy—my Jhetta—died on the journey to this village. This was the terrible time when the Brahmins had forced my family off our land—the land that we owned—in the Dang Valley. We had no choice in those days. If we had stayed, we would have starved so my family decided to join distant cousins in Rajapur. My husband paid the letter-writer in the bazaar to send word. Then we set out in the direction of the setting sun.

Sometimes we managed to buy rides on trucks but mostly we walked. Sometimes we'd reach a river and there was no ferryman for a few days. Finally, we reached the Karnali river and stopped to wait again—on the stony shore. We waited half a day before a fisherman agreed to take us on to Rajapur Island. He charged us too much money and frightened us with stories of all the things that might kill us.

He was right to warn us. The island was mostly wild jungle in those far-off times. It was a hard life and there wasn't much to eat. But we had no choice. We had to grow enough food to survive. We didn't have enough money to return, and anyway, there was nowhere to return to.

My next child died of fever, before her first birthday. The fever had been bad in those days and killed so many people, especially during the monsoon. Snakes also killed many relatives of mine. People were bitten as they cleared the land or cut ripe rice. That is what happened to one of my cousins. She was pregnant and so was night blind as is usual during pregnancy. She was bitten when she went out at night to piss. She died also. Sometimes wild elephants attacked. Ghosts and demons were also common in those days.

Now things are much better and, although I am growing old, I am happy, mostly—as long as the greedy, clever Brahmins continue to leave my family alone—so long as they take no more of my daughters. Daily still, I wonder where Maya is and what she is doing. I pray that she is happy.

I smile to see my husband's chickens pecking around the yard. Most of them are squabbling over insects that fall—constantly—from the deep shade of the mango tree. My youngest daughter is in the tree. She's with the black and white hen—the most intelligent one. It is getting the juiciest insects up there in the branches. The tree is strong and healthy. There will be many mangoes again next year, if the palm squirrels and the hornbills don't get them first.

These days we are quite rich. We have some rice in our storage bin and some maize in the rafters. The outside leaves of cauliflowers and cabbage are drying on the roof so that we can store them and eat them in winter. It is a long time since we had to go hungry. And these days when I become pregnant, I can still see in the dark!

Sonia

The sun wasn't that high in the sky but it was getting unpleasantly hot already. It was hard keeping up with Moti. I started to feel a little out of breath. I was so unfit. Moti must have sensed I was struggling, because she turned to allow me to catch up.

After a few moments, she asked me, 'Memsahib is angrez?'

'No—not angry at all!' I replied. 'But *you* seem angry. Have I offended you?'

Moti looked puzzled. She asked, 'Memsahib is no angrez? From which country Memsahib is coming?'

'England.'

'I think Ing Lan. Angrez. Blighty. Joo-kay. All the same; that is my idea.'

'Sorry, Moti?'

She spoke slower. 'Ing Lan. Angrez. Blighty. Joo-kay.'

'Oh! Yes, I see. I am from England—Ing Lan in the UK. That *was* my home.'

I'd misinterpreted her look. She wasn't cross; she seemed fine with me—thank God.

We walked on beneath scarlet-blossomed bottlebrush trees and past orange trumpet-shaped flowers where sunshine-yellow birds hovered and sipped nectar. A man walked past, looked me up and down, looked at what I was looking at and back to me again. Actually every man seemed to size me up—or was this paranoia?

Rhythmic tapping noises drew my attention to an area where an army of ragged women squatted at their work. One had a terribly bruised face. The women used hammers and chisels to chip away at gravestone-shaped stone slabs. Perhaps a hundred gravestones.

What was going on? Had some epidemic struck Rajapur? Was it bird flu or plague? Migrating wildfowl come through here, and there are outbreaks of real mediaeval bubonic plague in India from time to time…

I asked Moti, 'Why so many gravestones?'

'Grabestones? What is grabestones, Memsahib?'

'To mark a place where someone is buried.'

She knitted her brows. 'Berries, Memsahib? What kind of berries you like? We can eat mulberries?'

'No, not berries. After death. You bury people. Dig a hole and put people in the ground. Then you mark the place with a stone block—like these.'

'No, Memsahib. When Nepali peoples dies, we burn and throw hashes in the holy river.

'Hashish?'

'Truly, Memsahib. Hashes. Then, after some time, people are reborn.'

'So what are these stones for?'

'For making chutney.'

I felt so foolish. This was a kind of pestle and mortar factory. The stones were used to grind spices.

We walked a while in silence until we came to a place where various traders had spread their wares on the ground. One man squatted beside a huge heap of old clothes. On top was a bra that was almost big enough to carry your shopping home in—or a couple of babies; there was also a pair of y-fronts that looked designed to fit a rhino. These must be things that people in wealthy countries had donated; I would never have expected them to be *sold* over here though.

A child came running by, dragging an old cigarette packet on a string. How clever to improvise a toy from rubbish! A thin old woman pulled a nice-looking jumper out of the pile of second-hand clothes, and started the long process of settling on a price. Trader and purchaser were both enjoying the exchange.

Lots of strange and colourful things were on sale in various shack-shops, including an unbelievable range of beautiful dress fabrics. I stood undecided about whether to venture inside when that Ram-person, Rekraj's cousin, appeared from nowhere. He made me start. He said, 'Madam, now you are coming to the most important building in Rajapur!'

I didn't like him. I wanted to get away from him but at the same time I was ever so slightly intrigued, so I said, 'Ah. Good. How interesting.' What could the building be? Probably a temple. Definitely something very ancient.

He smiled in that chilling predatory way of his. 'I am delighted that I interest you, Son-i-ya. I shall enjoy having such an appreciative and attractive visitor in our unworthy village!'

Sickened, I tore my eyes away from his. I needed to change the subject to something neutral but my mind was blank. I felt the anxiety rising in me again.

We walked to a slightly more affluent-looking part of the village. Massive trees framed a dusty avenue. Before us was a small low concrete building where a wizened man in stained khaki stood smoking at the gate. He held a rifle like something from the First World War but neither he nor his weapon looked at all menacing. Another ancient, apathetic-looking guard sat in the shade of the verandah with a similar beaten-up weapon across his knees. Nearby, a huddle of shiny black crows squabbled over a scrap of goat skin.

I turned to the Ram-person and asked, 'Is *this* the most important building in Rajapur?'

'Of course.'

'What? The bank?'

'Correct: the bank. You will need to change your dollars there also.' I looked at him. He preened under my gaze. His moustache looked like a parasite that had flown onto his face and then stayed to grow fat on the slimy words that came from his mouth.

Then spookily, the letch melted away.

Moti, who must have been furtively following, magically reappeared. I felt immediately safer. It would be all right to continue my stroll, though the encounter with the Ram-person left me on edge again.

Dust rose in silent puffs at each footfall. Moti and I came to a crowded part of the market. Stalls offered pretty hair-slides and earrings and needles and thread and buttons and interesting colourful powders. I guessed from their exotic aroma that these were spices. One stall sold an array of tatty yellowing postcards—of Bollywood screen gods, real gods and wrestlers.

Far too many people were here although everyone was small, skinny and nimble so there wasn't that much jostling. Around us were women in saris, women in traditional Tharu dress, a nun in purple, men in loincloths and men dressed as though they were in London.

So many children wriggled past and between grown-ups' legs that it reminded me of something I'd read about the need for more family planning in Asia. It certainly seemed as if our government should help with that.

There were so many people pushing past that I didn't notice him at first but then I realized that Moti had disappeared and that Ram-man was standing beside me again. Standing far too close. I remembered some TV programme I'd seen a while back about the way different cultures have different comfort distances—and how us inhibited Brits need more space than any other nation. Even so, I was sure he was still standing far too close. He was brushing up against me. I didn't like it but the little alley of stalls made it hard to move away without seeming terribly rude.

I looked around, wondering where Moti was. I stepped back from him, as if I wanted to look at the next stall. He stepped quickly forward, and now I was sandwiched between him and the stall. I grabbed a wooden maraca-shaped object from the stall and held it out to him, trying to push him away with, 'What's this?'

'It is nothing,' he said taking it from me and replacing it on the stall.

I picked it up again and shoved it at him, pushing him an arm's length away, 'I really want to know what this is.'

'It is part for hookah pipe. Hubble-bubble you are calling it. For smoking. But I think you are not a smoking Madam?'

When he took it from me this time, his hand brushed against my breast. Now I knew that it wasn't any cultural difference that made me feel hemmed in by him.

'Don't you *dare* touch me!'

He put on an innocent butter-wouldn't-melt-in-my-mouth expression and held up his hands. 'I thought you would like to taste Nepali man. Are English women not passionate?'

'No! They are very reserved. And choosy. We have high standards—and you don't meet mine. If you come near me again, I'll scream. And I'll tell Rekraj!' I sounded like a schoolchild.

'I have done nothing. This is a small, small misunderstanding—of my hospitality.' Ram Krishna laughed as if he didn't care, as if he had no respect for me, or for womenkind in general, or anyone. He swaggered away, looking pleased with himself. The nearest stall-holders—all men of course—sniggered. I felt sick and vulnerable.

A tug at my elbow announced that Moti had reappeared.

'Did you see what happened, Moti?' I spluttered.

'I did see, Memsahib. He is bad man. We women can do nothing. No thing. It is our burden. It is our life.' She shrugged and led me on through the bazaar.

We shoved our way on until we emerged into daylight so dazzling, I was temporarily blinded. Something blew against my leg. A soiled plastic bag. Others flew around in the wind. An old horse chewed thoughtfully on a piece of newspaper. Coke and Fanta bottle tops lay in the dust.

A white cow was eating from a vegetable stall. The stall-holder wore a Muslim skullcap but even so seemed to tolerate the plunderer. Cleverly, he had arranged onions along the front of his display, hoping that the cow would steal from elsewhere. He tried to entice her away with some carrot tops.

Next to the vegetable salesman was a tiny wooden stall. The man squatting inside had a bulge in his cheek and blood-stained lips. I wondered if he had some horrible growth in his mouth as he couldn't speak. Whenever a customer approached, he took a shiny deep-green leaf, painted it with grey sludge, sprinkled on what looked like fragments of nutmeg and straw and powders, folded the leaf and then handed it to the customer who stuffed it into his mouth and was also rendered speechless. There were lots of red spit-marks around the stall. The seller added to them. 'You want, Memsahib?'

'No thank you!' I most certainly didn't 'want'.

From the corner of my eye, I saw someone approach, and thought, *Here we go again.* But the stranger wasn't that awful Ram-person. This man looked sickly, sweaty, anxious. I wondered if he had malaria or was a drug addict. He was dressed in trousers and a nylon shirt—like a westernized city Nepalese—but he wasn't stylish.

Then I realized—to my relief—that the stranger was interested in Moti, not me. I thought he was addressing her by name. She seemed to be challenging him, though. He looked at the ground and walked away. She spat, 'Lato!' after him.

'I guess he's not a friend of yours?'

'No, Memsahib. He is Dhan Sing. He is wanting to marry me. But he is old, and ugly also. This is why I called him lato!'

'And lato means?'

'Deaf and dumb.'

Next, and most unexpectedly, she turned and pushed herself in through a rusty old turnstile. I followed, suddenly breathless with anticipation. Where was she taking me?

Hardly breaking step, she slipped off her flip-flops and pointed to my feet. 'Off your shoes also, Memsahib.'

As we entered a verdant garden, incense filled my nostrils. It was like walking into another world, far, far away from the dust and noise and hassle of the bazaar. It felt safe.

The centrepiece of the little compound was a statue in the shape of a short rounded-off column decorated with red powder and flowers, and over it was a stone canopy. Moti bowed to it.

'What is it?' I asked her.

'Shiva lingam.'

'What's that?'

'Mighty Shiva is God of all gods. He destroy and he give new life. This,' and she pointed by pouting with her lips, 'is phallus—sign of Shiva, the Mahadev.'

'Phallus?'

'You no know this word, Memsahib?'

'Err—'

'It is male part that he use to make babies.' Giggling, she gave a suggestive thumbs up. I made a mental note never to use the thumbs up sign in Nepal.

'Um. Err. Yes, I do know the word.' But thought *she* must have got it wrong.

'And this,' she continued, pointing to the frying-pan-shaped base of the statue, 'this is yoni. It means vagina and womb.'

Then I considered—not for the first time—how sexually driven these people were. Do all of them think of sex *all* the time? It seemed like it! I felt like a defenceless little girl here. But surely no one would take advantage of me—unless that foul man Ram-thingamy tried it on. Maybe I should arm myself. My mother used to carry an ancient hatpin to defend herself. Perhaps I could find something like that in the market.

A snore drew my attention to a slumbering priest with a huge stomach. 'Is he drunk, Moti?'

'That is not possible. Brahmins do not take hard drinks.'

Later, when we walked past him, I caught a strong whiff of alcohol.

Regimental Sergeant-Major Bom Bahadur Gurung

The last memsahib had made us laugh so much that we'd been keenly waiting for the arrival of the new one—especially those of us in our community who, like me, are well-travelled and knowledgeable. Then when we'd almost forgotten she is coming, I see her in the bazaar.

She goes into the Shiva temple. I follow.

When I approach and introduce myself, I startle her. Perhaps I disturb a deep meditation on the gods. She looks a little scared also. How can I reassure her?

'I see you are enjoying our Shiva temple!' I say, endeavouring to sound friendly and welcoming.

She looks flustered when she replies, 'Oh, shouldn't I be in here? Being a non-Hindu...?'

I say, 'This place is for anyone who wishes to think and pray and commune with the gods. You are most welcome here and I am Bom Bahadur Gurung at your service, Madam.' I remove my topi, twirl the end of my moustache, give a little bow and offer to shake her by the hand.

She is, oddly, dumbstruck. This surprises me because all women talk too much. It is my idea that a woman talking is as happy as a pig in an open sewer. I also think that although a woman can never be a philosopher, foreign women are said to be assertive and can speak up for themselves. It may be, therefore, that they can have some interesting ideas. So I continue, 'Has Kamala here been explaining everything nicely for you?'

'Kamala? Who is Kamala?'

'Yes, please, this is Kamala standing beside you, Madam.'

The memsahib is looking troubled again and says, 'But this is Moti.'

Moti starts laughing and explains, 'Memsahib, Moti is my nickname. My real name, it is Kamala.'

'Oh, I'm so sorry. I shouldn't have been so familiar. Not so soon after meeting you!'

'It is no problem, Memsahib.'

'Okay, so tell me,' the Memsahib says while the Tharu girl continues to giggle, 'Does Moti mean something?'

'Most certainly, Memsahib. It mean Fatty.'

The memsahib now looks most upset and says, 'Omigod, I'm so sorry! I didn't mean to be rude!'

'It is no rude,' Kamala says, 'I am healthy and fatty. It is nice nickname!' she says, laughing some more.

The memsahib is stuttering like a cretin now and so I repeat, 'I hope that Kamala is explaining everything nicely for you?

'Yes, yes—very nicely; very nicely indeed. Everything.'

As she gabbles, I begin to wonder whether she can speak English.

I say, 'Now, let me ask your goodself Madam one question! Can you guess how I know English-speaking?'

'Did you serve with the British army?' she says. 'Were you with the Gurkhas?'

'You are a most clever and intelligent memsahib. You are exactly correct! Come sit and I can tell you stories about my regiment...'

We sit for a while and I tell her all about my times in the British army; how it is the best and most disciplined army in the world; how this discipline had led to so many Nepalis winning the Victoria Cross. She is polite and very attentive.

She says, 'Of course I know of Gurkha bravery. I think the Gurkhas have come to the aid of the British many times. I believe my great-grandfather might even have fought with the Gurkhas during the War.'

'He was with the Gurkha Regiment?'

'Actually I feel foolish to admit this but I really don't know which regiment he was in. He died when I was a child.'

I am mystified that she doesn't know the regiment.

She continues. 'Tell me though, Mr Ummm, what do you do? Is your family originally from here on Rajapur Island?'

'My origins are the Middle Hills. Rajapur Island used to be dangerous and junglee and very few people lived here. I first came to settle in Rajapur after retiring from my battalion. My military training was immediately useful. My first civilian action, in the Nepali year 2011 (that is in your year 1954), was to save Rajapur from the river. In those days, the town and the bazaar were further west—where now pumpkins and melons grow on the riverbank. I am used to giving orders on the parade ground. My voice, it is strong. I mobilized the community. After the flood, we all moved one kilometre inland, away from the river. In this way, the town was saved then. But the glorious days of Rajapur as a great trading post are finished. No one comes here and no one uses the ferry. Roads bypass us. Our community will become uncivilized again...' I shrug, look at her and venture a further enquiry, 'Now may I ask you one personal question?'

'Err...I'd rather—'

She looks troubled and I do not want this lovely English

lady to think that I might be a dishonourable kind of fellow. I hint at what is in my mind and ask, 'Are you a married lady? You see, I lost my wife also. I am alone for ten years. I am widower.'

She doesn't understand my question and instead she asks me about this temple only. I think this memsahib does not know how to speak pukka English. Maybe she is uneducated.

Sonia

Omigod, I feel so on edge in this country! I could have told this powerful, violent military man that my great-great-great-grandfather might have been murdered by someone like him. Maybe his ancestor did kill my ancestor. Think of that. I also felt stupid not knowing exactly where my great-grandfather had been stationed, although I know he was in Lucknow for a while. I never asked him and now it was too late. He is long dead.

I recited *'Cutty budgie hay'* to myself. It calmed me a little. I felt for my amulet. I steadied my breathing. The tingling subsided.

Contemplating the violence that had formed this region put me on edge but that wasn't all that worried me. First, there was the toilet incident, then the time they got angry about me touching the baby, then I insulted poor Moti (I can't even remember her real name) and now I am getting sexual harassment—*again*.

I was quite taken with this Bom-guy at first, he with his soft, colourful hat and his fine white handlebar moustache, which he'd waxed into two points. I thought he was going to be a gentleman like Rekraj. He was an upright distinguished-looking, older man. At first, I'd been fearful that he'd want to discuss phallic symbolism—but what was in his mind was worse, much worse. What would he do if he knew I was single? I wasn't going to lie but I didn't want to tell him I was fancy-free either.

That's why I asked, 'How old is this temple, please? Do you know?'

'Oh, it is very old.' His face folded into a thoughtful frown. He looked down at his right hand and, using his thumb, counted the joints, first in his index finger and then his middle finger. Then he looked up, beaming. 'I am thinking it is more than forty years old. But you haven't understood my question, Madam. I myself lost my wife. Are you also without a husband?'

'This is a very peaceful spot! I like it here. But I must go. Goodbye.'

Moti hurried to catch me up, 'You like this man, Memsahib? He is very *strong* man!' She giggled as she raised a suggestive thumb again.

'No, Moti, I do not like.' I was beginning to speak pidgin English. 'And I am not searching for a new husband!'

Why does everything—even here—get me thinking about that bloody man all the time, and my mother's accusation that it was my fault he was unfaithful. Just wait till I come home with a souvenir—a Nepalese toy boy. That'll show her! Oh, who was I kidding? That won't impress her. Nothing does. And anyway, for that, I'd need to look further than this Bom-bloke. He was no toy boy.

Moti and I stepped back out into the main street—if you could call it that—but I was so wracked with embarrassment and anxiety that she couldn't keep up with me. I stopped and waited for her and said, 'I really am so sorry. I didn't mean to be rude.'

'You no rude, Memsahib. It is no problem. I like it when you call me Moti. Then you are like my auntie! Come, let us see everything in the market! This way come!'

The next part of the bazaar looked lively and attractive. Colourful goods spilled from simple makeshift shops and out onto the dusty street. There were cloth shops, and plastic goods shops, and aluminium goods shops. At the cross-roads stood the most upmarket shop in town. It sold electronic gadgets, imported shampoos and creams to whiten the skin or treat frigidity. Outside, there were places where other vendors squatted, waiting for customers; there were roasted peanut sellers, umbrella repairers, watch repairers, barbers, tailors and a tooth-puller.

A man with a stethoscope around his neck was sticking a huge needle into the arm of a middle-aged woman. He attached the needle to a bottle of clear liquid that was precariously hooked over the corner of the warped door of his clinic. Other patients lay outside on string beds.

Moti saw where I was looking and said, 'That is doctor-sahib, Dr Dash—he is best bonesetter in Rajapur. It is not too costly to see him. He has certificates from India in his clinic. He has studied for a full six weeks there. My mother went to see him a few days ago. He also gave her this good medicine—by tube—for weakness. It made her little bit strong again.'

Someone had half-buried upended beer bottles to form a kind of miniature garden fence for this clinic-in-a-shack. Sawn-off mineral water bottles had been planted with crimson carnations to make an ingenious and delightful herbaceous border inside the bottle-fence.

Moti said, 'This way come! We will take some snacks. Let us buy samosas. They are tasty—and spicy also. You like spicy food, Memsahib?'

'Mmm—very much!'

'You can eat chillies also, Auntie?'

'Oh yes, please!'

She led me to an unhygienic-looking stall. A greasy individual threw anaemic triangles of pastry into a huge wok of boiling oil. He was the first really fat Nepalese person I'd seen. Within moments, he'd fished out sizzling golden samosas that made my mouth water just to look at them.

He fired four into a paper bag made out of the pages of a child's school exercise book. The child had been practising essential English vocabulary: poetess, seductress, actress, sorceress, temptress, marchioness.

If this is the kind of thing these local children are taught as useful English, I pity them. It also kind of explains why education isn't valued highly in this country. The teacher in me felt a pang.

I could do something here. No one knew my history nor why I'd had to stop teaching in Britain.

Moti intruded on my examination of the paper bag and asked, 'You need chutney, Memsahib?' She held a saucer of puce-coloured sludge. I must have pulled a face because she said, 'It make the samosas extra-tasty. Take! Eat!'

I nibbled at a crunchy corner of the samosa and tasted delicious lentil-flour pastry, the rich flavours of spicy minced goat and onions that were still just a little crunchy. I dipped into the puce chutney and more wonderful flavours burst onto my tongue.

I was about to comment when another sensation hit me. My mouth exploded like it had been napalmed. I couldn't see. My nose dribbled. I was hit by paroxysms of hiccups. I didn't know what to do.

Moti looked at me, wide-eyed, and then she choked. Chokes turned to giggles, and then she stopped even trying to disguise her mirth. The stall-holder started to laugh at me too. Wouldn't one of them do something to help? Might they think to offer me water? I was desperate enough to take it, even if it wasn't safe. I needed a drink. I could just make out through my tears that Moti was talking to the stall-holder. Grinning widely, he offered me a piece of dry white bread.

'Eat, Memsahib!' Moti commanded.

I did, and the hiccupping slowed. I started to be able to see again.

'But Memsahib said she likes spicy food. Is it not so?' Moti laughed.

'Hmm, there's spicy and there's explosive,' I said between hiccups. 'It has completely destroyed the inside of my mouth! Not sure I'll ever be able to speak properly again.'

As I sucked in air over my barely functional tongue, I decided that actually—masochistically—this was a rather nice sensation. The fire in my mouth was calming to an interesting tingling simmer. Even so, I should probably avoid the chutney next time.

4. PROPOSAL

Rekraj

Thinking about my situation, I shall make use of this visitor as well as enjoying the slightly sinful pleasure of looking at her. Her hair is the colour of ripe rice just before the harvest—as it is in the Kathmandu Valley these days. She dresses stylishly and wears makeup as fine as any Bollywood film star. I have noticed that she is nicely curvaceous. Unfortunately, Ram Krishna has also noticed her. I was a little shocked when he shamelessly commented, 'Her breasts are the size of juicy melons.'

When I came to know this memsahib would be staying in Rajapur, I thought we could give her some light typing duties but she has mentioned that she is not a typist. However, if I can involve her in my community work, this would be good for my political reputation locally. I will be admired, seen as modern and international—outward looking—not like those old fuddy-duddy supporters of the Panchayat.

I am facing one problem however. I am unhappy at the way my cousin talks freely about my plan to bring the memsahib to the office. Ram Krishna says he is most pleased. I assumed that he recognized the memsahib would be able to help our charitable work but he talks only of how, in this nice secluded place, he will have the opportunity to have interesting romantic conversations and get close to her again. He is so sure she will fall for his charms. He claims that he felt her melt just a little when he touched her and that it was only a matter of time—and opportunity.

When I reprimanded my cousin, he accused me of wanting the memsahib for myself. Sometimes I am ashamed to be related to this man.

I return to the Tharu house and see what might be arranged about these office duties. The old woman immediately begins complaining. She has no schooling and doesn't speak our national language nicely, so sometimes it is difficult to understand what she is saying. She seems to be telling how the memsahib had nearly drowned her baby in water. Now she is worried that the child will catch cold and die from fever.

Why would anyone do anything so dangerous as putting a baby in water? I shouldn't be surprised. My cousin did warn me to expect the foreigner to do strange things. Then, the Tharu told how the memsahib had chased a cow out of the vegetable patch and that retribution from the gods will surely follow. I give her money so that she can make a suitable offering at the temple. She can pray to Shiva or to Shitali, protectress of small children, so that the boy-child is not taken with fever; she can ask for forgiveness of the gods. That appeases her.

As I converse with the Tharu woman, I see that the memsahib is watching. Her brows are knitted and I am a little nervous that she will start prattling about some other unimportant thing. Or ask more boring questions. Or maybe she wants to learn to speak Nepali. She looks hot and tousled but rises now to greet me. She seems pleased to see me again and talks at length about the bazaar and what she had bought there. She shows me cheap trinkets of the sort low-caste women buy. Her eyes are bright with excitement and she looks beautiful again. It seems strange that such an exotic creature can take delight in plastic hair slides, glass bangles and two-rupee incense sticks but her enthusiasm is charming and makes me smile.

Then, surprisingly, she asks, 'Are there many snakes here?'

'There are not so many in this season,' I tell her. 'They come out at nighttime only. And sometimes in the afternoon. And on rainy days. Sometimes in the early mornings also. Many varieties are available here. We have cobra, viper, krait.'

She looks worried. She asks another stupid question, 'Are the snakes dangerous?'

'Of course dangerous,' I say. 'Many people they die from snake-bite in rainy season. We also have one creature; it hides in cracks and when you go nearby, it squirts poison in your eyes and you go blind—though for sometime, only. After some days, you can see again.'

With an odd look in her face she repeats, 'Only blind for a few days! Well, that's all right then!'

I am pleased I have reassured her but this conversation is actually not interesting, so I change the subject. 'I am so happy that you are finding amusement in this insignificant place! Now, I come today with one proposal—'

Her face falls and she starts to stutter something. I continue so that she is not embarrassed by not knowing what to say. I will not let her lose face. 'I am thinking that you, Madam, might soon grow bored here in our backward community and I am hoping that you will be gracious and help us with our work amongst the uneducated people on the island.'

'Ah, not *that* kind of proposal!' she says, looking relieved and then happy again. I wonder what she means.

'I'm here to help, Mr Rekraj,' she says, her face lit up with enthusiasm again. 'I'd be delighted if you could really make use of me.'

'Truly. There are many tasks...later also, you can help some of the High School teachers with English lessons.'

'Good. So, what shall I do first?'

'You, Memsahib, must come to the headquarters of our NGO and maybe help us fill out these long, long forms and proposals to secure money from the aid agencies. And I will show you our primary school and our income-generating projects—and you can also help with our health programme!'

'Wow! Slow down, Rekraj! I'm not really qualified to do all that! And what does NGO stand for?'

'NGO means non-government organization and our special NGO is called the Rajapur Gender Equality Forum. It will be good, therefore, that we have one lady helping us. It is no problem, Memsahib, that you say you have no qualifications.'

'No, yes, no. I am a qualified teacher—and a university graduate.'

'I am thinking you have been modest,' I say. 'You, Madam, can help with writing about our work—this only I find difficult in English. The aid agencies, they all like long reports in English. It is such a difficult language. You will be able to help us!'

'All right. Great. Starting when?'

'I shall come for you with my bicycle—tomorrow 6 am—and we will visit the school only!'

'Six in the morning! Why does everything have to start so early?' she asks pointlessly.

I find this an odd question but then I know that these godless westerners do not greet the day with prayer. I myself rise at 4 am to take a full body-wash in the river, then I pray and only then do I take a small snack before starting my duties.

I explain to her, 'Because this is a cool time of the day and nice for riding bicycle. Not so much of dust at that hour also.' I need to go. I say, 'Until tomorrow, isn't it?' I take my leave.

Sonia

I wanted to ask what the latest discussions had been about. Sister Sweet seemed to be remonstrating with Rekraj, who pointed to heaven in a questioning kind of gesture. But I didn't get a chance to find out what was going on. These people were strange. They seemed kindly enough though. I felt they'd look after me.

Sister Sweet approached me with a big friendly smile and said, 'Khana, Memsahib.' And put her right hand to her mouth in a mime of eating. Now that sounded like a great idea.

She had a brass pot in her hand. It looked like a teapot without a handle. She held its spout towards me. I reached out to take it but she pulled away from me making tut-tut noises.

I'd done something else to offend her and looked around for my guides—my guardians. Rekraj had left. I couldn't see Moti either. I was helpless and started to feel nervous again.

But then Sister Sweet broke into another of her disarming smiles and showed me that there was water in the pot and she demonstrated washing her hands with it. Then she started pouring water on the ground towards me. I wet my hands, she handed me soap and then she poured again while I rinsed the soap off and splashed a little water on my face.

'Shahbash!' she said as if encouraging a small child.

Soon I was installed in the chair. Sister Sweet handed me a battered spoon that didn't look especially clean but the delicious smell coming from the plate of food on my lap made my mouth water. I buckled up my courage and tucked in.

I had an enormous pile of rice, and some sloppy orange stuff and some fried mixed vegetables and meat in a thick rich sauce. I scooped up a spoonful of the most delicious chicken curry I'd ever tasted. It was far from tender though. As I chewed in vain I began to wonder whether some rubber bands had fallen into the sauce by mistake. Although the sauce was wonderful, I began to suspect that you weren't supposed to eat the pieces. I was having difficulty manoeuvring a spike of bone into a safe position in my mouth.

Sister Sweet's husband was now tucking into his food too but skilfully fired pieces of bone and gristle out of his mouth and onto the floor. Or he gnawed meat off the bone and threw it at a skeletal dog that had magically materialized in the garden.

I tried to avoid the gaze of an unknown, hungry-looking small boy who stood in front of me. He wore a tiny leather pouch tied around his neck with a piece of dirty string over a tattered T-shirt and ripped shorts. I could see his willy through the rip. Those must be the only clothes he owned.

He watched me intently while mining snot from his right nostril—and eating it. It wasn't exactly an appetizing view. I wished Sister Sweet would notice and take the child away. I coughed to try to draw her attention to the child, expecting she'd feed him but she seemed not to see him. Then I wondered if I should offer him food. Meanwhile, as I retrieved whole cardamoms and a bit of chicken-foot from my mouth, I started to feel comfortable and satisfied, and knew everything was going to be all right here. Sister Sweet smiled across at me as if she understood.

But then Ram Krishna walked over and took away my plate of food...

Guliya

I see the way that Ram Krishna Sahib is looking hungrily at the memsahib. This is a good development. Now he will leave Moti alone—at least for some time.

I wonder again why this memsahib has come here. She is completely incompetent. It is obvious that she is really ill so how will being here help her? What if she gets worse? What if she dies? It will be big trouble if this memsahib dies in my house. I will have trouble from the office in Kathmandu who sent the money, trouble from the Brahmins and also trouble from the gods. Maybe it is a mistake letting her stay here. She is so clumsy, she will probably hurt herself—even if she doesn't die. It is bound to end in trouble.

She even eats rice in a clumsy way, like a small, small child. Then she worries me further by coughing. I have prepared tasty spinach with her vegetables but this is a dangerous food for those with a cough. I wonder about taking it from her. I ask the Brahmin what to do. Ram Krishna grunts then takes the plate from her and passes it to me. It is jooto but I can give it to the hungry motherless child or my second cousin. It will not be wasted. When I return to the memsahib with a full plate but this time with no spinach, her mouth is opening and closing like a stranded fish. She is frowning. She does not understand that we have done this for her own good.

Sonia

The day was cooling. A lot had happened and I'd coped with it quite well. After my initial annoyance and thinking I'd been misled by the gap-year company, I made a decision not to make a big deal of this and to think positively. I told myself to go with the flow. I'd enjoy my time if I followed hippy Paul's example and just chilled. It would be interesting to discover what I would end up doing here.

Life felt a lot better once my stomach was full with Sister Sweet's excellent curry, even if they did do that strange thing of removing the delicious spinach.

I watched her busying about her chores. I wondered how old she was. Her poise made her elegant, despite her lined, weather-beaten skin and threadbare blouse. Her belly was wrinkled and slack from too many pregnancies but she didn't dress to disguise this. I admired that sort of self-confidence. Her thin stretch-marked stomach wobbled above her full, gathered skirt, whose colour had long since faded. The extra band of washed-out blue cloth stitched onto the bottom made it look as if the garment had been made for her when she was a child and had been altered when she'd grown up, or an extra piece had been added after the skirt had shrunk badly. I wondered how many children she'd had. How many she'd borne but had died. I thought of those I'd lost. The shameful termination. Then the wedding, the expectation, and the miscarriage.

I dreaded nightfall. I dreaded its ghosts. Every night I feared the darkness would bring more nightmares—and nocturnal visitors. I'd stow my protective amulet—my vajra—under my pillow and focus on chanting, *'Cutty budgie hay,'* to myself.

Even so, I felt my heart missing beats again, with the mere thought of the night to come. I tried to steady my breathing. But my heart galloped. It felt as if it was climbing up into my throat. Strangling me. My mouth went dry. I was shaking. My chest hurt it was so tight. I concentrated on my breathing. I wasn't going to collapse. I could control this. I had to. There were no doctors anywhere nearby.

My heart wouldn't stop. It kept pounding away.

I knew this feeling. I knew how to control this.

I felt for the amulet. I concentrated on breathing deep and slow. The world gradually came back into focus again. No one had noticed my panic attack.

My mother would have—and she would have criticized me and told me to breathe into a paper bag. Where would I find a paper bag here? I should have taken the sick bag from the plane. There I go again—I wasn't supposed to be saying 'should have' any more.

As I slowed my breathing, the nausea began to leave me and again I could see outside myself. There was nothing to fear here. I was surrounded by kindly, gentle people. Everything would be fine. The cockerel came charging by. The mad antics of the hens almost made me smile.

Sister Sweet—I must learn her real name—escorted me into 'my room' again. I marvelled at her flexibility as she squatted down to light a hurricane lamp. She smiled up at me and showed me how to turn the light up and down. She didn't need to show me. I knew how it worked but then thought that I had probably done something wrong with it the night before, as the lamp smelt a bit.

I was soon safely tucked up in my bed, so tired that I quickly drifted into blissful sleep.

Then, with a sickening jolt, *he* was there in my head and the life-sapping events of that awful Friday evening replayed themselves. There I was in that tumble of guilt and confusion. My husband had come home late from work, as usual. This time, he'd clearly been drinking.

He said, 'I have something to tell you.'

I should have guessed. Work kept him late so often, yet he never seemed that tired and never grumbled about it. He had just become ever more disgruntled with me and he had gone off sex completely. Yet sometimes, there had been a new sparkle in his eyes.

Why hadn't I sensed something was up? The whole thing was a complete shock.

He didn't explain or apologize. He just mumbled something like, 'I'm leaving you—tonight.'

I just stood there.

How could he? Why was he doing this—after all we'd been through? What had I done? Was there someone else? There had to be.

I didn't say anything, or at least I can't remember saying anything. I must have just stood on the same spot—dumbstruck—until he'd finished stuffing a few things into an overnight bag and slammed the front door. Then I went to the bathroom and vomited.

Since then, I've thought of so many questions that he never gave me answers for. I've even thought of some clever cutting comebacks. But I've never said them out loud—it would hurt too much. All I was left with was an auto-repeat in my brain, playing and replaying his heartless announcement, 'I'm leaving you.'

The hurricane lamp spluttered as if it were about to die. I watched it struggling. It gave a final fitful spit and went out. Blackness descended like a curse. I prayed that sleep would soon engulf me...

In the deep darkness later that night, I awoke to a strange sound coming from the corner of my bedroom. It was a scratchy noise that made me think of snakes again. I didn't move. I opened my eyes wide and rolled my eyeballs about to look for the author of the sound. I turned my head ever so slowly, so that it wouldn't know I was there. Should I, dare I, roll over and try to relight the lamp?

More scratching.

Rekraj had said that kraits live in this part of Nepal. He said that these highly venomous snakes can bite you in your sleep without you feeling it. You know nothing until you wake up, your muscles paralysed, unable to breathe.

What an unimaginably awful way to die.

I told myself to stop being so idiotic—paranoid, even. I was imagining things. All had become still. There was no snake in the room. There were no more sounds. I was so tired—exhausted. I drifted again—into a dream about a house that catches fire but the fire is warm and cosy. I toast crumpets on it...

Next time I awoke, I felt more refreshed than I'd felt for a very, very long time. Today would be good: a fresh beginning for a new dynamic me.

I was excited about the idea of working with the dashing Rekraj, and his charity. Until then, it hadn't occurred to me that I might still have some skills, that I might be useful. My only concern was that working with Rekraj would force me to spend time in the company of his cousin. I could see the family likeness between the two men but there was a great deal about this Ram-person that made me uneasy. Like Rekraj, he was good-looking but Ram Krishna knew it and preened irritatingly whenever I glanced in his direction.

I stumbled outside and around to the hole-in-the-ground toilet. The snake was still there by the pink loo roll. We ignored each other. I felt rather proud of that—being able to ignore it—almost.

As I peed, I got the feeling I was being watched. I couldn't resist looking around to check. I started. I saw an eye! It was a human eye looking through the thatch-grass that made up the outside wall of the lean-to. I screamed. A scream also came from the eye. We both screamed again. Then I saw the shadow of a small figure running away. Poor thing. I'd frightened an inquisitive child.

When I emerged from the lean-to, Sister Sweet was outside. She looked puzzled. I offered her a friendly 'Namaste, Gu-li-ya.'

'Tik chha, Memsahib?'

I smiled, reassured that she was there for me even if I didn't understand what she said. I mimed washing, and walked over to the little shelter that was the shower cubicle. Some kind, thoughtful person had left a bucket of water in there. I washed all over by dipping a tin mug into the water and throwing it at myself. The cold took my breath away but it was invigorating. By the time I finished sploshing, my skin was tingling and I was positively zinging.

I tidied myself and, staring into my own little mirror, applied a little mascara and eye shadow and lipstick. I looked at myself and—maybe it was the poor light or something—I didn't look too bad, considering. The sun was already beginning to lighten my mousy hair to something approaching an attractive blonde colour. The scar across my forehead didn't seem quite so purple and wasn't quite as obvious as it had been. Even so, I combed my hair across it to hide it as best I could. Actually, I felt quite sexy—for a change. I wanted to look attractive—for the first time in a long, long time.

It was strange how people seemed to just disappear sometimes. I was ready for breakfast now but everybody had vanished. It was after 6 am.

Where was everyone?

I sat myself down in a sunny spot and waited. I could see, now, how much better it was to work in the early morning light of the open air. It was lovely, actually.

The yard was shaded by a huge red bougainvillea, banana plants and mulberry bushes. Someone had planted a sunny border of African marigolds. The family's chickens pecked about; I could see chicken mess on the upended cooking pots. Close by was an upside-down conical basket with a cockerel trapped underneath. It looked unhappy. I should point this out to Sister Sweet. It made several unhappy pleas for help. I hadn't noticed its protests before and probably she hadn't either. Maybe I should let it out.

I decided. I walked over and released the cockerel. Immediately, it ran at the nearest hen and mounted her. I suppose all males have this urge to copulate. It must be natural but personally I think that there is too much sex in the world. Sister Sweet obviously thought so too, because all of a sudden she was back in the yard. She shot over to the feathery couple shouting '*Neramro Memsahib!*' and tried to stop the cock. He just ran off while Rekraj and Ram Krishna, who had also miraculously appeared, laughed like donkeys.

Then Rekraj turned and saluted me with hands held together as if in prayer. By now I knew that this was the way Nepalese greet each other—formally—although the men hug sometimes. It felt as if Rekraj was treating me like a proper, well-brought-up Nepalese lady. That pleased me. He seemed to be looking at me appreciatively. It certainly felt as if he'd noticed I'd made an effort.

I caught the delicious smell of roasting popcorn as Sister Sweet brought tea. Rekraj noisily slurped his, while Sister Sweet suckled two babies. Clearly, my guess that her age was sixty had to be wrong then. I was astonished to realize that she was such an Earth Mother. Her other little daughter was trying to climb into her lap to join the babies; she laughed and seemed to enjoy the attention. Had I ever had children, I would never have been that patient.

Ram Krishna asked, 'Why you did let cock out, Memsahib? He wants to be too busy with his girlfriends!' I was sure he was making this suggestive remark deliberately.

I tried to make my answer sound challenging, 'Because he was unhappy!'

'Cocks are not having feelings, Memsahib.' Ram Krishna considered me a half-wit.

'This is a bad cock,' Rekraj explained. 'He need stay in the basket.'

I'd done the wrong thing again. Everything was so different here. So, so different. This was not at all a good start to the day.

Rekraj then said conversationally, 'The baby is not sick today!'

'What? One of the twins?'

'There are no twins in this family, Memsahib. This other baby belongs to another mother.'

'What? A different mother?'

'This is the baby of the niece of Guliya who cares for the child while the mother works in the fields.

'Oh, that's nice,' I said, thinking that I must have misunderstood what he was saying. Surely Sister Sweet—Guliya—wouldn't breastfeed someone else's child?

'Guliya's baby son, he is healthy today.'

'Good!' This was also an odd thing to say. 'Yes, he looks healthy. I'm glad!'

'Perhaps the fever will come tomorrow—or the next day.'

I didn't understand why he was talking about the baby developing a fever. Maybe they had gone to see a soothsayer or something. The child seemed huge and very healthy to me.

Then I noticed someone else had arrived in the compound: a shifty-looking, emaciated stranger who seemed to be trying to shrink into the shadows. A skinny child with him looked scared to death.

Suddenly, Rekraj commanded, 'Come let's go!'

'Err—where?'

'My office, Memsahib. Come.'

Guliya

I go after the badmash cock, bring him back from the kitchen garden and put him under the basket. Rekraj and the memsahib start to leave for working. Then something very funny happens.

One of the pariah dogs that lives off rubbish in the bazaar pelts into our compound. It is running fast with a piece of goat hide in its mouth. This frightens the chickens. One flies up towards the memsahib's face. It makes some noise. She shrieks and thrashes with her arms to get it away, like she is being attacked by a cobra. It lands and runs off, clucking and hides in among the spinach plants. Memsahib is scared. This is something new for me. This is the first time I have seen someone being scared of a chicken.

It is my idea that this is why the neighbours' children come into my compound often to stare at the new memsahib. They come because she behaves most strangely. Always there is a chance she will do something interesting to entertain us and make us laugh. Perhaps she is a little mad.

She is having a big nose also—like a Mussalman's. Children like to come to look at that too.

Sonia

'It's okay. I'm all right!' I announced, trying to pull myself together and put on a brave face.

But people weren't concerned. They were laughing—laughing at me.

What if that horrible scabby dog had been rabid? Or the chicken had scratched my eyes out, or had some awful disease like bird flu? It was making a terrific noise, after all.

What if living in this unhygienic environment gives me worms or swine flu—or cancer. I am—after all—sensitive and allergic to all sorts of things.

The animals had scared me. My mouth was completely dry. I was fighting back tears.

Rekraj went into the house and reappeared with a wobbly, paint-splattered chair. Where had he found that? He made me sit in it. He was still grinning, damn him.

His cousin—that Ram Krishna—thrust a glass of water into my hand. It was warm and tasted disgusting.

Sister Sweet's husband arrived. Today he wore a normal sort of shirt but a Gandhi-esqe loincloth, which showed off his beautiful, impressively muscular but completely hairless legs. I had never seen a man with such smooth legs before but I couldn't imagine he shaved them. A dangerous-looking sickle stuck out of his cummerbund.

He flirted with Sister Sweet and made her laugh so that her whole face lit up, as if she was in the first flush of love—lucky woman! Laughing still, she pushed him away so that she could continue with her chores.

He squatted down and started trimming his toenails with the sickle. Watching him made me feel quite queasy. I didn't want to look in case he cut himself. I'm not keen on the sight of a lot of blood. Scraped knees I'm used to, but a big deep gash would make me feel ill.

Guliya

When his shadow falls across me, I think it is one of the Brahmins with even more work. Or that unsuitable Newar suitor. I look up. It isn't one of the maliks. It isn't the Newar. This visitor is the last person I expect to see. He is as welcome as a hungry mosquito. And he does look hungry. My mother used to call him the radish, because of his stupidity. He was never big but he is even skinnier than before.

A small unhealthy-looking boy stands behind him; the child's eyes look like a dead man's. Hari's wearing a new black tracksuit, big heavy glitzy jewellery and expensive sunglasses. His hat is at a silly angle so that the peak is over his ear—not shading his eyes as it should be. After all these years, he looks just as reckless, just as stupid. It looks as if this child has gone hungry to buy his fancy clothes. I am immediately angry with him. No other untouchable would have had the audacity to let his shadow fall across someone of higher caste. He is disrespecting of the fact that I am his elder also.

Despite myself I had liked him. I understood why my little sister had fallen in love with him, a mere Badi. He had been handsome; he still is. He was brash. He spent any money he had on clothes, on fine things—and on her. He made us laugh, too, with his clowning. That had been a long time before...was it seven, eight monsoons?

Now he is back and I know straightaway he comes with bad news. I know he will be a burden to our family. He will bring bad karma also. These days there are so many problems in my life.

I stand up from grinding the spices for the morning rice. I stretch. I do not greet him. What is it that I have done to offend the gods? How do I deserve this terrible karma? This morning my baby Kancha has a slight fever. I know that he is getting ill, and now this useless man is back. He is back and he has brought a child. I hadn't known he and my little sister had a son. I feel sorry for the child.

We look at each other. Nothing is said for a long while.

I think about that time, many monsoons ago, when he announced that he was going away to Kathmandu. Back then, he promised he would bring back money for the whole family. He'd said that there was lots of highly paid work in Kathmandu—and how, in the capital, caste didn't matter. He told us that there it is easy to hide the fact you are an untouchable. You change your name—no one knows. But we received not one paisa-piece. He promised he would make us proud. We heard nothing. He promised so much. He appeased us with promises but then he eloped with my little sister, and after that we heard nothing.

Nothing for all these years.

I can see that it hasn't been easy. I can see he hasn't eaten well for months. I know that look too well. I hate that look.

'Will you drink tea?' I finally say, though I am sure my husband will be angry if he sees this man eating or drinking in our compound. My husband won't have forgotten the slur this man brought to our family. 'You look hungry. I think you need rice also?'

He rocks his head in a way that says he needs and will accept anything I am willing to give. He looks famished. His eyes are wet.

'Sit—here on the verandah. Take this tea. And there is some for you, little one.' Poor scared little runt. Then I say, 'So there was a child? We didn't know there was a child.'

He looks away. He mumbles that there were two sons. He addresses me respectfully as 'bauju', sister-in-law. I feel a stab of pain when he calls me bauju, though he is truly my brother-in-law. Hari bhai says that the little one—my nephew who I'll never know—died last month. He didn't even see two years. Sorrow weighs heavily on me on hearing this news.

I don't want to ask the next question but I have to. 'And my little sister?'

He looks down again. He says that she died soon after

their second son was born—nearly two years ago. What did he expect but bad karma if he dishonoured the gods and the elders? He eloped with my sister without the blessings of our parents or a priest. They didn't walk around the sacred fire. Is it surprising that the gods cursed their union?

Sonia

Rekraj and I both had bicycles but the sand was so deep that we had to push them for the first few hundred metres. That gave me a chance to admire the countryside: the odd angular kapok trees, the morning glory and crown-of-thorns hedges and all the shy twittering birds. I saw a sleek black bird sweep out to scoop up an insect. I was moved by the beauty of a V of snow-white egrets flying against a clear blue sky as they headed off to the river to feed.

When we joined a road that looked as if it was used by vehicles, we were able to cycle again. Soon we overtook a cart pulled by two big black water buffaloes. They both looked as if they were dreaming of paradise, not pulling a cart piled high with a ton of timber. The cart had car tyres on the wheels, which explained why I saw so many tyre-tracks and so few vehicles and why the island was so beautifully quiet.

What an unusual experience it was to be somewhere where you couldn't hear traffic noise. The sharp sunshine made all the colours of the countryside bright and alive and I started to sing to myself as I pedalled.

For a while, we wobbled alongside a shallow irrigation canal. Wagtails ran in and out of the crystal clear water. Flowers the colour of forget-me-nots grew along the canal bank. I stopped to watch a superb turquoise-and-orange bee-eater flying in wide sweeps. When the bird caught an insect, it returned to a perch and carefully squeezed out the venom and then scratched out the poison sacs from the bee's backside.

Rekraj doubled back, smiling, 'This kind of bird he is so good at catching these small, small insects. And he never get stung!'

I was impressed—not only by that fact but by Rekraj knowing about birds. I'd read that bee-eaters catch a couple of hundred insects a day. Amazing, really.

A toned man in a loincloth squatted beneath the bee-eater's chosen perch. He was bare-chested and barefoot. A rough walking stick lay on the close-cropped grass beside him. He looked as if he was just enjoying watching the water flow by; clearly he had not a care in the world. These people have such a simple, natural existence. How I envied him.

Rekraj wasn't interested and, slightly annoyingly, chivvied me along. Then, when we'd cycled two or maybe three kilometres, he unexpectedly veered off the dirt road. He freewheeled down a tiny side-track that was overhung with banana plants.

'Look—their leaves must have unfurled some days ago, because they're in ribbons now.' I felt knowledgeable, to notice such details.

Rekraj glanced back and cast a crooked smile at me. Maybe he was surprised I would know something like that. These observations were interesting sidetracks to my journey along these back-tracks. I smiled at the pun I'd made.

We passed dugout canoes. We were far from the river or any navigable canals and it seemed an odd place to keep them. Then there was a slight rise in the path and we arrived in a small compound. Here a woman in a short red bodice and sarong was bashing a pile of dried beans with a stick. It looked like hard work but rather pointless. She stopped, dropped the stick, put her palms together and very formally said, 'Namaste Sahib, Memsahib.'

Seeing her was a bit of a relief. I had been feeling somewhat vulnerable. I was sure that Rekraj was an honourable sort of person but nevertheless it was good to realize that there were some women around. I felt safer in female company in this strange new country.

Although, I *had* found a weapon. Browsing in the market, I'd come across a 5-cm metal spike and decided that it would be a suitable substitute for the hatpin my mother used to carry to defend her honour. If a man got up close and over-friendly I could do quite a lot of damage with it. I kept it with me at all times.

We stopped pedalling and dismounted. I checked that my weapon was still there in my pocket, then pulled my hair over my scar.

We parked the bikes and Rekraj led me between several thatched huts and in through the door of a bigger wattle-and-daub building. There were about forty children inside. When they saw us, they stood up, giggling and chanted, 'Velcome, Velcome Madam So-nee-ya. How arrre joo today?'

I was struck dumb for a second. Madam Sonia: they already knew my name! Was *this* the High School? Only this? How did all these little ones learn to speak English so well? I was overcome with emotion. It was so wonderful that someone was giving these children the gift of education.

But I suddenly felt bereft. I had once been a person who changed lives. I had inspired children to look at the world—really look at the world. That had all been taken away though, by that strange embittered ten-year-old back in England.

Rekraj

The memsahib is still very weak. She cycles very slowly and rests often.

On the way, she had stopped at one place beside a tired old Tharu. I know this man. He has not done well since the benevolent system of bonded labour was outlawed. He has one small, small piece of land but it is not productive. It is at the end of that tiny useless irrigation ditch. Mostly, people steal all the water before it reaches his land, so he is going hungry. He cannot even afford to buy a shirt or shoes. He is wasting his time guarding the canal during the day. Does he not know that his neighbours will divert the water after dark? He should go and get some labouring work. Although he is so weak no one will employ him. What can he do?

The memsahib is also rather useless—like this Tharu man. I had arranged it all so nicely but this memsahib cannot even manage to do the needful. All that was expected of her was to say a few words to these children but she stands there with her mouth open like a goat that has just had its throat cut.

'Please make some small speech, Memsahib,' I prompt her. 'The children would like to hear your voice only.'

Slowly, she manages to speak a few hesitant words but it is not an interesting speech. The children are happy, though.

They have never seen a real American and they are looking at her, captivated by her, with her golden hair that forever wants to fly up to heaven, her tight blouse that clings to her breasts, and her skirt that shows her nice shapely calves and ankles. Maybe I am corrupting these children by bringing this foreigner here.

The schoolteacher, he is also looking with too much interest at Madam Sonia, and so I respectfully, shyly, touch her elbow and lead her out of the classroom to our workshop. Each and every one of the children follows us. They are very excited and noisy.

I show Madam Sonia where the destitute abandoned women are making children's clothes to sell in the bazaar. This is low-caste work but these village women, they don't mind. They are working hard treadling at our brand-new Indian-made Singer sewing machines. I notice that they are all well-dressed—too well-dressed, in fact. I expect that these women keep some cloth for themselves. I must talk to the manager about that kind of corruption. This manager isn't alert to these kinds of issues. He is quite lazy, actually.

'Come, Madam, I will show you how you can help us!' As I am leading her out, the schoolteacher arrives at last—wielding a big stick. He shouts at all the children. They run, screaming, back to the classroom.

Now we can talk again. I am distracted though as an eagle perches above us. This is an ill omen. I wonder whether I should go to the temple this night. Meanwhile I chat about that and this on the way to our fine pukka office. It is a proper modern office. I have visited similar up-to-date facilities in Kathmandu.

Sonia

Seeing all those innocent faces turned expectantly towards me, brought back the day I'd been told to leave my class. They came right in the middle of a lesson!

There was the awful disciplinary hearing. And then the trial-by-local-newspapers.

Worst of all was my husband's unsupportiveness. In fact, he even suggested that I might have lashed out at the child.

'Well you have been on edge lately,' he had said, 'and you fly off the handle so easily.'

That had really made me want to hit him. If he had said any more that day I would have. Now I imagined knifing him and then was shocked at the violent thoughts that boiled up from within me so easily. Where did *they* come from? Surely this wasn't really me? Was I going mad? I tried internally chanting my '*Cutty budgie hay*' mantra to see if I could clear my head. How was it that these memories could stay with me even in this remote place? How I wanted to make all this stuff—these echoes of my painful past—go away!

The ebullient Nepalese children jostled and shoved to get close to me. The entire school looked as if they were going to accompany me on my conducted tour and everyone else in the village came along too. All of them seemed to find my visit great fun. The eyes of children and adults alike shone with excitement.

I should have enjoyed being a celeb but all the pressing bodies and noise made me anxious. I felt overwhelmed and exhausted. There were just too many of them.

I was relieved when the schoolteacher chased them away, waving a big stick at the children. But then I felt bad about the teacher's behaviour. I don't approve of threatening children with a beating. Education should provide a model to help people rise above violence. That's what I had tried to communicate to my accusers at the hearing.

Actually, it was hard to imagine these gentle people being violent, although there did seem to be an undercurrent here—a potential for violence.

I suppose it comes from living in such poverty or maybe it is the climate that makes people lose control. That's what they'd said had happened to me—that I'd lost control—because there were bruises on the boy. It was no matter that I knew he'd got them at home. His stepfather, after all, was a drunk.

Civilized people are supposed to aspire to education and that's what I used to think. Yet what good is schooling going to do for the likes of my abused ten-year-old accuser? What chance did he have and what, exactly, had it given me?

I'd always loved reading but lately I'd survived on a diet of romantic novels which mostly made me even more dissatisfied with my life. I wished I'd had more love affairs. Going through teacher training and then straight into teaching, as a job, meant I didn't have time for escapist reading in years but I *had* absorbed articles about how parents ruin their children's lives.

There is always plenty about that in the newspapers and educational textbooks these days. Don't they know how guilty mothers feel already without adding to it? Actually, I think education made me less content—and certainly no more competent—as a wife, aunt and teacher. I don't know why these developing countries think it is so important. UNICEF has a mission to get girls to school but what's the point educating girls living in remote places like this?

As we continued our tour, I started to relax. Rekraj paused to admire a solitary fishing eagle. He enjoys watching wildlife as much as I do! He pointed out a home-made ladder leading up to rickety structure in one of the tallest trees in the area. 'This is elephant lookout post,' he told me. 'It is where, during harvest times, someone keep watch for wild elephants and he alert the villagers to light fires to scare them away. If they do not manage to make elephants go, they will eat the year's supply of food for the village. All of it. Everyone will go hungry. It is *too* difficult living next to national park!'

I had never thought of it like that: wildlife conservation versus a full stomach!

So far, the countryside had been alive with birds. Everywhere I went there were chirps and cheeps and whistles and all kinds of unfamiliar calls. But something very odd happened as we walked towards the ugly concrete box that Rekraj described as the office. An eerie silence fell. Suddenly there were no birdcalls whatsoever and there were no dogs barking either. The hairs stood up on the back of my neck. I told myself I was just being stupid—imagining things.

Rekraj hadn't noticed anything. He led me into a stuffy little office. It was only just large enough for a tiny desk and three chairs. The desk was laid out with an ancient manual typewriter, a pile of papers that had gathered a lot of dust and a pot of dustier plastic tulips.

Why hadn't someone cut a sprig of bougainvillea from just outside? That would have been so much nicer. Rekraj was clearly proud of his pokey office though and stood there grinning at me and watching me as I looked around. He then squeezed around his desk, sat down behind it and rather grandly gestured for me to sit too.

Almost before my bottom met the seat, there was a strange rumbling and my legs started to tremble. Was this some new kind of panic attack? Sometimes I did experience chest pain and breathing difficulties out of the blue. I didn't feel anxious now but these attacks never seemed to make sense. Even so, I couldn't understand why my legs should be trembling—until I realized that it was the ground that was shaking, not me.

Rekraj leapt to his feet, grabbed my wrist and dragged me out through the door. By the time we were outside again the tremor had stopped. The village dogs started to howl. The birds started up too, as noisy as any dawn chorus.

'I am sorry, Memsahib!' he said, looking agitated.

'Sorry, Rekraj? You didn't cause the earthquake. Why do you say sorry?'

'I am sorry for touching you. I hope you are not thinking I am disrespectful. I was thinking of your safety only. Usually, these small, small tremors do not cause any problem but sometimes these modern concrete buildings—they fall down. It is to do with the corruption in our country. The contractor tries to make a little money by using less concrete. You understand me?'

'I understand, Rekraj, and I do not think you have been disrespectful. You have heroically saved me!' I said.

I was shouting and wondered what this charming gentleman was thinking. He was blinking a lot and there was a tiny hint of pink in his cheeks that I hadn't noticed before. I didn't want him to feel awkward. I needed to move the conversation on quickly to prove that I really, really didn't care.

I blurted out the first thing that came into my head but quieter this time, 'Do you get many earthquakes here?'

'We have been having many. I think maybe...' and he

looked down, frowning, at his right hand and counted the joints of his index finger, his middle, ring and little fingers. 'Maybe eleven in this month. It is no problem but maybe Lord Shiva is angry with the Hills Peoples. My second cousin who lives in Kathmandu is very frightened about these earthquakes. If there is a big quake in the city many, many new buildings will fall down. He says it will be very terrible. Many people will die. These city people are always drinking too much of alcohol and eating too much of meat and sometimes they forget to make proper offerings to him.'

I didn't know what to say. I was still a bit shaken. I knew Shiva was often shown dancing in Nepalese religious statues and that he could be a destroyer as well as creator. He made things change and move. He was not a reassuring sort of god. Rekraj's matter-of-fact talk of earthquakes didn't reassure me either.

In that instant, I resolved to write to my mother. I would ignore her caustic comments and make my peace with her. I would explain why I had needed to come here—in case I never got back home again.

'May I ask you something, Rekraj?'

'Hunchha, didi?' he said smiling a smile that made him unbelievably handsome.

I wanted to ask him about the expression that my great-grandfather thought had kept him safe. He was quite convinced of its power. To prove it, he'd kept the bullet that had just missed his head when a villager had taken a pot-shot at him. That incident must have happened somewhere close to here.

I said, 'We have a saying in our family and I want to know what it means.'

'What is the saying, didi?'

'"*Cutty budgie hay.*"'

'This is no Nepali but Hindi.'

I was surprised that my childhood memory of my great-grandfather's odd expression was at least recognizable to Rekraj. He wasn't forthcoming about what it meant though, so I supposed he didn't speak Hindi.

Rekraj

When I was telling her that '*Cutty budgie hay*' is Hindi, not Nepali, she was looking strangely disappointed. I am puzzled also that she calls me a hero—a film star—but I suppose this is meant as a compliment to me. Perhaps she does not understand that film stars have no morals.

Perhaps she is thinking that I am like my cousin Ram Krishna. He has no morals also. Sometimes I think that maybe he is involved in sending girls to Mumbai—or dealing in drugs even. He certainly seems to know a lot about the terrible trafficking business. He told me some days ago that the men who use brothels in Mumbai like our lower-caste girls from the hills. They seem a little exotic, with their almond-shaped eyes and high cheekbones; he spoke of how these big city men are even sometimes satisfied with Tharu girls. How can he know these things? I am not sure where his money comes from also. He is not a good person. I hope Sonia Madam doesn't think I am like him.

I clap my hands and our women helpers bring the table and chairs outside so we can sit in the deep shade of the old mango tree. I explain how we are making applications for funding from international agencies—to help with our work.

'Already we are making a good contribution to improving female literacy. My cousin who used to work for Oxfam and also USAID in Kathmandu is always talking about the importance of female literacy. He says that if the women become better educated, they will drive forward the development of our nation. It is hard to believe but he says it is so. He says that empowerment of women through increased literacy is happening in India and now it must happen in Nepal. I think that we are too much overshadowed by India but he is very passionate about following their lead. He says that only in this way will we Nepalis have the strength to resist India's bullying! He knows these things because he has travelled a great deal and that has allowed him to see other cultures. He has been on many training programmes. He is well-read also. He was recently talking about the new Nepali translation of a book called *Mein Kampf*.'

Sonia didi pulls a face and so I ask, 'Do you know this book?'

'I haven't read it.'

'It is by one successful German. My cousin says we should be proud of our motherland—just like this writer. Maybe he is right.'

It is interesting talking about these things with Sonia didi but we must also think about the work we will be doing together. I explain how she can help us write good English proposals but the ground starts to shake again.

I wonder why the gods are so angry. Perhaps it is all the wrong things done by the memsahib. Perhaps it is her godlessness. Perhaps she is a sinful woman...but I do not think that she is a sinner. Perhaps Guliya did not make suitable offerings at the temple with the money I gave her. Perhaps it is my impure thoughts about the memsahib, when I should be treating her like an honoured guest. Perhaps it is connected with the fact that I, a Brahmin, am working with her, yet she is really and truly outcaste. This thought makes me feel uneasy. It is my idea that it is good that my parents will soon arrange a suitable bride for me.

Suddenly—out of the corner of my eye—I see a ripe papaya start to fall. It is disturbed by a clumsy young hornbill bird. I jump up and catch the fruit before it hits the ground and is spoilt. I am pleased. I bring it to Sonia didi.

'There! Shiva destroys but he also brings the gift of re-creation.' This is a good omen. I ask, 'Do you know this fruit? It is sweet and very tasty. Come, let us eat! This is a good fruit. Look—here is where the maggot has come out!'

She laughs but then says, 'Why do you say this is a good fruit—if it is maggoty?'

This again seems like a strange question. I explain, 'If there is a hole, the maggot has come out. If there is no hole, the maggot is still inside! Then it is possible to eat the maggot by mistake.' She pulls a face as I joke, 'This is not good for vegetarian people!'

But then she starts to laugh also. When she smiles, it is like the sun coming out from behind a storm cloud.

I cut open the papaya. She eats it most inelegantly. I have

to point out that there is a small, small piece on her chin. We laugh together about that also.

Sonia

Gosh—I found it hard to keep up with Rekraj's conversation—from *Mein Kampf* to maggot eating! I thought of that playground riddle:

What's worse than finding a maggot in your apple?
Answer: half a maggot.

Maybe that explains why Guliya took that food away from me so rudely on the first day I was here. Maybe someone spotted a maggot in the spinach!

'Oh and I am forgetting one thing…' Rekraj reached into the inside pocket of his jacket and pulled out a letter.

He said, 'This arrived for you, didi.'

I wasn't expecting any communications, especially so soon. He handed it over and I felt the warmth of his body on it. I turned the envelope over and noted the Queen's head on the stamp. Surprisingly, I wasn't interested. I was trying to avoid thinking about my previous life. I didn't know who I expected to write to me.

Recognizing my mother's hand, I was disappointed. I didn't open it. It would be full of accusations of irresponsibility. She'll probably mention the divorce again, even though she must have known that the spark had gone out of my marriage years before.

'It is a letter from home, I am thinking? It is from your family?'

'From my mother,' I told him.

'And your husband, he is…?' he asked, looking suddenly young and bashful.

'I have no husband.'

He looked confused when I said that but I wasn't going to explain. This letter had obliterated my joyous mood. *He* was back in my head again—even here.

I'd forgotten when I'd last made my husband laugh. I used to though—when we were first married. We used to giggle a lot. I used to have the whole family in fits. And my pupils too—I miss the little ones and their trusting innocence.

Now I'm saggy and spent. I've lost all my small enthusiasms, and my thighs wobble when I walk. I did consider—on more than one occasion—begging him to come back to me. But no matter how much I grovelled, I knew he wouldn't. He had replaced me—with a loud bleached blonde. What hurt was that she seemed so ordinary—dull, actually. Perhaps if we'd had children, things would have been different.

Fleetingly, after the divorce, I had thought of going to live with my forever-too-busy mother again but she would have had no mercy. She poisoned our relationship when she blamed me for my husband's affair. I was like my father, she said. He wasn't around much while I was growing up. He was always away on business trips. All he seemed interested in, when he was at home, was football. He didn't talk much. Or if he talked it was about football. I think he chose that subject just to annoy my mother.

'I have intruded, Madam!' Rekraj looked concerned and a little uncomfortable.

'I'm sorry?'

'I have intruded into Madam's private life. I did not wish to give offence or distress...'

'I'm sorry Rekraj. Don't worry. My head is completely messed up...'

'But your hair is beautiful, didi.'

'I wasn't...oh, never mind.'

I must have been sitting there in silence for ages. He looked concerned and confused but the nausea was rising in me and I couldn't explain. Not then. I just wanted to run away...return to Guliya's house.

When I got back to the house, the devious-looking Nepali chav had gone. I was pleased, because he'd been staring at me, which gave me the creeps. His skinny child though was playing shyly with Guliya's children.

My hostess greeted me formally, coldly and without her usual sunshine smile. I felt bad. Guilty. But for what? The nausea grew worse. I had definitely done something to offend her.

The baby was on her hip and wore a new necklace. It was a cheap-looking, home-made thing: a small leather pouch tied with a thong. Moti came to Guliya's side to say that little Kancha was still healthy and had no fever.

Why did everyone keep going on about the baby having a fever? They seem to be obsessing about him.

What is it about Asians and babies? I know that the Nepalis want lots of healthy sons but this was getting beyond a joke. Well, this was their problem, not mine. I wasn't going to get stressed about it.

Anyway, I had my letter to read. I was curious to see what my mother had written.

5. THE PROSTITUTE'S CHILD

Guliya

It was no surprise to me that my brother-in-law, Hari, wanted to change his fate. There was nothing for him in Rajapur. Everyone knows that Badi men live off the proceeds of their mother's, sister's and even wife's prostitution. That they do not know who their fathers are. What could he do except hope to find a fortune in the capital? How else could my sister take him for a husband? At least he tried.

Not like my cousin-auntie's husband who has been doing so badly since the landlord told him he wasn't his bonded labourer any more. Now times are so hard for them. They don't have enough to eat. I watch them all grow thinner and thinner. It is too difficult. What can they do? They must somehow bear their sorrow. They cannot appease the gods, or the landlords.

Hari bhai tells me the whole sad story between mouthfuls of my rice. He and my innocent little sister hadn't lived well in the city. It was more difficult to find work than they expected. Sometimes they lived on the street. He described the cold up there in Kathmandu: how it gets into your lungs and heart. How the valley is full of demons.

At first, Hari and Laxmi had the good fortune of finding work in a foreigner's house. Hari bhai became the gardener and watchman, and my sister did some cleaning inside the house. They got their food and were paid well for very little work; they lived in a hut in the garden. It was small—one room only—but it was dry. For a while, they had plenty to eat and life seemed good.

But then the sahib started getting angry. These foreigners are very excitable and shout a lot if their instructions aren't carried out within a few minutes. I have observed this also and I do not know why it is so. Brahmins avoid chillies and spicy foods, and nettles and strong drink. In that way they avoid becoming excited. These foreigners, they also avoid spicy food and they are not getting drunk all the time like some Nepali people. Even so, they are excitable. Perhaps it is because of all the potatoes and bread that they eat. Perhaps this makes them constipated and that makes them angry.

Sometimes Hari would decide not to sweep the leaves. Sometimes the sahib would catch him eating the air with the neighbour's gardener. Hari could never understand why it mattered if the leaves weren't swept. More leaves would fall the next day and there was so much filth in the street in Kathmandu also.

Then there was a problem with the house water supply. The sahib shouted at Hari bhai because he had used all the water in irrigating the garden, so there was none for the sahib's bath. The sahib got angry with my sister too. She didn't understand about what chemicals and which cloth she must use for cleaning. The sahib had an unnecessarily complicated system of different cloths for different rooms; there was one cloth for the kitchen table, another for the floor, another for the bathrooms and another for the toilet. The sahib shouted a lot at Laxmi about the cloths being in the wrong places. He shouted about bugs and insects. What was the point? A cloth is a cloth, after all. Finally, Hari told me how the sahib went completely crazy and told them to leave. They were out on the street again—just like that.

I know Hari speaks truly. These foreigners are quick to anger and they are very unpredictable also.

One day, while a foreign family was living here in Rajapur, they told my husband they would go away for a few days, and that he must guard the house and keep everything safe. My husband dutifully moved into the house and, to pass the time, he drank some strong drinks. He likes to drink from time to time. Where's the harm in that? He found a new tasty variety of vodka—made in India. Maybe he had a little bit too much of this strong drink but what does that matter, from time to time?

The problem was that the sahib came back early—while my husband was sleeping. The sahib banged on the door of his house but my husband was being a good guard and had locked himself inside. It was a long time before my husband awoke, and when he opened the door, the sahib was too, too angry. He shouted at my husband for a long time. He didn't understand how my husband's head was paining him.

They are so impatient, these foreigners. They cannot wait even a few minutes.

Hari is talking now of all the craziness there is in Kathmandu—in our nation's capital where so many people go. He says that the police are especially good at giving people sorrow. They use any excuse to use those long sticks they carry to beat people. Probably they like beating people. Sometimes they have a smile on their face when they are causing pain.

I ask Hari about the temples and other important and powerful holy places in Kathmandu. I ask him what merit there is to be gained by visiting these places but he says that mostly he was too scared to visit the holy places in case they found out his caste and beat him. He told me that in Kathmandu, even the priests beat people sometimes. I do not believe this thing that he tells me.

He could not change his caste so he even went to church a few times. The church people said that caste wasn't important—that their Lord Jesus doesn't care about caste and he loved everyone. Hari says that although it is a good thing to become Christian so that you are no longer untouchable, those churches are full of crazy people. He stopped going to church after he had become a real Christian man—when he was no longer untouchable.

I cannot understand how Hari dared desert his people's culture and make offerings to American gods—even for a short time. Surely Shiva will never forgive that boy for such behaviour? Hari bhai always did have so many stupid ideas. Still does. He doesn't understand how things are in the world. And never did.

He asks if the new memsahib who is staying with me now is one of these crazy people. I say, 'She is a little mad but she isn't a crazy church-person.'

He looks sad as he continues to talk about his bad karma. He wonders if it is because he went to church that the gods were angry and made Laxmi have miscarriage after miscarriage after miscarriage. He found out the gods at the church didn't want to help him.

Next, the family went to a free clinic in Bauda. This seemed like a very good place because they were given free medicines and food and warm clothes. The foreigners at the Bauda clinic could speak Nepali a bit but they gave lots of orders also. They were as bossy as Brahmins.

After some time they took the family to the big hospital in Patan. The foreign doctors there thought Laxmi had TB and they gave her strong medicines. These helped and she started to become a bit healthy again. Things seemed better for a while. Hari got a bit of casual labouring work. That was good. The foreign doctors asked the family to go back to the big hospital for regular injections and checks but that was too difficult. It was too far to walk and the bus was too expensive.

Their first son was strong and healthy but by the time my sister became pregnant for the last time, she had become very, very weak again. Even my slow-thinking brother-in-law knew that she needed good care.

He took good, worthy offerings to the golden stupa high up on the hill at Swayambhu. He hoped to buy favour and appease the gods. The offerings sent him into debt. But then when my sister went into labour, he took her to the big hospital. He said that it is the best hospital in the whole of Nepal—that lots of foreign doctors work there but again I am shocked. What use are these hospitals—run by Americans with no respect for the gods? Hari should have known this wasn't the way to save my sister. It is no wonder she died a few weeks after their second son had come into this world.

Hari doesn't talk about his sorrow but only about how he struggled to feed the baby and the older boy. How looking after them stopped him finding work. He had to work. He needed to work and the boys got in the way of that. He needed to give the boys away; then he could get another wife and start all over.

The foreigners kept saying that the younger boy needed to go back for regular treatment at the hospital. They said that the boy had TB—like his mother. The foreign doctors in Kathmandu said that it was TB that killed Laxmi but I know better.

Those foreigners offered to help him to give the boys up for adoption, or take them to the orphanage. They offered to pay for someone to look after the children while he worked but it was all too difficult. He couldn't decide what to do. He kept going back for more money and more baby food. That at least was a good thing that these foreigners did for the family. They had plenty of money; a few thousand rupees was nothing to them. He never quite got around to going back to the big hospital.

I feel so sorry that he—and especially my sister—went through all that pain alone and so far from the support of the family. My sister had no female relatives to help suckle her children—no one to share their burden. But this is the price they paid for leaving home like they did.

Hari says that when the Desai festival came around, the two usual foreign doctors were not at the free clinic any more. There was a new foreigner—a man. He said (through an untrustworthy high-caste translator) that he also came from the mountains, from a country called Switzerland.

Hari didn't care where the foreigner came from. His son was dying.

That foreign doctor from the mountains told Hari that all that was needed to stop the child's diarrhoea was to starve him and give him water only. He didn't give any strong medicines or injections. That doctor talked only. Hari's little boy became like a skeleton. The last time that doctor saw the boy, he said he weighed seven kilograms: seven kilograms and eighteen months old. What could my brother-in-law do? This foreign doctor didn't understand about the problems of Nepal and Hari could not fight against his karma. It was the will of the gods that the child became so ill and thin. Hearing this story makes me angry and full of sorrow all at once—though I say nothing.

What else should I expect? His attitude is typical of a Badi man. These Badi castes have lived for generations from the earnings of prostitution—living off those randi women. All Badi men ever do is a few small, small pieces of manual labour and some fishing. They are good-for-nothing. It is not their fault. It is not in their nature to do anything. It is their life.

Hari had said, all those years ago when he left for Kathmandu with my sister, that it was going to be so good for them. Him with his big ideas! He would make them rich. But that was all a crazy dream. I don't even ask him what he is going to do next. I don't care. I know he still has big ideas. This awful time has taught him nothing.

I feel so tired after listening to this story. I cry for my little sister, Laxmi. She was my favourite. It is good that my mother isn't alive to hear this story; it would have broken her heart.

Now I know that Hari has come only to leave the older boy with me. This is no problem for us. I will have a new son to care for me in old age and I won't even need to give him my milk. He is a little older but smaller than my Siru who has seen five monsoons. Little Hari and Siru will become fine playmates.

I stretch out my arms to the quivering bundle of bones. The child comes to me and melts into my lap—and cries. He is home again. He will become happy once more. He will have a good life. He will grow fat.

We will forget that his father is untouchable. His father is dead to us now.

Tomorrow I will take the boy, my nephew, to the temple to give thanks for his return. I should pay the priests for an amulet to protect him. I must find clothes for him also. Everything is so costly; I hope we can pay for it all.

Sonia

I brought the chair outside and placed it under the shade of the mango tree. I sat and carefully opened my mother's letter. It was self-absorbed, accusatory, inconsiderate. It was all that I had expected it would be. 'How could you go just like that?' 'What hope now is there of getting back with him?' What would happen if she needed me? Etcetra, etcetra, blah, blah, blah.

She wanted to know why I'd given up on my husband. She pointed out how going away would destroy the last hope of reconciliation. She seemed to have forgotten that the divorce came through months ago. In the next part of the letter, she returned to telling me about how abandoned she felt. It was always about her; there was never an exchange between her and me. She had never listened to me, never valued me, so why couldn't she let me live my own life?

I remember being stopped in my tracks many years ago when—out of the blue—she had suddenly said to me, 'Let me give you some advice, Sonia.' I was attentive, eager for some worldly pearl of wisdom. She continued, 'These green scourers,' she said, 'you should cut them in half. Half is enough...does the job and saves some money.'

We never had any real conversations—not about anything important or worthwhile. We never spoke about me, or anything that mattered to me. We never discussed the miscarriage, and she never ever allowed me to discuss the termination.

She made me so angry. I had a horrible feeling that all the emotions the letter had stirred up in me would make me have another dreadful, tortured night.

Then I remembered the letter that my GP had given me the last time I'd seen her. I'd gone to tell her that—finally—I was going off on my mini gap-year. She wished me well with a smile that made me wonder if she was laughing at me—or more likely doubting I'd ever leave. I was scared witless and needed her prescription to keep me calm on the flight. I should send her a postcard to prove I did it—to prove her wrong. She'd given me a letter to say I was all right to travel and also printed out something else, sealed it in an envelope and gave it to me 'in case a doctor out there needs to know about your medical history.'

I went into my room and opened the envelope. It read:

Patient no.: 22790
Mrs Sonia Agnes SWAYNE

EMIS no.: 22790
Name: Mrs Sonia Agnes SWAYNE
Age: 34 years
d.o.b.: 25.10.1976
NHS no.: 050 280 0303
Address: 37 Wilkin Street, Cambridge CB1 2RS
Telephone no.: 143271
Hospital no.: 77 31 64

ACTIVE PROBLEMS
Anxiety and depression
Irritable bowel syndrome
Initial insomnia

LAST CONSULTATION:
PROBLEM: Neurotic DEPRESSION with anxiety, hyperventilation and somatization.

HISTORY: Continuing breathlessness, chest pain, peripheral paraesthesia +++, colicky abdominal pain, initial insomnia. Isolated. Low self-esteem. Comfort eating +++; ruminating on 'allergies' despite negative testing; logorrhoeic. As before.
Reported that counselling was unhelpful. Continues to refuse prescriptions, except diazepam and sleeping pills.

EXAMINATION: Hyperventilating. Agitated. Pulse 110/minute. Sinus rhythm.

PLAN: Has booked a volunteer placement in Nepal. Very anxious about this. I said she was fit to go. Fit to Fly letter.

CURRENT MEDICATION:
Mebeverine 135 mg tds 100 tablets
Diazepam 2 mg qds prn 28 tablets
Zopiclone 3.75 mg prn intermittently 28 tablets

HEALTH STATUS

Occupation	:	schoolteacher
Height	:	165 cm
Weight	:	76 kg
Body Mass Index	:	27.9
BP	:	144/88
Alcohol	:	40 units/week
Exercise grading	:	avoids exercise
Smoking	:	never smoked tobacco
Rubella Ab	:	immune
Family history	:	nil of note

RECENT INVESTIGATIONS:

ECG	:	normal
CXR	:	normal

Blood tests	:	FBC, TFT, LFT, U&E, GFR, ESR, CRP, LH, FSH all normal
Pelvic ultrasound	:	normal

PAST MEDICAL HISTORY:
Adverse reaction—erythromycin—diarrhoea
Adverse reaction—codeine—sedation
Adverse reaction—amoxicillin—diarrhoea
Adverse reaction—ibuprofen—abdominal pain
Adverse reaction—paracetamol—constipation
Adverse reaction—contraceptive pill—mood swings
20.8.1981: chickenpox
21.11.1994: termination of pregnancy
13.3.1996: spontaneous miscarriage
30.1.2005: irritable bowel syndrome
2.8.10: initial insomnia
15.10.10: suicidal ideation

It was all so cold and clinical. I thought she liked me but it didn't seem like that now. What did she mean by writing 'as before' after listing and presumably dismissing all my awful symptoms? In what way was I neurotic? What did *that* mean? That wasn't exactly helpful or supportive, was it?

Stuff was going round and round in my head—about the judgemental GP, about my mother, about the hearing. There was now absolutely no chance I'd get to sleep later. Perhaps if I wrote back to my mother, and to the GP, that would clear my head. I started to compose a reply to my mother that would explain what I—me, myself—needed. I could tell her about the beauty here too—and the unjudgementalness of the people. I smiled. The word I'd just made up had 'mental' in the middle of it. Then I thought it was an awful, clumsy, stupid word.

I had only just picked up a pen when a throat-clearing sound made me look up.

That American—Herbert the anthropologist—was standing over me. Crap.

'Oh!' I said. 'I didn't expect to see you again—not so soon anyway!'

'Yeah. Hey.'

'Um...?'

'Hey,' he repeated.

'Do you want to come and sit with me?'

'Okay.'

'Here, take my seat. It is the only one. Don't worry about me. I'll sit here on the edge of the verandah.'

'Okay.'

Bloody hell—no manners here then. Here's another self-obsessed head case.

He sat. He talked—at enormous and tiresome length—about his problems. He droned on about how he was struggling to communicate, about what a difficult language Nepali was. He talked of his loneliness. He talked of his diarrhoea. Why the hell did he think I'd be at all interested in the details of his bowel movements?

He saw me—no doubt—as a mother figure. This was typical. People always seemed to think they could bring their worries to me, but no one cared when I needed some sympathy. I didn't want to be rude to him but I really, really couldn't care less.

I interrupted his diatribe with, 'I suppose you'd like some tea—but this isn't my house so I can't really offer you any hospitality.'

'I don't need tea—I'm sick of that nauseating syrup they call tea!'

I interrupted what promised to be another diatribe with, 'I quite like it, actually—it is fine as long as you don't think of it as tea! Although I must admit I haven't got used to the stuff with pepper in it yet. Have you tried the kind with cardamom in it? That's really delicious.'

'No I haven't—and I don't like any version of what they call tea. I could barely stomach it when I first got here; now I really hate it. What's wrong with coffee? Don't they grow it around here?'

'I don't think so. But I don't think I'd recognize a coffee tree even if I walked into one. Never mind; at least there is plenty of Coke in the market...I expect—being American—you like Coke?'

'Yeah, what's wrong with that? And what's wrong with being American?'

'Nothing, I suppose but it's not very Nepali.'

'American isn't very Nepali. Nope—it sure ain't! At least I know who I am. You sound as if you've gone native after being here less than a week!'

'I beg your pardon—' This boy was loathsome. Maybe being rude was going to be the only way to get rid of him. 'So...your researches aren't going too well, then?'

'No. It's pretty bad—the Badi women think I'm a client! Can you believe that?'

I shouldn't have but I started to laugh. 'What do you expect? They're prostitutes—trying to make a living! Surely a true anthropologist, one truly devoted to his work, would become a client as part of his research!'

He looked horrified. Then I could see him thinking about what I'd said, perhaps even considering my taunt to be good advice. He was the sort who wouldn't recognize good advice even if he stepped in it and wiped it all over his trousers.

Then my guardian angel arrived in the unexpected shape of that Bom guy I'd met in the temple. 'Good morning, Madam, Sir!' he said. 'Shall I ask Guliya to make tea for us?' His good manners immediately made me feel a little guilty for thinking uncharitable thoughts about Herb. Poor dear.

'That would be presumptuous—surely—since it's her house!' I said. 'But it is lovely to welcome another friend! Here, let me introduce you gentlemen! This is Bom umm, I'm sorry. I have rudely forgotten your full name,' I smiled at the Nepali and then, turning to the American continued, 'but I can say that this gentleman is a stalwart of the Rajapur community and an ex-Gurkha. He also speaks impeccable English. I think Mr Bom might be able to help you with your researches, umm, you know?' Then I turned back to Bom and said, 'Mr Bom, this is Basil.'

The Nepali gentleman responded, 'You are kind in your introduction, Madam, and my full name is Bom Bahadur Gurung.'

Bom Bahadur, at least, knew his manners. Actually, he was a real gentleman.

'And my name is Herb,' the American spat.

'Then,' Bom Bahadur laughed, 'the lady has made a clever jest—at your expense.'

'I noticed,' Herb said bitterly.

Despite my tease, Herb's eyes brightened and he launched into an interrogation. I watched as Bom Bahadur appeared to be absorbed in what the American had to say. At the same time, he managed to remain attentive to me and often tried to draw me in and involve me too. He was a very skilled conversationalist.

Bom Bahadur said, 'I must tell you one interesting fact. You, Mr Herb, are interested in our Badi ladies. The name of the profession of these ladies in the Nepali language is "randi", and it is my idea that this word has been stolen from the Nepali by you Britishers. But perhaps I am being indiscreet in talking in this way to a real British Memsahib!' He laughed rather flirtatiously, I felt. This time I was flattered. Clearly, I wasn't finished quite yet. Perhaps I wasn't so spent and unattractive after all. Perhaps that thought will lull me into restful sleep again tonight.

Guliya

This memsahib is causing a lot of interest. Men are coming like ants to spilt sugar. It is very interesting to watch. The two Brahmins look at her, and now there are two more admirers.

Which one will she choose? I hope she doesn't choose the American, who speaks that very loud, ugly language and looks so arrogant—standing like the king with his hands on his hips all the time. I do not like him. The Gurung is nice; he has a fine moustache but he is a little bit too old for her. The Brahmin might be most suitable but it is my idea that she may be a little old for him. Which one will it be?

What is good is that Moti doesn't like the idea of the Newar suitor. I had talked to her about the man who visited. Although she blushed, she quickly said she wasn't interested. She said, 'How can I marry a man I haven't even noticed—who has hardly spoken one word to me? Why doesn't he woo me? He must be a coward!'

I am pleased but I am surprised also that she has no

curiosity about this Newar. I wonder if she likes another man. I ask and ask her but she smiles and will not say.

I wonder if any of the memsahib's admirers have good foreign medicines. I need good medicines. These days I am feeling weak. I went to see Dr Dash and he gave me strong medicine. It looked like water but it contained something special. It went into my body through a needle and a tube in my arm. It was expensive. It gave me some strength but it was not enough. I need better medicines.

It is said that Dr Bhandari has some extra-powerful new medicine. It is an injection from India and it is the colour of rusty iron. If it is from India, it will be too expensive but I should ask my husband to find the money if it will help me.

Perhaps, instead, I shall ask the memsahib if she has any tablets for strength. Perhaps she also has some medicine that will make my husband's chest strong again. He has been having problems with his breathing for too long. Sometimes it is so bad he cannot work.

Last year he was so ill that I became very worried. I thought he was dying. I took offerings to the temple. I don't know why my husband has such bad karma when he is not a bad man. Maybe it is because he enjoys some strong drink once in a while but why not? Sometimes it is necessary to celebrate.

I begin to think that the gods aren't listening. Maybe my offerings are not worthy or expensive enough. Maybe it is the fact that my husband takes hard drinks they do not like.

We decided he should go to the big hospital in Nepalgunj. It was such a struggle getting onto the bus when his breathing was so bad. We had to leave before dawn to get to the road-head at Sati bazaar. The ferryman, he was also coughing and he wanted a lot of money for the crossing. He charged double because of the cold. And then when we got to the place where the buses wait, our bus was already full. You know what it is like: so many wanting to travel that you have to climb over people squatting on the floor with their children and chickens and luggage—and there was no room on the roof at all.

Once we got to the hospital, it was all pushing and shoving and trying to get a place in line with all the other sick people. There were many people, all jostling and crying.

We queued all day. It was so, so hot. Those who had done this before knew that two relatives should accompany the ill person—one can stay in the queue and the other can go to fetch food and water.

We got so hungry and thirsty that day. In that big, big city it was even difficult to find a water-pump that we could drink from.

Finally, we got to see the doctor-sahib as the sun was going down. He listened to my husband's chest and said he had pneumonia and asthma and allergies and that he was too thin and weak—and anaemic also. He gave my husband three injections; one caused great pain as it went into his body. The doctor also prescribed many strong medicines. The most expensive was a big bottle full of a yellow drink. It tasted of pineapple; my husband had to find four days of labouring work just to pay for that one. Then there were red pills and big yellow-and-white capsules and little white pills and triangular pills and some powders. He was also given a plastic thing that sprayed medicine; a nurse was ordered to show him how to use it but she was busy and didn't explain anything. She got angry when my husband asked a question about it.

I always find money very confusing because I never went to school and I cannot count. That is my burden. Even although I do not know numbers, I knew that this trip to the hospital was very expensive. All the medicines cost so much that my husband was worried about whether we would have enough money to pay for the bus to take us home. We had no money for food that day. We had no relatives there and knew no one in Nepalgunj and so there was nowhere for us to stay.

Finally, we caught the night bus back to Sati. We arrived home as the birds were waking up. It was such a costly trip, we decided we'd trust Dr Bhandari next time. He is clever and has many strong medicines. I do not think he cheats us. Maybe it is better to go to the temple also.

Rekraj

My cousin Ram Krishna has no morals. I wonder if I should say something. He has an appetite for women and I can see he is interested in the memsahib. This might cause problems but I feel shy to mention anything. Nevertheless I am worried.

His father—my uncle—was such a womanizer that his wife couldn't stand the shame of it. She poured petrol over herself and set herself alight. My uncle didn't care; he soon took a younger, more beautiful wife. I've even seen Ram Krishna flirt with her, his new mother. It is not respectful and it is not good behaviour. I do not like to see this. He debases himself also by paying attention to the Tharu's daughter.

Actually he has taken to hanging around the office rather too much, especially when Sonia didi is here. I notice that he dresses in his best coat-pant outfit. I don't trust him. I think he may do something wrong if he is left alone with her. It is inconvenient having to stay here whenever she is working in the office, although I admit that I do enjoy being with her. She makes my routine tasks pleasant, and the day passes quickly. We laugh a lot together.

I am perhaps being a little indelicate when I mention to her the terrible business of trafficking that goes on in Nepal. I tell her because I feel she is genuinely interested in helping Nepali women—even these unfortunate randi women.

I think she understands when I say, 'It is poverty that forces some families to sell their daughters. It is a horrible situation. Indians buy young girls and take them away to brothels in Mumbai. Mostly, by the time they are fifteen or sixteen, they have AIDS and get thrown out—sent back. They want to return to Nepal but they are too ashamed to go to their own villages. Some come here to Rajapur, because we are near Lucknow in India and the railway comes close to the border also.'

I can see that she is shocked. She doesn't speak for a while but then says, 'Lucknow. Is it close?'

'It is close. Lucknow is our nearest city. There is one good hospital there also, although the medicines there are more costly than in Nepal. There are other useful services...'

'I'd like to go.'

'It is possible but for you there will be some difficulties. For us Nepalis and Indians also it is no problem, we can cross the border willy-nilly, as you say. Foreigners may not cross into India but must travel to the border post near Nepalgunj. That is less convenient. The journey is longer but it is possible, if you need to. But why go there?'

'It would be interesting to see what it's like. My great-grandfather was there.'

'We will arrange this—but after some time. I am thinking, didi, that it is odd so many people cross into Nepal this way. Indians come to visit our Badi women and it is my idea that many returning randi women try to find their way back by way of Rajapur. Sometimes the Badi women let them stay in their part of the bazaar.'

I mention the difficulties involved in doing something to help these unfortunate women. 'We earn criticism from the Brahmin leaders,' I explain. 'When I raise this with them, they say that I pollute myself even talking about these women, that if I try to do something for them, they—the Brahmin leaders—will put barriers in the way of my other work.'

Sonia

I quickly got into the reassuring routine of cycling out to Rekraj's office and doing a few hours of typing each day. I'm not much of a secretarial type but I'm good enough at making documents look neat and official—and at least I can spell.

It was truly wonderful to have some structure and purpose in my life again. This and Rekraj's encouragement and respect did a lot to restore my confidence. Finally, I began to feel I might be able to come to the surface again. I was going to have something to feel proud of for once. Perhaps that was why I was sleeping better: the combination of a little exercise and some real work.

Hearing dogs howling at night didn't help though. They sounded like wolves. The wild country, the jungle, must be so close. Perhaps packs of wolves really did roam right into Rajapur town. I wondered again just how dangerous life here really was, and why the wretched dogs needed to howl all night long anyway.

I smiled to think that even in my younger years I had never been very adventurous. This was probably the most adventurous I'd ever been. Even in the days when I skied, I always preferred to look good on the familiar easy slopes rather than try anything challenging.

Being here now seemed like a dream; I kept wondering if I might wake up. Could I really be living and working hundreds of miles from anywhere? Even Kathmandu was two days away by bus. Was this really me? Could I really be living in the steamy plains where the heat chased the memsahibs into the Himalayan hill stations in colonial times? Where two of my ancestors from my father's side once lived?

Rekraj and I have already applied to some big charities and agencies for small sums of money for various projects here. Just a little money goes such a long way in Nepal. For some stupid reason most of the applications had to be written in English—and that's where I came in.

For instance, we've applied for money to build a decent toilet block in the High School. We're waiting to hear about that.

Meanwhile, Rekraj has had lots of ideas for helping some of the abandoned and widowed women and I've been working on applications for funding to help them make a living. It is such good work and I'm already part of it! Rekraj told me that I've already helped a great deal but probably he's just being nice. He's so thoughtful. He's always making plans and always includes me, which is lovely.

Some of the stories he tells might get me down a little, but mostly they've helped me put my own problems into proportion. Thinking that my vajra is keeping me safe here makes me smile. I haven't felt the need to mumble my '*Cutty budgie hay*' mantra for ages and I haven't been obsessing about my scar either.

I so enjoy being here in this little village of Chhetrapur on the outskirts of Rajapur bazaar. Rajapur town itself is quite compact so out here it feels very open and pastoral, although it only takes about twenty minutes to cycle from Guliya's house. The village is lush and I love being surrounded by exotic bird sounds as I work. And it's truly wonderful to have a worthwhile role. Already I seem to be accepted as part of the office furniture now, yet I've become quite a local celebrity.

You see, for a long time, I'd been trying to make contact with some of the ladies who work in the office, although Rekraj keeps telling me they are not 'ladies'.

'What, Rekraj? Are you saying these women are what you call randi?'

'No, no, didi. But they are uneducated village women.'

Without fail, every day, within ten minutes of my arrival here, a beautiful young woman brings me a glass of delicious, thick, steaming, cardamom-flavoured tea. At first she'd just scuttle in, leave the tea and scuttle out. If I attempted to talk to her she would seem frightened. After a while, her fear turned to giggles and finally, one day, she dared look at me and utter, 'How are joo? Waat iz jour name?'

'I am very well, thank you,' I said slowly and clearly. 'My name is Son-ı-a.'

She looked baffled and stared at me blankly.

I said, 'What is *your* name?'

She looked confused, then embarrassed and ran away, giggling some more.

The next day, having been briefed by Rekraj, I tried addressing her, 'Bahini?'

'Hunchha, Memsahib?' Wow! This was progress!

'What is your name? Timro naam ke ho?' I tried in both languages.

She looked at me, wide-eyed.

Then through a splutter of giggles, she said, 'Meero naam Binu ho!' This was a terrific victory. I'd asked a question in Nepali and someone had replied AND WE HAD UNDERSTOOD EACH OTHER! Now it was my turn to giggle. I didn't care even if her giggling was at me.

I even had the confidence to try, 'Meero naam Son-i-a ho.'

'Shabash, Memsahib!' I'd heard this before. I thought shabash meant I was doing all right.

I was feeling rather proud of myself when Ram Krishna strode into the little office. Binu fled. He came up and stood too close—far too close. I smelt alcohol on his breath. I felt sick.

'I have brought you a present!' he said, advancing towards me. 'That was sweet of me, wasn't it!'

Sweet was not a word that I had ever associated with him.

'Thanks.' I slipped my hand into my pocket and closed it around my spike.

'These are kimbu—mulberries, I think you call them.' He stepped closer. 'They are sweet—just like me!'

I took a step back. He was between me and the door.

He smiled, 'So...I see that you are trying to talk to the servants! You don't need to, you know. You shouldn't encourage them, actually. They'll only get ideas and start getting cheeky—and they'll ask for more money. Look, if you want to learn how to speak proper educated Nepali, like Brahmins speak, then I can teach you myself.'

'No, I wouldn't want...'

He came closer and I started to feel this was going to end really, really badly for me. I wondered if I'd have the courage to use my weapon. Stick it somewhere...effective.

'What's wrong with the lovely Sonia? Surely we can have some fun now...'

He grabbed me. The smell of alcohol, garlic and his sweat was overpowering.

'Leave me alone!' The words caught in my throat as it contracted in fear. Was there any hope that Binu would come to my rescue?

'Binu didi! Aunus!' I managed to shout.

She reappeared so quickly that she must have been waiting close by, listening. She was pulling another young woman along with her. The second woman put two fingers into her mouth and let out an ear-splitting whistle. More women came to the door. Several carried rather nasty-looking agricultural tools with sharp edges.

Ram Krishna was flushed and breathing heavily; he seemed to force a sickly smile onto his face. 'Sonia, let's just spend some time together...send your army away!'

'Why can't you just leave me alone!' I shouted again.

The women all started whistling. The noise was deafening. He put his hands over his ears. The uproar continued. They seemed encouraged by his reaction. More women arrived. They moved towards him. He pushed past them and fled.

I stood there, trembling. Binu hugged me. I clung to her. I wanted to hug them—all of them.

6. SISTERHOOD

Sonia

After that horrible experience with Ram Krishna, a whole string of young women came to see me. Each of them spoke his name and pulled a disapproving face, or did some kind of obscene-looking mime that had something to do with genitals. Or simply spat. Some tried to be more conversational with, 'Neramro mansi!' or, easier to understand, 'How are joo? Waat iz jour name?' I laughed so much with them. I was touched by their protectiveness. It felt like a powerful sisterhood. They understood, even if we had very little we could say to each other.

Thereafter, I would get completely engrossed in my two-finger typing on Rekraj's ancient black typewriter. I'd also spend time decorating the office with fresh bougainvillea and felt pleased with this small feminine touch. Sometimes I'd work in the shade of the mango tree. It was lovely being able to work outside. I relished having time to let my mind drift, to think. In Britain there is never enough silence. Each day I'd type until sweat made my hair stick to the back of my neck. This told me it was time to move somewhere cooler, perhaps to eat Guliya's delicious rice and curry.

'Rekraj?'

'Hunchha, didi?'

'Several of the ladies who live here have been squeezing me. Why do they do that?'

'Squeezing, didi? What means squeezing?'

'Feeling my arms—like testing a vegetable in the market.'

'They have given you pain, didi?'

'No, no, but why are they doing it?'

'Ah—it is my idea that they are feeling to see if you have bones inside, didi.'

'What?'

'They are thinking that you are looking so different that maybe you are different on the inside also. Sometimes people say that foreigners are white like clouds, and maybe they think you are light and empty like clouds also.'

'Do I look so different, Rekraj?'

'To them only.'

I pressed Rekraj to arrange a meeting with the staff at the High School. It took a bit of nagging to sort this out and I expected a quick interview with the Deputy Head, but that's not what happened. Rekraj took me to the campus, which proudly announced itself as the Amar Shaheed, Shree Dasharath Chand Higher Secondary School.

I was welcomed in the High School like royalty. I was escorted to a stage overlooking a kind of parade ground where everyone had gathered for a special assembly. There was a long, generous speech about me—in halting English. I was asked to respond. To still my nervousness, I convinced myself that most of the audience wouldn't follow what I was saying, so it just needed to sound fluent and fill some time. I thought of reciting 'The Jabberwocky' but then knew those who understood might be insulted.

Afterwards, I was whisked away into a large room where about twenty teachers waited. I was ushered to a lectern and told to begin my lesson. I wasn't prepared for this either but I suppose teachers are good at thinking on their feet. I thought I would try to showcase interactive learning, but caused consternation when I asked them to pull the chairs around in a circle. I knew I had a battle on my hands to win them over. I made a start. As I began, I looked at their faces. I tried to read their reactions but they were inscrutable. At the end though, the Head made another pretty speech and they invited me back—and asked me to run a weekly workshop for them.

Working with them was a delight. Interactive teaching was so new to them that they embraced it with enthusiasm and it was wonderful to hear their stories and experiences. I loved their language. They used words like thrice, goodself, and opined, liberally littered with excuse-mes. They asked about my 'native place'. They asked me about modern usage, citing words like wicked, massive, awesome, magic, cool, sick, guns and pants. We found things that made us all laugh.

For the rest of the week thereafter, I'd potter around with Rekraj. His team of helpers clearly felt more and more relaxed about coming by to greet me, or even sometimes feel my hair.

My favourite visitor though was the young hornbill that frequented the papaya trees. His head-feathers made him look like a punk and he was so ungainly, with his heavy-looking bill. He would have liked to hang upside down to peck at the luscious fruit but he could only cling on for a second or two, so often ended up tumbling to the ground, where he'd finish gobbling down his slushy orange prize. He was so funny.

Sometimes I'd cycle back with Rekraj. On one leisurely pedal back home, I decided to ask him about the spinach incident. 'Remember my first day here?'

'Hunchha, didi.'

'When Ram Krishna took my food away?'

'Hunchha.'

'That seemed a bit rude…'

'Hunchha?'

'Why did he do it?'

'It would have made you ill.'

'What? Was it poisoned?' I asked, laughing.

'You must not eat spinach when you have cough.'

'Why?'

'It makes cough more worse.'

'How?'

'It is fact of life.'

'What do you mean?'

'Spinach is hot food. Cough is sign of hot disease. Hot diseases must be treated with cold food. Yogurt is cold and buffalo meat is cold.'

'Cold buffalo meat doesn't sound very nice.'

'Buffalo meat is a cold food even when hot, after cooking. Fish and chicken are hot foods, even when cold. Some hot foods become cold when cooked, even when hot. Understand?'

'No.'

'You must take care because goat milk is hot and red lentils are also hot so you must avoid when you are having fever. Black lentils are cold so these can be eaten in this situation. It is quite straightforward actually.'

'Ah. The fact is you bullied me!'

'What? No! That, Madam, was never our intention. We were caring for you only.'

Poor man. My teasing obviously embarrassed him.

Quite often now, I had the confidence to pedal back alone. Actually this turned out to be nicer because more people greeted me. I loved that, and could even respond a bit when people asked me, 'What's new?'

That Nepali chav always seemed to be hanging around near Guliya's house, obsequiousness dripping off him like grease from a battered haddock. He was the skinny one with his bling and black tracksuit. He was there every day. He seemed to be watching or waiting for something. I didn't trust or like the look of him and I wasn't the only one.

Once I saw Guliya's husband shouting at him. Usually, he is such a mild-mannered man and I couldn't imagine what was making him so angry. I wondered who the chav was—maybe he was the black sheep of the family.

Late one morning while I was absorbed with my work in the office, I suddenly sensed that someone had come in and was watching me. I cringed, fearful that the philanderer Ram Krishna had sneaked back. I cursed, thinking how foolish I'd been not to have learned how to make that superbly penetrating whistle for help.

I turned, expecting to see him or one of Rekraj's helpers but this visitor was someone very different indeed. Immaculately dressed in a freshly pressed shirt and sharply cut trousers, he looked cool and impressively dust-free. He was gorgeous. How could he have got here without getting sweaty and grubby?

'Good morning, Madam!' he said, bowing slightly.

I leapt up, knocking my chair over. I offered him my rather clammy hand, then thought I shouldn't. He offered his hand to shake as I put my palms together and said, 'Namaste.'

He smiled at the muddle, bent to pick up my chair and gestured me to sit again.

'Don't be nervous,' he said. 'Rekraj has been telling me all about how you have been helping us! How you have been managing menial secretarial duties for our poor office in our primitive community.'

I wasn't sure if he was mocking me. I wasn't sure how to respond. I said the first thing that came into my head, 'No, it isn't menial. I love it!'

Rekraj appeared. I could see him over the newcomer's shoulder and he was smiling.

Encouraged, I continued, 'Actually I love Rajapur and I love Nepal!'

Since when had I become so gushy? I was shouting again, too. The stranger was blinking a lot, as if at the volume of my voice. He was smiling too, though. Maybe he was laughing at me.

He said, 'I have heard a great deal about you assertive American women!'

'I'm not American, fortunately! I'm British...actually!' I wanted to add, 'damn it!'

'Forgive me but the difference is not important.'

I didn't manage to butt in to correct him as he went into a long diatribe expressing a range of firmly held opinions. I began to think that he must be a politician. 'Actually, you, Madam, give me the opportunity to say that I am not liking so much names that you Britishers have left behind in settlements in the Plains—names like Waltergunj, Herbertpur, Forbesgunj, Bridgmangunj, Macleodgunj and even Sahibgunj.'

I needed to tell that American about Herbertpur. Laughingly I said, 'But these are splendid names—they are the names of British heroes!' But my tease fell flat and so after an awkward silence, I added, 'Don't worry, Mr Umm...I agree that Herbert and Walter are ugly names! Very ugly!'

'Yes, yes. Quite so,' he replied. 'What is most puzzling for me, Memsahib, is that Britain could operate, manipulate and dominate our region for three hundred years, but understand so little. I am not making that mistake. You, Madam, have first-hand, native knowledge of western society. You must do one thing, Madam. You must share some of your experience of capitalist systems. You have grown up in such a society but surely cooperatives are better? Actually, I am especially interested in issues regarding the hegemony of the Americans and how they can promote democracy—isn't that hypocritical?'

'Britain and America are very different.'

'I think not. Both embrace the capitalist model.'

I hadn't a clue as to what he was talking about. I found

myself just gazing at him and thinking how gorgeous he was. Gorgeous, but annoying. I could feel my colour rising and had to think of something to say. 'I'm sorry, I never have taken any interest in politics or world affairs but tell me, are you the person Rekraj talked about who was impressed with *Mein Kampf?*'

'Correct. I have recently read the Nepali translation. It was very interesting. There is always something to learn from any successful politician. Actually, Nepal has been isolated for too long from ideas from the outside world. It is good that such pieces of famous foreign literature are now available to ordinary Nepalis. We have suffered for too long from the arrogance that comes from—I should use the English expression: big fish in small ponds.'

I still really didn't understand what point he was making, yet I was dying to come up with some wise and witty remark. Embarrassed, I asked, 'Do tell me about how you came to be involved in all this.' And I waved my arm to indicate the funny little office in which we were having this conversation. 'I'd love to hear the whole story.'

Why was I saying love so much? He must think me really air-brained. Or is it hair-brained? That can't be right either.

'It was all my brainchild. Let me give you my card,' he said, proffering one embossed with gold lettering and the triangular Nepali flag. 'I raised the first sums that we needed to get started. As projects began to develop, I recruited my cousin here to run the Rajapur office. Meanwhile, I attend to fundraising and publicity in Kathmandu itself.'

'Oh, you're another cousin,' I said stupidly.

He said, 'It is best to keep things in the family. Families are most trustworthy, I find. Is it not so also in your native place?'

'Well if you are asking about MY family, I would have to disagree. I am sure though that it is wise to work with people you know and trust. I think I am a good judge of character and that's how I decide who is trustworthy.'

'Ah! Who would you trust with your vote then?'

'That is much more difficult. I think most politicians in most countries are corrupt! That's why I've lost interest in politics.'

'You speak from your heart. I can see this. Therefore, I can understand why you have become disillusioned with politics, but can you tell me what would make you interested again? What kind of person makes a good politician, in your opinion?'

This guy's intellect was too big for this poky little office. What could I say to satisfy him, and not make a fool of myself?

'I'm not sure what you mean by a good politician. If you mean a successful politician, I think you have to be devious and clever. I think I'd want any politician that represented me to be honest but I'd also like him to have a presence. Do you know what I mean?'

'I think the word you seek is charisma?'

'Yes, charisma,' I sighed. '*You* have it! I'd vote for *you!*' Then I started to giggle. What was wrong with me? I had to do something to hide my blushes. What had got into me?

There was a cough and Rekraj came to my rescue, before my self-esteem was trampled to a pulp and fed to the maggots in the long drop.

He said, 'Let us take tea now!'

Rekraj

My big-shot cousin from Kathmandu was—I am thinking—disappointed with Sonia didi. He was quite rude to her. Probably he was expecting some sharp, ruthless, politically astute campaigning type. I suppose those are the sort of foreign women he meets in Kathmandu. I expect he was looking forward to a long political debate with her, but he told me she was no better than a Nepali woman. I don't know why he is so critical; he is becoming like a foreigner himself. Sometimes I think that he has spent too much time in Kathmandu. He has forgotten his own community. It is also very strange that he considers it insulting to call Sonia didi no better than a Nepali woman. Where is his respect for our people?

It is my idea that Sonia didi is sensitive and kind and trying to help as best she can. I like her. She is innocent and she is a good person. Everything is very nice here in the office these days with her help.

That's another thing that attracts criticism from my cousin: he says we must get computers. Desktops, laptops! What is the use when we don't have electricity?

Sonia didi understands better. She understands service in the same way that Nepali women do and she is happy in this role. She is currently writing a very good proposal so that we can win funds to bring books to the school—and latrines also. One fine day, we will get this money. I think we will also receive money for the widows and the destitute ex-bonded labourers too.

Sometimes I watch her while she types—slowly, slowly. Often her tongue sticks out in concentration. I think she likes working in our headquarters: the very nerve centre of our Rajapur Gender Equality Forum. I think that it distracts her from her past troubles. She hasn't spoken of these but I know they haunt her.

This is one big thing that is different between westerners and Nepalis. I can see that people like Sonia didi live in the past and in the possibilities of the future. It holds them back from enjoying the moment. Even Brahmins are more spontaneous than westerners sometimes.

I am satisfied that tomorrow our proposals will be ready. We will visit my friend in the post office. We will send all the papers to Kathmandu. I feel happy about office matters.

However, something is different today. There are many vultures in the highest trees. I feel uneasy.

'Come!' I say to Sonia didi. 'Now we have finished the proposals, let us celebrate and have a small adventure. We will climb into the elephant lookout shelter—if it pleases you, only.'

'It pleases me, Rekraj dai.' She laughs. She looks at her most attractive when she laughs.

As we get to the bottom of the ladder, we both realize one big problem. She is wearing a western-style skirt. This is embarrassing. I think quickly. I say, 'I must climb first.' I start up before she can argue.

Sonia didi is a great expert at arguing, I have discovered. But then perhaps all women are expert at arguing. That is why some husbands have to beat their wives. I do not think it should be necessary to beat a woman though. There are other ways to exert male authority.

I am slightly surprised when her smiling face appears at the top of the ladder almost as soon as I have got there. She says, 'I am a little bit nervous of heights so I followed you quickly.' Then, after she's stood up, she exclaims, 'Wow! Look. Amazing. Hey, tell me, what's that village there?'

'This is Chhetrapur also,' I explain, 'it is a big village and the part where most people live is a little bit lower than here, by the office. Rice and lentils and bananas grow nicely there.'

'Look,' she says joyfully (it is my idea that she has become overexcited by the climb and the view and the air; women are quick to become overexcited sometimes). 'We can see the river...over there, and over there, and over there. Up here I can really appreciate the scale of the island. It is huge.'

'No, Madam, not huge.' I have to correct her again. 'Rajapur Island is 12 or 13 kilometres at its widest and 25 kilometres north to south only. It is the shape of a teardrop with the tip pointing into the mountains in the north and its rounded bottom cut by the Indo-Nepali border; 100,000 people live in the Nepali part. The Indian part is useless jungle.'

'But the river must be oh-so-powerful!'

'Truly, it has great power. It has the power to give life and also to take it away.'

She frowns and says, 'What do you mean?'

'The river brings water to make rice grow...'

But she is so excited that she isn't really listening. She points again, 'Hey! What's that thing that looks like a huge rusting box there?'

'That is the Chisapani ferry. There was a flood...and now a bridge has been built.'

'But how did the ferry get there?'

'The river brought it.'

'But it is a long, long way from the river!'

'Things are very different during the rains. The river becomes swollen. Small, small channels become rushing torrents. The river always changes also; it floods, it makes new channels; it isolates pieces of land; it moves its course so that some farmers cannot get water and people starve. It eats whole villages. It makes new land also. Slowly, slowly, the main rivers are moving to the east.'

Then, most unexpectedly, she says, 'I want to go up there!' She points now towards the mountains in the north. Her eyes shine with excitement again. I feel I'd like to kiss her but I must not. I will not act in a disrespectful way. It is my duty to protect her. I say, 'It is possible. There is a good path through the gorge and into the mountains. Can you walk?'

'Of course I can walk Rekraj dai, I am not yet so old and so feeble! I am used to working out: in the gym—occasionally.' Why was she talking of Jim? Was this the name of her boyfriend? Then she says something quite mad, 'I'll take Moti as my guide!'

How can she talk of taking Kamala as her guide? This really is too much. How can this weak incompetent foreigner go trekking with a young, inexperienced Tharu girl from the Plains? This will not and must not happen.

Women need to be guided in these kinds of situations—for their own good. This was my vision when I myself conceived our Rajapur Gender Equality Forum. It is to guide such misguided incompetent women.

Sonia

Suddenly I had a plan and when, later that day, I suggested going trekking to Moti, she smiled and said, 'Now, Auntie? Or maybe we can go tomorrow?'

That's the wonderful thing about Nepalis: their spontaneity. It took me aback actually. Then I thought more about it and realized her approach was refreshing. I found it liberating to be close to someone who could be so spontaneous!

I'd set out from Britain with a vague idea of finding out about the amulet and of seeing some of the places my great-grandfather had been to during the War. I thought I might even visit Cawnpore, where my great-great-great-grandfather died. I wanted to know more. Had he been hacked to bits in the massacre?

I'd already got the impression that life was cheap here compared to at home. There was so much violence and blood, death and disease. People died and that was that. I wondered if my ancestors were 'good men'. Had my great-great-great-grandfather deserved to die? Had he killed anyone? Did he really have a local lover?

Actually, I wasn't sure how many 'greats' my distant ancestor should have but I felt connected to him through the amulet—the vajra—I was wearing. It was a pity that I knew so little about him. Oddly, I'd even failed to find Cawnpore on Google Earth.

I am so ignorant—shamefully so, really. I suppose it was my depression that made me so lethargic. There—I had admitted it—I'd been depressed. My journey was giving me back my life though. The Indian subcontinent was so exotic, mysterious, full of potential, even if there was violence. My great-grandfather had loved his time here too. He had a wicked sparkle in his eye whenever he reminisced about the War. He was on my father's side of the family, so from the more broad-minded, dynamic branch. Why hadn't I learned more from him? Why couldn't I be more like him?

Maybe my husband had held me back. If I had suggested going trekking to him—my ex-husband—there would have been *months* of discussions and preparations and endless shopping trips to ensure we were properly equipped. Moti showed me that we didn't need to do much. I yearned to be as spontaneous.

Moti's priorities were so different. She didn't pack but she did insist that we must get up at 4 am to wash and pray! She explained that it is necessary to pray before breakfast.

Meanwhile, I grew more and more excited about our small adventure. If this went well, maybe I'd pluck up the courage to go on a solo hunt to search for the world my ancestors knew.

I wrote to my mother about our trip, knowing that, if I posted her a letter that day she'd get it quite quickly. Then at least, if anything happened, she'd know I'd been thinking of her. There would—after all—be risks on any journeying into the mountains. In my letter, I ignored all the critical judgements she'd written about me and instead simply enthused about Nepal, about Moti's family, about how important families are, and about how I was beginning to feel as if life was worth living again. I even rounded off the letter with a humorous sentence about how I'd had to come a long way to escape my chores, especially the loathsome ironing. It was a good letter. I was satisfied with it. She might even be impressed, although I don't suppose she'd find my celebration of escaping the ironing amusing.

I also bought a postcard of some sleazy-looking Indian film star and on it wrote a few cheery lines to my GP. She'd be amazed at what I'd achieved.

Satisfied, I snuggled up under my cosy cotton quilt that night, as excited and impatient as a child on Christmas Eve.

*

The dinner party was going really well and—for a change—all the other wives were complimenting me on my cooking, and on the house, the new furnishings and all that. Actually, I'd cheated a bit and fried some garlic in butter just as my guests were all due to arrive so that they were greeted by a mouth-watering smell. Then I got generous with the drinks and made sure my husband kept topping up the glasses so that by the time we all sat down at the dinner table, everyone was merry.

People laughed at my jokes and said how they adored my new jewellery. Unusually, my husband had brought back a lavish present from his most recent business trip and I could feel the gold earrings brushing against my neck. I was sitting tall, interjecting humour into the relaxed conversation around my table. Finally, I'd proved I could be a successful hostess. But some stranger had come into the room. He was shaking my shoulder roughly to get my attention. There was something wrong. He said that the kitchen was on fire. I didn't care. I wanted people to listen to the end of my witty story but they wouldn't. They had lost interest just before the punch line and just wanted to leave...

'Memsahib! Memsahib! It is time.' Moti was shaking me awake. She'd said she was going to rouse me before dawn but I hoped she'd oversleep. The bed was so cosy. 'Come Memsahib. It is time to wash!' she persisted.

I rummaged for my torch and stumbled out to the hand-pump. In the dark I could get away with no more than a lick and a promise. The water was—as I expected—freezing. I just washed around my eyes. I could make out that Moti thought this wasn't good enough. I wasn't clean enough to pray but the water was *so* cold. And I couldn't find my towel.

She led me to a little shrine: a rounded rock all smeared with red stuff. It was nestled in the shade of a huge, many-trunked tree. There was a lovely smell of incense. There were oil lamps burning nearby but even so, I could still hardly see what I was doing. Moti approached the reddened rock and bowed. She placed something at the foot of the effigy and seemed to be saying something under her breath.

She turned back to me and explained, 'This holy place is for Lord Ganesh. He is the most popular god because he is solving all kinds of problems for us. Without the blessing and grace and wisdom of Sri Ganesh, nothing can be achieved. It is necessary to bring offerings to him before starting any new undertaking. He has the power to take away obstacles but also he can place obstacles in the way of the unworthy.' She supervised as I placed hibiscus flowers and marigold heads in front of the rock.

'Is Ganesh the one with the head of an elephant, Moti?'

'Truly, Memsahib, but we should show some respect when mentioning Lord Ganesh's name.'

'Oh, sorry.' I blushed at my clumsiness.

'It is nothing. Sri Ganesh is slow to anger. He is also fatty like an elephant. He is especially fond of laddoos; you must also taste these delicacies. After some time we shall feast—like Lord Ganesh only!'

'Lovely,' I said, trying to sound enthusiastic. 'But Rekraj has already bought some for me and, well—um, I found them a bit sickly.'

'Sickly, Memsahib? Like illness?'

'Oh, no—just a bit too sweet for me. I'm sure children love them though.'

'Truly, Memsahib.'

'But tell me, Moti, why does Lord Ganesh have an elephant's head?'

'You do not know this story, didi?'

'No.'

'Then I must tell you, Auntie. Lord Ganesh is the son of Shiva and Parbati but Shiva was always busy making war. Now Parbati was very beautiful and she desired a son who could protect her honour while her husband was away war-mongering, so she created a boy-child out of what-you-call-this white stuff in the hair?'

'Dandruff? A god was created from dandruff?' I started to giggle—a disrespectful giggle, like a silly little girl. I couldn't help it. I tried to stifle my laughter with a cough while she remained solemn and reverent.

'Exactly so. Dandruff,' she nodded. 'In those far-off days, the gods lived in the jungle and did not have modern shampoos, I am thinking!' I could faintly see in the morning darkness that she was smiling. I hadn't offended her. She continued, 'Parbati created a son who guarded his mother very nicely. Then after many years, Shiva came home from the wars. Young Ganesh didn't recognize Shiva as his mother's husband and challenged him, so Shiva cut off Ganesh's head.

'Parbati was upset and cried and cried that her only son was dead. Wanting to pacify her and make his wife content again, Shiva said he would allow Ganesh to live and would give him the head of the next living thing who passed by. The next living thing to pass by was an elephant. Shiva cut off its head, placed it on Ganesh and breathed life into him. Now you will see statues of the happy family of Shiva, the beautiful Parbati and fat, healthy Ganesh sitting on her lap.'

'What a lovely story! Thank you,' I said.

'There are many more from the Mahabharata, the Bhagavad Gita and our other holy books. I will tell you one more about the wisdom of Lord Ganesh, if you wish it?'

'Yes—please. I'd love it!' I said with all the impatience of a little girl wanting a bedtime story.

Moti continued. 'One day there was a competition between Ganesh and his brother Karthikeya. Their father wanted to discover who could travel around the three worlds fastest. The prize was the fruit of all knowledge. Karthikeya set off at great speed while Ganesh simply walked around his parents three times. When Lord Shiva asked what Ganesh was doing, he explained that Shiva and Parbati were his world. This respect for his parents earned him the fruit.'

'That was a lovely story too,' I said, although I was disappointed it was so short.

'I am happy that you are liking this story also. It is an important moral story about how everyone should honour his parents and elders. It is a fine story. I will tell you others but after some time only.'

The story ended just as we reached home. We breakfasted on popcorn and sweet tea and set out on our adventure. The countryside was quite astonishingly beautiful with the low sun picking out rich saturated colours. Birds still screamed at each other in their dawn shouting-matches. The locals had no electric lights but I don't think that was the only reason they got up at dawn. It was such a wonderfully fresh time of day.

I'd dressed in my new Punjabi suit. That's what Moti called the baggy pyjama trousers and a long overshirt combination I had on. I found it cool, comfortable and practical. She said the suit was modern and trendy—old people like her mother never wore them. Moti made me smile when she talked of her mother as 'old' because Guliya must be about my age. Moti probably hadn't thought about what age I was.

She knew I enjoyed the same kinds of things she did—especially shopping; we certainly had that in common. The day before, for instance, I was really pleased to have found a terrific bargain in the bazaar. It was the perfect little backpack for our journey. It was quite fashionable, and practical too, and it only cost a pound. Having looked longingly—alongside Moti—at all the beautiful things the women could buy to put in their hair, I thought I'd grow mine again, as men find long hair sexier.

Unusually, it didn't take us long to walk the length of the bazaar that morning. It was odd to see the main street so deserted. It was probably just as well that the shops and stalls were still tightly shuttered, otherwise we would never have got away. As we walked through though, my nose caught a few pleasing whiffs of cooking, so behind the shutters, people were busy, always busy.

Then it was past the rice mill and on with the rising sun at our backs. The air was so still that trees were perfectly reflected in the clear blue water of the Karnali. I was amazed that there remained rivers in the world that were still this pristine. The smell now was mainly of dust, with an occasional waft of cow dung. We wandered between paddy fields, and through brooks, under drooping trees festooned with vines, past banana plants and huge thatched long-houses where pigs grunted disapprovingly. The scenery was astonishingly lush.

I hadn't a clue where we were going. I didn't care, actually. I trusted Moti absolutely. Then I thought about how young she was and wondered if I should. I was pleased to realize that we were to walk north along the riverbank for a while because it was so, so beautiful. There is something calming about water.

I paused to watch some men swinging lumps of wet cloth over their heads, hitting them down on makeshift wooden washboards. They start work early! When they saw I was watching them, they laughed and started shouting something that sounded not altogether polite.

I asked Moti to translate and, blushing, she said, 'These are Indian men. I do not understand what is being said.'

I knew then that she was lying and they were being lewd. I needed to learn to swear in Nepali! I decided that I must also try asking her about my mantra—but later.

Nature came to life as the day quickly warmed up. Lovely butterflies appeared, flying frenetically here and there and back again. Scarlet or powder-blue dragonflies patrolled their territories. A tiny iridescent blue-and-gold kingfisher perched on a root hanging beneath the undercut riverbank, outside her neat round nest-hole. She sped off upstream, wings not quite clipping the water. She looked just like the kingfishers I'd seen on the Cam river back home in England, but I'd forgotten quite how tiny these birds were, and how dazzlingly, gorgeously blue. Wild forget-me-nots grew everywhere. Odd cabbagey plants grew out of the silt; their leaves were thick and waxy and wore purple flowers. The women's clothes were as vibrant as the flowers. Even crudely hacked logs thrown across water courses to make footbridges were beautiful; innumerable feet had polished the wood to a rich deep red.

I wished I could paint this ineffable beauty but I had never been artistic. I hadn't even packed a camera and my phone was out of charge. It didn't matter. I breathed in the moment, savouring it. I looked towards the mountains—even these foothills inspired me with their stark grandeur. Suddenly, I knew that I'd enjoy many more moving moments and visions of beauty, and that they'd sustain me for the rest of my life.

A small movement on the ground caught my attention. A tiny fawn-coloured ball was moving along the path by itself. I went over to investigate and saw an enormous golden beetle was doing a handstand while resolutely rolling its ball of dung. It looked like hard work—and all to feed its babies. I wondered if it was a male or a female, and how you tell the sex of a dung beetle. I suppose only a dung beetle would care.

Moti smiled when she saw what I was looking at, but as I started to walk on, she grabbed my elbow and pointed at the ground two paces further ahead. I looked and saw nothing at first. Then I made out a black zigzag, then a diamond-shaped head, and then the whole snake. 'Danger—very danger, Memsahib,' she said.

What if I hadn't stopped to look at the dung beetle? What if she hadn't noticed the snake? What if I'd stepped on it? What if I'd been bitten? What if I'd died? As I backed away, I asked her, 'How dangerous is this place?'

'Little bit only, Memsahib. These snakes are lazy in the morning time when it is still cool.'

Despite the shock, I stayed quite calm. Remarkably calm. I told myself, the snake hadn't bitten me. It hadn't even moved. Probably, I would have walked right by it and come to no harm. Who is this inside my head now? A new calm Sonia? I smiled to myself.

Walking on, I kind of went into automatic pilot, placing one foot in front of the other, letting my mind wander. I thought about my vile liar of an ex-husband and his tart of a new wife. I wondered where my life might go next. There must be something I could do. I wasn't stupid, and a teaching qualification might still open a few doors.

After what seemed like hours of walking, I began to feel a bit faint—perhaps a post-shock reaction after the snake—or just hunger and thirst. I yearned for some sign of habitation. If we came across a village, we might be able to buy food or at least some tea but there weren't any houses anywhere. Had Moti planned for us to stop?

Maybe she is used to eating nothing when she goes trekking. After all, she had said something about this being a pilgrimage for her, and Hindus do a lot of fasting, especially when they are on pilgrimages, or bargaining with the gods for favours. I supposed that a bit of fasting would be good for me too, since I have become so fat. But the faintness was getting worse. And where were we going to stay that night?

Moti

We walk through useless uncultivated jungle. I am a little bit worried about the memsahib. She is like a blind woman. She stumbles often and never sees the snakes and hornets and thorn bushes. Usually, she just blunders into these things. She spends a lot of time looking at birds. Maybe she is worried that these mean some bad omen. I do not know how her gods speak to her. She says there are no gods in her country but how is that possible? She must live in a very poor and difficult place.

7. REMOVER OF OBSTACLES

Sonia

On and on we walked from grazing grounds dotted with mighty red silk-cotton trees into less wooded places where there were clusters of dusty thorn bushes. Then this merged into low forest where the trees were flat-topped acacias, like in wildlife programmes about Africa. Moti called this 'jungle' but it wasn't at all like the tropical jungles I'd seen on TV. It was lovely though: so wild, pristine, untouched. Maybe this is what Kipling's jungle was really like.

I put out my hand to feel a lovely feathery acacia leaf. Moti said something—too late!

'Agh! Ow!' The barbed thorns were already imbedded in my palm. I pulled at them. The pain got worse. They wouldn't let me go. Trying to release myself only allowed another leaf to get me, and another.

'Help me, Moti!'

By the time Moti came to my rescue, I was peppered with little bloody puncture-marks. How they stung!

'I need to find my wet-wipes!' I walked over into the shade and put down my backpack to sit. Moti shouted, 'No, Auntie! Do not sit!'

I wasn't interested in her advice. I sat. I jumped up. Dozens of tiny darts stabbed into my bum. My hands got pricked as I investigated. And in leaping up, I impaled my head in the acacia's low branches. This tree was attacking me too! I got into the clear and gingerly pulled fallen acacia thorns from my backside. The thorns had prickles on three sides—like those tyre-puncturing, anti-terrorist spiky stinger things the British army used in Northern Ireland and Iraq.

Already Moti was walking on. Her shoulders were quaking. She was laughing at me again. My throat was tight; I was on the point of tears. I wanted to stomp off in the opposite direction like a sulking toddler but I needed to stay close. I suppose it was just as well that it took quite a while to catch up with her.

We were so far from human habitation that we didn't meet any locals on the path—until we saw one standing with his head held high, challenging us, blocking our way. He didn't look as if he was going to let us pass, *and* he was well-muscled and armed. Delight turned to alarm.

Should we run? Should we stand and face him? He was handsome, tight-bellied, mostly black but with white around his eyes, nose, throat and belly. He was shorter than me but his long spiral horns made him look taller, much taller. His testicles were huge. He looked exceedingly powerful.

'I am thinking you were wanting to meet wild animals. Here is one blackbuck!' Moti grinned.

'He looks ready for a fight, Moti!'

'Maybe, Memsahib.'

This didn't reassure me. I said, 'Could he hurt us with those horns?'

'That is possible, Memsahib.'

I stood, too scared to move.

Moti then volunteered, 'He will run soon. He is giving his wives and childrens a chance to get away only.'

We stood watching him for ages. His nostrils flared as he sniffed the air. He seemed to be trying to decide how dangerous we were from our smell. He looked so proud. Finally, he bounded off like a gymnast. As he ran we saw his strikingly white behind.

Moti remarked, 'This antelope is the vehicle for Chandra, the moon god. See—there is the silver moon on backside of this animal.'

'What do you mean "vehicle"?'

'In heaven, each of the gods is having one animal for riding on. Kumar, the god of war, rides on peacock. Lord Ganesh, he rides on rat. Like that. Ganesh is the cleverest god because he is the Remover of Obstacles. He has four arms. Either he can trample down a problem or he can send his rat to squeeze through and solve it.'

I loved the way Hindus included the natural world within their beliefs—and the way they felt completely protected by their deities. They seemed to choose certain deities for certain problems, but then everyone seemed to pray to Ganesh. His paunch made him seem friendly and accommodating. Moti had told me he was the god of literature and jollity. That sounded like a brilliant combination.

Moti

I am happy to take my new auntie on this journey. It will be interesting for me also. Daily, I see people who come to Rajapur bazaar for shopping. These people come from far. They take some days to walk down from the hills. I have never seen their native places. They say that there are many easy paths into the hills.

When I asked my father about our pilgrimage, he said we must go to the holy cave in the mountains. There is a mighty Shiva lingam where we can worship and gain merit which will help little Kancha stay strong. After what Auntie did to him, it is good that she also can give an offering. I am happy. I am going on my first pilgrimage. It will be an important pilgrimage to help my baby brother.

We walk to the north of the island, closer to the mountains. I am seeking the ferryman. He is not in his usual place by the tea-shops. The nicely dressed Chhetri woman who runs the biggest shop explains that the river is very low; the ferry goes from further north these days, from the cobble beach at the very tip of the island. She says that it is very unusual and very inauspicious for the river to be so low in this season. This change in the river worries her. She expects it will cause some problem somehow. She also explains that because of the change, the ferry journey is shorter.

She has rice freshly cooked and there is no need to hurry; we can eat straightaway. We go inside and she serves us good generous helpings of rice and dal and vegetable curry, and tomato, onion and chillie chutney. I am hungry and it smells good. My mouth waters as I watch her put expensive Indian mango pickle on the shiny steel plate.

Sonia

The grubby tea-house owner was wearing a faded flowery garment that looked like her grandmother's cast-off night-dress. Her hair was greasy and her nails were black. She plonked an overfilled tray of rice and curry down in front of me. I couldn't imagine that this had been prepared hygienically but it was so gloomy inside that I couldn't really see what the food looked like. I was hungry but the thought of contamination worried me and the portion size was ridiculous. This was far too much for me. 'Isn't there cutlery, Moti?'

The woman brought a stained teaspoon in response to something Moti said to her. She polished it with her unwashed thumb before she gave it to me. I felt unwell. She also brought a rough earthenware bowl containing gelatinous whitish material with wood-shavings, dust and a few buffalo hairs strewn on the surface. Moti smiled a welcome to this stuff and remarked, 'Ah, good fresh buffalo yoghurt.'

Using her fingers, Moti was shovelling rice into her mouth at an astonishing rate. 'You are feeling some problem, Auntie?' She asked through another inelegant mouthful.

'Where can I wash?'

'Pani leeau!' Moti shouted.

In response, the woman gave me a small pot of water. I saw that I'd have to go outside and try to manage on my own. It wasn't easy, because you can't soap your hands and pour water onto them unless you grow a third hand—or someone pours for you. All I seemed to do was get soap on everything. But at least I had brought some soap, so I did get my hands—and the spoon—a little cleaner.

Back inside in the gloom again, I dipped the spoon into the food and it didn't taste too bad—even if there was a lingering aftertaste of soap. I scraped the top off the yoghurt and mixed some in with the curry. This improved the taste tremendously, but I then discovered that if I scooped too close to the edge of the yoghurt pot, bits fell off.

'Clay from the pot is stuck between my teeth,' I complained to Moti.

Moti said, 'This is not problem, Memsahib.'

'I'm not so sure. It is a problem for me—a most uncomfortable one!'

Once I finished eating, I fled outside. I couldn't stand the eye-stinging cooking smoke a moment longer. It was good to get some air. I must ask Moti to teach me more basic Nepali words so that I can ask for things myself at our next stop.

I stood waiting, wondering why Moti was taking so long, when she could eat so very fast. Movement above me caught my attention. I looked up, expecting to see another fine bird. It was a bird—a dead crow had been tied to a post with a bit of string and was blowing in the wind. How ghastly. Hindus are supposed to respect life.

Moti finally emerged. No doubt she'd been gossiping with the tea-house owner. I asked her about the crow and she said it was there to warn away other crows. It helped protect the beans and vegetables that were growing nearby.

'Come, let's go, Auntie.'

I thought and mused and wondered how I could encourage Moti to talk to me more. She seemed so shy and so reluctant to say anything beyond factual statements. Yet, she became animated when she spoke to other Nepali women. Why was she so monosyllabic with me? Maybe she found English difficult.

Moti

Auntie asks, 'Where do we go from here?'

'Little bit further, Auntie. This way come.'

As we walk, she asks, 'What is your father's work?'

Pleased that Auntie is interested in my family, I tell her, 'He is doing many things these days—now that he is no longer bonded to a landlord—now that he himself is a landowner.' Auntie stumbles on nothing, but recovers. 'He does all kind of work. But it is his choice only. We have land that he must tend, but he also takes money to work for others from time to time. Before, he had to labour for nothing—wherever the landlord ordered. Now everything is different and sometimes he is even paid good money. Yesterday only he went to the northeast of the island for digging.'

'Digging what?'

'He is working with cousins and he will have fun there with them. The landlord in that part of Rajapur is making a big piece of work to stop the river from taking his land. The men build shelters for themselves, by themselves, and sleep up there beside the river.'

Suddenly the memsahib shouts out.

I look around. She is staggering backwards and I am fearful a snake has bitten her. Then I understand. I point to the small, small animal that has frightened her. She has nearly stepped on a baby spotted deer. I point to the trembling outline of a week-old fawn.

Auntie is shaken. 'Something reddish shot out from under my feet. It sped away as fast as a bullet...'

'This is one chital, Auntie. The mother has left it alone while she goes to find food. Look how it shakes. It is also very scared—like you, Memsahib!'

'Oh. It gave me a huge shock, Moti!' She takes a water bottle from her bag and takes some gulps. 'That's better! But please finish telling me about your father's work.'

'We will go on also, Auntie?'

'Yes, of course.' And she strides off—in the wrong direction.

'This way come, Auntie,' I say beckoning. 'My father's work now only is not like it used to be in the days when Tharus like my father and his cousins were bonded to a landlord.'

'Bonded—what do you mean?'

'Bound to work for no money. Maybe one or two months before the rains, many men would walk to the north of the island. In those days, the landlord provided rice and meat and strong drink for his kamaiyas. Wives would go too, and cook while the children would play in the jungle and collect wild fruit to eat. It was a big party. I did look forward to those summer works, even if my father was always exhausted by the end. Sometimes he was tired because of all the work he had to do. Sometimes it was because his chest was weak and sometimes it was because he had drunk too much raksi! Sometimes he worried too much about his family—about what might happen if one year we didn't have a landlord to look after us.'

'So you're saying these—umm—kamaiyas weren't paid? They were slaves?'

'Little bit like slaves, yes, Auntie. Each January, landlords made an agreement with the heads of families and then that man's whole family had to work for that landlord for one year. For no pay. My father worried that because of his weak chest, he might not be taken on. If that had happened, we would have had nowhere to live, and no work also. We would have gone hungry. That was his worry each and every year. Now he has land, he has no worries—as long as he stays healthy.

'The kamaiya system has been stopped now—in your year 2000. Outsider-people said it was—as you have said, Auntie—a system of slavery. But not everyone is better off now.'

This nice conversation makes the journey go faster. To the north, I see one bus speeding along the East-West Highway. This is the modern fast black road that winds like a rat snake along the base of the hills. We will reach the ferry soon.

Sonia

It was brilliant that Moti was finally starting to speak to me. I had been talking about myself a lot thus far—in order to fill the silences. I had probably been selfish in burdening this young girl with the long, bitter story of my husband's betrayal. Yet she encouraged me; she seemed interested. She also seemed to agree that generally men are not to be trusted. That had encouraged me to talk more and I had indulged in a diatribe of accusations.

Moti talked a bit about karma and how fate is kind to some people, while for others it seemed to deliver only hardship. She believed there was no point in fighting it or blaming it. You just had to get on with life. This was easier said than done, although there was some wisdom in what she said. Perhaps not all my troubles were caused by others' maliciousness. Perhaps some were simply my karma.

I asked her, 'Will you get married, Moti?'

'Of course,' she said, simply.

Much later, we arrived, not at the harbour I was expecting, but at a silt and cobble beach. Other people were converging on this point too.

When I had first come to Rajapur, which already felt like half a lifetime ago, I'd crossed onto the island on a crude craft with the recycled truck engine driving it, but it had been big enough to accommodate a couple of four-wheel-drive vehicles and some buffaloes. This spot didn't look like the sort of place a ferry could moor.

Perhaps to pass the time and entertain me, Moti led me towards a man who was bent over a small dugout canoe. He was scooping water out of it with his hands. Beyond him, something moved in the river. It was oily-black and sinuous and it was swimming close to the shore. I made out a head and a long neck. It looked like some kind of water snake.

Moti led me to the man and his dugout. He pushed the boat out a little and beckoned us to sit inside. THIS was the ferry? There was still water in the bottom. I hesitated.

Others got aboard, sitting cramped one behind the other. Moti stepped in, too, and simply sat in the puddle. I couldn't do anything but copy her. I scrambled in and felt water soaking into my knickers. It was surprisingly refreshing. I looked over the side of the boat into the clear water and saw that each river-smoothed pebble was subtly differently coloured.

The swimming snake-thing seemed to be watching us. Maybe it was hunting us.

The ferryman took two rupees from everyone as several more people stepped aboard. He pushed off. The snake-thing dived, and I realized it was a bird. The ferryman squatted precariously on the tip of the back of the dugout and paddled us out into a huge and powerful Karnali river. It was a couple of hundred metres to the far bank. The boat rocked alarmingly as the current caught us. It didn't feel at all safe.

I'd been looking forward to another boat trip but this was no fun. The boat was tossed about like a bra in a tumble-dryer. It felt as if we could capsize at any moment. All the other passengers were cowering low and I could hear one of them mumbling as though praying. I looked out at the surface of the water as it whizzed by, too close. It made me feel sick and dizzy. My bum was actually lower than the surface of the river. I shut my eyes and started to think about believing in God. I knew that I didn't but wondered whether He'd accept late emergency applications.

Then after a long time, I started to register screechy music, children's shrieks and—astonishingly—the sounds of trucks and buses. There was a bump and a horrible scraping sound. I opened my eyes to see we'd made it to the shore again. Safely.

Everyone was scrambling out and striding over the cobbles and up the riverbank.

Rather than help me, the ferryman was staring, waiting for me to get out, I suppose.

Moti turned and said, 'Come, Auntie!'

I stood and staggered along the length of the dugout and onto the beach. From the river edge, I looked up to the blaring stalls of Chisapani bazaar. After a pause, while I gratefully readjusted to steady land beneath my feet again, I followed Moti and started to scramble steeply uphill towards the market, towards the noise. We passed naked toddlers and pigs luxuriating in the black sludge of a storm-drain. River water was dribbling down my legs from my sodden underwear. People would think I had wet myself.

'Err, Moti? Is there somewhere we could change?'

'Change, Auntie?'

'My wet clothes, Moti.'

'No possible, Auntie. This is busy place. Look—now we have come to the East-West Highway. It goes through the whole of the country...'

I then saw that I was standing on a real tarmacked road.

'We can take one bus to Kathmandu itself from here.'

'Have you ever been there, Moti? To Kathmandu?'

'Never, Memsahib. It is far—and costly also.'

I turned towards an odd circus-clown honk. The driver of a cram-packed cycle rickshaw hooted at men wobbling on bicycles piled high with fodder cut from the jungle—for their cows, I supposed.

It seemed strange to have left the island. There was electricity here. This was civilization. I wondered what interesting things there would be to buy. I found myself admiring the amazingly decorated trucks. Each had elaborate scenes painted on their sides, there were filigree aluminium decorations around the windows, tinselly things dangling from any protuberance, and—to help the driver judge vehicle width—antennae stuck out where wing-mirrors were usually positioned. A different Hindi film song blared out from each one.

Several buses were being loaded. A goat was being dragged inside one of them. People were on the roofs packing boxes, along with bundles of dozens of live chickens tied together by their legs. NICE BUS was written across the windscreen of one in large letters—though it didn't look that nice. All of them, I noticed, had HORN PLEASE on the back, with the words spelt in various original ways. One bus had LUCK in big letters on it. I smiled as I recalled how I'd thought we'd need luck to arrive at our destination on my first bus journey in Nepal. Another of the buses announced it was SUPER SONIC, just like the one I'd first come to Rajapur on; perhaps this was the same bus? That passing thought pleased me. I'd already been in this country long enough to recognize individual buses!

Hmm—Super Sonia, that's me. I'm becoming quite well acclimatized. Quite an expert.

We walked past a repulsive huddle of vultures, squabbling as they poked their heads right inside some large, recently dead animal's ribcage just beside the road. Nasty greenish drippy elastic stuff hung off their beaks.

A bus disturbed them from their revolting feast. They scrabbled to get away but they were clumsy from having eaten too much. One vulture ran along the road ahead of the bus, taxiing for take-off. It was so overfed that it couldn't get into the air. The bus driver honked his horn. The vulture looked round. People inside the bus cheered, which made me smile. Craning forward, the bird struggled to gain height. It kept looking over its shoulder and saw that the bus was gaining on it. It flapped frantically. The bird was half a metre above the road when the bus caught up with it and nudged its backside. More cheering. It thrust its wrinkly neck out straight ahead in an effort to accelerate and flapped even more desperately. Then it bounced off the bumper and gained a little more height.

People hung out of the glassless windows and seemed to

be shouting advice and instructions to the bird. Some were out of their seats, theatrically remonstrating with it. Everyone was involved. I felt sorry for it but couldn't help laughing.

Next, the vulture's slimy brown feathers hit the windscreen. The impact bounced the bird forward. It gained a little more height, bounced again and finally it was up above the bus. People applauded but it still wasn't clear. It got caught on the luggage on the roof and took a tumble before it was free. Then it circled round and returned to the stinking carcass.

This country must be simply seething with bacteria.

Moti

I like this place. It is a little bit modern. The way the stalls press up against the folds of the hills makes me think of scared chicks hiding amongst the feathers of the mother hen.

I say, 'Come, Auntie, let us take cold drinks!'

I see a sweet-seller with a beautiful pile of golden laddoos. I buy some and offer them to the memsahib.

'What are they?'

'Besan laddoos—lentil flour and sugar fried—very tasty. It is what gives Lord Ganesh the sparkle in his eyes!'

She takes one, examines the oil on her fingers, then nibbles at her laddoo as if it is poison.

'Now, look. This hotel is having one fridge, Auntie.'

I like coming to these places with good facilities. The owner of the Bageswari Hotel boasts he has the one and only fridge on Rajapur Island but it is never working. The cold drinks are always warm—even when the weather is cooler.

Now, after our small journey to Chisapani, we are thirsty and finish our cold drinks before the sweat has evaporated from the surface of the bottles. I watch the miracle of small, small drops forming on the outside of the glass. I crunch up the ice in my mouth. It makes me shiver. I love that feeling. I have heard people in the bazaar in Rajapur saying that, if you go into the high mountains, you can pick up pieces of ice from the ground itself only—and eat it just like I am eating ice today. Perhaps we will go so high that we can do this on our pilgrimage.

Drinks finished, I get up and walk around until I find one

Tibetan. Her hair is in two plaits. She mouths prayers in her strange language as she clicks her rosary. She is selling dried meat; she calls it deer meat. It is said that these Tibetans sell the meat of the cow but surely such pious people would not do this sacrilegious thing. I want to buy deer meat for our journey but the Tibetan is asking too much money—as they always do. It is dear deer meat. It is very hard to get a good price from any Tibetan. What to do? They are even more clever than the Brahmins. This Tibetan is also selling thunderbolts but why would anyone want to buy such inauspicious things? Thunderbolts bring great misfortune. It is odd also that Auntie wears one around her neck; perhaps in her country they have a different meaning or power. The Tibetans have different ways to ours too. Perhaps that is why this woman sells these things. Their men wear their hair in long plaits sometimes also. I like to talk with Tibetan women. They all seem strong and confident.

I ask this woman how many husbands she has and she gives me a long interesting answer. She says, 'I was fortunate. The man I wanted to marry had seven brothers. Our tradition is that when you marry a man you also marry all his brothers. I didn't want that. Luckily, two went to the monastery and two went to do business in Singapore so I live with only three husbands, but I spend a lot of time away—trading—because it is actually boring having even three husbands.'

I ask her, 'What do you think about one man having several wives, like we do in the Plains?'

She says, 'I like that idea: that way the work can be shared. It is good to have the friendship of other wives too. It is an interesting idea but there would also be a problem of too many children…'

'But children are wealth! They tend animals and cut fodder plants and bring dung to the fields and mind the younger children…'

'Truly, they do but there are many more stomachs to fill. Now tell me about your journey, bahini. It is a pilgrimage?'

'We go to save my baby brother. The memsahib bathed him in water and he will get a fever soon.'

'These foreigners have strange ways,' she says. 'But you

shouldn't go to the cave. That is not a power-place. You must go to a more important site with a potent, curative relic.'

'What place?' I ask her.

'All these kinds of places are high up in the mountains. They are far. Very far.'

'Then we cannot go to them. I think entering the cave will earn sufficient merit for our purposes. My brother is not *very* sick,' I explain. She is satisfied.

Sonia

The Chisapani bazaar was a lively, exciting place. There were lots of attractive glitzy or interesting things to buy. There were T-shirts and sweatshirts with random English words emblazoned across them, like Authentic Sport or Cowboys or U.S. Team. There was a huge range of hair ornaments, and those red things women stick on their foreheads. There were stalls with heaps of colourful powders. Actually, everything was colourful here.

Then I suddenly felt a little self-conscious. I was probably staring wide-eyed like some country bumpkin in London. What did I look like? My hair was unbrushed and I was unmade-up. And my knickers were still sodden.

After all the days I'd spent on Rajapur Island, the bazaar seemed almost cosmopolitan. The market smells were mouthwatering. The snacks looked tempting but the stalls selling cloth held my interest for longest. In my head, I started designing my next Punjabi suit. Maybe it would be lapis-blue with a navy trim. I was so absorbed in imagining the wonderful exotic wardrobe I'd take back home, that I hadn't noticed the approach of a neatly dressed man. Suddenly, he was standing in front of me, bowing.

'Oh—hello!' I exclaimed.

'Good day, Madam.' I looked to Moti for advice but she hadn't noticed this little man. Her attention was fixed on a spectacularly gaudy array of glass bangles.

'Hello,' I said again.

'I am Ishihara—development consultant, buildings and structural engineer.' He bowed again. 'I am happy to meet another foreigner.' What a cheek this man had, describing me as a foreigner. Then I thought and realized I was. I looked at him again and I saw that he wasn't Nepali, as I had first assumed. He was Japanese. He wanted to talk because we were comrades, both being outsiders. Maybe he was lonely.

He continued, 'Have you come also to work on some development project, please?'

'No, not really. I'm not qualified to do anything...' As soon as the words were out, I regretted them. Why did I always talk about myself in such a negative way? I quickly added, 'Although I *am* working as a volunteer—helping at a little NGO office on Rajapur Island.' I pointed south, downstream, towards the river we had crossed in that wobbly dugout and saw what a cat's cradle of waterways the Karnali was here, a veritable inland delta. I was surprised by what I saw. Even here, a few metres above river level, I had a good view of the countryside that Moti and I had walked through. To the north, the river was constrained by a 1,000-metre high mountain-corset but, downstream of where we stood, it splurged out, allowing innumerable islands to form. Thorn trees and bamboo tussocks adorned most of them and, even at this distance, I could see hundreds of birds picking around in the shallows.

The Japanese man wasn't interested in the scenery. He interrupted my reverie with, 'I see. If you are from Great Britain, you can teach these people about planning. They are most disorganized and cannot plan anything.'

'Mmm...maybe.' This was most embarrassing, but Moti didn't seem to hear. Her attention was on hair gadgets.

'You are living alone on Rajapur? Alone amongst these uncivilized people?' He put a handkerchief to his mouth. He appeared to have smelt something bad. 'This must be very hazardous for you. How do you eat?'

'Oh, I'm getting quite a taste for rice and lentils.'

'Mmm. I am nervous about eating their native food. I take only boiled eggs, bananas and whisky. That keeps me healthy.'

'Really? So what are you doing here?'

'Assessing our new clinic. One year ago, we built a state-of-art rural clinical facility. I have come to see how it is being used. We made it to withstand earthquakes. We Japanese have much experience and expertise about earthquakes. I have discovered these Nepali health workers are still using unhygienic huts instead of clinic. I do not understand why this is so. These people do not understand value of what the people of Japan have done for them.'

I was worried that Moti might be insulted by what he was saying. I looked for her but fortunately, she had wandered away at some point during his last little speech.

'Nothing gets done. Nepalis leave everything unfinished.'

I tried to turn around the conversation by saying, 'But I like the relaxed way Nepalis organize themselves. We have something to learn from them, I think.' I was desperate to get away in case anyone thought I judged Nepalis the same way. Edging away, I said, 'It was very nice meeting you, Mr Ishiwara. My friend and I must continue our journey. We have a long way to walk before dark.'

I walked off, not knowing where Moti was. I felt nervous and worried that I'd lost her, but in a matter of seconds, she rejoined me. She must have been keeping an eye on me from a distance, and for that I was grateful, deeply grateful.

Chisapani bazaar had no permanent buildings but was a lot bigger than it had looked from the riverbank; it overflowed from the East-West Highway in both directions and onto the bridge as well as north along the dirt track above the river that led into the Chisapani gorge itself. It almost looked like the gorge was trying to spit it out. We had quite a gauntlet of stalls to dodge and colourful awnings to duck under.

Eventually, we walked beyond the bazaar and into deep shade, and the blaring sounds faded. It was like wandering into a deliciously cool and green netherworld. I couldn't see the sky anymore, unless I craned my neck uncomfortably.

The Karnali river, which was now several metres below the path we were on, was held in by the beautifully fluted gorge walls. Lianas hung off ivory-white rocks. Trees grew out from every little ledge. The shrieks and whoops of unknown birds echoed off the cliffs. Lots worked the river; some looked like dippers. A squirrel bounded along a branch close by; it was big, and a rich handsome chestnut-brown.

Being out here in the countryside was a lovely change. I enjoyed the smell of the river and the mouldering leaves and the harsh squawks of parakeets. A soft sad *oooooing* call made me look towards a superb emerald dove. He shot off, quick as any MiG, banking at the last minute to avoid a branch.

Moti pointed down to a tiny pristine beach in an indentation at the base of the cliffs. There were a couple of logs on the beach.

'It is dangerous to harm these animals,' Moti declared. 'Anyone killing a crocodile will be reborn as a crocodile in their next life, and then they will eat only fish and dead bodies. I do not think this will be a nice life!' She walked on.

I looked again at the logs and one slithered into the river.

When we came out into the sun again, I said, 'Let's rest for a few minutes.'

Moti offered me a strip of dried meat that she had bought from the Tibetan woman. Flies had been crawling on it at the stall but the air was so pure here and I was so hungry that I didn't care. Not any more. It was chewy and tasted delicious.

I looked around me as I chewed. Close to where I was sitting, I spotted several clusters of carnivorous pitcher plants. 'Look, Moti!' I said. 'Do you know about these?'

'Of course, Memsahib. These are too bitter to eat.'

'Did you know these plants eat flies?'

'Not correct, Memsahib. This plant is also too bitter for the flies to eat it.'

'No, no. You have misunderstood. The plant eats the flies,' I explained.

'That is not possible.'

She really did think that I knew absolutely nothing about anything.

'May I ask a favour of you, Moti?'

'Of course, Auntie.'

'Teach me some Nepali! Teach me the words for please, thank you, yes and no—please.'

'Not possible, Auntie!'

'What?'

'It is not possible,' she said more slowly and clearly.

'Why not?'

'In Nepali, there is no word for yes, no word for no. Also we are not saying please and thank you also.'

'But how can a language not have those words? Without please and thank you everyone would seem very rude!'

'We speak respectfully and politely but we do this in the way we speak, not by adding one polite word like you do in English. Nepali is more respectful than English—foreigners often speak rudely to us!'

'Oh. So what about yes and no?'

'If you ask me one question like, "Do you like this meat?" I say "I like it", or "I do not like it".'

My heart sank. I recalled French lessons at school where we were asked a question and we weren't allowed to answer simply *oui* or *non*. We had to make up a whole sentence. French was hard enough but occasionally, just occasionally, you could guess what a word meant because it was a bit like English. I couldn't expect to recognize anything in Nepali. Nepali was going to be difficult. I felt like giving up already.

Electric blue and deep-sea-green damselflies flirted at the river's edge. Their wings sparkled as they caught the sun. I saw another swimming snake-creature, and realized it was a cormorant. Huge butterflies and superb dragonflies flitted about. A majestic bird flew over, which I recognized as an osprey. Another movement drew my eyes to a tree creeper. Moti saw where I was looking and said, 'This bird is Tree Doctor. It eats the insects that eat the tree. Plants cannot eat insects and flies but this is the job of the Tree Doctor.'

Then, she asked me suddenly, 'Did you like that Japanese man, Memsahib?'

'No, I didn't. He didn't seem to be the kind of person who should be doing development work! Did you hear him talking about the clinic? Do you know the one he was talking about?'

'Of course, Memsahib. It is a most famous clinic. It was costly. These Japanese people built it and there was a grand opening ceremony. At first, the outsider-doctors were happy to work there. Then monsoon came and rain poured into the clinic, and many medicines were spoilt. Government health posts only receive medical supplies twice in a year, so there were no medicines for many months. My friend told me the clinic is made in pieces so that when earthquakes come, the roof does not fall down. But rain comes in between these pieces. It is a problem. Big earthquakes maybe never come but the monsoon—it come every year. Our small, small houses are good when the earth shakes. The roof isn't too heavy and if it fall down, never mind. It is not a problem. Not like modern concrete houses. When they fall down, people die.'

8. THE PERFECT WOMAN

Moti

Auntie is talking again about her life and her sad times. Then suddenly she says, 'Ram Krishna seems to like you. Will you marry him?'

It is my idea that she is trying to be a little bit teasing but I am surprised that Auntie doesn't understand what a bad man Ram Krishna Sahib is. 'He is not a good man. I will never marry him,' I explain. 'He is not of my caste also.'

'I am sorry, Moti. I was dreaming, and thinking we might both find a good man, but you are right—Ram Krishna is horrible!'

I say to Auntie, 'That is true. He wants to lie with every womens. He even pays to go with Badi womens.'

'Men are like that,' Auntie says, 'until they settle for a while, at least, with the one they love.'

'What to do? He will never settle. Even after marriage he will not settle. Last week, he caught me in the field at the backside of our house. He kissed me and he wanted to force me to lie with him. I screamed and screamed. I got away and started to run to our house. I was so scared. I knew he would catch me. There is nowhere safe if a Brahmin gets these ideas into his head.

'The gods were with me that day. My mother heard my screams. Straightaway she knew. She had seen the way Ram Krishna looks at me and my screams told her something was happening. I saw her running towards me. She was carrying a freshly sharpened khukuri. She was angry. I have never seen her like this...with such—how do you say it—determination. Yes, determination. She was shouting as she ran to help me. By this time, Ram Krishna had caught me again. He had ripped my blouse. He was trying to kiss me again but he was surprised to see my mother shouting and running. He let me go. My mother reached him. Her face looked like monsoon thunder. She was going to cut him. I could see that she was angry enough to do that.

'She caught his hand. She got his smallest finger and held the curved cutting surface of the khukuri to it as if she would slice his finger off. She was still shouting, "You have already stolen away one daughter! If you want another daughter's body, then I will first take some of your body! You still want this daughter also?" This confused me. She was blaming Ram Krishna for the disappearance of my oldest sister, Maya. I did not understand what she was saying. She had never spoken to me of this. Later, when I asked, she would say nothing more.

'The colour drained from the face of Ram Krishna. He started to beg. My mother did not hear. She kept threatening him, "If you touch my daughter, I will cut you so that you cause no more trouble for Tharu girls. Your father is no good and dishonours your mother. You are the same. If I see you touch my daughter again—no, if I see you *look* at my daughter again—I will cut your banana! Into slices!"'

'Banana? What did she mean?' Auntie does ask lots of surprising questions.

'Banana is like phallus, no? And my mother looked so mad with anger that I think she could have done this terrible thing.'

'Wow, I can't imagine your mother threatening anyone. She seems so quiet and mild-mannered,' Auntie says.

'It is so. We Tharu people know that it is best to be invisible. Best to say nothing. But that day, all her years of holding onto her anger boiled over. I laughed and I cried at the same time when I saw her strength.

'It was only after some time that she let go of Ram Krishna's finger. Only after some time was he free to run away, like the dishonourable coward that he is. Like a beaten blooded fighting cock chased off by the champion.'

Auntie says, 'What a wonderful story of girl-power!'

I have to correct her. 'It is not wonderful. Now we will wait and see what bad things his family will do to us.'

'Why didn't you run to the police?' She asks me this strange question.

'They are all Brahmins too and they say that we flirt with Brahmin mens and so we deserve this kind of treatment. They say it is the fault of the womens! The last time that one relative made official complaint to the police, they insulted him and said he couldn't complain if he couldn't write and then they beat him up. Another time, a distant cousin once made a formal complaint to the police about a Brahmin—a Brahmin who had raped this cousin's wife. He himself was arrested and put in prison. After some time, he died there.'

'What do you mean…?' she looks horrified. 'Was he executed?'

'We have no capital punishment in Nepal. It is there in India, and in China also but not in Nepal. There is no official sentencing but lower castes do not do well in prison. People say that the prison staff organize the prisoners to be violent towards each other and in that way they have control. Many people die inside. It is said arrangements can be made if your enemy is powerful enough—or rich enough,' I explain, while Auntie sits open-mouthed.

She looks like a deaf mute.

'There is one other problem with our police and our prisons. If there has been some murder or serious crime and the criminal cannot be found, then the police arrest a relative of the criminal and keep him in prison to serve the criminal's sentence instead.'

Auntie continues to stand there with her mouth open, saying nothing.

'It was fortunate that my father did not see what Ram Krishna did. If he had seen this disrespectful thing then my father might have killed Ram Krishna. And that would cause much sorrow for my family. Even if he had only threatened the Brahmin like my mother had, our family would have been chased out from our house—our own house—never mind if it is ours by right and hard work. One good thing: I think that Ram Krishna is too embarrassed to tell people that he was scared of an old Tharu woman! Every time I think of what happened that day, my love for my mother fills my chest. I am so proud of her!' I say.

'You are so lucky to have such a loving family.' Auntie gazes at me. 'But what did your mother mean about Ram Krishna taking another daughter?'

'I cannot be sure but I think she is in Mumbai.'

'Oh, that's nice.'

'Not nice, Memsahib. Not good.'

'Why? There are lots of opportunities in the cities.'

I look at the ground and say nothing.

'So—err—did that experience put you off men, and marriage?'

'Not all men are like this.'

'So...who will you marry?' Auntie asks.

'It is not known.'

Next she asks a question that makes me giggle.

'Do you have a boyfriend?'

I do not reply. I think about the timid Newar man. I say, 'Do you remember that man who talked to me in the bazaar? My mother says he wants to marry me. Perhaps he will be nice. Did you think he is nice?'

'I hope you don't mind me saying, Moti, but I thought he looked a bit sickly—and weedy!'

'Weedy—what is weedy?'

'Weak... but if... do you like him, Moti?'

'He is Newar—from the Kathmandu Valley itself. I think that the idea of an exotic lover is interesting but you are right, Auntie. He does not look strong. If he hasn't the courage to talk to me properly, I don't think he is a manly man! He should bring me flowers and sing me songs like in the movies! I have seen that there is very little meat on his body. It is possible that he is a Big Man in his native place only. I am thinking he must live in a fine house in Kathmandu; isn't it so?'

The memsahib smiles and continues with her questions, 'Don't your people have arranged marriages?'

'Not always. The rich high-caste peoples, they have arranged marriages but we Tharus, we are free to choose.'

'So how will you choose?' she asks.

'It is not known, Memsahib. Maybe I will have a love marriage—like my parents. Love marriages are inexpensive. They are normal in ordinary families, like ours. Arranged marriages are also good. Everyone has a chance to find love. No one is left without a husband. Even ugly girls can find ugly husbands!'

'I'd hate to marry someone I'd only just met!' she frowns.

'All womens know that they must make sacrifices, like Sita,' I explain. 'All womens know they must work to fall in love. My cousin's marriage was arranged. Her parents found a suitable man for her. She has fallen in love with her husband. They are happy. Her eyes shine when she talks of him. I think that arranged marriages are best because sometimes love marriages don't last. They are not always good.'

'Really—why not?'

'It is not known. My aunt fell in love with an untouchable man and he took her away to Kathmandu when I was a child, so I hardly remember her. She's dead now. That is a sad thing—to be away from your real family. My big sister also, she fell in love with someone from a different caste. She fell in love with an old Brahmin. He was kind to her—not like Ram Krishna is to me. They made a baby together and so she had to move into his house with the senior wife and his mother, and his widowed sister. The Brahmin loved her but the Brahmin women were jealous and they were not kind. They made her do all the house-works and they beat her. When the baby came it was a girl. The Brahmin women took the baby away and it died. Then my sister came home to my father's house again. She is not happy anymore. My sister's name is Sita, and Sita in the *Ramayana* was unfortunate also. Let me tell you her story only.

'Sita was born out of the earth. King Janaka found her and saw immediately that she was so very beautiful that her marriage must be wisely arranged. He commanded that there be a test of manliness and Sita was the prize. Worthy Prince Rama won, Sita fell in love with him and for some time, they lived happily together in the palace at Ayodhya. That place is close by, in India, Auntie.

'Rama's stepmother made clever plans and got Rama banished. The couple went into exile in the jungle, where they lived a good life of prayer…'

I continue to tell the wonderful epic tale of love, magic, deceit, revenge, demons and kidnap but Auntie is impatient and rudely interrupts, 'Is there an ugly sister in your story, Moti?'

'There was one woman, Shoorpanakha. She fell in love with Rama but he was not interested in her seduction. In her fury, she attacked Sita but Rama's noble half-brother Lakshman saw and cut off her ears and nose!'

'What an awful thing to do!'

'It happens, Auntie. Husbands do cut off the nose of their wife if they are unfaithful.'

'No!'

'It is so, Auntie. Truly. It is there in our holy book, the *Ramayana*.' I wanted to get back to telling this epic story. Telling these stories improves the karma and makes the journey go quicker also.

I continue. 'Even in the jungle, the holy couple were not left in peace. The next problem was that Shoorpanakha wanted revenge and told Ravana, her unworthy brother, about Sita's beauty. Ravana kidnapped Sita because he desired her.'

Auntie says laughing, 'I wish someone desired me!' She makes me smile also.

'The righteous Rama came in a flying chariot with monkey-warriors and rescued Sita. After many adventures, they were crowned at the palace in Ayodhya. They were happy.

'After some time, Rama started to think bad things. He was influenced by other people and their talking. Rama understood the power of Sita's beauty. He thought that maybe Sita hadn't resisted Ravana's attempts to seduce her. He couldn't believe that after all that time in captivity, Sita was faithful to him.'

'Aggh! Men!' Auntie says, looking little bit angry now.

'Rama was wrong to doubt his virtuous wife. Sita had remained pure. She was so much upset by Rama's unfair accusation that she threw herself onto a funeral pyre. Her purity was proved when the flames did not harm her. Seeing this, Rama and Sita reunited but only for a short time. Next, Rama overheard a washerman discussing how impossible it was for a beautiful woman to sleep in another man's house and remain pure. Rama banished Sita without explanation. She returned to living in the jungle. Here she gave birth alone to twin sons, Lav and Kush.'

'That's just not fair!' Auntie's eyes show pain.

'It is our burden Memsahib. Womens are born to suffer.'

'Don't I know it!'

I continue my story, 'Fourteen years later, Rama met Lav and Kush. He recognized them as his own sons and invited them to live with him in the palace in Ayodhya. He recognized Sita also but did not embrace her.'

'What? Why not?'

'Rama had closed his mind to her. Then Sita knew that she has suffered enough. She asked Mother Earth to swallow her up.'

'This is *so* sad!' Auntie says with tears in her eyes. I am surprised that my story has made her cry. She says, 'Sita did everything to be a good wife but she was misjudged and abused.'

'Auntie is correct; Sita is the ideal woman. In the time of my grandmothers and great-grandmothers, widows would embrace sati and lie on the funeral pyre with their dead husband—because of Sita. This is why the nearest bazaar to Rajapur is called Sati. It is just across the river. My grandmother used to talk of a sati she saw in that place—the widow was very calm; my grandmother thinks she was drugged. But you see, our life is not so different; men control our karma.'

Sonia

'It is true,' I said. 'Even in supposedly liberated and liberal Britain, men dominate women's lives. But that doesn't mean we can't manipulate them!' Speaking like this surprised even me. I guess my old feminist self was waking once again.

'I don't know man-hip-you-light. Explain me, Auntie.'

My explanation made Moti frown then smile. Her new chattiness made me smile too. As we walked on I made a mental note: not only must I never ever give the thumbs up sign in this country (it was sexual) but I must also never ask a Nepalese man for a banana.

Moti's breathless teenage reflections made me recall my own glorious teenage years. They seemed a very, very long time ago, almost like another person's story. Back then, I had been able to launch myself coquettishly into a party full of strangers. In those days I could flirt so extravagantly that half the men in the room would be looking at me. The excitement of it all had been intoxicating. I'd been swept along by romantic notions that made me think that absolutely anything was possible. Maybe now, here in Nepal, I could rekindle that spark.

Almost as if reading my thoughts, Moti giggled, 'Auntie, it is my idea that you like Rekraj sahib? A little bit maybe? Is it not so?'

I felt myself blushing, then I giggled too.

'He is a good man, Auntie...'

I wanted to hug her. When I had first met Guliya's family, I had considered them ignorant and illiterate. Rekraj had almost encouraged this misjudgement. How wrong I had been about this quietly assertive, articulate teenager.

In Kathmandu I had met tourists who had talked of the laid-back Nepalese people, the happy smiling Nepalese people, but I was certainly getting a very different view. What I saw now was that their inscrutable faces hide so much worry.

Paul, the aging hippy I'd met on the bus, had described the Nepalese way of life as liberating Hindu fatalism but this was his male view. The inequalities in opportunities for Nepali women were nothing short of criminal, an expression of the global rule that all men are bastards.

How much should I believe of what I'd been told though? I had realized already that in Nepal rumour is rife and stories sometimes are just stories. Could she really be telling the truth about people being murdered in prison? She surely believed what she was telling me and I knew—after all—that some pretty awful things go on in British prisons...so would a husband really cut off the nose of an unfaithful wife? Could someone really do that?

Equally, what might a wife do to an unfaithful husband? Maybe I shouldn't think about that one or my jerk of a husband but I kept having really creative ideas! The banana-slicing image wouldn't leave me and I was fearful that I was now wearing a rather nasty grin. Time to think of other things. I interrupted my disillusioned analysis of the unfair state of the world by asking, 'Moti, tell me please, what is the meaning of "*Cutty budgie hay*"?'

She replied, 'Auntie is Hindi speaking! Shabash. But it is better you say, "*Katti bajay heh*"! This is more better. The *heh* word is coming through the nose also.' '*Katti bajay heh*' did sound much more like Hindi or Nepali or whatever—much more poetic.

Then she said without telling me anything more about my precious chant, 'Now, Auntie, tell me a story from your holy book!'

I told her about Adam and Eve and how womankind is blamed for all the evil and temptation in the world. I'd never thought of it like that before. It was quite depressing really, how institutionalized suppression of women was expressed in both our cultures. I wondered how much of a covert feminist Moti might be. Maybe she was the kind of woman who would have a career rather than a family.

We approached a single-storey concrete building at the edge of another village. The glassless windows had shutters but they were so badly warped that none could be closed. 'This is a danger place!' Moti remarked casually.

'What? Why?'

'If an earthquake come, this pukka building will fall down!'

'Gosh! Still, there must be a hospital nearby?'

'There is none.'

'Emergency services, then?'

'What is that?'

'Ambulance maybe?'

'There is none, Memsahib.'

'What happens if people are injured?'

'They must go to Nepalgunj. First, it is necessary to walk to Chisapani. Or relatives can carry them. Then they must take the bus for one or two hours. Only then can they reach the hospital. Maybe it is better if they to go to India.'

'But what about the clinic the Japanese built? Surely they could go there?'

'That place is for small, small problems only. The Health Assistant is not so skilled.'

When I had first come to Nepal, I had thought these people led such a carefree life but now I saw how precarious their existence was. If anything went wrong—an earthquake or a difficult labour—there was simply no help. They could only appeal to their gods. That's why they lived for each day. They grab pleasures when they can. That's why they smile so much.

I heard young voices chanting out their lessons but then there was a communal shriek. They'd detected our approach. A stampede of what seemed like hundreds of children poured out of the four classrooms. The schoolteacher followed—wearily. He seemed to be telling them to come back but no one listened. They were too excited about seeing me—it seemed.

'Where are the other teachers, Moti?'

'Mostly there is one only in these village schools. Government teachers like to work in the big cities—not in small, small villages such as this.'

'So this poor man has to teach all these kids?

'Why not? It is his job. He receives good salary and government pension also.'

'How many are there? More than a hundred?'

'It is my idea that there are maybe two hundred childrens, Auntie.'

One of the biggest of the children stepped forward and in loud halting English said, 'I must know your native place, Memsahib!'

'Oh,' I said, taken aback. I mustered my best smile and said, 'I am from England.'

'Ah, Englan, Scotlan, Vale, Irelan, Leever Pool, Black Pool, Lon Don, Birming Ham!'

'Very good—you know a lot!'

'And also Milton Keynes, I am forgetting.'

'It is easy to forget Milton Keynes. I'd like to!' Then I thought I'd try, *'Katti bajay heh!'*

'Ta chhaina, Memsahib.'

I was pleased this had earned a reply, even if I didn't understand what it meant.

Oddly, Moti chipped in and said, 'He is not having any watch, Auntie.'

The boy then asked me, 'Memsahib, how old is?'

'Well, how rude! It is not polite to ask a woman's age, young man!'

'Why not, Memsahib?'

'Because English ladies don't like people to know!'

'Why not?'

Cheeky little brat. 'How old do you think I am?'

'It is my idea that you have passed maybe twenty-five years?' He said this in all seriousness.

I laughed. I was delighted by his mistake but as soon as he realized his guess had been wrong, he seemed upset. Humiliated. He demanded to know the truth. When I admitted to an age of thirty-four, he said, 'Omigod. You are too old.' Where had he picked up such an expression and did he know he was blaspheming? Is it possible to blaspheme against Hindu gods?

The small boy continued doggedly, 'Then tell me, Madam, how many children and grandchildren have you been blessed with?'

Bloody cheek.

The stampede of children made me ask Moti, 'When you marry, how many children will you have?'

'That is the will of the gods but I expect I will have many.'

'Do you know about family planning?'

'Of course. Married ladies have a new baby every three years. They keep having babies until they go for the operation to have the womb turned upside-down. But this is a painful and dangerous operation and sometimes it doesn't work. It is also difficult to arrange. Sometimes there are family planning camps that come to Rajapur or Sati but they are cancelled mostly. Some say that real MBBS doctors are frightened to come here. They are frightened of dacoits. They are frightened of the fever.

'My mother was thinking of going for that operation last spring because my father is too scared to have his root cut off and my mother is becoming too old and tired to have more childrens. Also the old women of our village say that if you have many, many children then the blood becomes thin. If you have more than ten children the blood becomes very thin and usually you die soon after giving birth. Many of our relatives and neighbours have died in giving birth, like that. My mother wants the operation but the government doctors do not come. We are still waiting.'

I became aware of a wonderful perfume. It filled my head. *'Katti bajay heh,'* I said to myself. It distracted me from the shock of seeing this new real world that Moti inhabits. I inhaled more deeply and saw that we were surrounded by daphne bushes. I had seen single plants growing in gardens in England but walking through and amongst them was intoxicating. I broke off a sprig so that I could hold the little white flowers to my nose. Moti's talk of family planning made me think about our family history and I mentioned my great-grandmother, on my mother's side.

As we walked on, Moti's expression said she really, really wanted to hear a story of my family. 'Stories make the journey shorter,' she smiled.

'Okay but this story isn't a happy one. My great-grandmother lived too long ago to have the choice of family planning. She gave birth—slowly, painfully and frighteningly—to six children. When she conceived for the seventh time she decided she couldn't go through labour again. She was really scared. She went to see an old woman who gave her some special medicine. That medicine killed the unborn child but it stayed inside her. My great-grandmother died in agony, poisoned by the dead baby.

'My grandmother was only two when her mother died but knowing how her mother had died made her scared of giving birth too. She managed to deliver her first two children—slowly, painfully and frighteningly—but when she realized she was pregnant for the third time, she tried to cause a miscarriage by jumping off chairs and stairs and hitting herself in the belly. It didn't work but my mother has known all her life that she was unwanted. She always felt unloved.

'My mother, too, was scared of giving birth, and all my life she has talked of how painful it was and the risk and sacrifice she made by bringing me into the world. Other women talk of the joy of holding a new baby in their arms after the struggle of labour. She never has. She never talks of the joy of family life—but then she's never been a joyous person. She's always complaining about someone or something.'

Here I am now—just like her—complaining! I felt guilty as I wondered what my life would have been like if I hadn't had that termination? It was a mistake, I knew that now but I had been so young then. My mother had told me there was no other choice.

Moti was clearly enjoying my story. She said, 'It is like this in Nepal also. Giving birth is painful and frightening and dangerous. Sometimes girls who have lain with a man before marriage go to the old women. These women can take the baby away but lots of these girls, they die. Maybe thc gods are angry because these girls have taken away a life.'

I didn't know what to say but I did know I wanted to change to another subject—to something other than pain and death.

*

By the time Moti suggested stopping again, the sun had disappeared behind the mountains. She waved me towards a resting place beneath a huge old shade tree. The end of each of its waxy leaves had elegantly long points. I slumped down onto a stone seat. It was knobbly because of its carved patterns. Beautifully sculpted stones also rested amongst the sinuous tree-roots.

I breathed in new smells: flower scents, woodsmoke and leaf mould. The perfumes were delicious, sensuous. There was a straggly bush that I recognized as a hydrangea—how odd to see another English garden plant. I thought I'd spotted some spiky berberis bushes earlier too. I examined a great red wheal across my forearm. My skin had often been reacting like this lately. My immune system must still be horribly weakened.

It occurred to me—once again—that this trip might be the death of me but it was a dispassionate observation. I wasn't thrown into a panic by the thought. Actually, I really truly didn't care. This trip was doing me good.

There was still enough light to make out that we were up on a spur above the great river. A goat was grazing on a scrap of grass; she was near a dry stone wall that looked like an animal shelter. The ground was oddly soft underfoot. I was standing in a pile of droppings, though it didn't smell that bad at all. I knew—despite my fatigue, despite the view—that I didn't want to linger here. Cold was already creeping into my body from the rock I sat on. Sweat was drying on my face. I was beginning to shiver. I thought how utterly wonderful it would be to fall into a hot, scented bubble bath.

I watched Moti step up onto the verandah of a dilapidated thatched hut nearby and dive inside. She soon reappeared with the smiling tea-house owner. They brought rice-straw mats. I stirred my aching body in response to their beckoning. Creakily, I hobbled across to the verandah and collapsed onto the surprisingly thick, comfortable mat.

Moti passed me some tea. I curled my hands around the glass and felt the warmth flow into me. I let the steam flood my face. It tickled the inside of my nose. I paused before allowing myself the first sip, savouring the warm fudgy smell that made my mouth water. The tea was so hot and sweet and so delicious. What a treat it was to luxuriate in such simple sensations. There is just nothing like the pleasure of a drink when you are really thirsty or sitting down to rest when you are really, really tired, or getting warm and cosy and comfortable after you've been chilled to the marrow.

I didn't even much mind the faint whiff of cow dung you can always smell in these houses. It is normal for these people to use a mud and cow dung mixture to plaster the walls and floors—actually I can't believe I just thought that—not minding the smell! And anyway what is cow dung but processed grass! I felt rather proud of myself for thinking of it like that! I checked my arm and saw that the nasty allergic wheal had faded already; there was nothing but a slight scratch there now.

I found myself studying the two women as they babbled animatedly. The tea-shop owner had been so kind and welcoming that I didn't mind that their language excluded me. I studied the older woman's face. It looked as if it was moulded in terracotta. Her eyes were dark and almond-shaped, and her high cheekbones were sun-blushed and rosy. She looked so different from the Plains people—like Moti.

It was as if—by walking through the gorge—we'd entered a new country. The houses we had passed had been very different too.

I tuned out of the women's unintelligible chitchat and thought about the day. I felt good about myself, what I'd done, for myself.

I had spent years trying to impress my mother or my husband and seek their approval for any small achievement, which I seldom got. Now I realized how foolish I had been. Today I felt proud of myself, and I didn't need to tell anyone a thing. I knew I'd done well and that was enough. I'd achieved something, just for the sake of it—just for me. Actually, at that moment, I didn't care if I ever went home. If I had an accident—or met a desirable man—I wouldn't care. Falling in love or falling off a cliff, either way, I'd have no regrets. Dying now—or disappearing—would hurt no one, and this was a liberating thought. Really, I might never go home! Never.

I suppose that no one would want to go through a traumatic experience, but when you've survived something life-shattering and risen above it, it gives you a kind of serenity. I lay back on the mat on the verandah and closed my eyes, feeling smug and content.

A while later, I became aware of something tickling my hand. I looked down and saw a huge black spider. A tarantula. It was the size of a saucer. It was heavy. Its hairy legs were as thick as pipe-cleaners. I froze. It seemed to be looking up into my face with its row of glinting black eyes. Its jaws looked like wire-cutters. An enormous green dragonfly was struggling to get free from them.

I looked over towards Moti and mouthed, 'Help!'

She hadn't noticed anything.

I dared not move. Sweat dribbled off me. The spider started to walk further up my arm. That was it. I just panicked. I thrashed. I flailed my arms to get it off me. I ran.

Moti

I am just thinking that Auntie is happy—when she screams. She screams like she has seen Kali and all the thugs who worship her. Auntie jumps up, flapping her arms like a vulture that has eaten too much to get airborne. Then she takes off: she runs up the mountain, along a small, small goat path. She's still screaming. This is very strange behaviour.

The didi who owns the tea-shop asks, 'Your foreign friend—is she mad?'

I say, 'Maybe mad; my mother thinks this bideshi is possessed. It is hard to be sure. Mostly she is harmless—and quiet. But you can never tell what she will do next. She washed my baby brother in water!'

'Unbelievable!'

'*And* she chased a cow out of our vegetable garden. The mother cow came to bring blessings on our family and the foreigner chased her away!'

'This is very strange. She *must* be possessed.'

'Truly, didi.'

After the time it takes to cook rice, Auntie returns. Her face shows that she feels full of shame. There are little sticks in her wild-looking hair. Now truly, she looks mad. She is calm but she seems angry. She says something about not warning her. She is blaming me for taking her to a dangerous place. I don't understand what she is talking about. My mother and this tea-shop owner are right. This memsahib is possessed, surely.

While the memsahib has been away, I have heard about the life of this tea-shop owner. It is not a happy story. She married young, soon after her first menstruation but her husband was not a good man. He drank too much and beat her a lot when he was drunk. Sometimes there wasn't enough to eat because her husband spent all they had on strong drink. She said that although it may be wrong to think it, she was happy when he died of pneumonia. Then she was left to run her tea-shop alone, and now mostly she makes enough money to get by. These days her life is good.

The three of us now sit and eat good rice. We watch the full moon come up. I tell a story to soothe the memsahib.

'Auntie, have you seen the hare?'

'Err, yes. You have hair and I have hair.'

'No. Different kind. Animal with long ears and black

nose. It moves its nose like this.' I twitch and wrinkle my nose and she smiles in recognition.

'Ah—like a rabbit!'

'Truly. Long ago one hare lived in the jungle with his friends the monkey, the jackal and the otter. The hare was a kind animal and was always telling his friends to help others.

'One fine day Sakra, the Lord of the Heavens, came down to earth but he didn't look like a god. He looked like an ordinary Brahmin man. He went to the hare and asked for some food because he had travelled far and was hungry. The kind hare felt sorry for the hungry traveller and jumped into the fire that Sakra had lit. The hare wanted to cook himself. But the flames did not burn him. Sakra blessed the animal and said that now and forever, the goodness and self-sacrifice of the hare will show for all time. He took a mountain and squeezed it. Black ink poured out. Sakra lifted the hare, tucked it under his arm, used the mountain-juice ink to draw an outline of the hare on the moon. Then he let the hare go free. Now look,' I say, pointing up at the moon, 'See the hare in the moon, Memsahib?'

Auntie looks and smiles and sighs, 'That was a lovely story—quite lovely! Thank you. In England, we see it as a man in the moon. But you are right—it is a hare!'

Now this foreigner has become my auntie again. Sometimes it seems as though there are two different people inside her. That must mean that she is possessed. But it doesn't matter. It doesn't matter if she is a little mad. It is our life to cope with strange happenings. It is also our life to be controlled by Brahmins. I am used to crazy, over-fed Brahmins blaming us for everything. I have been worrying a lot recently, isn't it, about how Ram Krishna will get his revenge. It is not in his nature to forget. His family are always vindictive also. When I get home I might talk to my father about going away. We have distant cousins in Dang and others doing labouring work in Kathmandu also. Maybe I will go there. I would like to visit Kathmandu. I would like to see our king. I would like to see the world, one day.

Sonia

Still writhing with embarrassment, I pulled out my sleeping bag and struggled into it there on the verandah. My rice-straw mat cushioned me and made a surprisingly comfortable bed. It smelt nice—like fresh hay. Seeing me settled, Moti went inside. I expect she wanted to chat some more to the tea-house owner. I heard laughter—they were probably laughing at me.

I tried to snuggle down to sleep but had to sit up again and pull little sticks out of my hair. My arm was itching. I think I was having an allergic reaction to the spider. I was so sensitive.

The sun had set. It was quite dark now although it was still far too early to sleep. I would have liked to have read the trashy novel I'd stashed in my bag to take my mind off the day's events, but there was no electricity here and my little torch didn't give enough light to read by. I lay back. Clouds now covered the moon, and the stars too.

Mosquitoes whined. They flew around my head, waiting to land and feed on me, on my life-blood. I whisked them away but they weren't bothered by anything I did. I covered myself in my sleeping bag liner and hoped—uncharitably—that they'd go in and bite Moti and the tea-shop lady. The heat inside my sleeping bag made my arm itchier. I needed to resist the urge to scratch.

My mind moved from the squirming embarrassment of the spider incident to recalling another humiliation. It was the last party that my husband took me to. It was a really posh affair and all the other wives had bought dresses especially for the occasion. My husband had told me we couldn't afford yet another new outfit—I had plenty. I could dress up in one of my old favourites.

The trouble was, I had been comfort eating, big time, and I'd grown out of most of my nice clothes. The only smart outfit that I hadn't already worn hundreds of times before was an awfully snug fit. I had squirmed into it all right and the cloth held me in quite well. It was actually slimming, I felt.

The party turned out to be a really dour occasion. It was mostly my husband's colleagues or blokey men that his workmates thought might help sales or something. The only two wives that I did get on with a bit must have realized what kind of a party it would be because they weren't there. The place was packed with men in suits, and there was a sprinkling of over-made-up flirtatious young women and tarted-up ambitious wives.

I started drinking, out of boredom mostly. The nibbles were good too. I noticed a quite presentable man eyeing me up and I was drunk enough to wink at him. My marriage was at the stage where I didn't care what my husband thought. My new admirer was older but I could see he was a bit cultured. He came over and brought me another drink. He was attentive. He told some great jokes. He was deliciously rude about the boss's wife. The drink slipped down easily. He made me laugh so much and I was vaguely aware that I was laughing really loudly. People were looking but I didn't care. I was having fun.

Then someone grabbed my elbow. It was my husband. 'Okay, Sonns. You've had enough,' he snarled. 'Time to go home—before you embarrass me anymore.'

'I wouldn't want to embarrass you, darling,' I spat. I tried to pull away from him. There was a bit of a struggle. My dress burst open all down one side-seam.

'That's YOUR fault,' I told him loudly. I should have been embarrassed. My fat was spilling out of the rip in my dress. I didn't care. I was liberated by the drink. I started to laugh. I laughed until I wet myself...

It was very, very dark—pitch-black—when I woke. Mosquitoes were still massing around my face. My bladder was bursting. What a curse insomnia was. I rummaged for my torch and squirmed out of my sleeping bag. Why do they make them so narrow?

Gingerly, I shuffled towards the long-drop. I had a feeling that I was not alone. There were rustling sounds close by. And snuffling noises. I shone my torch around. I saw nothing at first. Then, in the trembling spotlight, I made out a round spiky creature. It was as startled and confused as I was. For a few seconds, it was frozen to the spot. It didn't even twitch a whisker. It stared at me with big cute eyes. Then, as I started to laugh, it returned to its work, sniffing around amongst the onion skins and wood shavings and dry leaves as if I wasn't there. It wasn't frightened of me at all. Those long, long quills must defend it well. After a few minutes, the porcupine sauntered away into the darkness. I was so sorry it had gone, although my laughter had put pressure on my bladder and reminded me forcefully why I had got up.

9. MAKING AMENDS

Moti

After completing my morning wash and my prayers, I return to the verandah. Auntie is sitting up but still in her sleeping bag. I look into her face. It is as if nothing unusual has happened. We eat roasted maize and, after some time, she also gets up. She tells me that she will not wash this morning, and this is a surprising thing to me. I did not expect foreigners to be so dirty in their habits.

We start walking again. We leave the main path by the river. The tea-shop owner has explained nicely to me that here the river is called the Bheri but it becomes the Karnali before it flows though the Chisapani gorge.

Soon we are climbing up through jungle where spiky pieces of rock stick out of the ground between the sal trees. The tea-shop owner has told me to look out for bears. There are bad spirits in this part of the jungle also. This is quite a dangerous place but I don't tell Auntie.

Sonia

Next morning, I couldn't look Moti in the eye. No doubt she thought that I'd gone mad. Perhaps I was mad. She seemed as relaxed and uncritical as always though. I pulled on my clammy clothes. They didn't smell good. I thought about asking for some hot water to wash but then decided I couldn't be bothered. There was no one around that I wanted to impress. So Moti led me off, deeper still into the mountains. It felt good to be walking again. I was a bit achy but I was feeling fit. Activity took my mind off my embarrassment. Now that I was well-rested and calmer, I saw more. There were aquilegia and gentians. I suppose some Victorian plant hunter must have brought these back to grace English gardens. Nepal is a flower-lover's paradise. Purple primroses and aconites grew close to the path. I loved the blue flowers. I also came upon a purple-and-white orchid growing out of a crook in a rhododendron tree. It was quite astonishingly beautiful.

Further on, I paused to watch two large animals gambolling amongst the rounded boulders at the edge of the river. They looked like overgrown weasels but were much lovelier: a rich, red-brown colour with luxuriously long tails, and yellow chests that merged into white under the chin. They were playing chase and clearly having great fun. Such sights of nature lifted my spirits and distracted me from ruminating on recent events. Then Moti started talking again. 'Memsahib?'

'Hmm?'

'This spider?'

Omigod. Why does she want to talk about that? And why is she calling me Memsahib again. I thought we'd got over all that formality.

'This kind of spider, it is not very dangerous. Spider bites heal after some weeks.'

'Well, that's all right then—a hole in your flesh that only takes weeks to heal.' I hoped she'd miss the sarcasm in my voice. But then as her words sank in, I wondered what she meant by 'not very dangerous'.

'Also, Memsahib,' Moti continued, 'this spider, it could not bite while it had food in its mouth!'

I just hate spiders—that's all. What's wrong with that? Lots of people are frightened of spiders. What should I say so that we could talk about something different?

My counsellor had told me to do that whenever anxieties were building up. Perhaps I shall ask Moti to tell me another story. No, I didn't want that either. It would probably be another distressing tale designed to keep women subservient and unchallenging.

The rhythm of walking soothed me again and my brain switched into neutral at last. I just walked and looked. Birds identical to the kestrels you see hovering beside motorways in Britain played here on updrafts from the river. And there were wagtails. We walked over hard red ground and passed women collecting leaves, sweeping them into baskets that they carried slung from a headband. Some carried babies too.

'Moti, what are they going to do with the leaves?'

'It is for fertilize their fields.'

'Do they live nearby?'

Moti asked them and translated the answer, 'Their houses are one hour walking from this place, Auntie.'

I stepped over a column of red ants and then saw a horrifying giant orange wasp-of-a-thing dragging away an even larger hairy tarantula. How common were these spiders? Then I smiled maliciously—pleased that the spider had got its comeuppance. Until that moment, I hadn't liked wasps.

We passed boys watching cattle. A group of children in blue school uniforms came charging down the mountainside. All the girls wore their hair in tight neat plaits tied with ribbons. Their hair shone with oil. Even the boys looked freshly scrubbed—not like me; I needed a bath. Then there was a family group, all dressed up in their Sunday best. Rather than having changed into some practical garment for their journey, the women wore gorgeous flowing saris. It was interesting to see that the women and even the small children carried the luggage—never the men. Moti stopped to talk with them and discovered that they'd already walked for a day-and-a-half. They were going to a wedding.

A mule-train came by, bells ringing and hooves clopping on the rocky path. The mules wore fluffy ornaments on their bridles—seemingly dressed to accompany cabaret dancers, not carry salt.

'These animals are not good!' Moti suddenly announced.

'Why?' I queried, wondering how mules could offend anyone.

'Because there is less work for people. Now strong men can sometimes find work carrying the most awkward loads but ordinary loads are mostly carried by mules. The owners don't have to pay them and they never strike. Those Maoists are always trying to tell people to strike. That just makes more problems. There are less and less chances for us to get work. The best work is portering for tourists. The loads are very light and you only have to work for half of the day. The pay is good also.'

'Can you work on the land?' I asked her.

'Landlords don't like to employ womens. They say that if women dig out irrigation canals, we pollute them. This work must be done by men only. There are very few jobs that women can do. It is a big problem for us.'

Nobody came along after that for ages and I returned to thinking about nothing but the soothing rhythm of walking.

I noticed the ease with which Moti moved, wondering at her grace and perfect coordination. I doubt she was aware of just how beautiful she was to watch. I'm sure I looked disabled by comparison. I forever needed to monitor where I was planting my feet. I stomped along, jolting my joints, stumbling often. While we climbed up, I longed to be climbing down and when we reached a part of the path that took us downhill, I longed to be climbing again. My knees and thighs and heels ached on the descents. My back and calves hurt on the ascents.

Moti

Auntie has asked who owns the land in Rajapur. She frowns when I say, 'Mostly it is Brahmin families.' I do not say that sometimes it seems like Brahmins own the whole world. I tell Auntie one sad story.

'My cousin-auntie's husband had some bad news. His landlord told my cousin-uncle that he wasn't his bonded labourer any more. He said that the government stopped the kamaiya system. Until that day, my cousin-uncle's family had had their half-katha of land and his ten sacks of rice as payment for all the work he did on the landlord's land throughout the year. There were also meat feasts after the rice was transplanted, and again after the harvest. The landlord controlled who got water and it was his problem if anyone tried to steal what was needed to irrigate the crop. And if the harvest was bad, the landlord looked after his labourers and their families, and loaned money if anyone got sick. It was not a bad system. These days our community is forever fighting; no one knows what to do. Caste fights against caste and everyone loads even greater burdens on poor Tharus.

'The landlords are forbidden to employ their kamaiya, so now my cousin-auntie's husband grows thinner and thinner and the family survives on the little bit of money my cousin-auntie earns carrying bricks to build big new houses for rich people who have come to live in the bazaar. These days it is easier for womens to get labouring work because womens are not paid so much.

'Daily now, my cousin-uncle squats beside the irrigation canal guarding the small, small dribble of water that keeps his mustard and vegetables alive. I do not think this is a useful thing to do because mostly people block and divert the irrigation water after dark—when no one can see who is responsible. It is too difficult. These new responsibilities weigh heavily on him. Soon he will get very ill. My mother and I, we worry about that family.'

Sonia

I'd sweated so much that new sweat was mixing with the old. I really stank. It felt as if the salt cracked when I grimaced. It was unbelievably luxurious to simply splash water on my face whenever we came to a stream. Actually, the tiny trickles of water that came off the mountain and dribbled across the path were miniature havens for plant life and I was astonished to recognize delphiniums and—further from the water—some little plants that looked like saxifrages. There were huge, yellow-flowering mahonia bushes too, and a lovely perfume drifted from them. All of them looked as if some Englishman had transplanted them from his garden—but they were growing wild here.

We were making good, steady progress up a deep V-shaped valley. The countryside was bare; sparkly bits in the ground reflected sunlight. Tufts of giant bamboo and a few gnarled plants that looked like stunted chestnut trees grew out from behind boulders here and there. Two vultures soared in graceful spirals above us with their three-metre wingspans. Maybe these are the ones that take scavenged bones to great heights and drop them onto rocks so they can feast on the marrow.

The river seemed to have chewed its way between awesome crags and pinnacles, and then had left what it didn't want as sheer slopes of glistening white silt sweeping down to the pristine water. Birds that looked like swallows played in the updrafts. It was so wild and so stark and so very beautiful that I wanted to cry. I breathed in another wonderful moment to keep safe in my heart.

Moti

The trees become smaller and fewer in number while the rocks and pieces of mountain grow larger. There is nothing for animals here. Even goats would find little to eat. But I am satisfied. Our pilgrimage is blessed.

I look back. The path that we have taken winds away like a frightened rat snake. The way forward is around a sheer outcrop of light-coloured rock. There are political symbols on it.

Then in the shade of that rock, I see something light-coloured and glistening. I walk over and see that it is ice. I squat down to take some. It is very hard. It is not like the pieces of ice that fall from the sky during hailstorms, when the Great God Indra is angry. This must be something different.

I break a piece off the edge and put it in my mouth and crunch it, like I did in Chisapani. It is wonderful. Sonia didi takes some and giggles as she puts it into her mouth. We laugh together, enjoying this gift from the gods.

Sonia

Hours later I heard children's voices again. That was quite a relief. I hoped Moti would let me rest for a bit. I was feeling so tired. Perhaps it was the effect of the altitude. We had been up and down and up and down all day and I reckoned we must have climbed the equivalent of three Ben Nevises by now, not including all the horizontal distance covered.

We had come to a little village in the middle of nowhere, and the place was in an uproar. The central street was a bog—the source of at least some of the water was a communal tap that was left running. Big black hairy pigs, grunting joyously, wallowed in the mire. A child lay face down in it—having an epileptic fit. No one helped her.

I asked Moti what was going on. I've no idea how she always knows the answers to the many questions I ask, but she replied, 'These people are celebrating.'

'Good,' I said, slightly hesitantly. There were certainly plenty of drunks about. 'What are they celebrating?'

'It is one funeral.'

I didn't know what to say that would not give offence. I looked around, searching for something different, safer, to talk about. Many of the outside walls of the tiny whitewashed houses were daubed with crude representations of ploughs, suns, trees and bicycles.

Moti saw where I was looking and explained, 'People who know writing and people who do not know writing, everypeople can understand and recognize these signs. Each represents one political party.'

We took tea at a hut that looked as if the daubers had done battle over whose symbols would go on top. Displayed in the gloom inside were the meagre things for sale: battered dusty packets of local cigarettes and chewing tobacco and biscuits and funny little packets of some red stuff for Lord-knows-what purpose. There was also a basket containing shrivelled little pieces of something brownish. I asked Moti about them.

'This is proots, Auntie. You want to try please?'

'Proots?'

'Proots,' she confirmed.

'And what are proots?'

She looked puzzled when she answered, 'You no having proots in your native place, Auntie? Many trees are having proots. There are kimbu, orange, lemon, apple, like that. Try. These are sweet and tasty also.'

They looked dry and exceedingly dirty. She took some and fired three pieces into her mouth from a foot away. Tentatively, I picked up a piece and nibbled the edge. The tangy taste of apricot announced itself on my tongue but it wasn't the sweet, slightly slimy sensation of apricots you get at home. This was sharp and delicious. I took more. 'Mmm, they're really good.'

Moti then announced, 'Let us sleep here only. I am thinking this is a good place.'

I'm not sure I agreed but I was relieved we would be stopping for the day.

Even though it had been so hot out in the sunshine all day, I soon cooled down and felt quite shivery sitting in the shade of the verandah. Now was the time to do a strip wash but all I actually did was pull out my sleeping bag, take off some clothes and climb in. I stank but it was lovely and cosy. I decided I'd ask for hot water to wash, come morning. When Moti brought food to me it felt utterly luxurious not to have to get out of my bag.

The sun was rising when I awoke. What a treat it had been to sleep right through the night—again. Busy sounds were coming from the kitchen. I could smell the fire and roasting popcorn. I was so snug, it was delicious. I raised my chin and saw my breath turn to clouds in front of my face. The air must be cold at this altitude. There was a heavy frosting of ice crystals on the cattle pen. Moti came out onto the verandah holding a steaming glass. 'Bad tea, Auntie!'

'Mmm.' Wonderful bad tea!

Moti

Auntie is very lazy this morning. We must pray before breakfast, the temple is close by. We start and soon, close to the path, I notice holy marks drawn by an ascetic. 'Look, Auntie! Here is one drawing of a vajra, a thunderbolt. It is the weapon of Indra who rules the rain and the lightning and the sky. This is like the small, small vajra you wear.'

Scattered around are a few old, dry sal-leaf plates. These have been used to bring offerings. We have reached the shrine.

Auntie has walked so slowly that it has taken a very long time to reach this place, but arriving now gives me a good feeling. Now I can help my baby brother. First, though, I must arrange for my auntie to purify herself.

Sonia

As soon as I'd got up out of my sleeping bag, Moti said, 'We must buy coconuts and incense sticks.' I also bought two plates, which were made by stitching thick waxy leaves together with delicate slivers of wood; they themselves were works of art. They contained coloured rice and the bright orange pom-pom heads of African marigolds.

Suddenly Moti seemed to be in a tremendous rush. I wanted to take more tea and wash, but she was insistent that we pray first. I wasn't very keen but before the tea-shop owner had heated water for me to bathe (had Moti even asked her?), we were off, continuing still further on our 'pilgrimage', as she called it. Moti strode on.

The rocks on the path were slippery with ice. The path took us up, and at one point I got a view—to the northwest, I guessed—of wild, broken, ocean-green country. It looked like an oil painting of a storm-tossed sea. I couldn't see any villages, or roads. From here, it was obvious why people walked down south to shop for Indian goods on the East-West Highway or in Rajapur. We walked on further up into oak forest, as far as an outcrop of light-coloured rock. There was a gaping black hole at the base of the cliff. Had we arrived, finally? The entrance to this cave was decorated with colourful prayer flags. Flowering shrubs grew all around and the place was twittering with birds. The smell of incense filled my nostrils and Moti began to mumble under her breath. She was praying.

Internally, I recited *'Katti bajay heh!'* too. On the cliff to the right of the cave there was a fine mural of scary-looking devils and foul monsters. Close by, more orchids were being visited by gorgeous fast-moving iridescent birds. There was fragrant, cream-flowered clematis growing over some rocks there too. I got my breath back and then took a great lungful of scented air. This was such a special place.

Moti led me past the cave entrance, saying, 'I will bring you to a place where we can take bath.' Was my stench that obvious? She guided me through the trees to a spot where someone had built a small mud dam at the cliff base. Butterflies were drinking there.

Fortunately, Moti didn't make me take a cold bath but we did wash our hands and faces. The water made my skin tingle delightfully. I marvelled at the cool tranquillity of the place. Huge tree-roots embraced the crags and boulders; long-tailed scarlet birds flitted delicately between scented bushes.

Back down at the cave, Moti pointed to some of the gaudily clad figures in the murals. She said laughingly, 'These ghosts, they are your brothers and sisters! They are looking just like you, Auntie! They also have white faces like you only.'

I wasn't sure whether I should feel insulted, though her face said this was a harmless tease. Another painting caught my eye; it was of a seated figure with a halo, and in his hand was another object that looked remarkably like my amulet. I'd ask Moti about it later. Below the paintings, and fixed in an alcove in the rock, were brass cylinders, covered with beautiful lettering. Moti turned each one and encouraged me to do so too. These, surely, were Buddhist prayer wheels. This seemed strange because Moti was Hindu and she talked of making offerings here to Shiva, the ultimate Hindu god.

The smell became acrid and less-than-pleasant as we entered the cave shrine. I hoped we wouldn't need to stay inside long. There were scuttling noises from the floor deeper inside the cave. Those had to be rats. Rats don't attack people, I reasoned. I astonished myself by thinking I was okay with rats. Then, squeaking noises came from the roof of the cave, maybe ten metres above me. Something wet landed on the top of my head. I now had bat poo in my hair.

Moti walked forward and placed the leaf plate in front of a huge phallic stalagmite. If you could forget the smell, it was actually quite beautiful. Everything was smoothed by an icing-like covering of white rock. Drips from the ceiling made interesting echoey sounds, which suggested this was quite a cavern. It was too dark to make out just how big it was. The wet made everything treacherous, especially since the cave floor sloped. I was careful about where I planted each step. Moti smashed the coconut on the ground. Three sleek, healthy-looking rats ran in to feast on the white flesh. Moti turned and beckoned me towards a different part of the cave. 'This way come, Auntie!'

This place was beginning to give me the creeps. We stood amongst the stalagmites; in places, some had joined stalactites to make weird shapes that made me think of people who had been turned to stone by Medusa or petrified for some frightful sin. Dancing candle flames made the scene eerier still. One column had formed close to the cave wall and, smiling, Moti beckoned me closer to see. She had the look of someone about to show a secret treasure. She said, 'Passing behind this column brings merit, Auntie. We must try!'

'What do you mean "we"?' I grumbled.

She didn't answer but began to wriggle between the stalactite column and the wall. It looked tight and difficult but in no time she had popped out the other side. 'Now Auntie must try! It will surely bring good fortune!'

I looked. The space looked ridiculously small but then I thought why not at least *try*? Yes, Sonia, why not *do* something?

With some trepidation, I pushed the top part of my body into the gap. It wasn't as small as it looked although I needed to breathe out to get my ribs through. Then my waist slipped through easily. It suddenly occurred to me that there might be big spiders in here. Then what would I do? I felt a clonk as my hips hit cold unyielding rock. I knew I was going to bruise. I couldn't go on. I scuffled backwards. I got jammed by the bottom of my ribcage.

I was stuck.

Cold dread seized me. Why had I even thought to try this? Panic surged through my body. My mouth went dry. Things started happening down below and I wondered if I'd wet myself. 'Moti, I am stuck!' I stood there, awkwardly balanced sideways on one leg. Already, the chill of the wet rock was seeping into me like a disease.

Moti came over, grinning broadly. 'It is no problem, Auntie!'

I felt a surge of fury. 'It is a problem. I AM STUCK! I can't get out!' Immediately, I started thinking of the rats I'd seen and imagined them nibbling my toes, and fingers, and nose.

'If you angry, Memsahib, you will never get out! When people angry they are swelling up. Calm happy people, they can get through only.'

I was furious with her but not so furious that I was deaf to her advice. She was right. I tried focusing on *'Katti bajay heh, katti bajay heh'*.

'Give me this bag, Auntie!'

I unbuckled my bumbag and passed it to her. I took deep breaths. The gap seemed to get bigger. Suddenly, it wasn't pressing in on me any longer.

'It is no problem, Auntie. The hole, it is bigger higher up!'

I'd slipped down into a V-shaped slot. I thought about this. I wriggled.

Then I discovered that by standing a little higher—on tiptoe—my hips slipped through, albeit at the expense of leaving a little skin there in the cave. With a bit more wriggling to get both legs clear, I was free again.

Moti seemed delighted. And, once I'd calmed down, I was too. I felt really pleased with myself! I couldn't imagine managing that a year ago.

Then I thought about what this little trial was about. Surely the greedy and gluttonous wouldn't be able to squeeze through the place that I had just managed to negotiate. The underfed, self-deprecating lower echelons of Nepal would slither through easily. Those who lived simply were thus rewarded with feeling as if they had been judged worthy. How excellent Hinduism seemed! It was so simple and attractive, if this really was all you needed to do to be a good Hindu. It was so much healthier than all the guilt stuff of Christianity.

I wanted to ask Moti all sorts of clumsy questions about religion. I was about to ask her about the prayer-wheels, and my vajra, when my feet slipped out from under me.

I thumped over onto my back. Oopphh. My head was fired back against the rock and hit it hard.

I started to slide over smooth rock lubricated with drip-water and bat poo. Everything went into slow motion. I was winded. I couldn't scream. I slithered down sideways. My feet caught on a rocky corner. I spun around and continued down into the depths of the cave, as if riding the flumes at the swimming pool. My stomach was left behind. Then suddenly it was all over as my feet smashed into solid rock. My legs took most of the impact.

I lay there waiting for the pain to start. It didn't. Nothing seemed to be broken. That was something. I *was* shaken though. I was certainly shaken.

I couldn't see anything. There had been an enormous jolt

when I landed. My head hurt. Had it taken my sight away? I blinked. I rubbed my eyes. This made me see stars. My hands were covered with something foul-smelling. I tried to blink away the stinging sensation and the blindness.

I got unsteadily to my feet. I turned. I now made out way, way above me that there was a smudge of grey. My ears were ringing, echoing, but not from within. Someone was shouting.

I heard, 'Auntie! Any problem, Auntie?'

There was a slithering noise and a sort of whooshing. I heard the strike of a match. I was momentarily mesmerized at the miracle of being able to see again. Moti was there, standing beside me. She and her beautiful young face had blossomed into my vision. She was laughing, as usual. 'Any pain, Auntie. You no hurt?'

'Thank you, Moti. I am not hurt—not much.'

She grabbed my disgusting hand. It stung a bit so I knew it was grazed. She half-dragged, half-led the way back up and outside the cave. We were both plastered in black stuff but she looked radiant out in the sunshine once again. Daylight emphasized the perfection of her flawless skin. We looked at each other. She was pointing and laughing, which was a bit much, but her mirth was so infectious that I couldn't resist laughing too. She was such a tonic!

She grinned, 'Your face, Auntie, it is not so beautiful! You are looking little bit brownish—like Nepali lady.'

She handed me my bumbag. I pulled out my mirror, thankful that it was unbroken. I had two black eyes where I'd rubbed them with my filthy hands. It was quite a contrast to my sun-bleached hair. 'Maybe I can start a new fashion,' I said, 'Cave-gothic!'

She said, 'What was that, Auntie?'

I smiled but didn't elaborate.

A fine gentle drizzle was falling from the sky now. It was light and refreshing. Moti spread open her upturned hands to feel it better. 'This is a blessing from the gods. They are pleased with your offering in the cave. This is a most auspicious sign.'

I couldn't imagine any Brit thinking a drizzle was good in any way.

Then Moti suggested, 'Let us return to the place where we took bath before—yes?'

She led me back to the pool amongst the trees at the base of the cliff. Butterflies still flitted there. We washed in the pristine spring water. I felt elated. What an adventure!

'Come, let us sit,' she said.

We found a smooth inviting boulder under a vast banyan tree, and sat in companionable silence. There unexpectedly, on that rock, I saw the secret of contentment. I didn't know (or care) whether the insight came from the mountains, the journey or the feeling of escape, I only knew that true happiness is only ever possible if you have been unhappy. And there, at that moment, I couldn't remember the last time I had felt so peaceful. It wouldn't have been possible for me to take in any more happiness.

Moti turned to me and smiled as if she knew. I realized then that this moment and this wonderful feeling would sustain me for a long, long time.

10. HOMEWARD BOUND

Sonia

It is odd how when you're retracing your steps, when you are returning over familiar ground, when you're homeward bound, the journey seems so much shorter. It was also odd that I thought of going back to Rajapur as being homeward bound!

I was certainly looking forward to seeing Rekraj again—and Moti's mother, brothers and sisters. They made me laugh with the joy of life.

We seemed to cover the distance in no time, or maybe it felt easier because now we were walking downhill. Soon we were at the familiar tea-house on the high spur where the spider had attacked me. Moti said that we must stop and eat again because, 'The didi here is best cook.'

I checked carefully before I sat on the verandah after our late breakfast. I watched an orange admiral butterfly slurping at a goat-dropping. An odd taste for such a beautiful creature! Moti seemed relaxed and at ease. Visiting the holy place had given her a new glow.

I decided to be bold and asked her, 'The shrine we visited, Moti?'

'Hunchha, Auntie?'

'Is it a Hindu place of worship?'

'Hunchha, Auntie. It is a place to be with God, with the Mahadev.'

'But is it for Hindus?'

'It is for Lord Shiva, the mightiest of the gods. We saw his lingam inside the cave, no? You remember this word, Auntie?' She made the thumbs up sign to remind me. She was talking down to me again.

'Yes, yes,' I said, 'I know all about lingams; you talk about them a lot! But if that cave was a shrine to a Hindu god, then why were Buddhist prayer flags and prayer wheels there?'

She looked at me as if I was a little mad for asking and

then replied, 'It is a place for being close to God only. It is for any peoples who want to want to worship—Hindu, Buddhist, never mind. We don't care. Christians can find peace here also. It is my idea, Auntie, that you are a Christian lady? True? Why are you wearing one vajra? This is the sign of the Great God Indra. He is throwing these thunderbolts at the bad gods and the demons.'

'Isn't it a Buddhist thing?'

'Buddhist, Hindu, Christian, never mind. All are worthy gods.'

We sat looking out from the verandah of the rude little tea-house. I breathed in the mountain air. Only from here—in taking the time to stop and really look and absorb the scene—did I fully appreciate the precipitousness and the huge dimensions of the valley. Straggly weather-beaten trees clung onto the earth at crazy angles, growing out of any scrap of soil. Steep as it was, there were places where some desperate soul had dug terraces to grow hill rice or maize or beans.

Sunlight sparkling back from the ripples in the lapis-blue river below made me blink, it was so bright. I could have thrown a stone into it to make a splash, although it was at least 25 metres beneath us. Small birds swept and manoeuvred between patches of white-water and boulders down there. Cuckoos were calling across the valley and, closer, crickets whistled their love songs. A cicada started up in his strange metallic voice; another grated back. Yet another sounded almost like a whistling kettle. A huge orange butterfly flapped sedately by. The day was perfect—tranquillity itself.

Then oddly, unexpectedly, I heard rumbling in the far distance. Thunder. I looked up into the clear blue sky. There was not even a streak of cloud. Maybe it was thunder in another valley.

Weather is strange and localized in the mountains I'd read—even in Snowdonia. But was it thunder? Perhaps the noises were inside my head. Is this what tinnitus sounds like? Or was it another earth tremor?

The ground wasn't shaking. The birds and crickets hadn't sensed anything bad—they were still singing. It wasn't at all like when we experienced that tremor in Rajapur. Then, everything had gone ominously silent.

I asked Moti, 'Did you hear thunder?'

'Maybe it is the gods fighting,' she suggested. 'Sometimes they make war and throw thunderbolts at their enemies.'

She looked up at the cloudless sky and I read doubt in her face.

'Could it be a landslide, Moti?'

'This is not landslide, Auntie. Landslides, they come during rainy times, isn't it.'

'A flash flood then?'

Moti frowned and said nothing more. The rumbling must be thunder—a long way off—I decided. The sound continued though, and went on and on. How could thunder continue for so long like this? It was definitely coming from further up the river.

'What is it?' I asked Moti.

She didn't answer but I could see that she could hear it. She was also looking upstream. Still she said nothing. She looked down at the river, way below us. She frowned again.

The next time I looked upstream, the scene had changed. The head of the valley had become strangely indistinct. It was as if—suddenly, mysteriously—some kind of cloud had formed. And all the while, the sound was growing louder. Then I saw that the cloud had substance, and a kind of sparkling quality. Something massive was moving in it—way upstream. I couldn't make out what it could be, until I realized that the sunlight was reflected from this thing. I felt for my amulet. I always found it reassuring to run my fingers over it.

I looked and stared and saw that light was shining back from an impossibly huge wall of water. It filled about a quarter of the steep, V-shaped valley. It was surging down towards us. The thunder became a roar. Growing ever louder.

Even at this distance, I could see that bits of houses and trees were tumbling in this awesome wave. It was mesmerizing.

Moti grabbed my wrist and dragged me to my feet. She shouted something but I couldn't make out what she'd said.

We sprinted up the crazily steep goat track behind the tea-house. The tea-shop owner, whom I'd taken to be slow and decrepit, ran past us with her skirts hitched-up. The roaring noise seemed to pursue us.

My lungs were bursting by the time the ground levelled off a bit. We stopped on a shoulder of land. It looked solid enough. The tea-house owner was here too—breathing hard.

Hands on hips, panting still, I looked down from our safe vantage point. A shock wave made me stagger. I dropped to my knees. The water had hit the sheer cliffs beneath us. The impact felt like the whole valley side was crashing down.

Then the noise really arrived. We covered our ears against a deafening roar. Way below, branches, whole trees, logs, a dugout, parts of houses and fence-posts were all tumbling around in the foaming brown water. Bits of brightly coloured cloth might have been people—drowning or drowned.

The ground trembled as the insatiable death-wave went on. It swept away everything beneath us. It tumbled over a grassy promontory that forced the river into a bend. A topknot of bright green maize plants grew on it. The greedy water piled up momentarily behind it and then the whole lot disappeared, devoured. A whirlpool formed below it and a rainbow above it.

Unsatisfied, the water scoured out a new pool. More riverbank collapsed into the ravenous river. My nostrils filled with the scent of fresh rain although there was none. The smell of dust had also returned. Huge chunks of valley wall crumbled into the river—in slow motion—like the sea taking back a sandcastle on the beach. I crouched, cowering speechless as the thunderous flood moved on south.

A huge crack appeared in the ground close by. I didn't know where we could run to. Moti tugged at my arm. She was shouting something. I couldn't hear what she was saying. All I could hear was thunder. She dragged me on again. She pulled me towards a rocky outcrop maybe 150 metres away. There were strange ripping and thudding sounds mixed with the awful endless roar from the water. I ran. I gasped to suck air in. This was the longest 150 metres I'd ever run. I was finished. I couldn't run anymore. I couldn't pull in enough air but still Moti dragged me on.

The tea-shop owner ran past us again. I saw her reach a grassy ledge beside the rocks. Her hands were on her hips as she fought to get her breath back. I wanted to be there, standing with her. She looked back towards us and I read fear and shock on her face. She gestured to us to hurry.

There were more terrifying tearing and cracking sounds behind us. The earth was shaking again. I really couldn't run any further. I felt dizzy. It felt as if the ground was moving under my feet. No. It really was moving.

Moti wrenched my arm and threw me towards the rocks. I collapsed at the foot of the outcrop and thought of nothing but getting air into my lungs.

Moti was with me now, with her hand holding my arm. I looked up into her face. I followed her gaze. I couldn't work out what had happened. Then I saw that the spur where we'd just been standing wasn't there anymore. I crouched; numb, incredulous.

I looked down from where I lay. There was a yawning chasm half a metre from where I was cowering. I peered over the edge. Roots waved impotently in the updraft. Brown water boiled and seethed beneath us. Whirlpools formed and disappeared and formed again. Stricken branches waved from the river as if begging to be rescued.

The world started to spin and I was sure the ground was moving under me again. I caught a hold of the rocks behind me and hung on for dear life. Then the movement stopped. I dared to release my grip a little. I chanted, '*Katti bajay heh*,' and felt for my protective, magical amulet.

Slowly, the realization of what had happened sunk in. That wall of water must have swept down faster than an express train. Nothing at the bottom of the valley would have had a chance. The path we had taken that very morning had run close to the river. If we had walked that route only a few hours later, we would have been swept away. If Moti hadn't dragged me to the rocks, I would have died.

I looked around. We had escaped the wave but I couldn't see how we could climb down from here. I thought again. I imagined how the water would have surged down, ravaging the valley and everything beyond. I wondered about rescue teams, helicopters. There wouldn't be any. Not here.

Then I thought some more and imagined how the devastation would continue as the flood powered further south. 'What will the river do to Rajapur?' I asked Moti.

She said simply, 'Many people will find their way to a new life this day.'

'Omigod—your family!' I cried.

Guliya

I run to the river with a heavy heart. The gods have already seen fit to take three babies from me. I have lost poor, lovely Maya also. It is so long since she was taken. Surely that is enough? What have I done in this life or in previous lives to deserve even more punishment? Have I not given so many good offerings in the temple lately?

I arrive at the river breathless. It is hard to make out any familiar landmarks. Then I see the point of higher ground where the children often dive in. There, wedged in the mulberry bush, are Siru and Atti's flip-flops. My husband, their father, has told the children a silly story about how vultures like eating flip-flops. After that, they always wedged their shoes in this bush when they went swimming. Little Hari—their new-found cousin—has left his shoes and catapult there also.

The children had gone swimming. Now they are gone. It is my karma to suffer. I have lost so many children now. Maybe Moti is also dead. Also, I do not know where my husband is. He went north again to dig out the main irrigation canal. He will have been close to the water when the wave came. He might also have been drunk—often he gets drunk when he goes on these work parties. He moves slowly when he has been taking hard drinks. Why do the gods punish us so? Is there any harm in a little strong drink, a little fun? And why would the gods take my innocent children. They have done nothing to offend the gods.

I turn. I walk back to my baby, my Kancha. My mind is empty. I am empty. I have lost everything.

Bom Bahadur

I am sitting drinking tea and eating the air with my friends in the Hotel Bageswari. Actually that Newar man, Dhan Sing, he has joined me again. He is a government man—in the Irrigation Department or Agriculture or something like that. I understand now why he spends time with me. He has come to know that I am familiar with Kamala Tharu's family. I am like a family member to them. We have seen good and bad times together and we have helped one another. Dhan Sing has noticed Kamala and he aims to marry her. He wants me to talk to her—to persuade her. The problem is that he hasn't even found the courage to talk to her himself. Not one word of love has he offered her. I know that he has spoken to Guliya but what is the point in that? Kamala is of the age when she is influenced by the love stories in the Bollywood movies. Dhan Sing will not win her by being shy and conventional. In my opinion, he has no backbone; he is typical of these educated types. He studied in Russia, I am thinking.

I was trying to advise him about making himself known to Kamala when we notice that there is some commotion. People are running into the bazaar. They are very excited about something. These people of the Plains are very excitable. This is something that I myself have observed. Maybe some Indian is coming with a dancing bear, or ices. Maybe a film star is visiting!

A runaway donkey gallops through—scattering people. That is an unusual sight. Normally, donkeys are too lazy to run anywhere. Something has scared it. Could there be a big cat on the loose? Sometimes rogue leopards and even tigers dare to steal cattle. We had one man-eater on the island in the past—some years back. Government men came and took it to the zoo in Kathmandu.

More men and women arrive. There is shouting. I stop one man. He says that the river has taken large pieces of Rajapur Island. These rural people are always exaggerating, isn't it? It is typical behaviour for civilians. They hope for compensation from His Majesty's Government or from some international NGO. I ask him for more information but he does not linger. He calls a child to him and hurries away.

It is only then that I see the flood. How can it be then that water is flowing in and along the main street? It is rising steadily also. We are accustomed to wading through water during the monsoon season. Sometimes it is knee-deep in the bazaar. This is our life; we are used to this and we know that this water brings wealth to Rajapur. It makes the rice grow. But the rains are over now. The skies are clear. What can be happening? Have the gods sent some terrible punishment?

People have talked about how low the river has been lately. Why then should we have a flood? I do not understand. I cannot guess the origin of the water. Perhaps this is Indian mischief. Perhaps I need to go to the barrage: the barrage across the river that was built by the Indians and is controlled by them. Maybe I must speak against the Indians. I must be an advocate for all the people of Nepal!

I leave my tea and quick-march over to the temple. It will be dry there. It is built on the highest point in the bazaar. People will go there for guidance from the priests. The streets are full of people going this way and that, in utter confusion. I must find out what is happening. I decide not to go to the temple but walk on to the town water tower. From there I will be able to see. Perhaps I will be able to mobilize the community and somehow stop the water. Being a regimental sergeant-major (retired), I can organize and motivate these people. But first I need intelligence. Perhaps there will be some informative report on the radio?

Rekraj

I have a sense of foreboding. I have seen inauspicious things. Vultures fly overhead and small birds are silent. I notice the smell of wet mud in the air. I have no understanding of these strange happenings.

I am weary of my work also. I have been sitting on the verandah of the office typing. I am getting bored without company. I miss Sonia didi's chitchat and giggles. Ram Krishna should have come to help today but once again he has failed to fulfil a simple duty. I don't know what to expect of this useless cousin of mine. But what to do? It is our burden to tolerate and accommodate slothful family members.

I go to the elephant lookout. Since that nice time I had there with Sonia didi, I like to climb the ladder and look out.

The air is fresher and I feel like a god up there. The platform is a good place to be. The view from there is very far, and it is cool also.

This afternoon, the scene is not good. At first I cannot believe what I see. I think my eyes have become somehow blurred with too much work.

The day before, the landscape was a beautiful patchwork of lush green winter wheat and bright yellow fields of mustard, with mango, silk-cotton and the flame-of-the-forest trees here and there. Today, everything is brown. I am uncertain whether it is the river that has swollen or whether it has eaten huge pieces of the island. In the distance, wherever the ground is lower and close to the river, uprooted trees are strewn around the landscape as if some demon has ripped each one out and, unsatisfied, has dropped it where he plucked it.

This place and our NGO headquarters are situated on a small rise. It is one of the highest points on Rajapur Island. This place has itself become a small, small island. A thousand confused images crowd my mind. The Indians must have done this thing. Some years ago, they built the barrage across the Geruwa river. With this, they control the water, our water. They must have closed the gates and so flooded Rajapur. The Indians do things like this to Nepal. They are always bullying us in this way or that way. They like to taste our women—dishonourably. And now they destroy our land.

Bom Bahadur

I walk on through the bazaar. There is so much of water in each and every place. I see lots of stunned, wounded people. The worse cases are being brought here in buffalo-carts. Some walk nursing broken arms. Some are badly cut. Many are covered in dried mud. A few are wet.

Vultures are circling. There has been some great and terrible happening. I think many casualties are coming to Rajapur for help. I think that this is only the start. I try to ask people what has happened but all are hurrying and some look a little mad. Finally, I manage to catch the arm of one man. He says that the river deities became angry. He says that the whole of Guptipur village has been swept away. The radio mast has come down also. Communications will be difficult and there will be many, many injuries. It is good that Sonia Madam and Kamala are safely up in the hills.

I think of Dr Bhandari. I must check with him. He has an excellent shortwave radio. There may be news on this, or broadcasts about an evacuation plan. Dr Bhandari and Dr Dash, the best bonesetter on the island, will need help. Dash is the one with political ambitions—he will be thinking of how to profit from the disaster but he will be providing a good service also. Even so, these two will not be able to attend to all the wounded. If there are many casualties, perhaps we can arrange a first-aid centre in the Shiva temple. There is a water-pump inside, in the courtyard garden, and we can clean and dress wounds and simple cuts. I can do this because I am trained for the battlefield. Actually, I am highly trained. I was part of the best army in the world. In former years, when I was in my prime—at the very peak of physical fitness—I served Her Majesty and now I am serving His Majesty—and his esteemed subjects. First, I will talk to Bhandari about what must be done. He is a good man. He will provide wise advice.

11. MATING SNAKE-DEITIES

Moti

The gods have shown us that they are very angry. I do not know the reason. I have the idea that Indra thinks it sacrilegious for a non-Hindu to wear a vajra but this is a small, small transgression by an ignorant foreigner. Surely this cannot have provoked such divine wrath? Especially as Sonia didi wears it like an amulet—for protection. Perhaps it has been blessed by one of her American priests. It is not important now. I tell her, 'I need go to my home, Auntie. I need go quick.'

She understands the words I speak, but she doesn't realize that I need to go very fast. She doesn't know how slowly she walks. She looks around. I can see that she is fearful of moving from this place. She says, 'How do we get down from here?' She is still clinging onto the rock face. She is quivering like a trapped hare.

'Up! We must first climb up,' I tell her. 'It is no problem, Auntie. Come!' I smile and take her hand again to encourage her. Her eyes are big. I tell her, 'Come! Stand!' She is scared of falling. 'Let us go this way. It is easy.' I lead to show her. 'There is a little bit of climbing up around the rock but it is no problem.'

Sonia

My ears were still ringing from the incredible noise of the wave but now there was a strange background quietness. I could hear the river below us but the birds weren't calling and the insects had gone quiet. Someone—on the other side of the river—was wailing. It was a horrible, haunting cry of despair.

The tea-shop owner nimbly climbed up over the rocks above us and Moti also left me. She left me alone with that awful crying. Moti didn't seem to have heard it.

She told me to follow her. I can't. I know I will fall to my death. I was sure that the scrap of ground I was on was moving. I sat down again and clung onto the rock—shaking, wondering when the ground I was on would fall into the seething water below. Just as I was beginning to think that I should start to pray, Moti returned. She was smiling, as usual. 'This way come, Auntie!'

'I can't.'

'It is no problem—come!' She pulled me to my feet, and said, 'This time Auntie goes first and I will come backside and push!' She started to laugh.

I thought her mirth must be a sign of madness at first but soon couldn't resist her laughter. I started to giggle myself. I turned and found that the rock was so craggy that it was easy to scramble upwards, especially with Moti literally bringing up the rear—her head often bumping into my bum while she shouted, 'Up, Auntie, up!'

Then, 'Shabash! Brave Auntie!'

We'd made it.

A little above the rocks that had saved our lives, I saw a small goat track. The ground was covered with short spiky grass, and an occasional battered-looking gentian. There didn't seem to be enough soil for trees or even bushes. We followed that tiny path for a while, one behind the other. I tried not to look down to the river that was way, way below us now. It wasn't difficult walking but one slip would mean plummeting hundreds of metres. There was nothing to grab on to. One slip was all it needed. I concentrated hard on placing each foot down carefully, safely.

Moti

From higher up we can see that the tea-shop where we had stayed, it is gone. The owner is standing still at this vantage point. Tears fill her eyes. She has lost everything. My heart feels her pain but it is her karma. 'Come with us, didi,' I say but she shakes her head. Maybe she has somewhere to go. I can do nothing. I do not know if we will find shelter. I take my leave from her. I must return to my family. We must find a way quite high up on the valley wall. This will be a little bit difficult. Sonia didi manages to walk quite well—better than I expected. We make good speed at first.

Auntie tries to talk as she walks but she has no wind. She says, 'Yes. Of course. You must. Go back. I want to walk. With you. I will try. Not to slow. You down. I have money,' she pats her money-belt, 'that will help us. Speed us. You need money. To get back. To your family.'

'I think Auntie is wise.'

I feel some small comfort when we rejoin the main path. We see more people. It is good to be amongst people at times like this. Many are hurrying south. After no time at all, we find another place where the path has been washed away. The path is gone in many, many places. It is rarely possible to cross low down because the steep shifting slopes of rock, broken trees and debris end in a drop straight down into the river, maybe 300 metres below.

This is not so unusual in the Hills, but people haven't yet made paths across so it is dangerous. The big problem is that we often have to climb up high above the river and across new scree. Trees and big boulders are still moving and settling. We do a lot of slow, difficult scrambling over the scree-slides. Others, too, are trying to find easy routes. Sometimes other people advise us on the best way. Sonia Auntie manages quite well.

Sonia

Moti headed back at astonishing speed. I hadn't realized she could walk so fast. I'd recovered from the mad run up the mountain but I was soon breathless again with trying to keep up with her. The tea-shop lady walked with us until we came to a place where we looked down to where her shop had been. Her face showed no emotion. I pressed a 500-rupee note into her hand and ran to catch up with Moti again.

We seemed to be making quite good progress—despite the terrain. I wasn't that unfit. The death-wave had taken enormous pieces out of the valley. All the way back downstream, there were great white scars where chunks of mountainside hundreds of metres wide had gone. They'd tumbled into the flood and just gone. Large birds were circling overhead—vultures, I supposed.

Moti

We reach the gorge. I see that the wave has come through and swept over the main path but it has stood firm against the water. Here the valley is narrow and cut into solid rock. Many other people have also reached this place. Several paths meet here. We have to climb through stranded trees that the river has left on and across the path. Their branches have acted like sieves and have caught dead oxen, goats, dogs and chickens. A snake dangles there, limp as a hot dog's tongue.

There is a woman also. She is from the Hills. Auntie says we should push her in. This is a good thing to do. She will float downstream until she reaches the waters of the holy Ganga river. Then she will be reborn. Perhaps in her next life she will have the good luck to be reincarnated as a man.

Several of us work together to move the tree she is in. It is heavy. It takes some time. It rocks on the edge of the path. Finally, the tree tumbles. We send the Hills-woman home with a splash. She looks as if she is smiling as she sinks silently into the purifying river. We walk on, feeling we have done one small karmic task. One small contribution. I look ahead, expecting to come to the bazaar sheltered in the entrance of the gorge.

I step out from the gorge. The sunlight is dazzling. I screw up my eyes. I rub them to clear the fog, to see more clearly. I cannot believe it. The bazaar at Chisapani has gone—every stall. The place where the buses take on passengers is not here. A big part of the East-West Highway has slipped off the incline and lies in pieces in the river below. This place was built on scree and river cobbles—the river gods have taken them back. I look south. I recognize nothing. Nothing. All I see is moving, muddy water. Fallen, broken trees and trucks and buses stick out from the water. There are bits of road and big rocks. I think of a man driven by lust who takes a woman against her will and afterwards leaves her broken. The river and the lustful man are the same. It is always like this.

Dogs and vultures are fighting over carcasses. It is my idea that some of the flesh they are ripping apart is human. A crocodile pulls something the size of a person into the water also. Downstream, unconcerned, an Indian man is squatting by a dugout canoe. I tell Auntie we must go to him. There is no easy path. We follow others who are scrambling over rock-piles and debris.

After some time, we reach the ferryman. His face is dark as thunder. I greet him. I ask politely if he will take us to Rajapur Island. He is hostile and unhelpful.

He replies, 'It is possible—if you can pay.'

'We can pay. How much money will you take, brother?'

'Two thousand rupees,' he says, looking at me coldly. He knows I cannot pay such an enormous sum. A man would have to work for three or four months to earn that much; I would have to work for maybe half a year.

'These are hard times,' I tell him. 'The gods are angry. How can you ask for so much money when you must know I need to return to my family? Why do you try to make money from others' misfortunes? Such deeds will be repaid with bad karma.'

He spits disdainfully. I have never talked to a man like this before. Maybe Auntie's demon possesses me now. Today, I do not care. The ferryman may be a man but he is no better than me! I stand tall.

Auntie asks what has been said. When I explain, she laughs. She says she feels proud that I have spoken up for myself. She shows him we have money by snatching 2,000-rupee notes from her wallet and, using her left hand, she waves them rudely at him. He deserves to be treated badly. He says nothing as he paddles us across. He is facing some difficulties.

The water is swirling, as if all the river deities are mating in the depths. The crossing is frightening. I hear Auntie saying *'Katti bajay heh,'* as we cross. Maybe this helps her not worry so much but it is a strange mantra to choose. Finally, the ferryman runs the dinghy up onto the shore of Rajapur Island. Auntie pays this greedy man. I curse him under my breath.

We walk south. It is difficult to find any familiar landmarks. There are so many broken things. I see the twisted wheels of a tanga. I wonder if the horse that pulled it is buried beneath. Half a truck is sticking out of the mud also. There are splashes of colour where awnings that once covered market stalls lay half-buried beside big pieces of road. Everything is covered in silt. Everything is the colour of mud. The land lies ravaged.

The smell of death is everywhere. Slimy black children of snake-deities writhe in the mud. The usual packs of dogs that always hang around on the edge of every village are howling and fighting with each other. One pack looks as if it will challenge us. The pack leader is an old, scarred fighting dog. You know such creatures because owners cut off their ears so that opponents can't catch hold easily. The whole pack seems a little mad. How quickly these dogs have learned to disrespect people. I show no fear and they do not attack; they have had enough to eat from scavenging in the debris.

The only things that are still standing in the northern part of the island are a few red silk-cotton trees and shrines. The gods have protected the places where we bring our offerings.

Sonia

I scrambled out of the dugout. The ferryman didn't bother to help me; he just stared as I struggled. I didn't care. I was pleased to leave him behind and grateful to have my feet back on dry land again—if you could call it dry land. Sticky revolting grey stuff coated everything now. The mud-laden river was still beautiful though, sparkling where the sun caught it. There it was, always moving, but remaining unmoved by all the desolation and distress it had caused.

Straightening up, I unstuck my wet clothes from my bottom. A black-and-white bird plummeted vertically into the river, surfaced and flew off with a small eel wriggling it its beak. Everything else on the island was in a state of devastation. Maybe the flood looked worse than it really was. Maybe this happens every year. The mud that covered everything must nourish the land. Maybe new shoots will soon start peeking through, stimulated by all the nutrients in the silt. Rekraj had explained to me that Rajapur Island was part of an inland delta. He said that there are often floods, especially at the north end of the island. Sometimes parts are washed away, and sometimes new pieces of island are created.

This looked really, really awful though. Surely *this* didn't happen often? Everything was the same colour. Everything looked like it had been carved out of sticky beige mud. The mud was thick and grass wasn't sticking through it. Most of the scrubby stuff that we'd seen growing here only a few days before had gone, and so had lots of trees. Some were uprooted. Many had just disappeared.

Odd unidentifiable things poked out from the sludge and the river. There were also bits of stick and sacking and wheels and branches and tree trunks and house timbers and pieces of metal and doors and boulders and great pieces of tarmac. There was no sign of any paths. Had there ever been any?

Rekraj

Slowly, I gather the story piece by small, small piece. It is my idea that those tremors we've felt over the last days and weeks have caused a landslide in some remote place, high up in the mountains. This would block the river, but only for some time. The water must soon overflow and in overflowing, it would scour away the landslide. Then all that has backed up behind would be released. Suddenly. A surge wave would come down through the mountains, tearing away everything. It happens thus. Our grandparents talk about it and I have read about it in the newspapers also.

The force of such a wave coming through the gorge would be terrific but, once out of the foothills, the river could spread out and some of the power of the river would dissipate. By the time the wave reached the level of Rajapur bazaar, 30 kilometres south of the gorge, it would be slowing down and depositing all that it has stolen from the Hills.

Even so, it will have swept away parts of the north of the island—maybe large parts. All the ferries will be gone.

The Indians may not be directly responsible for the problem, but their dam will have made the flood worse and I am sure that if they had opened their barrage and released the water, then the damage would have been less—much less—for us here in Nepal. It is odd that there is nothing on the radio about what has happened here. Has the flood taken away all communications?

Help will be a long time coming to Rajapur. Maybe it will never come. We are too far from Kathmandu here.

His Majesty's Government will do very little. Those radishes in their grand houses in Kathmandu will not lose face for Nepal by asking for help from the Indians. And the Indians will not help Nepal before their own people.

We will need to look to our own resources. We will see who has the ability to lead in this crisis.

People will be converging on Rajapur bazaar because that is where they think they'll find help, direction and leadership and maybe some comfort too. There they may find their loved ones—or news of them. These are bad times.

I feel sorrow that the gods have sent this terrible flood. Perhaps it is because there is so much strong drink on this island. Each and every Tharu village has one or maybe two stills. The Tharus like to celebrate in this way.

Food and clean water will be important. But who will care for those who have been injured? And cremate the dead? How will we manage?

Then I think about the schoolchildren. There is no sound from the classroom close by. This is odd. There is no parental wailing either.

First, I must go to the school. I shall make sure the children are safe and then I will go to the bazaar and see what can be arranged.

I could put Ram Krishna to work here and now, but he is never around when he is needed. He is such a useless fellow. Even though he is my cousin, I feel this criticism of him is justified.

Sonia

'Will we be able to find our way back, Moti?'

'It is not known, Auntie. We must walk with the morning sun on our left side.' She strode out again, purposefully. We walked past a truck and something that looked like a footbridge. Revolting things, eels perhaps, writhed in the puddles of muddy water that had been created around it. Above it perched a huge dull-green kingfisher with a beak so big it looked as if it would topple forward. It was watching things in the river, deciding whether they were worth eating. Mynah birds were picking about. A pathetic, lost-looking horse with a broken leg was trying—and failing—to find something to eat. It was nuzzling at a patch of those odd waxy-leaved plants with purple flowers. They looked poisonous.

Another posse of skinny dogs sprinted by. The one in the lead barked as if issuing an order. Moti stooped to pick up a stone and told me to copy her. The stone I found was surprisingly light. The dogs sped past.

Something sharp stabbed into my hand. I shrieked in fear and surprise. My stone scratched me. I dropped it. Moti looked at me as if I was mad. A clawed foot poked out of my stone, then another. Then a tiny grey-green head emerged tentatively. The small mud turtle scuttled away, plopped into a puddle and disappeared.

There was a bad smell as I stepped on something soft. The smell got worse. I stepped back, and made out brown hair sticking out through the mud. This dead thing was an ox, and it was starting to stink.

We came upon another soft heap. My stomach dropped to my feet as I realized that this one wore clothes. This one was a person. A small person. At the same split second, Moti and I both saw that the girl wore Tharu clothes. She was the same size as little Atti. Her arm was raised over her head as if to protect herself. My hand went to my mouth and I staggered backwards. I was nearly sick. I looked on in horror while Moti walked forward, squatted down and tenderly wiped mud away from the child's face. Moti dipped her hand into a puddle to smooth away the river silt more effectively. Then she covered the little body with a huge battered palm leaf.

'This is not my little sister.' Moti said, apparently to herself.

I didn't know why Moti expected Atti to be here. I lurched on, numb. I wanted to wake up from this nightmare. My head was whirring. I don't know for how long I walked. I was vaguely aware that we were now progressing along the bank of the main river.

I became aware of a voice. It wasn't saying anything I

understood. It was speaking Nepali. It was Moti. She was talking to a woman. The woman was standing on the river bank. She was looking out across the river. The woman didn't seem to be saying much back to Moti. I walked on. I kept hoping that I was in some awful dream but I knew this was foolish. I was a very, very long way from my cosy bed in Cambridge.

Some time later, Moti caught my elbow and steered me towards a tiny building.

'Let us ask for help here, Auntie.'

'Is someone living inside such a small place?' I asked, incredulous. She didn't reply. 'Did you get any directions or news from that woman you talked to?'

Finally, Moti said reluctantly, 'That woman said she was looking towards where her house had been. Her house has gone. Her children have gone. Her husband and his brothers have gone. Everything is gone.'

Moti turned and ducked into the gloom of the tiny building. Blindly, I followed her into this strange little structure. As my eyes slowly grew accustomed to the dark, I made out splashes of colour—red and gold. This was a shrine to Ganesh. The floor inside was covered in sticky mud but the elephant-headed god was pristine. I mimicked Moti as she put her hands together in salute. I prayed too—for the first time in my life. Surely if there is a God—or gods—they would show compassion and help us now?

'Do you know this place well, Moti?'

'I know this place.' She didn't look happy. She was fearful but didn't say why.

Outside, again a little girl had materialized. It was as if she had been waiting for us. She might have been about three years old, maybe more. Her face was blank, her hair thin and matted. She didn't respond when Moti spoke to her. Maybe she was in shock.

'It is my idea that she does not understand the Nepali or Tharu or Hindi languages.'

'Where can she be from?'

'She is wearing clothes of people from the Hills. We must take her with us. And look here!' Moti pointed to fresh pugmarks. A big cat had walked around the shrine, probably while we were inside. Moti—unfazed as ever—threw the child up onto her shoulders. We walked on.

There were countless huddles of vultures, picking at God-knows-what. I didn't dare look. We disturbed a couple of weird, warty-headed ibises. Their red disfigured faces made them look as though they had some awful skin condition. Why Egyptians think these birds are sacred, I don't know—they're so ugly!

Panic was beginning to rise in me again as I thought of plague and man-eaters. Surely all around us were jackals and wild dogs and leopards and even tigers? Maybe there were other flesh-eaters I had not heard of? And now—all these shattered human lives. How I wanted to go home!

Then, as if to heap more troubles upon us, we came upon a huge swollen irrigation channel. I knew Moti was going to say we must get across it somehow. It was flowing fast and furious. To my great alarm, there was no discussion. Moti hardly broke step as she slipped off her sandals and adjusted the child on her shoulders. She just walked forward, straight into the rushing brown water. It was flecked with yeasty foam. Quickly, she waded out until the water was waist-deep. She walked steadily forward while the tiny girl shrieked with glee. I heard Moti laughing with her. The surging water was soon up to Moti's armpits, but the child wriggled, trying to splash with her feet. She was enjoying it! The two of them rose up out of the water again, but as soon as Moti put the child down she ran back to splash some more.

'Come, Auntie!' Moti shouted, laughing at the little girl's antics.

I took off my trainers, tied them together by the laces and dangled them around my neck. The mud on my soles was surprisingly hot and slug-slimy. I slithered down into the water. I felt pieces of stick and leaves washing past my legs. I started to imagine creatures in the water that might bite me. Crocodiles. Snakes. Water scorpions. Leeches. Other unknown beasts.

Tentatively I stepped forward, aware that the rushing water wanted to sweep my feet away each time I took a step.

I shuffled on, going deeper and deeper. More of me was now accessible for some aquatic creature to bite. And I was being pushed rapidly downstream—away from Moti. I turned back towards her, broadside to the stream. I was going to shout for help but as I opened my mouth, the full force of the water took me. I fell backwards. I went under. I began to choke. Water surged up my nose. All I could see was brown—mud brown—as I thrashed to stand again. I tried not to splutter. Something hit me. Was it some creature? Would it bite me? I curled up and in that way I felt stable enough to lower my feet. By the time I'd managed to put my weight on my feet and get my head above water again, I'd been swept 50 metres from Moti and the child. Miraculously, I hadn't lost my trainers.

It was several more minutes before I could scramble onto the mud bank on their side of the torrent. It was so slippery that I slithered back into the water several times. My clothes were heavy and clung to me.

Moti and the child were not a bit concerned. Had they not seen that I had nearly drowned in that raging, swirling water? They merely waited for me to put my trainers on again and rejoin them. Moti made no comment at all about the crossing. That seemed so odd after I'd been in so much danger. Surely she could see that I was still shaking from the shock of it—the shock of nearly drowning after everything else that had happened. I wondered whether to say anything but she was already walking on.

As we got further away from the water, we startled a peacock. He trotted away for a few paces, then turned, raised and spread his tail. He quivered it so that it caught the light. In my relief to be back on dry land again—alive—surrounded by mud and death, his beautiful shimmering sea-greens and electric blues were mesmerizing and brought tears to my eyes. I wanted to stand and watch. I wanted to lose myself in his beauty but Moti pressed ever onward. I hurried after her.

Then a movement off to one side made me look towards a small-scale explosion of zebra stripes and cinnamon-orange. The bird had been probing with his long, curved beak, searching for food in the mud and we'd disturbed him.

He lifted his crest with a disgusted complaining *poo-poo-poo* as we came close again. The exhibitionist flew away in undulating flight, mocking us. With his noisy departure, beauty left us again.

My mind wandered as I plodded on relentlessly. My life had been a mess when I came here. Now, my bitter past didn't matter. The misjudgement, the isolation, the lack of appreciation I had experienced were unimportant. Suddenly, I no longer saw myself as a victim. How could I, amidst this devastation?

I was in the middle of a real-life drama and I did not want to be a bystander. Somehow I was going to help. But what could I do? I dismissed one idea after another. What could I do with no skills and little chance of making myself understood, not knowing much Nepali? The first-aid course I'd done to run the school netball team wasn't going to help much in all this.

I walked mechanically, not noticing where I was putting my feet. Then unexpectedly, the child on Moti's shoulders shrieked. She pointed just ahead of me. Less than two paces away lay a big snake. Clumsily, I scuffed the ground as I stopped. That alerted the snake. It snapped around towards me. It reared up and spread its hood. It hissed. It rasped threateningly.

My knees turned to jelly. I couldn't move. I couldn't breathe. I couldn't even take a step backwards. I thought I might be sick. The snake rasped again. I was frozen in terror. I was going to die.

Then out of the corner of my eye, I saw something move. A bigger object. A brown blur. A dog—a mad dog—charged in and tried to bite the snake's tail. The dog was canny and fast. The snake struck out but missed. The dog sunk its teeth into the snake and tried to drag it away. The snake struck out again. I saw in slow motion as its huge spring-loaded fangs, dribbling venom a little, sank deep into the dog's side. The snake hadn't missed the second time.

I started as Moti took my elbow and pulled me away. She said, 'In saving us, this dog will surely die.'

I watched in horrified fascination as the snake chewed at

the dog. The mutt released the snake and howled. It lurched about, as if trying to shake the snake off but it held on. As the animal staggered away, the cobra dropped to the ground. The dog limped off, tail between its legs, whimpering. It didn't get far. Soon it fell. It twitched a bit and lay still.

'Lord Ganesh is protecting us.' Moti said in a matter-of-fact tone. 'He will protect us from tigers also.'

Omigod. Not tigers too.

Moti

I am nervous now. Lord Ganesh will protect us from wild animals but not from the Brahmins. Brahmins honour him with many expensive offerings. We are close now to the village where Ram Krishna's family own many bigga of land. His youngest brothers live here. And some cousins. They are all the same. They are all no good. They are all womanizers. I am frightened now.

Before this day, he and his brothers and cousin-brothers could do whatever they wanted with any Tharu or untouchable girl, but if they were too bold their relatives would have something to say. They would control them. They would not have been allowed to bring shame on the family name. But now the family will not care. They will be thinking of finding their loved ones only. We had a little bit of protection before. Now we have none. Anything can happen.

It is my idea that on this day of disaster when their crops are ruined and their houses are broken, they will look for the comfort of a woman's body, never mind if that woman is not looking for this kind of comfort also. This is a very dangerous place today. Shadows are also long now. It will grow dark soon.

Then, as if my thoughts have brought him here, I see him. He is walking towards us. He looks out of place in his coat-pant outfit in this junglee area. His mind is somewhere far away. It is a long time before he sees us. I am angry with myself. If I had known that he wasn't paying attention, we could have hidden. Now it is too late. I look around for a rock. I need to defend myself. But there is sand only.

He stops. He says, 'Greetings. I was not expecting to meet

anyone here in this junglee place. How has this day treated you ladies?' He is polite. I realize it is not Ram Krishna. He is some other person. A relative, probably. I say a small thank you to Durga, and to Lord Ganesh also. These Brahmin men all look alike with their big noses and their city clothes. My mind is playing tricks on me. This Brahmin is not interested in me. He continues pleasantly, 'Where are you walking to today?' Then, 'You must take great care. There are many snakes! Go with good fortune, bahini.' He bows to Sonia didi and takes his leave.

I hurry on. Sonia didi looks confused and maybe a little disappointed. I think she is hoping that we'd stop and talk. She is weak. I can see she is very tired. She has tried hard but now she is finished. She is not used to this life. She is used to riding in cars. She is used to servants doing everything for her. I don't want to leave her but I need to get to Rajapur bazaar. It will be most dangerous here after dark. We must go quickly. We need to get where there are many people. We will be safe once we reach the bazaar.

Then I see him. I know immediately it is really him this time.

There is a lot of debris. The river has left several trees here. He is standing amongst them. He is waiting there beside the path. It is as if he is expecting me. Perhaps one of his relatives has told him I am here. Again I cast around, seeking a rock. Again there are none. I wonder if I can run away. Running won't help me though. I know this.

Ram Krishna is lounging up against one of the fallen trees. His hand is resting along its now-horizontal trunk. He is looking at the ground some distance in front of where he stands. I put down the tiny girl who has been riding on my shoulders. I push her away from me. Then I notice that someone else is here. Another man—a Tharu—is squatting close by. He looks as if he is waiting to take orders from Ram Krishna. Then I think how odd it is that the Tharu is so relaxed in the presence of the Brahmin. I feel fear. Has Ram Krishna made some kind of arrangement with this Tharu? Have the two men set some kind of trap?

12. KARMA AND RETRIBUTION

Moti

The Tharu man turns and smiles. He gets up and offers a formal greeting, 'Ram Ram.'

I stare hard at one man then the other. Something is very wrong. It is strange that Ram Krishna remains silent. Being a Brahmin, he thinks it disrespectful for Tharus to talk together in front of him like this. I look at him. I see that he is quite, quite still. His colour is not good. He hasn't moved since we arrived at this place. He hasn't even raised his head or found a new insult for me. And there are flies around him.

The Tharu also says, 'I am so pleased to see that you are well on this terrible day, Kamala cousin-sister...' He knows my name. He is some distant relative but I have hardly ever spoken to him.

'Ram Ram, my cousin-brother. I am also pleased to see that the day has not treated you badly.' The Tharu youth has greeted me in a most friendly way and I ask him, 'What has happened here?'

He nods towards Ram Krishna, 'I found him, some time ago. I did not want to help him at first because I know what pain he caused you, my cousin-sister. I know that he is a bad man. But he asked for my help and I could not walk away. In my heart though that is truly what I wanted to do. I tried to release him but he was caught between two big trees. Both trees were heavy—too heavy to move without a big work-party, or a team of buffaloes. I went for help but there was no one close by. He begged me not to leave him alone.'

Auntie has been standing beside me, staring at Ram Krishna. She says, 'I think he's dead—dead as a dodo, Moti.' I do not know what is dodo.

'And good riddance, I'd say!'

Is it possible? Is he dead? Cold spreads through my body, but the air seems to go out of it also.

He *is* dead. Now the warmth comes back into my body. I can feel it as if the rays of the first hot sun of the year are pouring down into my stiffened limbs, making me grow subtle and lithe as winter leaves my bones.

I look at the Tharu man and ask him how he avoided getting trapped in the same way by the flood.

He shrugs and mutters something about the will of the gods and then tells me, 'He talked about you, Kamala-sister. He said he was sorry that he might never lie with you—that he desired you still. Then I saw that he was badly injured—below the waist. He knew he would never lie with a woman again. This was his karma. His manhood was gone. There wasn't much blood so I didn't know how badly injured he was.

'He talked and talked of all the women he had enjoyed. He smiled as he spoke of them. He said that he wondered how many bastards he had fathered. He talked of the Tharu girls he had trafficked and all the money he had made from this. He said he was crazy for you also, that he truly loved you, but it is my idea that the Brahmin never came to know the meaning of the word 'love'.

I shudder. I look again and see that Ram Krishna has a small smile on his face. How is it he had an easy death? The gods are truly unjust. The Tharu continues, 'Then the Brahmin stopped talking. His head tipped slightly to one side and rested on his own shoulder, then rolled forward. He hasn't moved since. I have been watching him for a long time now. Look—there are vultures waiting in the tree above him. You are safe from this man now, my cousin-sister. This is a good day for you.'

'Truly, this is a good day for me, cousin-brother. This was the karma of the Brahmin. It is what he deserved. We will leave him like this—for the vultures. We will not help him to the next life with fire. I think in his next life he will come back as a woman.'

'This would be a true and just retribution!'

I wonder why I have never noticed this, my cousin-brother, before. He is my age, strong and handsome. I like the look of him. Sonia didi is sitting on the ground and is staring at the body of the Brahmin. Tears drip from her face. The lost child has gone to sit beside her but she is not looking at Auntie; she is looking up, towards the circling vultures.

I turn back to the Tharu and say, 'Will you walk with us? We will go now to the bazaar and seek news of my family.'

'I will walk with you and help find your family, my cousin-sister. It is getting late now. Rajapur bazaar is still far. We must hurry or spend the night in the jungle. Come, let's go.' He walks over to Sonia didi and surprises me by saying in English, 'Come, Madam!' and helps her to her feet.

The lost child doesn't move. She continues to gaze at the treetops. Then I see what she is staring at. There is another child—a child of maybe six—stranded in the high branches. Her big ebony eyes are shiny with fear. My cousin-brother looks up too, and nimbly climbs up to coax her down.

Sonia

I watched flies running over Ram Krishna's face and in and out of his nose. They had even crawled into his mouth. I started to cry but it wasn't for him. Life was cheap after all. I'd killed my baby. Life had been taken away from him too, and I just kept thinking that at least Ram Krishna deserved to die. My baby didn't—what had it done? Nothing evil. What an awful, cold, hard person I was.

Was it the shock of seeing his body? What was this doing to me? Was I really heartless and callous? What had I become?

Rekraj

When I get to the school I hear the children quietly crying inside the classroom. I am not surprised to find that the teacher has run away. His behaviour was always predictable. He is a buffalo with no sense of duty or decency. I have long thought that he is a useless fellow. He is a little bit like Ram Krishna. This teacher fellow has deserted the children and—poor things—they are so scared. They whisper and whimper and don't know what to do. I speak to them and explain what has happened. I tell them that they must be brave. Several cry louder now. I tell them that we are in a good place. The river will rise no further. More sobs.

I tell them we must be calm and patient and wait for help to come. I assign two of the biggest boys to be in charge and explain to them that I need to go to Rajapur bazaar to get help. When I say this, the littlest ones begin to cry, very loudly. A small girl runs up to me and grabs my legs and clings desperately. I pick her up. I tell the children that they should pray. I tell the children that they should eat their tiffin and wait for their parents to return.

I instruct the older children to organize the classroom so that they can all sleep here tonight. It will be a distraction for the children to gather rice-straw to make the place comfortable. Finally, I warn them that there will be a lot of cobras. Cobras are always a problem when the river rises and in the rainy season. During the monsoon, several people each week are bitten by cobras on the island. The wise old guruwa saves some with his charms and potions but most die before they can get help. Children die fastest.

I turn to leave the classroom, feeling as if I have done one small useful thing but I feel distress about deserting the children now. What to do? Surely I must go to the bazaar and see how things are there but I also feel it is my duty to stay with the children. Where are all the responsible adults in this chaos? Where are the parents? Have they all drowned?

Moti

We walk south, Sonia didi, my cousin-brother, the two children and I. We walk towards Rajapur bazaar. I make conversation to pass the journey time, 'I have seen you in the bazaar but tell me, where is your house?' And, 'What is your good name, cousin-brother?'

'I am Ganga Lal Tharu,' he says. I like the fact that he is proud to be a Tharu. Some men take names that are not truly theirs, to hide their caste. Uncle Hari does this. He is ashamed of his family.

I say, 'That is a fine strong name—like you, cousin!' We laugh together. I feel a little wicked for flirting with him on a day like this.

There is another swollen irrigation canal but even Sonia didi can manage to cross without falling in—and with a child on her shoulders. I know that we are getting close to Rajapur bazaar. I am feeling easier in my mind. I feel strong again but this feeling doesn't last for long.

There is a rustling in the bushes to one side of the path.

Immediately I think this could be a bear or a leopard or wild dogs. There are many kinds of hungry wild animals that might take us. The sounds are clumsy though. It can't be a leopard or dogs. It is something large. I feel certain it is a bear.

Three big Brahmin men with stout walking sticks step out of the undergrowth. They block our way. Ganga Lal reaches for the catapult in his belt.

I recognize one of the men as an older brother of Ram Krishna. I know we are in for a beating. His mouth is pulled back into a vicious snarl, like a rabid dog. He says, 'I am so happy that you have come this way, Kamala Tharu.'

'I wish you good fortune also, Sahib,' I say, trying to appease him.

'You dare speak to me, you witch! You are the one who enchanted my poor brother. You bewitched him so that he fell in love with you. Then you cursed him. He was having endless problems in his belly...I know that he had the Evil Eye. Now you have killed him with your black magic.'

'It was not like that, Sahib. He...'

'Shut your mouth, witch!' He steps towards me. I see Sonia didi take a step back. Out of the corner of my eye, I see also Ganga Lal putting down the child he had been carrying. He stoops to pick something from the ground and whispers to the little girls. The two lost children link hands, run and climb up the flimsy branches of a tree. Then Ganga Lal steps to one side, and out of my view. He will leave me to face this trouble alone now.

Sonia

I didn't know who these new men were or what they were saying but I was sure they meant us harm. They were dressed like they had money. I looked at their faces and saw family likenesses with Ram Krishna and Rekraj. But why were they so angry? Why did they wield those big sticks? If they're related to Rekraj they must be Brahmins, and Rekraj told me that theirs is the caste of priests. Shouldn't Hindu priests be gentle? They looked half-mad. Maybe the disaster had turned their minds. Maybe it had turned my mind. But surely they wouldn't attack us? Surely no one would dare attack a British woman?

Then I considered just how stupid and naive that thought was. If someone were even to find a body in a situation like this, firstly, would anyone care? Secondly, if they did care, wouldn't they assume that any damage had been done by the flood rather than those nasty-looking staves? Dread filled me again. My great-great-great-grandfather had died not far from here. Perhaps he had been murdered. At this moment in this situation, I felt strongly that the cholera story was just a story. His death had been a violent one. Were my bones also going to become part of the bloodied, blood-red soil of the subcontinent?

I felt for my trusty amulet. I slipped my hand into my pocket and closed it around the 5-cm metal spike I'd found—the one that I had planned to use to defend myself against Ram Krishna, if necessary.

Moti

Ram Krishna's brother continues to pour abuse on me. I say nothing in my defence. It is always this way with Brahmins. There is no point in trying to explain anything. Then it is as if he remembers something important.

He says, quite casually, 'I have news of your oldest sister: the beautiful one.'

'Of Maya? How? Where is she? Have you seen her?'

I don't know why I expect the Brahmin to tell me anything I want to hear but I am so desperate for news of my beloved sister. 'What have you heard? Did she elope?'

He smiles. He is enjoying the pain he is causing by reminding me of her disappearance.

'Where is she? Please tell me what you have heard, Sahib.'

'How is it you ask if she eloped? She had no lover. These days, she is enjoying Indian hospitality only.'

'What are you saying! How do you know? Perhaps it was you who arranged it!'

He smiled and said only, 'It would be better if she was dead.'

'Don't say that, you heartless jackal. It *was* you who arranged it!'

I feel great pain. I don't want him to see how much he is giving me sorrow. I don't want to cry. I am scared also. Murder is in his heart. Sonia didi surprises me by stepping forward. She is standing close to me. I look at her and see that she has no fear. She truly feels like my older sister now.

Suddenly there is a sound of a catapult somewhere in the undergrowth. There is a small smacking sound. One of the Brahmins holds his hand to his head and staggers a little. A small trickle of blood comes from his cheekbone. I try to keep my face blank, though I want to laugh and clap and dance. I am wrong about Ganga Lal. He is doing his best for me.

The man who was hit turns. He looks into the jungle. Half-heartedly he goes grumbling after Ganga Lal. Now there are only two of these angry Brahmins. Maybe if we are clever we can split them up. Maybe we can outwit them. One is fat. I think we can run faster than him.

There are more sounds in the undergrowth but from a different place. I am impressed that Ganga Lal can move so quickly and quietly, like a spirit. But then I am puzzled. The noise is more than one man would make. I wonder if there are more Brahmins.

Again, I am wrong.

A huge grey form bursts out of the bushes. It is a full-grown cow-elephant. She is angry. She is flapping her ears aggressively. She makes an ear-splitting trumpeting sound. Another elephant appears behind her, and others—with calves. They are between us and the Brahmins. I grab Sonia didi's wrist. She has a small metal spike in her hand. This is a useful weapon against men. We run. I hear more trumpeting and blowing. I hear the sound of heavy feet. The elephants are not coming after us. Lord Ganesh is keeping us safe.

Bom Bahadur

There is so much of crying and wailing. Brahmin women make most noise. It is high-pitched and enough to give everyone pains in the head. The lower castes carry their burden of sorrow and loss quietly but they, too, are suffering. There is too much suffering in our community. All the children have streaks on their muddy faces where tears have dribbled down, but their tears are used up. They have stopped crying now.

Dr Bhandari has a long queue already. Battered, bloodied people stand or squat. Some cradle broken arms. He and the dispensing assistant are expertly dealing with every person who comes to them, one by one. His wife is helping also. This shows how broad-minded Bhandari is, allowing his uneducated wife to do this work also. The three of them are managing well. Bhandari tells me that still there is nothing about us on the radio. There was a passing mention on All India Radio about some laundrymen being swept away in Manjhra and the river bursting its banks near Colonelganj in India but nothing about Rajapur Island or events in Nepal. Is it possible that no one knows our plight?

Bhandari is not a real MBBS medical doctor but has been trained for three full months. He is also wise and experienced and he knows these people. He has helped them through many epidemics. Doctor sahib is a Brahmin but he is a good man nevertheless. He reminds me of one MBBS doctor I used to talk to in those glorious days when I served with the British Gurkhas. He was a physician and he was a bit of a philosopher also. I could listen to him for hours. Perhaps I am becoming a philosopher also. Actually, he was unusual for a British man—he had interesting conversation. This British doctor, he himself told me that seeing human suffering changes you. It either makes you compassionate or it makes you hard.

Seeing suffering has certainly made Bhandari compassionate. Everyone on the island knows he is a good man. He has become rich—not through swindling like so many Brahmins—but by his honesty and care, and his excellent dispensary. They knock on his door at any time of the day or night and they know he will help them; they all trust him.

Some years ago, a woman was brought to him. Her relatives brought her in a buffalo-cart, as is usual with these kinds of emergencies. It was her first baby and she had been in labour for a week, maybe more. She'd lost a lot of blood, of course, and the baby wouldn't come out. The traditional midwife said she could do nothing more and the woman would die. The family thought they were fortunate because there was a small military unit posted near their village. With them was a Brahmin MBBS doctor—Russian-trained. They took the woman to this doctor and asked for his help. He said that nothing could be done. She needed an operation and that was not possible on Rajapur Island. That military doctor, although he was a properly qualified MBBS physician, had been hardened by seeing suffering. Her pain and crying did not move him.

So they brought the poor suffering woman to Bhandari. He told me how scared he had been when he saw the baby's arm outside. He could see that the baby was dead. He knew that if he didn't get the baby out the woman would die—in agony. He also knew that he didn't have the skills to save this woman, and he had very little experience in these kinds of cases. He also knew that he was the only person around who could possibly save this woman. He had to try.

He is very intelligent and isn't proud like some Brahmins. He called the traditional midwife from Gumna village close by. Her work with delivering babies pollutes her and strict Brahmins can have nothing to do with these women, but Bhandari knew she was well-trained and had some knowledge. They worked together. Bhandari took a big risk and injected some powerful medicines. He'd never done this kind of thing before but knew enough to know that these medicines themselves can kill people. They can stop people breathing. They stop pain and they bring peace but they are dangerous, he knew that. Even so, he gave her a big dose of medicines and the woman's muscles became relaxed just enough to start getting the baby out. They ended up having to cut it. It was very horrible. But they saved that woman. She lived—and she has even had three more children!

Bhandari is a good man and he knows also that I have some basic first-aid training from my army days. He thinks my idea to set up a first-aid post in the Shiva temple is good. He gives me antiseptic. We both know that infection will be the biggest problem in this situation. I do not need many other supplies for doing this work. I am pleased that I have formed a good plan of what to do to help these people. I am not of these people but I have become close to them. They and I are blood-brothers; we suffered together in those early days of taming the island. Those were hard times, when the fever and Evil Eye took many, many good strong men.

Although I am competent and well-trained, I quickly see that I need help. I meet that lovelorn Newar, Dhan Sing. I ask him. He doesn't hear me. He asks about Kamala. He fears she has been drowned. He doesn't seem to be able to do anything except wander around uselessly looking for her. This is no way to win a woman's heart—especially a woman of Kamala's calibre. If she has survived and returns, she will not be impressed. It is unfortunate and a waste. He is an engineer; we could use his skills.

Dhan Sing will not help but I continue with my mission. I visit one tailor in the bazaar. My army days have made me broad-minded and so I can ask this untouchable to give me new needles and thick thread for sewing wounds and lacerations. Some other members of the Gurung caste—distant cousins whom I have met in Pokhara and Kathmandu—are very particular about who they deal with. Many are very superior about mixing with lower castes. They treat untouchable castes badly.

Then while I am talking to this tailor, a good idea strikes me. I tell him to come to the Shiva temple also where I shall turn him into a doctor! Stitching wounds will be easy for a tailor! He is happy. He says it will be good for his karma. He says that he seldom has the opportunity to do things that will gain him merit. That is mostly what high-caste people do only. He is my first recruit. He is overjoyed to follow me.

Moti

It takes some time to circle around and get back to the children but Ganga Lal is already with them. The new child told us how the Brahmins had run for their lives. The she-elephants seemed especially angry with them. The gods are truly with us this day.

We walk on, knowing now that we will reach Rajapur bazaar safely. We come—unexpectedly—to one community that is a little higher and so has escaped the water. There is an elephant lookout post marking it out. I can hear that children are still inside the school.

Sonia

I was utterly exhausted. There were probably good reasons for pressing on towards Rajapur bazaar but I'd begun to doubt I'd make it. I became aware of a hissing sound. Another snake. I hadn't enough energy to worry whether it bit me or not. I looked towards the sound and saw a bloated buffalo carcass. There was no snake. Gas was escaping from the buffalo's decaying body. I was too tired to be disgusted.

Suddenly I felt as if we were entering the world again—the world as it had been before the flood. We had gained a little height: just enough to have emerged from the hellish landscape of mud and pieces of trees. There were even some glimpses of green. Not all the bushes were covered in mud. There were even a few patches of grass, and one could hear bird calls. As the ground subtly continued to rise I realized we were entering a small village. It seemed to have escaped the destruction. A woman was busy at a hand-pump. She was absorbed in washing a child.

As we got closer, I saw that the water that ran off the child's head was blood red. The child—a little girl—was not crying but her scalp was split open and I thought I could see her skull underneath. I stood and watched in horror as the woman teased out strands of hair on either side of the gash and tried to pull the wound together with them. The woman mumbled to herself. She straightened up and beckoned Moti over. 'Aunus bahini!'

Together, the two women managed to push and pull the wound together and secure it by tying knots of hair across it. Finally, the treatment was complete. There were neat little hair-knots in a line across the child's scalp and only a slight trickle of blood dribbled down her neck.

This village was a teeming and vibrant island. Blood-coloured bottlebrush trees and scarlet hibiscus looked too bright for this devastated new world. I was overcome with the beauty of this place and tears ran down my cheeks—tears of joy and relief. I wondered whether I could stay, and at least rest awhile. The village was half-familiar. Then recognition dawned. We'd arrived in our village, where I'd been doing the typing.

Then he appeared. He looked calm, immaculate as ever, and unbelievably desirable. My fatigue evaporated in an instant.

Rekraj

As I come out of the schoolroom and into the sunshine I am astonished to see her again. The soft orange light of the sinking sun is shining through her golden hair and she is radiant—a little smeared with mud but radiant. She is crying but she also looks overjoyed to see me. 'I was frightened that you might be dead!' she says.

I don't know what to say. I am too shy to say what is in my overflowing heart. We look at each other for what seems like a long time, but it is only moments. Then I say, 'I am relieved to see that you are unharmed only. Kamala is all right also?'

'Yes, she is, but it is strange to hear you call Moti by her real name! Now I think she must go to find her family,' she says. Sonia didi looks tearful and tired but then she smiles. One of the children inside the school starts crying louder than ever. The other young ones join in. Sonia didi shows concern and asks, 'What can I do to help?'

'I do not know. It is a very horrible situation...I have spoken to the children and told them that I will seek help in Rajapur bazaar. Let us first go there together.'

'We'll leave the children, Rekraj?'

'We must—to send help to them.'

Kamala takes her leave. Then I say to Sonia didi, 'First you must go to the pump. Wash your face a little. It will make you feel fresher. Drink water also!'

She is being very brave while I am feeling nervous about what we will find when we reach Rajapur bazaar. I am expecting a terrible scene.

We start walking in silence. I think about my duties. It is my duty to help this woman to safety. I like her very much also. It is also my duty to serve my community. I wonder if buses are still running from Kothiyaghat and Sati. I think there may be no buses for some time so it will not be possible for injured people to get to the hospital in Nepalgunj or Lucknow. Perhaps she will be able to walk out to Lucknow. After such a flood, the border authorities will surely let a foreigner cross into India?

After some time she says, 'I've been thinking a lot, while walking back here with Moti—I mean Kamala.' She makes me smile by trying to be so correct all the time. I like that. She continues with a very serious expression on her face, 'I don't know much but I think that food and water will become a big problem.'

'True. All the grain stores will have been destroyed.'

'Yes. So could we prepare and dry the meat of any dead or drowned cattle? This would be one way of starting to dispose of the dead animals.'

I find her opinion most interesting. It is good that she wants to help, but I tell her, 'Meat is a problem in our country. We Brahmins and Chhetris also cannot eat cow. Cow is holy for Hindus but we can eat buffalo except on certain holy days and on the eleventh day after the new moon also. Tharus, they cannot eat cow or buffalo but they like to eat pig very much. We cannot eat pig and Mussalmans cannot eat pig. And for Mussalmans to eat meat it must be killed in a special way. I do not think they may eat drowned animals. Everyone can eat goat and chicken only—except for the vegetarians. They cannot eat any meat or eggs or fish. Mussalmans they kill and prepare meat. They can eat cow and buffalo and goat.'

She is undaunted by these complexities and says, 'Then we need butchers who are Muslims and butchers who are Brahmins. Right?'

'I am sorry but you are incorrect. Brahmins cannot take life.'

'But they are not taking life…'

'You are correct. Tharu people can prepare pig and goat and there are many of these animals on the island. It is Muslims who are often our butchers.' And then I think a little more and say, 'Of course, there are Brahmin cooks who kill chickens…' Our culture is quite complicated. Perhaps this Sonia didi is actually quite intelligent, for a woman. She has quickly got some ideas about our lives.

She interrupts my thoughts. I had forgotten that actually when she is excited she talks too much. She says, 'I had lots of ideas when I was walking. We need to dispose of the dead—people *and* animals. In that way we might be able to stop disease and infection. We need to pull all the dead things out of the waterways: cremate the bodies. Can we do that? Could we organize working parties—to protect the water supplies? I walked by so many carcasses here on the island. They're stinking already.'

Moti

It is good to have found that Brahmin who has been at our house so much. He is the cousin of Ram Krishna but he is not bad like the rest of the family. The gods have made sure that we met. Sonia didi trusts this man. She decides to stay with him. This is easier for me and I continue with Ganga Lal and the two children.

We are passing more and more people as we get close to Rajapur bazaar. There is destruction and mud everywhere we have been but what shocks me is the expressions on people's faces. They wear the awful face of hopelessness.

Ganga Lal has been so attentive and such a hero—*just* like in a Bollywood movie. I am thinking that I could fall in love with someone like him. I wonder what I should say to him. I am just practising something to make him smile when suddenly he takes his leave. My face must show disappointment and surprise because he quickly explains his worries about his family and tells me exactly where his house is 'so that we can meet again soon, bahini.' He shouts, 'Go with good fortune my cousin-sister!' over his shoulder as he strides away. He leaves the lost children with me—of course. I turn towards our house, and encourage the children onwards. They are very tired.

Finally, we arrive. It is not the joyous homecoming I hoped for. My home is empty, apart from the loud American. He looks surprised and then pleased to see me. I do not care about him. I want to know, where is my mother, my father and my brothers and sisters? Are they all dead? I call to my family but there is no one. My heart shrinks into pain and fear.

The American then stands up. He doesn't greet me. He is so rude. He starts talking about himself. In turn I am also rude to him. I interrupt him by asking if he has news of my family.

He has no news. He says nothing to give me comfort. He ignores the children also. How can any person ignore the distress of small children? Has he no heart? I tell the little ones to wait here at the house while I search for my family. I need to find food for them also.

13. EASIER THAN PATCHING JEANS

Sonia

Rekraj was quiet. I hoped he wasn't angry with me—I upset people so easily. I always worry about that. During the hours I'd spent walking the whole length of the island, I had thought and thought about how I could help. I needed to keep my mind busy so that I didn't ruminate on the horrors I'd seen and the new horrors to come. In that way I suppose I was selfish but I was also now desperate to help—somehow.

I had recognized one problem. The countryside had been so changed by the flood, with everything covered in mud, that it was difficult to find your way around. I imagined children—like the little girls we had found, children who had been swept away—wandering lost and distraught and unable to find their way back to their parents.

When I talked to Rekraj about this and suggested raising flags on the mosque and at the temple, he said, 'This is excellent thinking, Sonia didi. Come—let us first go to our holy places and arrange everything.'

We hurried on. Being with him energized me. I was ready to walk with him all through the night if need be. The closer we got to the market, the more people we saw. We dodged between endless streams of villagers. I looked into their faces and wouldn't have guessed they were in the middle of a disaster. Their expressions told me nothing.

It didn't take us long to reach the main temple. I looked up at the flag. Its horizontal dark blue, yellow, green, red, gold and light blue stripes caught the breeze. Rekraj shouted a few orders and, not many minutes later, a man materialized with a huge bamboo and started lashing a green flag to it. Rekraj said something about hoping it wasn't sacrilegious to raise this new flag above Shiva's but the priest was watching and nodded approvingly.

'Putting this Muslim green here in the Hindu temple will be a strange sight for our people. Thus they will come to know something unusual is here and they will be attracted to this meeting place. We will instruct some small child to sound the temple bell and we will speak with the muezzin and suggest he makes announcements also!' Rekraj said enthusiastically.

It struck me that Rekraj had found new inner resources. He had transformed from a quiet, self-effacing man into someone who could be an inspirational leader. People immediately responded to his commands. His authority was recognized. They already knew that he was a good, trustworthy man.

In this small tight-knit community, they must know who is worth following, and who will exploit a situation. Or do caste differences keep everyone at odds whatever happens?

I gazed in admiration at Rekraj whose new-found strength shone out of him. I was in danger of becoming completely besotted, but knew that even if I was reckless enough to tell him how I felt, this wasn't the time or place to make any kind of announcement. And he was still so young—and innocent too, I guessed. I couldn't lead him astray, could I?

'Rekraj dai?'

'Hunchha, Sonia didi?' Suddenly he was looking deep into my eyes. He was looking at me as if he knew exactly what I was thinking. I had to look away. I was blushing like a teenager. I stammered, 'I—I want to go back to see if Guliya is all right—is that okay?'

'Surely. You must go.' He gave my arm an affectionate squeeze and, blushing too, turned to his tasks again. 'I will find you again—at sundown.'

That simple promise made my heart leap. It suddenly felt to me that all the birds around were squawking in celebration.

I found my way back to Guliya's house. The place was empty apart from Herb the American, and the two lost little girls. They were sitting in the dust, holding hands, quiet and wide-eyed. You could see tracking in the dust on their faces where they had been crying. Herb was ignoring those poor scared children.

Then that all-too-familiar feeling of dread struck me. The birds had fallen silent. No dog howled. The hairs stood up at the back of my neck. I was paralysed with fear. Not again—

please! The ground started to shake. I staggered over to the children. I hugged them close to me. We were in a safe place. We were out in the open. Herb was sitting on the verandah. He should have moved. At first he didn't really react. Then he just started crying like a big blubbering baby.

The tremor passed. Dogs started howling and the birds became noisy again. It must have been just like the 'all clear' sounded during the Blitz. How did the animals sense that this was only an aftershock? The children stopped cowering against me and looked about them again. They seemed less frightened. But Herb's crying continued. 'What has happened, Rosemary?' I ask him, feeling I should say something but not a bit interested in what he had to say.

'Can't you skip these crappy jokes?'

'Sorry but I do find Herb such a funny name.'

'Are you mad?'

'Yes, probably—a little— after what I've seen today.'

I thought of telling him about struggling to untangle the body of that woman from the tree and how difficult it had been to roll her into the river. I could still smell something of her on my hands. With a shudder, I also recalled that feeling of softness underfoot when I trod on a half-buried body. I didn't say anything because he could have seen worse. So many had died on the island that day.

Wearily, I stood up and asked him, 'What has happened to *you?* Are you hurt?'

'No,' Herb replied, tight-lipped.

'Have you lost a loved one?'

'No.'

'You must have seen some horrible things?'

'No, no, no!'

'What, then?'

'Why the inquisition?'

'I was concerned. I wondered why you were crying. I thought I was showing a little compassion…'

He blurted out, 'My notes are gone!'

'Your notes!' I spluttered. 'What do you mean—your notes?'

'My work is lost. Everything I've done here. I'm trapped

here. Everyone says there are no ferries. There's no food. There will be epidemics. There's no escape. I don't want to die here.' He looked as if he was going to cry again.

I wanted to pull him up by his lapels. I wanted to slap him as hard as I could but, of course, I didn't do that. Instead, I burst out, 'You selfish bastard! How can you sit there feeling sorry for yourself when you are surrounded by people who have lost everything? *Everything!*'

'*I've* lost everything too!'

'You've only been here a *month!*'

He started crying again. Pathetic creature. I wanted to say I was glad his work was flushed away. I longed to slap some sense into him but I wanted to find Guliya and the rest of the family more. Had they all survived? Where could they be? Maybe at the temple?

'You could swim across river!' I suggested sarcastically. He looked at me again as if he knew I was mad, but that just made me smile. 'First though, you *could* try to cheer up those scared kids.' I threw that last remark back over my shoulder as I walked away. I felt bad about deserting the kids yet again.

'I don't know anything about kids,' Herb whined.

'No time like the present. High time you learned!' I shouted back.

The main street was a sea of bewildered, shattered people; it was hard navigating through this human tide. I passed a long queue of battered people, waiting—patiently—to see one of the so-called doctors: Dr B-something; I could never remember these Nepali names! There he was, sitting out in the sunshine, treating and tending and plastering and dressing. It must be wonderful having those skills, so that people trust you like that. He had a smug smile on his face and I could see that he was an untroubled sort of guy. I don't suppose he had seen much hardship or suffering in his life. He'd be well paid too, I guessed, though I saw no money changing hands.

I was dragged from my contemplations by bumping into a numb-looking woman. She recoiled from me as if I was a leper. That upset me. Rekraj had explained to me once that some villagers thought I was a witch because I was white. I walked on, dodging between all the expressionless people. All the while I was wondering if I'd be able to help, just a little.

Then I spotted her.

She walked like all the life had been sucked out of her. She was carrying Kancha on her hip but he was limp as a rag doll. I hoped he was only asleep. Guliya's head was bowed low and her free arm dangled lifelessly too. I called to her. She didn't react. I ran up and took her in my arms. She was wooden in my embrace but there was warmth in the baby's body.

I said, 'Moti ramro chha.' I smiled and nodded and gave her a thumbs up sign. I hoped she wouldn't misinterpret it. I hoped she understood that I knew Moti was all right. Guliya looked blankly at me. 'Atti, Siru giyo—moriyo.'

'Oh no; they can't be dead,' I choked.

'Meero siriman, punni.'

'Not your husband too!'

She started to cry, silently. I hugged her again. We sobbed all over each other. Kancha stirred, thank God.

I wanted to tell her that her other children could still be alive but I couldn't communicate that much in Nepali. Maybe she knew somehow that they had drowned. My heart overflowed for this poor lovely, loving woman.

I don't know how long we stood there for but the next thing I registered was a shout—in English, 'Hey! Sonia! Is that you?'

I turned to see Paul, the aging hippy who had so charmed me on the bus, half a lifetime ago. I sniffed and wiped away tears with the back of my hand.

'Hey!' I felt ill and dizzy and dazed. He was clearly delighted to see me. I should have been pleased to see him too. He seemed like a nice guy. I liked him. After all, he spoke English!

'Hey,' I repeated, sniffing again. 'I never expected to see you again—let alone here in the middle of all this!' I sniffed louder and tried again to wipe away the snot and tears. I started to introduce Guliya but she was already walking away.

'No. Yes. Mmm. Our karmas must be linked. It is all ordained you know,' he grinned.

'Really? I'm not sure...' I said.

'Hey, hey. Don't worry—I'm not getting heavy on you. Are you all right?'

'I'm okay, but that lovely woman is the person I've been staying with here, and two of her youngest children are dead...and her husband too. They were obviously so much in love. I wish I could have said more, given her some words of comfort.'

'I reckon your tears said much more than words,' Paul solemnly looked down at me. 'Christ, this is a mess but I'm *really* pleased to see you! You look great! I'm impressed you are coping with all this.'

'Well...' I couldn't believe that someone like him was impressed with me!

'I think "mess" is a bit of an understatement,' I said. Then I suddenly felt prudish—school-teacherly—correcting his take on the disaster like that. Lighten up, Sonia, I told myself. I asked him, 'How on earth did you get here?'

'I told you I was going fishing—I hitched a ride on one of those bloody great mahseers I told you about.' He was kind of laughing, trying to make a joke but realized it wasn't working. 'No, look, I'll tell you all about it one day but I need something to drink. Is there anywhere I can get some water?'

I pointed to a hand-pump in a Brahmin's compound.

'Can I just help myself?' He suddenly looked uncertain and lost. That surprised me. He'd seemed so self-assured before.

'It'll be okay—as long as you don't put your lips to the spout.'

Once he'd quenched his thirst and pumped water over his head he said, 'Now...is food a possibility?'

'That,' I said, 'is going to be a bit more challenging.' Then my previous idea came back to me and I said, 'I'm sure a gregarious guy like you can help get things organized! You can speak a bit of Nepali, right?'

'Yeah, well I've learned a few words. *Om mani padme hum*...nah, but that's probably Tibetan, isn't it?'

'I think so.'

'I know "ow" means come, "jow" means go, "cow" means eat and "pee" means drink...which is mighty confusing...'

Even amidst all this grief and chaos he was making me laugh!

'That's great!' I said to him. 'All you need to do is put "nuss" on the end of the words and you'd even sound passably polite!'

'Okay teacher!' he chuckled.

'So...how are you on spit-roasts?' I challenged him. 'We all need to eat something after everything that's happened.'

He raised a questioning eyebrow and then realization spread across his face. 'Ah, now *that's* worth talking about!' He rubbed his hands together in blissful anticipation. 'Yeah, it sounds like it's time for a campfire. Do you fancy goat or beef steak?'

'Anything!' I said. 'I've heard snake is quite tasty! You know, I think I'd even manage rat as long as it was cooked properly. But who knows what the locals will eat...'

'Yeah, yeah, but remember Nepalis are pragmatists. I'll call it deer meat, then most of them won't mind.' He laughed again—infectiously.

Moti

The bazaar is full of people wandering blindly here and there. It makes walking slow. Where will I find food in all this chaos? My belly is empty and the foundling children are faint with hunger. I walk out towards the rice mill. Surely I will find some rice at the mill? After some time, I arrive at the big iron gates.

I am surprised that there is a lot of damage to this pukka building. There must have been too much cement stolen at the time it was made. It is leaning at a strange angle. I squeeze between the distorted gates and push open the big main door. It creaks. There are other creaks from elsewhere in the building. As my eyes adjust to the darkness inside, I see that all the full sacks of rice have already been taken. There are scuffs and tracks in the dust where people have dragged sacks away. Little is left but a small amount of grain that has spilt onto the floor. I go inside. I find an empty sack. I squat down and start to pick up rice, grain by grain.

I am absorbed in this task. It takes time to pick up rice in this way but I'm getting a small pile—enough already for a meal for one, so far. The building is creaking like an unoiled buffalo-cart. Then there is an odd sound. Someone is behind me. I turn to see who is there in the doorway. The light is behind him so I cannot make out who it is. Dust floats down. The creaking sounds become louder. Things are moving overhead. There is a terrific noise. Timbers are falling. Something hits me. Everything is black.

Bom Bahadur

I am making my way back to the main temple with the tailor and I am having one idea after another—lots of excellent ideas. But then my plans and contemplations are interrupted by someone catching hold of my arm. It is Dhan Sing. He is asking about Kamala again. I have no news for him. I ask him once more to help us. He says that he cannot. Useless fellow. Another thing is that I haven't seen the police. What can they be doing? They have a few motorbikes and radios but there is no sign of them, nor the army. Where are these people? Have they fled?

Perhaps instead we must utilize the traditional midwife. She is low caste. She deals with polluting things. She is a woman also so it may cause too much trouble to involve her—although I know she would be calm and competent. It is an uncomfortable thing to say but sometimes I believe our caste system is a handicap to our nation. I have been to training courses that talked about empowerment and community mobilization. This is what we need here, but it is difficult to get all the elements of our community to work together nicely. Muslims can't work with what they call infidels. High caste will not work with low and women cannot work with men.

Actually, Brahmins are the worst; they do not want to work with anybody. Not that they ever do any real work. And the Brahmin landlords of Rajapur mostly seem angry with each other—all the time. They are busy with their squabbles over water and with their political agendas. It is all too, too difficult. The ear doctor might be of use though, and certainly the tooth-puller, perhaps the barbers also. These are people that everyone needs to use—from time to time. They will be tolerated. Truly we have many skilled people in our little community—even if some of them lack the correct qualifications! It is up to me to mobilize them all!

I am musing like this when I spot her. I am pleased to see her again.

'Ah, Sonia didi, I am happy to find you in good health!' She is not alone. She is walking with another foreigner: an interesting-looking man with a cheerful face. I turn to him and say, 'And I am thinking that this is your husband only, Sonia Madam?'

She looks shocked and says, 'No, Mr Bom Bahadur. We met on the bus journey here. He is just an acquaintance!'

I am pleased that the memsahib can remember my full name now. I am amused also to see this new foreigner protest but with laughter in his eyes.

'Ah, Sonia—you stabbed me in the heart! Am I really only an acquaintance?'

They are both laughing. They are easy in each other's company. While they are laughing I have one more clever idea.

I say, 'May I make so bold as to ask if I can put you to work, Sonia didi? And your—err—friend also perhaps?'

'Sorry, Mr Bom Bahadur, where are my manners? This is Paul.'

'Good to meet you, mate!' this man Paul says as he shakes me warmly by the hand, 'and thanks for the offer, but nah, I'm off to set up a barbeque!' And he walks away, rubbing his hands together and chuckling. He seems like such a happy, carefree chap. He is giving a good example to those who are suffering this day.

Sonia didi looks back towards me as if she is seeking my guidance and leadership. I can provide this service for her. We walk together back to the temple. Soon I have organized an orderly British army-style queue. The tailor and Sonia didi are soon doing a good job of cleaning and stitching wounds and lacerations.

Sonia

I couldn't believe it when Bom Bahadur said he was going to turn me into a doctor. When he explained about stitching, I thought, 'No way,' and the conversation jolted me back in time to when that spotty young doctor in England stitched up my forehead after the cat attacked me. It had been awful, watching him coming towards me with a big syringe and thread. But after ruminating endlessly about that awful night, it was a relief to realize that I hadn't actually thought about it for ages. That bit of my life might be behind me at long last.

I decided, on the spot, that I would make up a really good story about how I got my scar—should it be a tiger, or a leopard or a crocodile, or leaping into a snake pit to save some guy?

Coming back, I worried now that all the blood and gore I would see might make me vomit. It didn't. But then why should it upset me? I was used to cleaning grazed knees in my teaching days and had even coped with a broken arm when a child fell off the climbing frame. Soon, I was so intent on what Bom Bahadur said I needed to do that I forgot I couldn't cope. He was a good teacher too. He made me feel competent.

Bom Bahadur showed me how to clean gashes by pouring water into them. He said we had to make sure nothing was left in any wound, otherwise it would never heal. He taught me to probe—ever so gently—to make sure. He showed me how to stab the needle a centimetre or so deep into the skin—he said it hurt less if you plunged it in quickly—then I had to pull it through from underneath on the far side of the wound so that the edges came together. I was surprised how strong and thick skin is and how deep the needle needed to go. Then he taught me about compression bandaging—to stop any bleeding. It wasn't long before I was operating solo.

I was so absorbed in the stitching and on tying the knots and trying to distract my patients from their pain that I'm embarrassed to admit that I began to enjoy what I was doing. I was surprised at myself. I was doing something really important—for the first time in a very long time! I was really helping. I was useful. Actually, I think I probably stopped several people from bleeding to death.

The cringing low-caste tailor whom Bom Bahadur had also turned into a surgeon was similarly delighted with what he was doing. And our stitching was neat—neater than the doctor in Cambridge had done on me!

But it was hard not to inflict further pain on these injured people. Not that you would know that they were suffering from the way they reacted. They were so stoical and uncomplaining. I suppose they had to be. What else could they do? What else could we do? We had no anaesthetic. I just tried to get the job done as quickly and neatly as possible.

Sometimes the probing took a lot of time and I was astonished at what and how much was inside some wounds. I picked out pieces of glass, plastic, broken bangles, corrugated iron or other bits of metal. One man came wincing in pain from a small cut in the palm of his hand. I was puzzled at the way such a small wound seemed to be distressing him so much until my probing tweezers hit something hard and I pulled out a great wedge of wood. I nearly vomited as it emerged. As he and I recovered, a woman I didn't know slapped me on the back and cackled a congratulatory, 'Shabash, Memsahib!'

Meanwhile, patients arrived on foot, family members carried some, others came in wheelbarrows, in buffalo-carts, on bicycles, on horseback: a steady stream of human suffering. After we'd been stitching for an hour or so, Bom Bahadur returned. He looked pleased with himself.

'Ah, Sonia Madam, I see that you are nicely settled into your work...Look! I have found another volunteer.' This wizened little man was about half the regimental sergeant-major's body weight. He cowered, knowing that the soldier was quite mad and might shortly eat him. This new 'volunteer' was an ice-cream salesman who wore a kind of beaten-up aluminium box on his back.

Issuing sharp orders all the while, Bom Bahadur got the nervous little salesman to remove the metal backpack. His eyes went up to the temple flag, perhaps in an appeal to his gods, and I saw that Rekraj's green flag had been replaced with a large white sheet with a big red cross painted on it.

The two men squatted down and started mixing nasty-looking chemicals which didn't smell good. They steamed—threateningly. Bom Bahadur explained as he worked that this device was used to make ice, using the cooling properties of ammonia—that was the awful stink. We had no anaesthetic but he thought that by applying ice to people's wounds, we should be able to stitch painlessly. I was incredulous at first but it really did work. I saw fewer silent tears thenceforth.

The queue of people waiting for us was endless. I didn't have time to wonder how long we could keep going. I realized—with some satisfaction—that I was getting really confident though. I stitched each person much faster now. I was becoming especially good at getting the raggedy skin edges together properly.

The human body is much more forgiving than the average needlework project. Suturing was actually—surprisingly—much easier than patching jeans. Skin came together much easier than worn cloth. The body seemed to kind of know how it went back together again, and the stickiness of the congealing blood helped everything stay where it should.

By now, Bom Bahadur had organized a team of women to wash all the wounds before we attended to them. This made us faster and more efficient, most of the time, although sometimes the women argued about who needed to be stitched next.

There was no question about one victim though. He was ushered towards me by three of the helpers. He staggered, dragging one leg. He was obviously in a lot of pain. Sweat streamed off his face. His main wound was in his buttock. Blood trickled from it. I felt around with my fingers. This made the man cry out, yet the wound didn't look that bad or deep. I probed gently inside the bloody gash. My probe went deep. It hit metal. We applied some sulphurous ice to cool the area. Gently I felt inside with my fingers. More muffled complaints. One of my fingers closed around a metal rod. I felt some kind of handle. The man cried out again as I started to try to move the object. I knew I had to just pull—and pull hard. He screamed. I gagged as I hauled out a complete door latch. There was blood spurting everywhere. I needed to apply pressure but I could see that my patient immediately felt better. The blood flow slowed remarkably quickly too.

He became quite relaxed and started chatting to one of the lady helpers as I stitched him up! The women seemed to be amused rather than shocked by what was happening and it was obvious from the gesticulations that they were now teasing the man for having a door in his backside. Even children joined in the hilarity. They performed a kind of mime of the whole thing and made the man laugh. Meanwhile I was still thinking, how can you lose something of that size inside someone's flesh?

Once I'd finished stitching his wound and done my best to apply a compression bandage, he hobbled away, proudly waving his bloody door latch. How I wanted to hear his story…but I just had to imagine the forces he had survived in that awful death-wave.

We soon developed a routine. Our patients were washed. The tailor and I stitched. Women leaned over us and offered advice. We probed. We stitched. The ice-cream man mixed his potions. Women kept us supplied with thread—and patients. They sang too.

It looked as if patients would never stop coming. Despite all the chaos though, things seemed to happen when they needed to happen. Children played around us. Rekraj and others like him were busy in the background, helping as many people as possible. Eventually, I realized that the casualties who obviously had broken bones were being redirected to Dr Bhandari or Dr Dash. Present everywhere, there was patience, not panic, and everyone seemed to be contributing as much as they were able.

Someone had organized a kind of crèche in another corner of the temple compound and from there came sounds of contented and not-so-contented tiny voices. I had confidence about Bom Bahadur's managerial skills but I did begin to wonder what we would do when the light failed. I didn't have time to think or wonder much though. I needed to concentrate on my work.

After a while came an incongruous vision of a tall, imposing old man walking towards us across the temple courtyard. He was dressed in a beautifully pressed white shirt and sarong. His white hair was tied into a neat bun. In one hand he carried a paraffin pressure lamp and in the other, a stripy plastic shopping bag. He approached me, bowed slightly and offered me a solemn greeting. Then he said, 'I am Ayurvedic doctor, Madam, and I am bringing some useful herbs. This one you must break and bruise and apply to wounds that are bleeding too much. It will halt the bleeding. There will be less pain also.'

Then he simply left the lamp and the shopping bag next to me, bowed again and walked away. I watched him go, wondering, albeit briefly, if I should have said or done something. But there was still an enormous queue of people to treat. I looked inside the bag. It was full of scruffy little bits of weeds—of the sort you'd pull out of any herbaceous border. Encouraged by the gesticulations of my helpers, I tried scrunching up the not-very-special-looking plants and applied them as a kind of poultice. It did—miraculously—stop the bleeding and that made it much easier for me to see what I was stitching. Wounds also needed fewer stitches and so now I inflicted less pain.

We'd been stitching for what seemed like hours when a small boy ran towards me. He pushed between the casualties. I wondered why no one had told him to wait in line properly, until he presented the tailor and me with two sizzling hot steaks on a banana leaf.

The boy said, 'Paul Sahib pakkayekko!' And then he danced away, chanting. 'Paul Sahib, Paul Sahib!'

I looked up above the roofs of the temple courtyard, saw smoke and smiled. The gregarious and multi-talented ex-hippy must have managed to organize another bunch of people. I suppose they had all you needed to butcher the drowned animals. They'd got a fire going and were working on the barbeque of a lifetime.

I stood, stretched and walked over to the hand-pump to sluice my patients' blood off my hands. I turned to see that the tailor was already eating his slab of meat with great enthusiasm. He hadn't even bothered to wash first.

Maybe in Britain we are over-obsessed with hygiene. I

smiled to myself as I sank my teeth into the best beefsteak I'd ever tasted.

Rekraj

I had been uncertain how people would react to me myself only taking charge. I almost expected some of the Tharus to use this opportunity to resist Brahmin authority but people welcome my orders and instructions. Many of them continue to behave like lost sheep.

While I have been working with all members of our community, I have been thinking. I see the suffering on all their faces. One Brahmin doctor friend of mine—a clever fellow, I thought he was—told me that low-caste people do not feel pain in the same way that we Brahmins do. It is true that low castes do not complain but maybe that is because they cannot. It is my idea that in this way this doctor keeps aloof from the people who suffer most. Actually, we should show the lower castes some respect. Sometimes I feel ashamed of my people; we can be unkind. Actually, that makes me think about my big-shot cousin from Kathmandu. He acts like some great philanthropist but where is he these days? Why has he not come to help with the rescue work? This is his community, after all. He should be here but I know he will not come now.

My cousin isn't here but that outsider Bom Bahadur Gurung has been calm and has managed so many things through all of this. I know him to be an excellent fellow. His authority comes from his experience as a soldier. I hear men joke that even his moustache is fierce and frightening but he has already done a lot to help. He has even trained Sonia didi so that she is carrying out the duties of a Health Assistant! She also is a fine example in these difficult times.

I must speak to her about how she could leave the island now. It is possible that buses are running close by. It might take her one day to walk to the road-head and it would not be easy, but one of my countrymen would be sure to help her. I am full of admiration for her. I have feelings for her also. It is my duty to look after her. She should go home—to where she will be safe. I am uncertain of what to do. I am nervous of telling her. I do not want her to leave, but now is not the time to speak about my feelings and what I want.

It is fortunate that the Tharus have all the skills that are necessary to survive in this godforsaken situation. All the boats have been washed away so we cannot get the injured off the island. I am arranging several work-parties—they are putting up shelters. Many homes have been destroyed and we need shelters to shade the injured from the sun, shelters for field hospitals, shelters to store any food that isn't already spoilt, shelters for orphanages, shelters to cook under. These simple people are so skilful at this kind of much-needed work. I sent one small work-party to build a shelter near the river, near where Paul Sahib is making a party of butchering and cooking so much meat. He seems to have good organizational skills. He can make people laugh also. I helped him put up green flags where Muslims can eat, orange flags where Brahmins can eat and blue flags where Tharus can eat, and everyone is looking a little happier. Actually, I am surprised that this hippy-type is acting responsibly. He is a good man also. I have heard him talk about karma and I realize he knows about the important things in life.

There is one new problem. These activities so close to the river are attracting dogs and jackals and crocodiles and vultures also. It is good that some Brahmins are starting to arrange funeral pyres. They are beginning thé prayers and the Tharus are gathering wood.

Guliya

I am wandering in the bazaar for hour upon hour. People are walking back and forward, here and there, hither and thither. There are so many people looking for their loved ones. That Newar man who wants to marry Moti, he stops me. He asks if I have news of her. I have nothing to give him, not one word. He starts to talk of his marriage plans. How can he think of his wedding at a time like this? The disaster must have sent him mad but what can anyone do? I do not care about him. He is not of my family. He is not of my caste. I turn away and see another buffalo-cart filled with children. Some of them are crying. Mostly, they are quiet. The driver stops outside the Shiva temple. These are lost children but mine are not amongst them. How will they find their parents in all this chaos? Maybe Shitala can bring my children back to me. I will go to her shrine in the temple of Saraswati. But what offering is suitable for such important and powerful goddesses? What can I possibly give?

Sonia

Life assumed a routine of working all day, sleeping a little—work, sleep, work, sleep. The meat started to taste very strange—it was beyond 'gamey'. I'd lost track of time. I wondered when any kind of rescue effort would reach us. Surely the army had helicopters? Where were the British Gurkhas? Surely aid agencies knew we were in trouble? Why did no one come?

I hadn't counted the number of days that had passed since the wave, but tiny green shoots were poking through the mud here and there. Already the cycle of life was replenishing itself, nourished by the debris of disaster.

It had been a long time since I'd seen Moti. I wondered what had become of her. I wondered if she had found her mother. It suddenly struck me that some accident might have taken her. It would be so easy for a tree to fall on someone, or there was the daily possibility of a snake-bite, or an attack by a pack of those half-wild dogs.

I asked Bom Bahadur who might know. 'You must not worry, bahini. Moti is a clever and resourceful woman. She will come back after some time.' He had other things on his mind. He marshalled the casualties. He organized them by priority so that the wounds were steadily getting less horrifying—but more mucky and infected. Some were positively smelly. My team of wound-washers stayed busy. They were bossy and issued what sounded like sharp orders to the patients. 'Ow-ow,' they'd shout then, they would say gently, 'Slowly, brother—the memsahib will heal you soon.'

They had collected more miraculous Ayurvedic herbs too. The Ayurvedic doctor had brought other remedies; he said that they would control infection. I hoped and prayed he knew what he was doing. Meanwhile we probed. We cleaned.

We stitched. Paul and his team of bloodied butchers joined us when we collapsed into exhausted sleep in the temple courtyard.

Then we'd wake with the dawn. We stitched. We even occasionally washed ourselves under the hand-pump, beside the beautiful richly scented jasmine. I'd often catch wafts of its perfume even while I was stitching. I thought about Rekraj a lot, and looked forward to snatching time with him. We were both so busy though, our meetings were always much too short.

14. ANY GOD WHO MIGHT BE LISTENING

Guliya

I have cut my hair. I will fast until I see them again. This is what I have vowed. I will pray at the shrine to Shitala until they come back to me. If I pass on to the next incarnation before I see them again, then so be it. The priest gives me sugar-water once in a day; he says that someone brings it for me daily. He does not say who. It is not that young Brahmin, although he visits often and tries to persuade me to eat—for the sake of the baby. He tells me to go home. I have no home while I have no children. I will stay. I will pray. Maybe my husband will find me here also—if he is alive. It is my idea that he is dead.

Sonia

A while back, Rekraj called me away from my work. He said he had something important to say to me. He led me to a secluded corner of the temple. I was mystified. What could be so important or private between us? I knew what I wanted him to announce but I also knew that couldn't be the message he would deliver. He stood in front of me, suddenly looking almost childlike in his shyness. He made a pretty speech about how honoured he'd been to work with me, how much I'd helped his people and his community and how he was full of gratitude and admiration, but...

I knew that his charming speech would come to a 'but'...

'Now, finally, Sonia didi, it is possible for you to leave. A few new dugouts have been carved from fallen simal trees. Buses have started running once more. A few are leaving from just across the river at Sati. More are leaving from Kothiyaghat. And so I can arrange that you get one bus to take you to Kathmandu—and home.'

He stood in front of me looking guilty and embarrassed.

I asked, 'Would it be best if I left Rajapur?

He gave that annoying non-reply, 'It is as you like, Sonia didi.'

'Please, Rekraj! Tell me—am I a burden?'

'It is my duty to keep you safe from all harm, didi.'

'But tell me honestly, Rekraj dai, am I becoming a burden—an extra mouth to feed?'

'Most certainly not, didi!'

His eyes said that he spoke from his heart. I could restrain myself no longer. I was done with clumsy stilted English. I took a step towards him, slung my arms around his neck and kissed him.

He pulled away from me. He looked at first shocked, then confused.

I felt dreadful. I'd gone too far.

He frowned and stutteringly said, 'It would be better...'

'...and it would make me very happy if you, Sonia didi, would stay for some time longer with us—with me.' He was smiling broadly now. His eyes had welled up and he held his hand against his lips as if to keep the kiss there a little longer. 'We must return to our duties, Sonia didi. Later we will be together only.' As he turned and walked away, my hand went from my lips to my amulet. I mumbled the grateful words *'Katti bajay heh'* to any god who might be listening.

Guliya

I am weak. I am not seeing clearly. It is good that the bazaar—and the world—is far from me now. I think about when I was young. I think about my children. I focus on an insect that is struggling through the thick green grass here in the temple compound. Poor thing. It is so tiny and it has to work so hard to get nowhere. This must be how the gods see us. Perhaps we are their playthings.

Sonia

I'd been doing this work for so many days that some of my first patients had come back to show me how well my handiwork was healing. They embarrassed me by touching my feet, but it was so uplifting to know that what I had done for them was worthwhile. I had helped—just a little.

One day—a day like any other—when I knew I'd been stitching all my life, I registered an unfamiliar noise. It was deep and continuous. After so many days, this new sound was worrying. My first thought was that it must be another wave, although strangely this time I wasn't particularly frightened, not at first. I was fatalistic. It wouldn't really matter if I died this day.

The people around me had heard the sound too. A few looked scared but no one was running. Most were talking excitedly about the sound. Some pointed to the sky. Kids started running around pretending to be aeroplanes. They started playing war games too. They pretended to shoot each other and some fell down and feigned death. How could they play dead here, and after all the deaths there had been?

I felt the nasty familiar sensation of panic starting in my stomach and rising to my throat...this was a feeling I never thought I'd have again, not after all that had happened. I wondered where Paul was. If he was still down by the river, would he stay safe?

Then at last I recognized the noise. It was the sound of a chopper, or maybe two helicopters. Soldiers must have arrived to help. My heart slowed again. I went back to my stitching. My sense of duty to these people overcame my curiosity. I couldn't just get up and leave a patient with a needle still sticking out of his leg, now could I? I reasoned though that if most of my patients had now gone to see the choppers, then surely I too, could take a quick look.

I didn't need to though. Just then, a soldier walked into the temple courtyard. He did a cursory genuflection, looked around and left. He was a British Gurkha. This was good news. They would organize everything. They could talk to the locals. Thank goodness.

I was quickly absorbed again in my work, trying to stitch a particularly jagged rip in a man's thigh. He joked with the tailor—at my expense, I suspect—while I was stitching him. These people are astonishingly stoical. I'll never get over that.

Suddenly I became aware of an American voice—an unfamiliar American voice. A TV camera was pointing at me. Some journalist-type was talking about the woman who was living in a real episode of *ER*—in Nepal. He seemed to be talking about me! Damn him. My tongue was sticking out with concentration. He was distracting me from getting an awkward corner—a bit of skin on this thigh—back into the shape it was supposed to be.

He shoved a microphone in my face.

'Please! I can't see to operate if you do that. Can't you see I'm *busy*!' I spat. 'Just wait a minute, won't you!'

The reporter held up his hands in surrender and stepped back. I ignored him until I'd finished and had sloshed water over my needlework. I looked up to see the reporter examining his fingernails and picking dirt out from under them. He pulled out a little bottle of hand-sanitizer and rubbed some in between his fingers. He looked at his Rolex.

My patient then got up and despite the huge gash in his leg, stooped low and touched my feet. I *do* wish they'd stop doing that. It seems so humiliating for them. I was particularly embarrassed to see that the gesture had been caught on film.

I stretched my back. Stood. Stretched the rest of me, and suddenly felt exhausted. I walked the familiar five paces to the hand-pump, washed my hands and bloodied forearms. I rinsed my face and took a long, delicious drink.

I turned back to the reporter and asked, 'Now. What was it you wanted?'

'Is there any mineral water around?'

He was holding an empty bottle. Did this idiot really expect to find mineral water here?

'Water, you said? As you can see—it's in the pump…'

'Is it safe?' he asked with a deep frown.

'Maybe. There isn't anything else, and I'm drinking it, aren't I?'

He pulled a face and said, 'Yeah, but you're probably immune by now, what with working shoulder to shoulder with the locals and stuff.'

What an interesting thought. Me with my stressed immune system and unacclimatized body? Even amongst all this trauma and infection, I had actually found that my work had been a terrifically powerful tonic. I got to the end of each day feeling tremendously tired, but all my sensitivities and allergies and unhealthy feelings had melted away.

Maybe it is the work. Maybe it is Rekraj. He and I always eat together and I am totally and absolutely in love with him—in a platonic way, of course. Though that kiss wasn't exactly platonic. What a contrast there was between his manners and considerateness and this uncouth journalist. I simply couldn't be bothered to explain to him about the water. I just looked at him. I was profoundly wearied by this man. He reminded me of my husband, my ex-husband. How did he not see all the suffering that was going on all around him?

He said, 'Never mind. I'll skip the drink. Look, can I just ask you a few questions?'

'Okay.'

'I'll start with a little intro. What's your name, by the way?'

I told him. He smoothed his voice for the camera and began, 'I am here on Rajaypore Island, Nepaul, minutes after being choppered in, courtesy of the British Gurkha regiment. Here, I have the privilege to encounter Ms Sonia Swayne, housewife from Cambridge, England, who has single-handedly set up this field hospital and is administering the only medical treatment in the whole region. Tell us, Sonia, how you came to be here. How you had the confidence to take charge.' I was irritated that he had described me as a housewife but stifled the urge to argue the point.

'I came for a complete break—to escape problems at home…an unfaithful husband, trouble at work, that kind of thing. It is laughable really, isn't it, given where I am now, and what's happened?' He didn't look amused, let alone interested. I continued, 'And about taking charge—I'm a schoolteacher, after all, and used to multi-tasking. But you mustn't make me out to be a hero. I haven't done much. I am nothing—just a tourist really. You should interview the locals. It is these people who are brave and resourceful. Talk to Sergeant-Major Bom Bahadur Gurung! It is he who set up this clinic here. And Mr Rekraj Dixit got teams together to build shelters for the homeless and arranged meeting points for families who have been separated. And Paul...gosh, I don't even know his surname...he's been helping to organize food and cremations and burials and such. There are others doing tremendous things for the injured too. Dr Bhandari and Dr Dash, they're also busy treating the worst wounds and plastering broken limbs and administering anti-venom to all the snake-bite victims. These are the heroes. Not me.'

The journalist had completely lost interest. He was waving his hands at the cameraman, gesturing throat-cutting to indicate he should stop filming.

'Look, sweetie, I want to hear *your* story,' he said, making camera-rolling gestures again. 'How did you find out what had happened?'

'What? Oh, I saw the wave actually. It was awe-inspiring—totally unstoppable.'

'So what caused it?'

'It was probably a Glacial Lake Outburst Flood. Whatever, the Karnali—or the river further into the mountains, the Bheri most probably—must have been blocked, maybe by a landslide. Then the water would have backed up, and by the time the blockage collapsed, there would have been a huge amount of water collected. When such a temporary lake is liberated all at once, the result is disaster. Locals know all about these events and can explain it better than I can. Look, let me find Rekraj Dixit and Bom Bahadur Gurung for you—they'll make much more interesting interviewees!'

'Nah, thanks, sweetie. You *are* kind but I don't expect I'd understand them. Let me just take some more footage of you working.' He waved meaningfully once again at the cameraman as he walked away. He seemed to be mumbling complaints about the climate and lack of water or something similar. I hated him.

I went back to work. I had more important things to concern me. I yearned for news of Guliya and the children. I so wanted to set eyes on Moti again. I beckoned my next patient over. I didn't like the camera following my every move but what the hell—I had work to do. I gestured for my patient to sit down. He had a horrible gash on his shoulder that would take me some time to stitch back into the proper shape. Actually I was looking forward to the challenge of this one. I started by filling a jug from the pump and poured lots of water into the wound to wash away the clotted blood. I pulled out a good-sized piece of wood. He hardly winced at all, though I knew I'd hurt him. I was aware that they were still filming but I became absorbed in the operation, chanting inwardly my comforting mantra, *'Katti bajay heh.'* I really, really needed to find out what it meant.

A while later, I looked up to move a crick in my neck and realized that the cameraman had gone. I was thankful for that. Someone else, a soldier this time, was walking towards me now. He was white-skinned, smiling, and was holding out a bar of Cadbury's chocolate. My mouth watered just looking at the purple wrapper.

'Wow! This is impressive.' His upper-class English was strangely heart-warming. 'How long have you been doing this for?'

I paused to wipe sweat from my brow with my bloodied forearm. 'I dunno. Two or three weeks. I've rather lost track.' I couldn't take my eyes off the chocolate bar.

'I'll bet you have. And sorry—I mustn't tease—take the chocolate!'

'May I?' Unceremoniously, I took the chocolate and bit off a third of the bar. I put my hand over my mouth and started to giggle as that wonderful taste exploded into my mouth. I probably dribbled a bit. He was still talking but I heard nothing.

I let out a muffled apology. 'Sorry. Mmm...this is unbelievable.' I bit off another inelegant mouthful. 'Mmm, this is so good.'

He was laughing now. 'You know I'm enjoying watching you eat that more than if I'd eaten it myself!'

'Sorry. Mmm. Thank you. You're a gentleman! But what were you saying?'

'I said that the main quake was thirteen days ago but we've only just heard about the wave. Sorry we've taken so long to get here!'

'So the flood wasn't from a glacial lake then?'

'My—how impressive...lady-surgeon *and* geomorphologist! Sorry—that sounded patronizing but, as a matter of fact, no one knows. So far, no one's gone up into the mountains to take a look, so there are several theories. Maybe they'll work it out from satellite images eventually, but at the moment the boffs are undecided. Most people seem to be saying that a quake caused a landslide that blocked the river, until it overflowed—then woosh…'

As he talked, I wiped my nose on my sleeve. Then self-consciously said, 'Ooops—sorry! Standards have slipped!'

He laughed, 'I'll let you off! Actually you look wrecked. C'mon, I think it would be all right to take break and have a bite. Our medics are setting up and will be taking over very soon. Come and join us in the Mess Tent in an hour!'

I caught a waft of jasmine. A gentle sprinkle of cooling rain was descending upon us. It was delicious. It felt like a benediction. My patient turned his face up to heaven too—and smiled—despite what I was doing to him.

A rainbow appeared. I knew we were both thinking about how the rain and the sun are life-giving and how Rajapur would recover. The rice crop next monsoon would fill the bellies of the 100,000 people living on the island. It will be like reincarnation really.

Across the temple courtyard, the line of people waiting for my attention was still very, very long but they waited—squatting mostly—with complete patience, like they were simply queuing for the bus. I realized with a bit of a start that Rekraj had arrived and was standing close, looking at me. He looked concerned. I leapt up and restrained myself from hugging him, though every time I saw him now I longed to hold him. Instead, I smiled at him, and then put on a mock serious face. 'Rekraj bhai, how long have you been watching me for?'

He just smiled his gorgeous smile.

'Look, will you please—once and for all—answer a very important question for me?'

'Ask anything, Sonia didi!'

'You don't really mean that, Rekraj!' I said mischievously, flirtatiously. He smiled even more broadly, if that was possible. I continued, 'Look, I need to know the meaning of this phrase, "*Katti bajay heh*".'

'Ah, Sonia didi, you are no longer speaking like bideshi. Your pronunciation is excellent but now you are sounding like an Indian!'

'Is that an insult or a compliment?'

'An unintentional insult. Forgive me,' he laughed.

'Forgiven, but *please* tell me what it means, Rekraj!'

'It means "What is the time?", only!'

I started to laugh. The myth was exploded. The mantra that had kept me sane meant 'what's the time?'! Only that. I laughed until the tears streamed, while poor Rekraj looked more and more concerned. I made an excuse to go to the pump and wash my face and the blood off my hands. I pulled myself together and decided I must also ask him about my amulet, although I was a little nervous that he might also destroy another mystic image for me.

He seemed pleased to tell me what he knew though, and adopted a respectful, sombre face as he explained. 'This vajra is a most important and honoured object. After some time, I shall take you to some of the important holy places in Kathmandu and there you will find these vajras in Hindu temples and Buddhist holy places also. It is the mace and represents a thunderbolt and a diamond also. It cuts but cannot be cut. Sometimes you will see Tibetans selling these things.'

'Yes, you're right, I saw a Tibetan woman selling them at the Chisapani market.'

So my family heirloom truly did have some significance. That was something! That moment though, I knew that I didn't need any talisman or magical phrase. It was time to look for meaning in my life but not through keepsakes and karma. I was strong enough to do anything I wanted—and be anything I wanted—not to impress my ex-husband or mother, but for myself.

Rekraj continued, 'Now I think is time. Come, didi—let us take rest together, and some special Gurkha tea and heavy military snacks also!'

As we walked away together, I saw three shrieking children sprinting towards me. They were shouting something. I made out the words, 'Auntie, Auntie!' There was something familiar about them. Then, with a surge of joy, I realized who they were. 'Atti! Siru! Little Hari!'

They ran straight into me, shrieking still. We did a big hug and the four of us laughed and cried all at once. They'd survived! I was so happy. They were so happy. It was so good to be together again.

I desperately wanted to know how they'd come through this but I'd have to wait for their story. I needed to help the children. They were expecting me to find their mother but where should we start looking? How were we going to find Guliya in all this chaos? The last time I'd seen her, she looked as if her heart had been ripped out. She was in danger of just wandering off and drowning herself.

Bom Bahadur

Sonia didi is looking fatigued, so clearly, I am arriving at a most timely moment. I watch her finish her work. Sometimes she sticks out her tongue, she is concentrating so much. I observe until she is finished stitching that particular man, then I tell her that she can rest for some time. I have found two more tailors who are willing to become surgeons. They are very keen volunteers. I didn't even need to threaten them much. These low-caste people are good men—they understand where their duties lie. They have compassion also. They know what it is to suffer.

I have just seen that useless Newar Dhan Sing trying to persuade the helicopter pilot to give him a ride back to Nepalgunj. The Newar doesn't care. He is running away, back to his own people in the valley. He is not even staying long enough to speak to Kamala. I am surprised that he never felt it was his duty to help here. It is strange to observe this when our foreign friends have done what they can.

I see a British officer chat to Sonia didi for a short time and then take his leave. Then Rekraj Dixit arrives and takes her away from work. As they walk across the courtyard, three children run to her. I ask them why they are not more respectful. The biggest boy says, 'This foreigner has been staying in our house. She is our friend, our Auntie.'

I wonder if, these days, the memsahib understands some

of our language because she kisses him and says, 'Don't you recognize them, Mr Bom Bahadur? They are Guliya's two and that poor new-found nephew. They've returned! Guliya thinks they are drowned!'

'I am pleased to hear this, Sonia didi. Now I think you must all return to the house. Go! Take your tiffin—take rest also. The Gurkhas are distributing food rations. Soon they will have evacuated the bad casualties also. The worst is over now I am thinking.'

She says, 'I hope so...but where is Guliya? I'm so worried about her.'

'She is safe. She is at the Saraswati temple—praying.'

I speak to the children and tell them to go to the temple by the High School. There they will find their mother. When—finally—they understand what I am saying to them, they look at each other. Then they start to cry. Poor things...I think they will have a long interesting story to tell.

'Come,' I tell them. 'Let us go to your mother.' As we walk away from the Shiva temple they seem to be laughing and crying at the same time. It is difficult to tell. I do not know about how Tharu children behave. Sometimes I find their language a bit too difficult.

Guliya

The hunger has gone now. It is quiet here in the temple. Others who have lost everything lie still and silent. Their tears are dry now. My Kancha also doesn't cry anymore. There is a thumping in my head, like someone is using it as a drum. There is the sound of the rushing river in my ears. I hear the *kag-kag* of a crow.

Then I think I hear a shout. I am mistaken. Why would anyone shout here in this place of worship? But there is another shout. Several shouts. They are children's voices. I turn. My head spins with this small movement. Everything is blurred.

Three children are running towards me across the temple compound. I do not understand why children would be running in the temple. At first I do not recognize them. I feel sure it must be some cruel hallucination. But then they reach me and embrace me and I can smell them, the warm familiar smell of my own flesh and blood. The gods have returned my children to me!

I am too shocked to say anything. My head is swimming. I am unsteady. I go down on my knees so that I can hold my children better. My eyes mist over completely. I chant a prayer. I do not want to faint now.

After some time, I realize that the memsahib and the Gurung soldier with the big moustache are here also. It is they only who have brought the children here to me at the temple. Still I cannot take it all in. I cannot really believe that this nightmare is all over so quickly. I am waking from a terrible, terrible dream.

Then I see that the memsahib has come inside still wearing her leather shoes. The children are so excited that even the priest says nothing to her. The priest is actually smiling to see us reunited. That is a rare sight! A Brahmin smiling!

The useless Badi man, Hari, is skulking in the background also. I thought that he had left Rajapur. I was wrong in thinking that. He has been loitering close to the temple, waiting and waiting. Perhaps Hari has lied about his caste. Perhaps he is telling everyone that he is a Christian man now. Whatever the priest knows, he has pretended not to recognize that Hari is untouchable. Everyone knows that it is impossible to change your caste. The only way to change caste is to enter the purifying flames of a funeral pyre. Only then can you change your caste. If you have earned enough merit in one life, then perhaps you will be reborn into a higher station in life. Everyone knows this.

Perhaps it is to gain merit that Hari bhai has been bringing the sugar-water to keep me alive. Perhaps he wishes to give a little back after all the sorrow he has caused me and my family. It is my idea that Hari bhai hopes to make amends for taking my sister. After all, he is not a bad man. He is just useless, good-for-nothing.

It might please the gods if we take him in but I cannot. Not now. He will not earn forgiveness from us like this. He is not of our caste. He cannot enter our family. I do not know, or care, what will happen to him now. He has brought this bad karma upon himself. There is nothing for him here, not since the system of bonded labouring was made illegal. It is my idea that he must return to Kathmandu, or maybe he will go to India and find work there, or in some other foreign place.

It is strange that my nephew, little Hari, shows no interest in his father...perhaps I remind the boy of his poor dead mother and that is enough for him. That is what I wish for.

The memsahib and the children and I return to our house, slowly slowly. Hari bhai trails along behind us like a hungry pariah dog hoping for some scraps of food. Two strange children are waiting there at the house. They recognize the memsahib and run to her. The memsahib says something about Moti but I do not understand her. I think these must be lost children. Probably they are orphaned. They are polite and respectful and they can live in our house. They say that the loud mad American man has run away. I do not care about that foreigner. I am happy that he has gone.

Then there is a cough. I turn, wondering who is there. Who is visiting our humble house on such a day as this?

It is my husband!

He has a black eye and a big cut across his face. He is very dirty also. He looks very tired but he is smiling. Another strange child is with him too. I tell him—laughing—that if he has brought yet another child to feed, he must promise to have a vasectomy. He agrees—straightaway. But I know he will not do this thing. He will not have his root cut off. Men are too scared to go for the operation. It is my karma to have another child. Our compound will be full of the happy sounds of many children playing together. Perhaps we will make another child tonight.

He turns a little to show me that someone is standing behind him. Her head is bowed shyly. She looks so much older that I do not recognize her straightaway. She is dressed in oranges and yellows and pinks, like an Indian, and she wears make-up like a Badi woman. She looks up at me briefly and there are tears in her eyes. She must have read confusion in my face because slowly she turns, as if to walk away.

'Maya!' I shout. 'You have come home! Come to me!'

When I embrace her, I feel how skinny she has become, my poor darling daughter. But she is home now. Things will get better now that she is home. I force a smile through my tears and say, 'Suddenly our house is full again. My heart is overflowing!'

Sonia

I was getting so confused about who all these people were but it was clearly a happy reunion. I expect I'd be able to get some of the story later—from Rekraj. In fact, I wondered whether I might be able to sneak away and meet him before all the excitement had died down. But then I decided it would be polite to wait. Maybe I'd just spend a bit more time tidying myself up so that I looked presentable for our evening together. I felt like a teenager, counting off the minutes until I could see him again.

Guliya

My daughter will only say that she has spent some time in Mumbai.

I say, teasing, hoping, 'So you became a Bollywood star!'

She looks down at the ground again. She cannot talk of it. She says briefly that Ram Krishna promised her so many things, including fame, but all his promises were broken. She quickly came to know that there was no easy way out. It was her karma to bear this burden for some time. She was quiet and submissive and obedient. She forced herself to smile a lot. In that way she became popular and slowly gained their trust. Then finally she was given enough freedom to be able to escape. But that was only the beginning.

Coming home—travelling as a lone woman through India—wasn't easy. As she travelled, she came to see that she had changed. People disrespected her wherever she went. She knew that she would not be welcome even in Rajapur. She didn't want to bring shame on our family but she needed to see if we were all right. She came as close as Lumki, and got a job helping in a tea-shop at the bus station. The Rajapur buses stop there so she thought there would be a good chance of some news. Most of the travellers were Brahmins though, with no interest in Tharu affairs. She got no news but she did earn a lot of abuse. The men there, because they were passing through and because no one knows their relatives, they were lewd, so very lewd. The truck drivers were the worst. They often touched her. Daily they said disgusting things to her. But still she had to smile at them.

Then when reports came through about the wave, she knew she must get home. She had to know if her family—our family—had survived. Rajapur bazaar was only a few miles away but it wasn't easy getting there. She walked up and down the river before she found a ferry. Then it was difficult to find her way back to Rajapur bazaar. The gods were with her when she saw my husband, her father, also making his way home.

I am so overwhelmed to see my daughter after three long years that I've hardly spoken to my poor husband. He doesn't care. He wants to hear Maya's voice as much as I do. Finally, I ask him how he escaped the wave. He looks down, smiling guiltily. He clears his throat and says, 'There was a lot of good interesting storytelling while we were working and digging the sediment out of the main canal up in the north of the island. The local men had been telling tales about elephants attacking the villages nearby. I took notice and decided to keep myself safe. The landlord paid us well for the work we'd done so I celebrated by buying a little pineapple-flavoured wine. Just one small bottle. It is a new variety from India and the taste is most excellent. To keep safe from the wild animals of the jungle, I climbed up into one elephant lookout platform. It was very sturdy as it was built against one of the biggest red silk-cotton trees on the island. I enjoyed my drink up there. There was a very good view out over the river and the rice fields. After some time, I fell asleep.

'When I woke, the world had changed. At first I thought that the drink had destroyed my eyesight. Sometimes it happens if you buy strong drink from certain tea-shops. But slowly I saw that everything had been swept away. Everyone seemed to have gone too. There was no sign of the ladder up to the platform either. I shouted for someone to bring a ladder. I needed help to get down. But no one came. No one heard. I wondered if I was the only one left alive in the world.

'I waited a long, long time. Everyone seemed to be dead, or they had fled. Finally, I realized that I had to jump. It was a long way but I had no choice. Either I could stay there and starve or I had to risk jumping. It was a long way to the ground. It was the height of two elephants, maybe even more.

'It took half the day to summon the courage. After some time, I made the jump. I jumped into a great pile of broken house timbers and thatch. I don't remember landing. I was knocked out maybe a long while, I don't know. My head was hurting a lot when I awoke. I felt ill also. Finally, I knew I must get up and try to find my way home.

'The journey was long and it was difficult to recognize anything. All the time I was walking, I was thinking that I would find all of my family gone. I prayed and prayed that this would not be so. Then I found this boy on the way. He had lost everything also but I saw that he was a good boy. We walked together. I thought that the gods meant me to find this child and look after him. Now I am thinking that because the gods have treated us kindly we must show our gratitude. It is good that they have also given us more children. We are indeed fortunate and blessed.'

My husband knows how I love children and he knows how to get round me. I am so happy he has returned. I weep with joy.

'I have only one sadness,' he continues. 'I left one bottle of pineapple-flavoured wine up in that tree on the elephant lookout platform. Perhaps I will return to that place tomorrow. Maybe it will be there waiting for me to bring it home!'

I laugh. I want to throw something at him but before I can, another wonderful thing happens. To complete my happiness, Moti comes home also. Her arm is in plaster. She is scratched and bruised but she is all right. She is accompanied by a Tharu boy that I recognize. He is a distant cousin. I know his uncles and they are good men. Moti is looking at him as the boy carries a small sack of rice for her. I can see immediately that there is love between them.

I run to embrace her. My heart is overflowing and I am weeping with joy—again. The gods take but they also give great happiness. I will make a good offering at the temple tomorrow. Moti is also crying tears of joy. She, too, is amazed to find our whole family at the house now. There is a lot of laughing and hugging but now we need to hear her story.

Moti tells us, 'I reached home safely and thought that the gods were smiling on me. They had kept us safe but we were hungry. The two little lost girls were crying because their bellies were paining them. I decided to go to the mill. It was my idea to take just a little rice from there. The gods were angry and punished me because I was stealing, but I was only trying to get food for the children. It was only the fallen grains that the rats would have taken. Was it such a sin? I didn't know what else I could do.

'The floods or maybe the tremors had weakened the building. The ceiling collapsed on me. Everything went black. Maybe the gods thought that was punishment enough because Ganga Lal found me. He helped me get out. He took me to Dr Bhandari. It was Bhandari only who put my arm in plaster. He gave me medicines for my paining head also.

'Now the Gurkhas are giving out food rations so I have brought this bagful for us. We will take rice together after so much time apart.'

I say, 'Now, my daughters, you must teach the memsahib how to grind chillies for the chutney.'

Maya, Moti and the memsahib smile. This foreigner still cannot speak but I think she understands. I see Hari walking away. Finally, he has accepted he is not welcome here. I thought of offering rice to him but he is not of our family. His son looks silently at his retreating back. Little Hari gets up and comes to embrace me again. He is a good boy.

It feels like such a long time since I ate rice with my family. Moti and the memsahib will make special chutney and rich thick lentil dal also. After some time, we will eat good rice together again.

15. THE SMELL OF FRESHLY MOWN GRASS

Sonia

I am exuberant with the beauty of Cambridge in spring. I've just spent a lovely afternoon cycling along the towpath, watching rowers on the Cam. Everyone who is on the river today looks so fit and beautiful, if a little pallid. Even in the eights rowed by older people, they look healthy and happy, carefree even. I smile to myself, realizing that I am classifying people of my own age as 'older'. I might take up rowing again, though not immediately. I know I'll find kindred spirits amongst the rowers—people who aren't scared of going out in the rain.

My already good mood is raised still further today. It must be something about the soothing qualities of water. The river is such a tranquil place, a place to sit and think of romance and the beauty of nature. Enjoy the elegance of the swans and the chance of a glimpse of a kingfisher. I'm feeling quite chuffed that I've finally attracted the attention of my family and friends. They were impressed at seeing me on the TV news, even if my mother made a mild swipe at me for not having put on any make-up before I went on camera. Her jibes amuse rather than depress me now. I cycle homewards, feeling in love with the world.

Suddenly, some idiot steps out in front of my bike. He's waving his arms at me.

I am jolted back to an ugly reality. 'Hello, Sonns!'

I skid to a halt and nearly drop the bike.

'Are you mad?'

It is my husband. Or should I say my ex-husband.

'Hey! This is brilliant,' he says grinning stupidly. 'I wanted to talk to you. Heard you were back from Tibet or wherever...great to see you! I'm so pleased you are back!'

He's grown fat. I don't care if he is pleased or miserable. Anyway, why's *he* pleased? He abandoned me.

'How did you know?' I say flatly, trying to stem the tide of fury that I thought I'd dealt with. 'Let's get off the road so that we don't go under a bus or something,' I say, as if to a primary school child.

'I saw you out cycling yesterday. I didn't recognize you at first. I just noticed this attractive, bronzed woman hurtling down Hills Road. You were certainly moving—and you've lost so much weight!'

'I'm quite aware I was fat before.'

'That's not what I meant at all. You know that! You look so tanned and fit—quite some transformation for my cuddly, faithful, stay-at-home wife. You've done something with your hair. The trip has done you good. You look gorgeous.'

Patronizing bastard.

'I'm glad you think the sun-bleached look suits me! I do feel good.'

Or at least I did until I ran into you.

'All the allergies and fatigue that were haunting me, those are long gone. I'm a new woman!'

'I can see that—you really do look great!'

'You've put on weight,' I challenge him.

'Mmm, well, err, life's been…difficult. But hey! I saw you on the news! They covered that disaster that you got caught up in and they showed a short clip of you being helped to safety.'

'What? Being helped to safety? I wasn't—'

'Yes, you looked pretty beaten up then, I should say! After you, there was a long interview with that American—you know, the guy who organized the rescue efforts? He was called Herb something-or-other. It must have been great having someone with such presence of mind and leadership skills in a disaster situation like that. He described how he'd suggested building shelters and setting up first-aid centres and putting flags up so that people could find their way home. He said that the locals couldn't get it together so it was really fortunate that he happened to be there doing his research. He explained how he might never be able to finish his thesis—because he'd given so much to the people. He'd known that the sacrifice was worth it. What a man, eh?'

'Mmm-hmm, quite a character,' I say sarcastically. 'Actually it is a pity, because I was quite looking forward to reading his book—his Great Work. That also promised to be an interesting piece of fiction!'

'Eh?'

'Oh never mind. I don't suppose the world will be any poorer for it not being written.'

'You've changed.' He gives me one of his meaningful looks. 'Hey, they also interviewed a Brit—looked like a burned-out hippy-type. He explained how he'd barbequed the animal carcasses so that people would have something to eat—otherwise everyone on the island would have gone hungry.'

'Hmm. That was Paul—and it was my idea, actually.'

'I should have guessed—you always were good in the kitchen department.'

'Are you *trying* to be patronizing?'

'Course not—I'm paying you a compliment!'

'Huh, some compliment! So, tell me, which locals did they interview? They had a bit of a different story to tell, no doubt?'

'Nah, they didn't talk to any locals. I don't suppose any of them could speak English—or would even know what a TV was. Right?'

'No—actually...' My blood boils but I can't be bothered to explain what really happened. My ex-husband prattles on, 'So...where have you been today?'

'What?'

'Where have you been?'

'Not that it is any of your business but I've been...enjoying the river...listening to the church bells and blackbirds singing. There is something calming about water. The Cam is so lovely at this time of the year, and it's a simply an idyllic evening. The sunset is going to be superb too. You know what's great about being away?'

'What?'

'It's that you see home in a fresh new light. I've even been enjoying the amazing choice of things in the supermarkets. How weird is that! I think the smell of freshly mown grass on Midsummer Common is just out of this world. And have you seen all the wonderful blossoms along the towpath—the hawthorn and may, the willows, celandines and forget-me-nots?'

'I haven't forgotten you!' he interrupts. He hasn't caught my poetic mood. But what did I expect? He wouldn't recognize a poem if it slapped him in the face.

'I was talking about flowers, colours and beauty; you never did understand my artistic side and my passion for nature, did you? Look, I've got to go. Meeting...someone. See you around, maybe.'

'I'll call you!' he shouts after me. I don't respond. It's more like a threat than a promise. Bastard. He's wrecked my blissful mood.

I kick up my pedal intending to cycle on, when I hear, 'Mrs S! Oi. Over 'ere! Can I 'ave a word, like?'

I turn, knowing immediately who this is.

'Good afternoon, Conner.'

'Mrs S! You're back! Hey, I saw you on TV! You're famous!'

'Kind of. So, how are you, Conner?'

'Yeah. Well. Ya know.'

'No, I don't know really. So what do you want? I don't suppose we're supposed to speak to each other.'

'Yeah, yeah, yeah, I know. Sorry. But Cambridge is a small place. These fings 'appen eh? Anyway, I fought I should say I'm not proud of what I did...what I said wasn't good. It just got—you know—confusing. Then Mum started really doing my 'ead in, right? And 'er bloke; 'e was always drunk and shouting. I was angry. Wanted to 'urt someone.'

'Yes I know. I could see you were suffering.'

'Yeah, and things got even worse after that 'earing thing. I got in trouble, proper trouble, like. Got a social worker. She was okay. After I 'eard you was some kind of 'ero in India, I ended up telling her, ya know, what I done. What really 'appened. She said I should tell people, right? So I went and 'ad a talk to old Dick 'ead.'

'Old Dick Head?'

'Suppose I shouldn't call 'im that in front of a teacher?'

I try half-heartedly not to smile.

Conner smiles back. 'I reckon I've sorted this out, Mrs S, and 'e ought to be giving you a call soon. Said 'e would. To clear the air, like.'

*

I can't work out what had had most influence on Old Dick Head. Was it Conner's revised statement or my new celebrity status? Whatever the reason, the Head is slimy-sweet, promising to clear my name, and even says that—if I want it—he can organize a job, teaching at a neighbouring school. Apparently they need someone to cover maternity leave or something. And maybe I'd like to give a talk about the work I had been doing in Nepal.

I say I'll give the matter some thought and that I might ask him for a reference some time. It feels fantastic not having to beg anymore.

Later that day, my ex phones. I can tell from his voice that he has his charm-the-girls face on. 'I want to hear about Tibet. It must have been great?'

'Yes it was. And it was Nepal.'

'So tell me, what was it like?'

'You wouldn't have liked it.' I say trying to shut down the conversation.

'Oh? How so?'

'You know...terrible roads, clapped out cars, dodgy plumbing, poor TV reception, awful beer, no steak—beef is actually an illegal substance in Nepal. You'd have thought it uncivilized.'

'But you didn't?'

'Not at all. I found it beautiful, wonderful, bewildering, heartbreaking, exciting, tranquil—everything really. The trip has given me a lot, made me more self-confident, made me understand what in life is important. I've put the problems at the school behind me and got my self-respect back. It's made me feel so much better in oh so many...'

'Good.' My attempt to summarize my life-changing trip hasn't moved him. He's impatient to have his say. 'I suppose you've gone vegetarian and meditate now?'

He is talking to me in the belittling way he'd always talked to me. I don't like it. I don't like it at all.

'No, but what's wrong with that? What's wrong with a bit of spirituality? Surely it is better than shutting down your brain by watching the telly every evening?'

'I don't. Actually I've just joined a gym...'

'And have you been?'

'Err, I've only been once but...anyway I'm pleased you are back—*really* pleased.'

'You already said that. What do you want?' I sigh.

'Look I want to say sorry. I was a complete pig...'

'I agree.'

'Mmm, yeah and while you were away I realized how much we had, and what we threw away.'

'We?' I say indignantly.

'Sorry—not we, I...what *I* threw away.'

'She's dumped you then.'

'No. Yes. That's not the point.'

'Isn't it?'

I am mildly surprised that I feel nothing for him now—not even pity. We'd had some good times but that was all a very long time ago, like another incarnation.

'Can we meet?'

'I don't think so.'

'Why not?'

'Don't want to.'

'Why not? Let me take you out to dinner. Somewhere really nice...expensive...romantic.'

'No.'

'Why not?'

'You won't want to know.'

'Why not? Tell me!'

'I've moved on.'

'Come on, Sonns. We had it all...'

'It doesn't seem like that to me now. We don't have anything in common any more...actually I wonder whether we ever truly had anything in common...'

'Give me another chance. Just supper—that's all.'

'No. I am not interested.'

'What have you got to lose?'

'My temper. Look, my new man will be arriving soon. He'll be living here with me. We're starting a new life together.'

'What?' There was a long stunned silence. 'You mean you paired off with that American?'

'Yuck—credit me with some taste.'

'Omigod—not the unwashed, washed-up hippy!'

'No—and he wasn't washed up. He made me laugh. I got on well with Paul. And anyway, you'd have had a problem washing in those conditions! We were in the middle of a disaster, you know.'

'Yeah, maybe.' There is a long pause and I hear the realization sinking in. He stammers, 'You're bringing some immigrant back here...'

'Look...There's no point in continuing this—or in meeting.'

I am thrilled to have the spunk to say this to him, to take control. I wouldn't have dared before. And I can't keep the satisfaction out of my voice.

'But...how *could* you?' he almost shouts.

'What?' How dare he react like this! 'Look, it was *you* who was unfaithful, you know. It was *you* who left *me*... Remember? How could *you*?' I find his selfishness tiring rather than upsetting now. I put down the phone as he blusters on. I don't care and I am in danger of being late for my appointment with the GP.

*

'You look fantastic, Sonia,' my GP says. 'Are you okay—after all you've been through?'

'I'm good. Excellent actually.'

'I'm pleased. Hey, I was astonished to see you on TV. You're definitely my most famous patient! You must be quite a celebrity now?'

'No, not really...I've kept my head down. The press aren't interested in the real story of the genuine heroes—the Nepalis.'

She smiles, knowingly. 'Mmm. I can see that the experience has given you your self-esteem back.'

'Yes I really think it has, although the idea of me revisiting the places of my ancestors was a bit of an anticlimax. Kanpur was a sprawling concrete mess. They call it the Manchester of Northern India. I couldn't imagine that it could possibly have been the Cawnpore where Brits were hacked to pieces by a hoard of sabre-waving mutineers!' I say this without shuddering now. 'I did find the Memorial Church but his name wasn't there. I tried the phone directory and thought I'd made a breakthrough when I thought of spelling Campbell with a K but there were so, so many Kambles...'

'So you didn't manage to meet up with any distant relatives?'

'No, that only happens in novels, doesn't it?' We both laugh at this. 'I was left wondering, though, how Britain could operate in India for 300 years and take so little back from it in terms of understanding...'

Suddenly she looks serious again. She is back in doctor-mode when she asks, 'Are you really okay? Sleeping all right? No souvenir stomach bugs?'

'No, I suppose there are a few rumblings and I'm *going* a bit more frequently but I really do feel great. Yes, there was horror but so much more positive stuff...loads to savour for a very, very long time.'

'Great. And how about the scar?'

'Scar?'

'On your face. You were terribly upset about that, weren't you?'

'Upset! Obsessed, more like. How could I be precious about a scar when I've met lepers with no noses, children with half their faces burned away, and kids with unrepaired harelips and cleft palates? That cat-scratch is nothing! Look, I'm fine. I've been reincarnated, don't you know!'

She laughs again, 'There's nothing like seeing others' difficulties for putting your own into perspective! I'm so pleased that it all worked out. And thanks for that postcard you sent early on. It made me quite envious.'

'What, even that sleazy film star?'

'Mmm. Made me smile. And they call them heroes!'

'I'm not surprised,' I say.

'I understand now, just why you spent so long there. I expect you were reluctant to leave too?'

'I was, especially after I got back to some teaching in the High School. And also one of my first proposals got us funding to put latrines into the primary school. You know, I loved it there but I was grown up enough to know I couldn't stay forever.'

'You were very wise to leave while you still loved the place...'

'Yes and actually, I even wonder whether all those conversations I had with my teenage friend Moti might have heightened her ambitions. She married recently and she's going to train to become a teacher...so I feel I've given a little back on several levels.'

'Excellent. Something to feel proud of—for a change!'

'Mmm. But I have a little medical complication...I'm sorry—I haven't shaved my legs—I've gone a bit native...'

My GP smiled a gentle smile and said, 'Don't worry. That really doesn't matter!'

Patient no.: 22790
Ms Sonia Agnes SWAYNE

EMIS no.	:	22790
Name	:	Ms Sonia Agnes SWAYNE
Age	:	34 years
d.o.b.	:	25.10.1976
NHS no.	:	050 280 0303
Address	:	37 Wilkin Street, Cambridge CB1 2RS
Telephone no.	:	143271
Hospital no.	:	77 31 64

ACTIVE PROBLEMS
Gastro-intestinal unease
Amenorrhoea

LAST CONSULTATION:
PROBLEM—Gastro-intestinal unease
PROBLEM—Amenorrhoea

HISTORY—Just back from Nepal. Mild gripey abdominal pain. Usual vague, post-travel gastro-intestinal symptoms. Unlikely to be significant. Amenorrhoea for several months. Looks well. Sleep and appetite good. No longer any biological symptoms of depression. Seems to have made peace with her family and herself.

PLAN stool tests x3; u/s scan

CURRENT MEDICATION:
Folic acid 5mg daily + OTC vitamin D

HEALTH STATUS

Occupation	:	school teacher
Height	:	165 cm
Weight	:	64 kg
Body Mass Index	:	23.5
BP	:	110/72
Smoking	:	never smoked tobacco
Alcohol	:	4 units/week
Exercise grading	:	enjoys heavy exercise
Rubella Ab	:	immune
Family history	:	nil of note

INVESTIGATIONS:
Stool tests requested

After the GP finishes examining me, she says, 'Well, that wasn't quite the outcome I'd imagined when you left here! Are you quite sure that you want to keep the baby?'

'Absolutely. I've always wanted children and I know this baby'll be as dark and handsome as his father. I'll just have to imagine the moustache!' I don't know why I'm so sure I'm expecting a boy. Remembering Rekraj and that one wonderful night, makes me feel warm inside. He was the prince of my fantasies.

I recall what he said just as we parted. He was facing the prospect of an arranged marriage and I was deeply concerned for him. He was so naive, in many ways. But he had said, 'I have met her twice or thrice. My parents have made a wise choice. She is young and innocent and open—just like you only. We will be happy.'

My face must have shown my mood because my GP smiles with her next question. 'Does the father know?'

'No.'

'Will you tell him?'

'No. No, I'm grown up enough to recognize that my love affair was with Nepal, really. The passion would not have lasted. He was lovely, but...' I trail off with a lovelorn sigh.

'You're right. I know of lots of women who have gone to Nepal and fallen in love with their trek leader. Some have stayed to live in poverty in Kathmandu while their husbands continue to work as trekking guides and so, are never home. The wives become effectively enslaved to their mothers-in-law, or they live miserably alone in a tiny unheated flat. But you have had the sense to avoid that fate. Will you manage all right on your own?'

'Oh, I won't be alone. Becky was house-sitting while I was away. We've been good friends for years and she's broken up with her long-term man. We decided there was no reason for her to move out when I came home; we get on well and she says being an auntie will be a brilliant distraction, a laugh. The arrangement will suit us both, and it'll help my finances.'

My eyes must be sparkling again because the GP gives me another knowing smile.

'Are you very close?'

'Yes, err well, not in that way. We've been friends forever and she's often been there for me. Now she needs company,' I said, feeling the baby move and the flutterings of love in my heart again. 'It'll be like living in a student house-share all over again.'

'Excellent,' my GP says. 'The baby is due in five-and-a-half months, and there's just time to get a detailed scan done...Becky can go along too if you want, although you might get mistaken for a couple.'

'Wouldn't be the first time!' We laugh again.

'Good. You'll both enjoy it. It's absolutely wonderful to see the baby's hands and even the tiny heart beating... miraculous new life...'

I leave the doctor's thinking about my next challenge. I have to tell my family. I am still putting this off. I am strangely nervous about sharing my joyous news because my mother's reaction will be something about me needing to act my age. But it really is nothing to do with her. I might even tell her that. This is my life, after all, and it is a good one. It really is.

I'm determined to laugh when she criticizes me again, and I'll tell her that we could be close again. All I've done has renewed me, and what I've become has made me more able to love, and forgive. I think I'll be able to make her see that now.

That night, I serve up good Basmati rice for Becky and me.

'You nervous about tomorrow?' Becky asks.

'No—not really, surprisingly. It'll be interesting…And I'm looking forward to seeing Paul again.'

'Ooh…do I see a sparkle in your eye?' she teases.

'Maybe. He's fun, and attractive but not in a come-and-be-the-stepfather-of-my-baby kind of way. More like in a one-night-stand sort of way!'

'Oh my! Listen to Sonia, woman of the world!'

'Hmm—so speaks this woman of the world who's never ever had a one-night stand in her life.'

*

The studio building is grand and imposing. I look in through the vast glass frontage. Paul is sitting, waiting on red velvet furniture. He leaps up when he sees me and we hug. He still has that lovely musky fragrance about him. His sun-bleached hair is shorter now, his clothes pressed and ordinary, to fit in with London life. Paul says, 'You're even more gorgeous than the last time I saw you. Pity that a beautiful and talented woman like you wouldn't have time for a nomad like me!'

'If you never ask, you never get, Paul!'

'Oh, *really?* You're on then!'

We look at each other and simultaneously splutter into laughter.

'Nervous?' I ask.

'Nah. You?'

'A little.'

'You'll be fine,' Paul smiles. 'After Nepal, this is a piece of piss. And Raj is a real pro anyhow. You'll like him. Actually I reckon you'll *really* like him. A real charmer. Nice genuine guy too. He'll fill any awkward silences, no probs.'

'So you've been matchmaking, have you, Paul?'

In answer he holds up his hands as if in surrender. 'You know my philosophy...everyone needs a bit of lovin'—you'd be good for each other!'

We settle into a soundproofed room with padded scarlet walls and a lot of microphones and high-tech stuff. Raj is charming and seems genuinely interested in me. Paul and Raj clearly have some history. 'So what happened to the dreads, mate?'

'Ah, Sonia cut them while I slept and now I'm totally under her control!'

'Sounds lovely,' Raj chips in, winking at me. I hardly have a chance to open my mouth. Actually their man-banter is hilarious. They almost seem to be competing for me!

Raj then gets serious and says, 'We're on in about a minute...just to say...this is informal. We'll try to make it feel like a bit of chitchat between friends but if we stray into any difficult stuff just shake your head and I'll change tack, okay?'

Suddenly we're on air. Live. Raj is doing an intro, describing the disaster. Spouting numbers of people killed, numbers injured, sketching out the current relief efforts in the region. There are film clips showing as he speaks. They show the huge extent of the devastation.

I'm back there, yet understanding more fully now what happened to the people in that place that I love. I choke up. Then there's the clip of Herb taking credit for the start of the rescue efforts...and I realize Raj is talking to me.

'It must be hard revisiting this, Ms Swayne?'

'Yes, terrible.' I cough. 'For the Nepalis especially, of course. So many lives ripped apart...' I trail off—recalling the corpses and the many I couldn't save, the dead children's bloated faces, the body of the woman I disentangled from the tree so it could be swallowed by the rushing river, remembering Rekraj—then quickly I pull myself together, take a deep breath and continue, 'Still, it's good to know that I did what I could to help. Possibly saved a few lives…'

'That's not what official reports are saying now.'

'What?'

'Reports suggest you helped save *hundreds* of lives!'

'Oh? Really? I don't suppose that's true…'

'But it is, absolutely true.'

He encourages me to describe the makeshift clinic, and gets Paul talking of his barbeque and cremation service.

'It was actually Sonia's idea to build bonfires to cook the dead livestock—nah, not exactly livestock,' Paul chuckled, interrupting himself. 'We reckoned decomposing carcasses would cause some god-awful plague or cholera or something, so barbequing seemed like a great way of getting rid of the dead animals while feeding the starving survivors. And me—I'm always hungry, as you know, Raj!'

Raj smiles, uncertainly and continues, 'But we should also talk of the efforts of the American anthropologist, Herbert Friedman. He, too, was making considerable efforts, wasn't he?'

'Err well…' I hesitate and start to shake my head so he'll change the subject, but something in me wants to be honest with this man, so I shrug and make a face instead.

'No?' Raj leans forward, eyebrows raised.

'He was terribly young,' I said. 'Even before the flood, he wasn't doing too well. He found the conditions difficult, and didn't really manage to get very far learning the language.'

'But Dr Freidman claimed he headed up the rescue and relief efforts.'

'I've heard that.'

'You mean he *did* head up the rescue?'

'Err…I mean he *claimed* he did, yes.' I look across to Paul, wondering how much to say. I did want to put the record straight, but I didn't really want to call Herb a liar on air. How dare he suggest he was so much better than my Nepali friends, though. How dare he!

'Actually, we should talk about the real heroes—the Nepali community leaders…'

'Yes, we'll come to them but how did Dr Freidman help, in fact, Ms Swayne?' Raj presses.

'Uh, I'm not aware that he did. And—umm—I don't think he should be calling himself 'Doctor' either. From what he told me, I don't believe he was able to complete his thesis—for his PhD, which is what he went to Nepal to do.'

'Now *that's* interesting. So who *did* coordinate the response to the disaster?

'The leaders were undoubtedly Regimental Sergeant-Major Bom Bahadur Gurung and Rekraj Dixit. They were absolutely amazing at mobilizing the community and keeping everyone calm. It was Bom Bahadur who trained me to stitch wounds. He was in the Gurkhas and was incredibly good at improvizing. He even worked out that we could make a kind of local anaesthetic with the materials the ice-lolly salesman provided! And then there was Mr Vaidiya with his knowledge of local herbs...he was amazing too.'

'So, Ms Swayne, how long did you operate your Gurkha field hospital, as it were?'

'You know, Raj, I really couldn't say. I guess I could work it out, but the whole awful business has become a blur. When you are in the middle of something like this, you don't dwell on the hard stuff—or timetables. We were working from dawn till dusk and then some. Day after day. We just kept working until the helicopters came. And then I reckon I must have slept for a week!'

After the interview is over, Raj apologizes. 'Look, I pressed you to speak out. I hope that was okay, Sonia?'

'Yes, I think it was. It feels good to have put the record straight, even if I feel slightly bad because of what I said about Herb. He was actually a pathetic creature and he shouldn't have lied. He shouldn't take the credit for all that Bom Bahadur and Rekraj achieved. That is simply not right!'

'Yeah, that came over...and it was good to speak out for your Nepalese friends. Thanks so much for doing this. I think it went really well. It'll help raise funds too—with that plug we did for the Red Cross.'

'Great! You made it easy—thanks. And fun, in an odd sort of way.'

'Absolutely my pleasure. Hey, are you hungry? I know I am. Fancy a bite?'

'Yes, I do...Paul? You hungry too?'

'Nah. Three's a crowd, I reckon.' And he turns to leave.

'Come up to Cambridge some time, Paul—we'll go punting!'

'Okay—you're on, Sonia. Have a wonderful evening, you two,' he said, winking at me. 'See ya.'

Raj guided me out into the fresh evening air, along tiny London backstreets and into a smart-looking restaurant, 'After you, Memsahib!'

'Oh—I was thinking we were in search of a beef burger or something.'

'Won't this do, then?'

'Yes, it looks lovely—but err—I wasn't really expecting anything quite so formal.' I run my fingers through my hair and adjust my blouse.

'Don't worry—you still look lovely!'

'Nice of you to say that...'

'Ouch—*nice?*'

'Sorry—embarrassment makes me ungracious. Even so, if you call me Memsahib again, I'll leave!'

He laughs an easy laugh and we settle at a secluded table. 'Don't worry. Don't read anything into this. I just didn't want our conversation to end. I so enjoyed interviewing you... and anyway, Paul will give me a hard time if I admit to only buying you a beef burger!'

'Yes, today's been fun. But I am at a huge disadvantage, Raj. A poor innocent single woman alone in London...set up by an ex-dope-head. Oops, but maybe you imbibe too?' I flutter my eyelashes in mock alarm. 'And I *really* dread to think what Paul's told you about me!'

He laughs. 'It was all good, don't worry. So...am I safe to assume you *are* single then?'

I feel uneasy. He is certainly a charmer but how much of philanderer is he? And what was I getting into?

He says, 'What shall we have to drink? Red or white?'

'Ah, I won't—thanks.'

'Ooh, sorry. Antibiotics or antidepressants?'

'Does there have to be a reason!' I'm rattled. I don't feel right about not telling this man the truth, but don't want him to know too much either, not yet.

'Well, since you ask...' he frowned, 'yes, usually there is—an alcoholic ex, for example!'

'Err...'

'Sorry—that was out of order. Could we cut that bit? I'm really sorry. It's the investigative journalist in me. Hard to switch off, especially after such a brilliant interview tonight. And I promise, I wasn't scheming to get you drunk.'

'Good.'

'Forgiven?'

'Maybe...' I shrug off his intrusion and turn the tables on him. 'Why don't you tell me about yourself?'

He smiles. 'This is the sort of question I ask all the time, but it is hard to answer...surprisingly hard to sum up a life in a few sentences, especially when that life isn't particularly interesting.'

'But I'm guessing it's complicated?'

'Err...certainly complicated!'

'Well, I think complicated sounds intriguing, personally. So...I won't let you get away without answering, you know!'

'Clearly! So...I was brought up in a moderately dull London suburb. Did okay at school. Good at the blag. Good at cricket, fast bowler. Worked my way up from local newspaper hack to local radio, then got a big break...'

'But are you single?'

His eyes meet mine as he says, 'Yes. Yes I am.'

'So why's a gorgeous guy like you single?'

'Wow, that's straight to the point!'

'Yes... well, that's me...two feet—straight in!'

'It's okay...since you asked, so persistently...I divorced—quite recently, actually.'

'Oh, I am sorry.'

'Don't be...it's okay.' He looks hurt and vulnerable—so different from Raj, the self-confident journalist. 'It was a relief for both of us, as it turned out.'

He stares at the tablecloth, while I feast upon his milk-chocolate skin and liquorice hair. Then I wonder what's going on inside my head—I loathe liquorice. I need to temper this uncomfortable moment. 'Hey Raj, let's order some food! I'm starving!'

His head snaps up and his gorgeous smile is back.

Over dinner we danced around in conversation, and skilfully avoid talking about the complications of our lives. Then...to find neutral ground, I ask, 'What do you know of the subcontinent?'

'You'd think, given my complexion, I'd be an expert, wouldn't you? But my grandparents were Ugandan Asians. We have no close relatives in Asia—that I know of anyway. I keep thinking I'll go on some kind of pilgrimage one day but it'd be weird, going somewhere, where I'd look like a local but am not. I keep putting it off...'

'You should go on your pilgrimage! I did after my marriage broke up. It clears out all the grime of hurt and disappointment. A pilgrimage is a fine thing. Often sorts out complications. A great adventure. Opens up a million possibilities. In fact, it's how I met...all sorts of important people...'

The evening continues into the small hours and in my head I am analysing him. I recall the fantasies I had at the start of my time in Nepal. Raj could be my eligible prince. It even occurs to me that he'd be the ideal stepfather for Rekraj's baby, because he'd look like the natural parent. But what was I doing? I'd only just met this guy!

Finally, he pays the bill—reluctantly, it seems to me—and we leave. We wander out into the crisp night.

'May I take your arm, Sonia?'

'Mmm, but it will be complicated, Raj.'

'Great—I love complicated.'

GLOSSARY

MAINLY OF NEPALI WORDS

aunus: Come here, please.

Ayurveda: Ancient system of traditional herbal medicine used all over the subcontinent.

Badi: Caste of hereditary prostitutes who live in the lowlands of Nepal.

Bahadur: Brave; often the second given name for Nepali boys.

badmass: Naughty; mischievous.

bahini: Younger sister; used to address a younger female.

banyan: Multi-trunked fig tree with aerial roots, *Ficus bengalensis.*

bazaar: Market (used in Arabic, Nepali, Hindi and other languages).

bears: The sloth bear, *Melurus ursinus,* and the Himalayan black bear, *Selenarctos thibetanus,* found in Nepal.

bee-eater: Gorgeous insectivorous birds; we saw the chestnut-headed *Merops leschenauti,* the green *Merops orientalis,* the blue-tailed *Merops philippinus,* and the blue-bearded *Nyctyornis athertoni* in and around Rajapur.

bideshi: Western foreigner.

bhai: Younger brother; also used to address any younger male.

blackbuck: Attractive small antelope, *Antelope cervicapra;* stands 60–82 cm at the shoulder and weighs 25–45 kg. Males have fine spiral horns up to 50 cm long.

Brahmin: Highest Hindu caste, mostly priests. Strict Brahmins are teetotaller vegetarians who eat no eggs.

Buddhism: In Nepal, Buddhism is of the Mahayana (or Vajrayana) form, popularly known as Lamaism, which has had

Hindu influences. Many temples in Nepal contain shrines for both Buddhist and Hindu worship.

bulbul: Several varieties of crested birds with strong bills; they eat fruit and insects. They form affectionate couples, and so feature in Oriental love poetry.

caste: Exclusive social position that Hindus are born into and can never change, except by converting to Islam or Christianity. Since it is no longer illegal to change religion in Nepal, numerous low-caste Hindus have converted, in the hope of improving their lot. Caste is usually indicated in surnames.

chital: Spotted deer, *Axis axis;* like a fallow deer, but their coats are more golden and their antlers less complex.

cobra: Both the Indian cobra, *Naja naja,* and the king cobra or hamadryad, *Ophiophagus hannah,* occur in the lowlands where Sonia stayed. Both species are killers.

dai: Older brother.

dacoits: Bands of robbers.

didi: Older sister; someone who is older and therefore, is addressed with respect.

Ganga: The Ganges river; a popularly given name amongst Hindu men and women.

Gangetic: Of or related to the Ganges river.

Ganesh: The elephant-headed Hindu god of wisdom and jollity. His mount is the bandicoot.

GP: General Practitioner; a British family physician. After studying for five years, doctors wishing to become GPs spend two further years training while working in various hospital specialties, and after that, they work for another year in supervised family practice. GPs perform minor operations, fit contraceptive devices, take Pap smears, and act as the first point of medical contact for patients of all ages. GPs also manage and support patients with long-standing conditions, including diabetes, asthma, vascular disorders, epilepsy and mental health problems. Their roles are similar but more extensive than primary care physicians in the US.

guruwa: Local healer.

Gurkha: Regiment of Nepali mercenaries in the British army, originally recruited from the town of Gorkha in central Nepal. Gurkhas now come from any hill village in Nepal.

guru: Teacher. This word has come into English to mean a spiritual teacher or guide, but in Nepal, it is also used to mean a schoolteacher.

hero (or **hiro**): Male film star, but literally a 'star' or 'diamond'.

himal: A mountain that always has snow on it.

Himalaya: Place of eternal snows.

hoina: Frequently used expression meaning something like 'isn't it?'

hookah: Water-pipe or hubble-bubble. Tobacco or cannabis smoke is cooled by being drawn through water.

hotel: Place to eat, sometimes just a shack. In Nepal, this is not always somewhere to stay.

jungle: Wild, useless and uncultivated land (in Nepali, Hindi). The meaning of this word has become more evocative of adventure since being adopted into the English language.

jooto: Polluted; Hindus avoid sharing cups, for example, for fear of cultural pollution. Consequently, impressively, they are experts at pouring drinks into the mouth without their lips touching the vessel.

kamaiya: System of bonded labourers (slaves, effectively) outlawed in Nepal in the year 2000.

kanchha: Last-born male child. 'Kanchhi' is the female form.

karma: Effect of former deeds; the good or bad luck people have; fate.

khana: Food, generally implying a substantial meal including plenty of rice.

khukuri: Short, curved blade used as a hatchet.

krait: A big, black—though not very aggressive—snake, *Bungarus caerulus*. Their venom is said to be capable of killing a human in five to twelve hours; they rarely grow much more than a metre long.

lato: Deaf mute

lingam: Phallic symbol of Lord Shiva in his role of divine creator.

long-drop: Hole-in-the-ground toilet without a ceramic footplate and often lacking water too. They are usually built as outhouses away from the main home.

mahseer: Largest member of the carp family; weighs up to 80 kg. A popular freshwater game fish.

malik: Landowner.

mantra: Mystic incantation (from Sanskrit).

MBBS: Bachelor of medicine and bachelor of surgery qualification equivalent to the American MD.

memsahib: Married European lady (from Hindi).

moriyo: Dead.

Moti: Pearl; a man's given name, or when used as an affectionate nickname for a woman, it means 'fatty'.

Mussalman: Muslim.

namaste: Very formal Hindu greeting, literally—'honour to thee'. It is said with hands placed palms-together as if saying a prayer.

Newar: People of the Kathmandu Valley who have their own language, which is also called 'Newar'.

NGO: Non-government organization; often charitable and involved in community work.

peepal: *Bo* tree; a kind of fig, *Ficus religiosa*, with long 'drip-tips' at the end of each leaf, and which is of great religious significance to Hindus and Buddhists.

pukka: Proper; a permanent structure or something made of concrete as opposed to a temporary construction; adopted into English to mean proper, genuine, good, straightforward.

queerie (or **kuiré**): White-skinned foreigner.

randi: Prostitute.

sahib: Gentleman, Sir or Mr; a term of respect for people of rank and Europeans.

sal: Ironwood trees of the lowlands, *Shorea robusta,* straight-trunked with wood so dense it sinks in water.

samosa: Spicy puff pastry triangle.

sati (also spelt **'suttee'**): an obsolete ritual when a widow was burned alive on the funeral pyre of her husband; from the Sanskrit for 'virtuous wife'.

shabash: Well done.

Shiva: Mahadev, great god of destruction and re-creation, and the most powerful of the Hindu trinity.

simal: Red silk-cotton tree, *Bombax ceiba*. It flowers in March, and it has very soft wood so is easy to carve and is often used to make dugout canoes.

tanga: Horse-drawn taxi with two wheels and often a four-poster sunshade; called 'tonga' in India.

tarai: the Gangetic plains, the lowlands of southern Nepal and the adjacent plains of India; often also spelt as 'terai'.

Tharu: Indigenous peoples of the Nepali lowlands—a disparate group with different languages.

thatch grass: Much of it is *kãs (Saccharum spontaneum)* or 'elephant grass', which grows by rivers and has attractive white seed-heads.

thug: Caste of violent criminals, worshippers of the Goddess Kali, the demoness who represents the dark side of Parvati. Thugs practise *thuggee*—making a living by strangling their victims with a silver rupee rolled in a silk scarf.

tiffin: Luncheon, from an old north of England provincialism that entered eighteenth-century slang, and thence adopted into Indian English. Indian and Nepali children go to school carrying shiny steel tiffin tins containing their lunchtime snacks.

topi: Hat.

untouchable: Lower than the lowest caste of Hindus; outcastes who 'pollute' higher caste people if they eat together. These people are called Dalits in India.

vajra: Thunderbolt (from Sanskrit).

vultures: There are eight different species that live in Nepal. In the lowlands, the Indian griffon (or long-billed) vulture is common and it clears up a lot of rotting flesh. In the mountains, the bearded vulture or *lammergeier* can be seen. There are also, among others, yellow-faced Egyptian vultures.

ACKNOWLEDGEMENTS

The idea for this novel arrived in my consciousness around the time that my memoir, *A Glimpse of Eternal Snows,* was first published. The idea was to try to get inside the heads of some of my Nepali friends, neighbours and chance acquaintances by writing about them. I wanted to give voice to the illiterate and the untouchable. I also conceived of a journey for a British woman—Sonia certainly contains parts of me—who could be someone who needs to reinvent herself in order to survive. Working as a doctor in Nepal and Cambridge, I certainly learned a lot about what it is like to feel worthless and abandoned.

Although this novel is set in a region I know intimately, it wasn't easy to create this tale. However, I have enjoyed the process, especially revisiting the amusing cross-cultural misunderstandings. And some of the adventures that Sonia gets tangled up in were quite a surprise, even to me.

Good writers are like magpies, storing away pieces of dialogue and experience, which pop up from memory unexpectedly. One such nugget, which became an important theme in the book, was Sonia's mantra. This originated in a conversation at a family party with a distant cousin, Pat Barlow. I am indebted to him.

Writing is a tough, lonely business but I've had huge amounts of feedback and encouragement from fellow authors: Sally Haiselden, Francoise Hivernel, Stephanie Ledger, Josephine Warrior, Thure Etzold and other members of Cambridge Writers, as well as from Penny Speller, Victor Watson, Rosemary Hayes and Gabrielle Palmer of Walden Writers. They and others (including Jane Bailey, Mary Styles and Simon Howarth) bravely volunteered to read or listen to early drafts of the book and helped form the story. It is all too easy to lose confidence in any writing project and I am deeply grateful to everyone who has encouraged me, and helped me keep the faith.

Big thank yous go to my editors, Amy Corzine (author

of *The Secret Life of the Universe)*, and also Aruna Ghose and Kartikeya Jain from Speaking Tiger, for making sensitive suggestions to improve the book. Thanks to Anurag Basnet for helping to bring this story to the reading public.